Prisoner of passion...

Before Caro could divine Rowland's intentions, his strong hands were drawing her close into the circle of his arms, his hard lips on hers. For a moment she swayed in his embrace, blood thundering in her ears, hating him and hating her own body for the treacherous way it responded eagerly to his touch. She knew she would not fight back, could not resist him. Instead, she matched her passion to his: her strokes to his caresses, her kisses to his mouthings. By the time he drew her toward the bed, she had never been so perfectly primed for love.

Abruptly, Rowland cast her down and stepped back.

"So that was what you came for after all, my lotus. What a pity we have no time to indulge our appetites any further. *No, Caro!*" His voice cracked like a whiplash. "Stay where you are or I'll call in a trooper to guard you like any other traitor!"

INDIGO NIGHTS

OLIVIA O'NEILL

A BERKLEY MEDALLION BOOK

published by

BERKLEY PUBLISHING CORPORATION

Futura Publications Limited
110 Warner Road
Camberwell, London SE5 9HQ

SBN 425-03629-4

*BERKLEY MEDALLION BOOKS are published by
Berkley Publishing Corporation
200 Madison Avenue
New York, N. Y. 10016*

BERKLEY MEDALLION BOOK ® TM 757,375

Printed in the United States of America

Berkley Medallion Edition, OCTOBER, 1977

Cast of Characters

Lady Caroline March	Caro
Lady Marchmain	Caro's mother
Lord Marchmain	Caro's father
Georgie, Jamie	Caro's younger brothers
Amelia Hamilton	Caro's friend, Rowland Steel's sister
Tom Hamilton	Amelia's husband
Azimullah Khan	Moslem-Indian envoy to London
Captain Rowland Steel	Captain, 46th Irregular Bengal Cavalry
Lady Marvell	Caro's companion on voyage to India
Brook Vyner	Assistant Collector, Civil Service, East India Company
Philippa Thynne	Caro's older sister
Captain Andrew Thynne	Philippa's husband, Captain, 42nd Queen's Regiment
Prince Chandranaya (Prince Bahadur)	Aspiring Rajah of Patelbar

Rajah Jahan Bahadur Shah	Reigning Rajah of Patelbar
Nana Sahib, Rajah of Bithoor	Recently deposed Indian Prince, Ally of Prince Chandranaya
Bhalat Ram	Caro's manservant
Fionn Kelly	Irish doctor in Patelbar
Sher Dil	Indian servant of Phillipa's household
Bulbul	Proprietress, Joyhouse of Kali and Rowland Steel's former Indian nanny
General, Sir James Steel	Rowland Steel's father
Adeen Rao	Prince Chandranaya's father
General "Tiger" Elliott	Commander of British forces at Baburpore
Sita Ram	Bulbul and General Steel's son, Rowland Steel's half brother and companion
Abdur	Bulbul's servant
Lewis Allan	Rowland Steel's fellow officer
Captain Willie Arbuthnot	Rowland Steel's cousin, Scottish officer
Gul Mohammed	Rowland Steel's manservant

INDIGO NIGHTS

OLIVIA O'NEILL

Chapter One

A SUMMONS TO her mother's bedroom before the hour of noon was a rare enough event to cause Lady Caroline March a degree of alarm.

What had she done now? What could she have done to make her mother want to see her so early?

The Countess of Marchmain—a fading porcelain beauty whose constant fight against the ravages of the years forbade her to rise before the clock struck twelve—took little interest in her children beyond appointing nurses, governesses, and servants to attend them, and saw her offspring privately only to criticize or scold.

When Sarah, her mother's dour Scots maid, told Caro she was to go immediately to Lady Marchmain's room, Caro ran quickly through her mind a number of possible reasons for the summons, but try as she might she could fasten on no particular misdemeanor serious enough to warrant her mother's reprimand.

She had not gone riding unattended, or overspent her small allowance or danced too long with any one of the gentlemen who sought her hand—or with the very dashing Captain Thomas Hamilton, who didn't. She had worn her bonnet against the summer sun, and spoken prettily to all those tiresome old aunts at Mama's tea party yesterday.

On all these points, her conscience was clear. Nevertheless, as she changed her shabby brown holland dress for a more becoming, and cleaner, morning gown of lavender cotton, and smoothed her thick dark hair into a shining coil at the nape of her neck, Caro felt a nagging unease. She could see it reflected in the long-lashed brown eyes gazing anxiously back at her from the looking glass. Remote and uninterested in her children Lady Marchmain might be, but she had—like Queen Victoria herself— an uncanny knack of detecting wrongdoing, and Caro feared that somehow, somewhere, the Countess had divined that her younger daughter's feelings toward recently widowed Captain Hamilton had become warmer than mere sympathetic friendship warranted. Not that she was in any way in love with Tom, thought Caro, rubbing the toe of her somewhat scuffed shoe against her stocking in an attempt to give it a shine. How could she be, with poor, dear Amelia scarcely a month in her grave? Yet there was something about Tom's powerful frame, the touch of his hands—not soft, like her father's, but hard and muscular from contact with reins, swords, pistols—and the way his heavy-lidded blue eyes followed her, that made Caro keenly aware of his presence no matter how many others were in the room.

"Your mother's awaiting, my lady." Sarah rapped smartly on the door.

"Coming!" Caro rammed home a final hairpin and hurried down the passage, hung with portraits of Marchmain forebears, to her mother's bedchamber. She scratched softly and was told to enter. As she had expected, Lady Marchmain was still abed in the great rose and gold fourposter. A cup of chocolate cooled on a side table, and two small spaniels rolled and scratched on the rug.

"Ah, Caroline." Her mother turned a languid head to greet her, and Caro dutifully pecked the cheek still redolent of Madame Guillaume's Venus Unguent, which Lady Marchmain believed to be a sovereign remedy for wrinkles. "I have some good news for you, dear child. Your father and I have decided on a match for you."

Since the London season had ended in July, Caro had been aware of her parents' increasingly anxious efforts to find a husband for her, but none of the young men under consideration had proved rich enough not only to support Caro in becoming style, but also to pay off Lord Marchmain's racing debts, which, since the failure of his heavily backed colt Cicero, to win the Derby, had reached enormous proportions. Now there was an air of certainty about her mother that Caro found even more disquieting than if the conversation had opened upon the subject of Captain Hamilton.

"Decided, Mama?"

"Yes, you are a very fortunate girl. Imagine it—in only your first London season, you have attracted the attention of Sir Robert Anderton, whom every scheming mother in the country has been trying for years to snare for her daughter. He called here yesterday and asked your father if he might address you, and of course we were delighted to give our permission. It seems that he was introduced to you at poor Amelia Hamilton's birthday party in June, and was so struck with your looks, my love, that nothing would do but he must go home and consult with his daughters and, their approval being given, hurry back to London to speak to your father. I was never more astonished in my life than when he announced the news to me, but we have talked it over and agree that it is the very match for you."

She surveyed her daughter appraisingly. No one could deny that Caro was the beauty of the family: in her slim yet rounded figure and glowing dark eyes Lady Marchmain saw a younger, more vivid version of herself in the long-gone days when suitors had queued to address her. Yet there was in Caro's expression a certain willfulness—a disquietingly headstrong quality—which called for firm handling. She should not be allowed to go her own way or she would soon grow out of hand. Give her an inch and she'll take a foot, thought Lady Marchmain grimly—but not with a strong-minded, experienced man like Sir Robert. He'd know how to hold her in check.

She went on. "Sir Robert is a good deal older than you, Caroline; indeed, he has daughters near your own age, but an older man will suit you very well, believe me; especially since Sir Robert is blessed with a large fortune. My dear," she said, clasping her hands in a semblance of ecstasy, "he is immensely rich. You will want for nothing. Now kiss me and tell me you are pleased."

The color drained slowly from Caro's cheeks, and she swayed, catching at the back of a chair to steady herself. "Marry Sir Robert?" she said faintly. "Mama, you cannot be serious. Why, he is old, and fat."

Lady Marchmain permitted herself a frown. "Do not be pert, Caroline," she said warningly. "This is a great opportunity for you—for us all. Neither Sir Robert's age, nor his figure should cause you to hesitate. He is hale and hearty, and fifty-five is no great age for a man in any case. What matters is that he wants to make you his wife. He has large estates in the North Country—Cumberland, I believe—where you will be able to indulge your passion for riding"—she condemned it all with a sniff—"and other bucolic pursuits. Sir Robert is reputed to be generous; and best of all, he is utterly besotted with you. He said so to your father with the utmost frankness. No lovesick boy could speak of you more extravagantly: your night-dark hair with copper glints; the grace of your figure; the delicacy of your features; you would blush to hear him."

She cast a dissatisfied glance at her daughter's

4

simple cotton dress—made over from one of Philippa's, she was certain, and showing signs of wear, as were Caro's shoes and stockings. She said, in a softer tone, "Just think, Caroline. You will be able to command the best dressmakers and milliners, and spend whatever you wish. Is it not worth a few extra years on your husband's age to allow you so much power and wealth? Have you not dreamed of such a match?"

But Caro's dreams had been very different. Of a knight in shining armor to carry her away to his castle, certainly; but a knight young and handsome, debonair, gallant—somewhat in the manner of Andrew Thynne, the young cavalry captain who, four years ago, had won her sister Philippa's heart and carried her off to live with him in the exotic East. Not of a slobbering, fat, bald Scottish banker nearly thrice her age.

"Mama, I am obliged to Sir Robert for his—his *interest*," she said in a choked voice, "but I cannot marry him. Please do not try to make me. Truly, I would do anything to please you and Papa, but not this. I must beg of you to tell Sir Robert that his offer is refused."

In her heart of hearts, Lady Marchmain had half expected this reaction, and was prepared. "I am deeply grieved that you should prove so ungrateful, Caroline," she said icily. "I did not believe you so selfish as to consider your own inclinations alone. I see I must be frank with you. Sir Robert's offer is generous in the extreme, and in addition to a most substantial marriage settlement on you, he has agreed to pay off the mortgage on Marchmain House and provide the money to send both your brothers to Eton. This will enable Papa to repay his debts to Mr. Padwick; so you see how your marriage will benefit us all."

Numbly Caro shook her head, not trusting herself to speak.

Her mother's voice hardened. "Go to your room, then, Caroline. Do not let me hear any further talk of refusing Sir Robert. It is all arranged, and your father would be extremely vexed if he were to hear of your childish objections. I will tell Sarah to serve luncheon in your room, so that you may have time to think over your unmannerly behavior—that is, unless you prefer to apologize for it at once. No? Then go to your room immediately."

Alone in her bedroom, Caro paced the floor in helpless rage. To be trapped like this, just when life seemed to hold such promise—it was too much to bear. In two years' time, at twenty-one, she would be independent of her parents and no further burden on their finances, but they could not wait, and instead chose to sell her in this way to the highest bidder. And, argued her mind shrewdly, when she was twenty-one and her own mistress, she would be no further use to Lord Marchmain as a bargaining counter. He was trying to marry her off—and make money out of it— before she achieved independence. Her nineteenth birthday was not two months past, and as a minor she knew that, as far as the law was concerned, her parents had complete control over her. She could appeal to no one to overrule their decision.

As far as the law was concerned ... Caro's natural resilience began to reassert itself; she shook back her long dark hair and thought furiously. By the time Sarah appeared with a meager tray of food and the information that Lady Caroline might leave her room only when she felt prepared to apologize to her mother, Caro had the glimmering of a plan.

She wished that she could have confided in her older sister. Though Philippa was her parents' favorite— being naturally gentle and biddable—Caro felt sure that in this instance even her mild-tempered sister would encourage her to rebel. But Philippa was six thousand or more miles away, living on the hot, dusty Ganges plain in the garrison town of Baburpore, from which she wrote long, colorful descriptions of Indian life and the afflictions borne by English memsahibs ranging from dishonest servants to prickly heat. Philippa could do nothing to help Caro, might not even know of her sister's fate until the wedding was over.

The other person to whom Caro would naturally have turned was Amelia Hamilton—as Amelia Steel her sister's schoolmate and greatest friend—who had always taken a kindly interest in Philippa's younger sister. During Caro's first London season, Amelia frequently invited her to join small, diverting parties at her pretty town house, where the guests were chosen for their gaiety and charm rather than their wealth.

At these parties of Amelia's, her husband, Tom Hamilton, seemed curiously out of place. His tall, broad-shouldered figure and heavily handsome features seemed to belong to a savage world of primitive action and violent excitement, far removed from the frills and flounces of his wife's drawing room. Amelia's friends were a little in awe of him, and vivacious Molly Kettering, who knew all the latest gossip, whispered to Caro that she should beware of Tom Hamilton. He was wild. There was even a rumor that he had killed his man in a duel, though the whole affair had been hushed up.

Tom never seemed to take part in the singing, card playing, or other diversions Amelia organized, and Caro often wondered why he bothered to attend such social gatherings, which he plainly found tedious. Just once, when Amelia had consented to play waltzes after supper, Tom detached himself from the mantelpiece, where he had been observing the company with his brooding gaze, strolled over to where Caro was sitting with Molly Kettering, and invited her to dance. To her

7

surprise—for she would not have expected him to dance well—their bodies moved in excellent harmony together; and as Amelia, laughing, played faster and faster, Tom spun Caro dizzyingly around the polished floor until the other dancers fell back to applaud their performance.

He did not speak, but held her eyes with his as they swooped and whirled, his hand firmly on her back and his hard, muscular body close against her so that, as the long moments stretched out, Caro was aware of Tom's somber eyes as the one fixed point in a spinning world. When Amelia brought down her hands in a final crashing chord and everyone began to laugh and chatter again, Caro found her heart was pounding from more than the exertion of the dance, and her knees would scarcely support her. For a moment after the music had ceased Tom's arms continued to hold her fast and his eyes to stare fiercely—almost hungrily—at her upturned face and the pulse drumming in her white throat.

Then, as she made a small movement to free herself, the spell was broken, and Tom was his formal, withdrawn self again as he bowed stiffly and escorted her back to sit with Molly.

Caro often wondered, after that dance, whether Amelia noticed how Tom seemed to seek her company in preference to that of all the other ladies who made up Amelia's circle of friends, and if she did notice, whether she minded. He escorted her riding in the Row, accompanied by a groom, much to the annoyance of Charlie Harper and Blake McIntyre, who considered this their special privilege; he talked to no other lady after the farewell dinner that Lord and Lady Marchmain gave to mark Philippa's departure for India. Caro could not help being aware that, limited as their opportunities for conversation were, he found her attractive, and while she still felt faintly uneasy in his presence, it was certainly exhilarating to have a grown man with Tom Hamilton's dangerous and uncertain reputation dancing attendance on her in place of the blushing, stammering boys fresh from school who had previously been partnered with her.

On the whole, she doubted if Amelia saw anything untoward in her husband's relationship with Philippa's vivacious little sister.

Warm-hearted, generous Amelia was herself a natural flirt, always the center of a laughing circle, and a most successful hostess. Her parties were reckoned the gayest in London, and her invitations eagerly sought after.

When Azimullah Khan, an affable, silvery tongued Moslem envoy, was sent to London by a recently deposed Indian Prince known as Nana Sahib, of the now-subdued Mahratta tribe, for the purpose of negotiating with the directors of the Honourable East India Company for the renewal of Nana Sahib's pension, he was soon drawn into Amelia's lively circle of friends, and often to be found at her parties and entertainments. But then, Azimullah Khan was quite the rage that summer of 1855: no party was counted a success without his splendidly dressed, turbaned presence, and he moved in the highest level of society.

Although it was common knowledge that the East India Company had no intention of reauthorizing his dethroned master's pension, it did not stop the sophisticated, pleasure-loving Azimullah Khan from cutting a notable dash with his armies of uniformed servants and apparently unlimited funds. Everyone vowed he would never forget the summer when Azimullah Khan had delighted them so.

Then one day came the stunning news that Amelia Hamilton had been brutally murdered. Her maid, returning from her day out, had found a box of flowers in the hall, and had run upstairs to tell her mistress. In the boudoir she had found Amelia, lying dead on a chaise longue, her head grotesquely twisted on a broken neck. The room was in chaos, drawers pulled out and their contents flung on the floor, the jewel box ransacked, and the open French window with curtains billowing out onto the balcony showing how the murderer had made his escape.

Caro, shocked and disbelieving, heard the details from a solemn young policeman who made routine inquiries at the homes of Amelia's closest friends in the hope of discovering some motive for the crime.

"Head bent over at a terrible angle, poor lady," he said with gloomy relish, "and the Captain away on a fishing trip in the country. Didn't know nothing about what had happened to his wife until he drove up to his own front door and found his house full of policemen. The sergeant tried to break it to him gentle-like, but there's no easy way of telling a man that someone's done in his lady, and sergeant said he thought the poor gentleman was going to fall into a fit. Then he started shouting and yelling at the servants to know why they hadn't protected their mistress better, and there was no reasoning with him that day."

Caro could imagine the scene: Tom frantic with grief, the servants frightened and sobbing, the police in their heavy boots searching Amelia's pretty boudoir with its filmy net curtains and pink silk hangings. Her lucky, lighthearted friend, the lovely, vivacious girl, lying still and silent, her face covered by her own cashmere shawl. But who would have killed Amelia? She had not had a single enemy in the world. Yet there had been many who loved Amelia; now they were deeply suffering the pain of her loss, chief among the grieving being Tom Hamilton.

In the weeks that followed, Caro's feelings toward Tom underwent a subtle change. Whereas before Amelia's death she had been a little overawed by him, now he seemed greatly subdued by the tragedy of losing his wife and she found herself able to talk more freely to him. She thought him wise to move from the house where everything reminded him of Amelia.

"I'm off to France, you know," he told her when she called with her mother on a visit of condolence. "A soldier-of-fortune can always make a living in one of their colonies, and it may help me to forget."

Caro's heart had ached for him. She put an impulsive hand on his arm: "You will always be welcome at Marchmain House, Tom, will he not, Mama?"

Lady Marchmain's cold eyes fastened on Caro's hand where it lay on Tom's black-banded sleeve. "We will certainly be happy to see you there," she agreed, but her tone belied her words. The countess did not approve of Tom Hamilton, and only her daughters' well-known friendship with Amelia had persuaded her to make the gesture of offering her condolences in person. She gazed speculatively at the young widower. He certainly was a fine figure of a man, she thought; over average height, with the muscular swell of his broad shoulders straining the seams of his broadcloth coat. Trained, she had heard, by one of the foremost pugilists of the day, he had the power and grace of an athlete, yet he was not handsome: his complexion was too swarthy and those startlingly blue eyes close-set under heavy black brows. But it was not his looks that Lady Marchmain disliked so much as the suppressed violence she sensed within him, as if a dangerous animal had been trained to an appearance of good behavior still remained, deep down, as wild and menacing as it was when it was born.

On this point, Lady Marchmain and her husband had been agreed. Though they shared the same gaming club, she knew that Lord Marchmain would not play at the same table as Tom Hamilton. "Never fear: I don't play with a man who isn't governor of his own temper," he'd said briskly, when she voiced to him her misgivings. "The wonder is that Amelia ever married him. But I suppose he is an attractive enough fellow, even if he is a bit of a scoundrel."

He was certainly attractive to her daughter, Lady Marchmain had reflected, watching them both. She wondered whether to reprimand Caro for forward behavior when they were alone, then thought comfortably that there was no need. Once Caro was married to Sir Robert Anderton, Lady Marchmain's maternal worries would be at an end, and her daughter safe from the kind of temptation that Tom Hamilton most assuredly represented.

Briskly pulling on her gloves, she had bidden Tom farewell, adding her hopes that his journeying would be pleasant, then swept out with a somewhat reluctant Caro, who had been enjoying the conversation, trailing in her wake. Tomorrow, thought Lady Marchmain, she would announce to Caro the glad news of the match they planned for her, and begin arrangements for an early wedding. But thanks to that willful girl, nothing had gone according to plan.

Alone in her bedroom the next day with the remains of her bread-and-water luncheon, Caro flung herself on the elegant little fourposter bed she used to share with Philippa, careless of crushing the smooth chintz counterpane patterned with bunches of forget-me-nots. She would never marry that flabby old miser, she thought defiantly. No matter how they starved and beat her, she would continue to refuse Sir Robert. If only she had someone strong to protect her—to take her side. Then she thought of Tom, and instantly, fully-fledged, a plan sprang to her mind. Tom Hamilton would help her, she was sure of it.

On impulse she sprang off the bed and went to her writing desk, pushing aside the half-finished letter to

Philippa she had begun last night. On a fresh sheet of paper she scribbled a note to Tom, begging him to meet her by the garden gate of Marchmain House at four o'clock the following afternoon, since she had something important to tell him.

Do not fail me, she concluded dramatically, *for my life is in your hands*, and after considering and rejecting several formulas assuring him of her affection, she signed it simply *Caro*. She sealed the letter with a wafer and tucked it into the pocket of her dress. Then she rang for Sarah.

Anyone who knew Caro well should have been suspicious of her meek, obedient demeanor for the rest of that hot summer's day. Having dutifully kissed her mother and begged her pardon for making such a foolish, ungrateful speech that morning, Caro obtained permission to walk down Bond Street with the footman in attendance, to see the new creations of her favorite milliner.

When the footman's attention was temporarily diverted by seeing Prince Albert drive past in a four-in-hand emblazoned with the Royal Arms, Caro seized the opportunity to slip her letter and a shining new penny into the grimy hand of a little street urchin, with the whispered information that he'd receive a second penny when he called at Marchmain House to report the safe delivery of the letter into Captain Hamilton's own hands.

"Captain Hamilton, yes'm," said the child, promptly memorizing the two addresses with slum-sharpened wits. "I'll give it 'im right away."

"Go around to the tradesmen's entrance of Marchmain House, and I'll see that Cook has something for you," murmured Caro, and away sped her letter bearer just as the footman reluctantly pushed his way out of the crowd cheering the Prince.

Satisfied, Caro sauntered on a little farther, looking

in shop windows, then turned for home.

At six that evening, the street Arab returned and reported that Captain Hamilton had said he'd be there. Caro interviewed him in the kitchen under the indulgent eye of Cook, who had a weakness for small boys since her own son had been early snatched from her by the smallpox. She was a simple woman, and Caro had no fear that when she made her escape Cook would connect her disappearance with the street Arab's message.

The child left Marchmain House with a paper bag crammed with delicious scraps—ham, a chicken drumstick, several apples, and a slice of rich fruit cake—and a firm resolve to run further errands on behalf of Lady Caroline March should the opportunity arise.

So it was, that cloaked and hooded, Caro slipped through the garden gate while Marchmain House and its inhabitants dozed in the August sunlight, and found Tom Hamilton waiting on his handsome weight-carrying bay horse at the far end of the street. She hurried toward him.

"Good day to you, Caro," said Tom, swinging lightly down from the saddle and clasping both her hands in his. His eyes raked her shrouded form. "Don't you find that cloak a trifle warm for August? Now, what's it all about? You see me here in obedience to your message, though your choice of messenger was a touch unusual. Could you not have secured the services of your father's footman to carry your letters?"

"Oh, Tom, I am in deep trouble," gasped Caro, breathless from her run down the quiet street. Thankfully she pushed back her hood and loosened the cloak. "I am so glad you came, for I need your help to make my escape."

"Escape? What can you mean?"

She saw that she had caught his interest and hurried

on. "Papa and Mama are determined to marry me to Sir Robert Anderton! Oh, it is so unjust! He is old and fat and has daughters as old as I. I could never love him! He is rich as Croesus and has promised to pay Papa's gaming debts if I marry him, and send the boys to school—though I am sure they have no wish to go. Now do you see why I asked you to meet me? You must help me! Help me, I beg of you!"

Tom listened in silence, chewing thoughtfully at his fingernail. He glanced up and down the street, but it was empty apart from a loitering street child, busily intent on searching the gutter.

"I'd do anything in my power to help you, Caro, of course; but what do you wish me to do? As you know, I am shortly departing for France. My house is sold, and I have told the landlord of the inn where I'm staying that from tomorrow he may have my room. I've nowhere to shelter you, even if I wished to."

Caro moved closer to him and put all the appeal she possessed into her big dark eyes. "But you *do* wish it, Tom, I'm certain," she said softly. "You would not like to see me married to a man old enough to be my grandfather. *Please* help me."

Tom regarded her still more thoughtfully. "Are you asking me to take you to France? To be sure, I can imagine nothing more delightful, but what of your reputation? Even if you escape this marriage, your parents will soon wish you to marry someone else—a confirmed spinster daughter, even one as lovely as you, Caro, is hardly what Lord Marchmain would want."

"Oh, don't concern yourself about my reputation!" she exclaimed inpatiently. "I think I can look after that myself. No: all I ask is that you should take me with you when you leave for France, and set me down at the home of my friend Cecilia Furneaux, who lives at Alton, in Hampshire.

"I have it all planned," she went on. "Mrs. Furneaux

has two younger daughters, and I believe I can persuade her to give me a situation as their governess until I attain my majority. For as I daresay you know, my sole fortune now consists of the Portland sapphires, which my dear grandmother left me; but when I am twenty-one, half the revenues from her estate will be mine, and I shall be perfectly independent of my father. It was because my grandmother Portland did not wish to see her estate gambled away that she left it equally to myself and Philippa, since Jamie and Georgie were born after her death. Naturally, when I inherit, I shall allot a share to my brothers, just as Philippa did when she married.

"I must hide for two years, that is all. Please help me!" she repeated.

The Portland sapphires! Caro was too engrossed in her own recital to notice the sudden gleam in Tom's eyes. He controlled his excitement with an effort, responding coolly, "You say that in two years' time this fortune will be yours? Will it not equally become available to you upon your marriage?"

She laughed. "Available to my husband, you mean! Oh, it is no great fortune, I assure you, merely an independence which my grandmother Portland wished me and Philippa to possess so that we should not be forced into the kind of loveless marriage my parents now desire me to make. Mrs. Furneaux was a dear friend of my grandmother and she will understand perfectly how I am placed, though I dare not write to warn her of my intention for fear of the letter being seen and my whereabouts immediately guessed. For the same reason I dare not travel there openly, but if you are to take a ship from Southampton next week, and intend to travel there by easy stages, I would be infinitely obliged if you would set me on my way."

Tom's highly developed hunting instinct and quick grasp of opportunity were the only things that had kept him one jump ahead of the law during the past ten of his twenty-six years. He never consciously planned ahead, but seized his chances as they came along. It was surprising how often, he thought, fate seemed to play into the hands of a man who was strong, determined and, above all, reckless. Tom liked danger; without it he felt only half alive, but he was uncomfortably aware that here in England the net was slowly, inexorably closing around him, and that soon he would be trussed and entangled in its meshes like a tiger bound to spend the rest of its life in a cage.

Since Amelia's death he had felt that his lucky streak had run out. Old friends avoided him, suspecting what they could not prove. His debts had snowballed alarmingly. And now he had heard that Amelia's brother, Captain Rowland Steel, had returned from India and was inquiring into his sister's death. The only course open to him seemed to be a quick, quiet departure for some land less dogged by officialdom and the trappings of civilization—a place where he could hunt, fight, and wrest a fortune from those weaker than himself without exciting the moral indignation that such conduct would provoke here in England. The trouble was that he was most cursedly short of the ready. Though he had sold his house and Amelia's jewels, there was hardly enough left to pay his passage to France, let alone carry him to Canada, India, or some other distant land of opportunity.

Until Caro, the most alluring little minx to leave the schoolroom for many a long year, had offered to place herself and her jewels in his care!

Hiding his jubilation, he took Caro's gloved hand in an extravagant gesture and pressed it to his lips. "Sweet Caro, your slightest wish is my command. I will do anything you say. If you will meet me here on tomorrow afternoon, with the smallest amount of luggage you can contrive, I undertake to escort you safely to Mrs. Furneaux's country house. As you say, it is no great way from Southampton, and will not cause me to delay my own departure by more than a day."

Caro's eyes filled with grateful tears, and Tom felt a sudden impulse to crush her to him and tear back the cloak that covered that tantalizing white throat. Sternly he held himself in check. That would be the worst folly, to give in to his cravings before the time was ripe, especially since fate, which had treated him so shabbily of late, now seemed ready to play into his hands.

"I knew I was right to come to you," Caro exclaimed. "You are a true friend." She gave him a radiant smile. "I will wait here for you on Friday, and bring only the smallest portmanteau."

"And the jewels," he interposed. "You may find them of use as security in the next years should you need it. But a word of warning, Caro; if you so much as hint of this to anyone—your brothers, say, or a faithful maid—your parents will be on your track before you can reach your destination, and I will suffer for it, too."

"I shall tell no one," she promised, and he believed her. Young as she was, Caro had the air of one accustomed to make her own decisions. She blew him a kiss and skipped back lightly to the garden gate, which closed with a soft thud behind her.

The urchin removed his intent gaze from the gutter to stare after her billowing cloak. He hadn't caught all of the conversation, but he'd heard enough to tell him that Lady Caroline was up to something and on Friday she'd be meeting this dandy again, and bringing a portmanteau that time... Deep in thought, the child had to make a sudden spring for safety to avoid being ridden down by the bloke, who whipped up his horses and drove down the street at a reckless pace, his lips drawn back in a grin that was almost a snarl.

*　　　*　　　*

The next day crawled by, for Caro, once she had taken her decision to leave home, was in a fever to be gone. Time and again, when her maid was below stairs, she packed and repacked her tiny carpetbag, wrapping the Portland sapphires carefully in a square of chamois leather and placing them at the bottom of a small reticule. Feeling their comforting hardness under her hand gave her courage as, once more, she glanced swiftly round the rose arbor before slipping through the gate in the garden wall. Steadying her breathing, trying not to hurry, she strolled along, keeping close to the wall and avoiding the eyes of passersby, till she reached the corner of the street. Tom's post chaise loomed beside her, the impatient horses pawing at the cobbles. He had not failed her.

"Get in quickly; you're late." His tone was brusque, preoccupied, and his eyes roved restlessly up and down the street as he handed her into the closed carriage, but all was peaceful in the afternoon sunlight. A few women returning with laden baskets from their shopping, a child in buttoned boots bowling a hoop along the pavement, while his nurse gossiped with a dapper young man in a billycock hat, a ragged waif leaning against the sun-warmed brick wall; nothing to disquiet even a man who knew a warrant had been issued for his arrest.

Tom had been obliged to leave his lodgings earlier in the day than he wanted to, owing to the attentions of a party of police who had called there that very morning and, finding him absent, proceeded to ransack his possessions most thoroughly. This he had learned from his landlord on his return from hiring the light post chaise, complete with horses, which was to convey him to the coast. Deciding that it was too risky to take his own equipage, he had left it with the accommodating landlord in lieu of rent, and pausing only to snatch up a few necessaries from among his tumbled clothes, he had driven the hired carriage by a roundabout route to the alley behind Marchmain House and there waited, burning with impatience, for Caro to emerge.

A close call, he thought, slamming the door and springing quickly into the driving seat. But provided he kept calm and did not alarm Caro's suspicions prematurely, all should yet be well. He leaned down, peering through the small half-open window to where Caro was disposing herself and her bag in the cramped interior.

"You have the jewels?" he called softly, and was rewarded by her quick, confident nod. He touched his whip to the horses' backs, and the chaise bounded forward.

For the first hour or so, Caro kept her mind off the jolting discomfort of the carriage being driven too fast over cobbled streets by rehearsing in her mind how she was to present her case to Mrs. Furneaux. She knew she had plenty of time to think it over. When she had last visited Cecilia's family, the previous year, she had traveled in Lord Marchmain's heavy, outdated coach-and-four, and recalled that the journey had taken from early morning until ten o'clock at night, and had necessitated no fewer than four changes of horses.

Now they were traveling much faster, in a lighter conveyance, and Tom was a notable whip, who could be relied on to get the utmost out of his cattle; even so, she guessed it would be full dark before they saw the lights of Grammary House. In her mind she pictured the mellow red-brick facade of the handsome Queen Anne building, with its clock tower over the stableyard and noble cedar trees sweeping low branches down to the velvet lawns.

Fortunately, Lady Marchmain was not intimate with Mrs. Furneaux, whom she considered a blue-stocking who had exerted an undesirable influence over Lady Marchmain's mother, encouraging her to provide a measure of independence for her grand-daughters by her absurd will, which effectively bypassed her spendthrift son-in-law and gave over the entire revenues of the late Lady Portland's estate to Philippa and Caro when they attained their respective majorities. Lady Marchmain did not even know how earnestly Mrs. Furneaux had besought Caro, on that last visit, to make the most of her grandmother's legacy, and not to surrender—as Philippa had—to the first man who took an interest in her. By English law, a woman's property became her husband's upon her wedding day, and though Mrs. Furneaux freely admitted that Andrew Thynne had loved Philippa more than her inheritance, she pointed out to Caro that fortune hunters abounded and that young girls were easily deceived. To be enabled to enjoy a few years' independence before submitting to the shackles of matrimony was a privilege few girls were given, and Caro would be a fool not to take advantage of her grandmother's generosity.

This argument had greatly impressed Caro, and she felt sure that Mrs. Furneaux and her daughters would give her practical as well as moral support in her stand against a forced and loveless match.

The chaise halted at last, and Caro descended stiffly to pace around the coachhouse yard while the steaming horses who had brought them from London were unharnessed, and a fresh pair put to. Tom, pushing a dark bottle into the pocket of his greatcoat, appeared from the inn just as her circulation was beginning to run freely again, and hustled her back into the carriage.

"Don't show yourself in such a fashion," he hissed, "or all our work may go for nought. Stable lads have eyes and tongues, and a posthouse is the first place where inquiries would be made."

Her eyes stung with tears at his unexpectedly harsh rebuke, and at her own thoughtlessness. Although she was cold and cramped, she stayed hidden for the rest of the journey.

It proved shorter than she expected.

Having steeled herself to endure the bumping and jolting for at least two more hours in the summer twilight, Caro was astonished when, soon after sunset, the horses stopped before a lodge gate. Mindful of Tom's warning, she kept the window shut and her face hidden as he spoke briefly to the lodge-keeper, and the heavy iron gates creaked open. She rubbed her eyes and stared through the growing dusk at the tree-lined avenue leading up to the house. A gravel sweep, smooth lawns—yes, but where were the cedar trees she remembered? Surely the stables were on the left wing of the house, not the right?

Now the chaise clattered and rocked over cobbles and under an arch. A groom came running to hold the horses' heads. Caro's heart began to thunder and she had the terrible sense of having gone to sleep in a dream and awakened to a nightmare. Why was Tom conveying her into the stable yard instead of handing her out at the front door? Why didn't she recognize Cecilia's home, where she had spent so happy a summer, exploring every building and outbuilding?

The terrible truth dawned, though for a moment or two she refused to accept it. This was not Cecilia's home. Tom had brought her to an unknown destination. She was at his mercy; and nobody knew where she was. Before her wildly chasing thoughts could settle on a plan of action, the carriage door was opened.

"Come," said Tom. "We have arrived, and I for one could do with some refreshment."

His tone was level, yet she sensed the taut excitement behind it, like a man whose daring gamble is about to pay off. She had heard the same suppressed yet hectic note in her father's voice when he'd staked more than he could afford on a single throw.

She controlled her shaking hands as well as she could, and said, "I fear that I must have misdirected you, Tom, or you have mistaken the way. This is not Grammary House."

He laughed, a harsh low rasp that set her nerves on edge. "Not Grammary House, no, but it will serve for a night's lodging to one as careless as you of her reputation. Come, milady."

His hand closed on her wrist, and she pulled back for a second, then gave in to the relentless pressure that threatened to crack one bone against the other. "I can manage very well alone," she murmured, but he did not relax his grip, and she just had time to snatch up her little portmanteau with her free hand as he dragged her out of the chaise.

A side door opened as they approached, and Caro caught a glimpse of an impassive-faced manservant holding a branch of flaring candles to light their way. Then the door thudded shut behind them, and Tom, still keeping a tight grip on her arm, led her into a paneled dining room where the long gleaming table was set with two places.

"Allow me to take your cloak," he said, with a dreadful pretense of courtesy. He ripped it roughly from her shoulders and flung it to the servant. "No doubt you are weary from your journey and would prefer to eat at once. A glass of wine?"

She sipped warily, glad of the wine's heartening glow but well aware that she must hoard her strength and keep her wits about her if she were to escape unharmed from this new and frightening Tom Hamilton. How right her father had been to see it was more than mere wildness that set Tom apart from the other men of her acquaintance. She wished she had listened to her mother, to Molly Kettering's whispered warnings. Almost she wished herself back in her own room at Marchmain House—at least the threat of marrying Sir Robert was sufficiently remote, to allow time for maneuver. The threat from Tom seemed alarmingly immediate.

The silent servant piled her plate with food and glided out of the room. She made a pretense of eating while covertly watching Tom, who ate heartily.

"Where are we?" she ventured at last. "Whose is this house?"

"It wouldn't help you if I told you to whom it belongs," he said curtly. "Call it Bluebeard's Castle, if you wish." The thought seemed to amuse him. "All you need know is that I am free to treat this house as my own, and that the servants here are chosen for their—*discretion*. They will not help you, no matter how much noise you make. I promised myself that my last night in England should be one to remember, but I little dreamed whose company I'd enjoy that night. Lady Caroline March is certainly a better conquest than some tart from the stews of Southampton." He rose and stalked round the table to stand behind her, his strong, sinewy hands caressing her neck. Caro sat rigid, scarcely daring to breathe. He would not—*could* not—mean to attack her here.

"By heaven," he growled, his voice sunk so low that she hardly caught the words, "I have waited so long for this, and thought my chance would never come. I used to watch you throughout those dull parties of Amelia's, and dream of possessing you." As he spoke, his hands moved roughly, purposefully, over her bodice and down to her breasts, grasping them, kneading them, heedless of her pain or pleasure.

Steeling herself to remain calm beneath the pressure of hands that threatened to turn her giddy, Caro raised her head quickly, as if she'd caught some sound outside.

"What's that?" she cried in a high, breathless voice. "There's someone at the door. Are you expecting company, Tom?"

The dizzying pressure on her breasts relaxed suddenly, then dropped away as Tom growled a curse and strode to the window, pulling aside the heavy velvet curtains and leaning out into the night. Quick as thought, Caro slid from her chair and sprang silently to the door. Before Tom turned from his puzzled survey of the quiet carriageway outside, she was halfway across the hall, her slippers making no sound on the square black-and-white tiles. Three closed doors confronted her, and she paused for an instant to try the handle of the nearest. It did not budge and she knew she had only seconds in which to find a hiding place. She cast a quick glance around, noting the positions of the doors and the wide, shallow staircase, then she picked up a heavy vase and flung it with all her strength at the oil lamp that hung from a thin chain in the well of the hall.

Her aim was true. Just as Tom emerged into the hall, the vase knocked the lamp from its support and together they crashed onto the tiles, plunging the hall into blackness. Caro ran lightly up the stairs, one hand feeling for the banister, the other clutching her precious portmanteau.

Below her in the hall, Tom was bellowing like a wounded bull, shouting for lights, and footsteps hurried in all directions, doors slammed, and from the tinkling crunch of breaking china she knew that more than one person had blundered into the debris from the vase. She gained the landing and paused. A long corridor stretched in front of her with doors, presumably bedrooms, on either side. Moonlight streaming through an uncurtained window illuminated every corner; there was nowhere to hide on the landing, and she had no desire to be trapped in a bedroom like a cornered rat.

Picking up her hampering skirts, her heart pounding wildly, she ran up a second flight of stairs, hoping she could find some attic to give her temporary refuge.

Beyond that, she couldn't plan; she only knew that she must get as far away from Tom as possible.

Lights were flickering downstairs again as she reached the top landing and slowed, trying to control her labored breathing. Here, at the top of the house, the polished boards of the ground floor and thick carpets of the second gave place to thin jute coverings and a smell compounded of dust, carbolic soap, stale sweat, and tallow which Caro recognized immediately as belonging to the maids' quarters. The floorboards were uneven and the ceilings low, and she moved with caution, trying first one locked door and then another. At last a door gave to her touch, and cautiously she opened it, ready to draw back in an instant should there be anyone within.

It was empty. A maid's room, apparently, the small window uncurtained and moonlight shining on the narrow lumpy mattress with its iron bedstead, the basin and chipped ewer, the rail on which hung two or three print dresses. She glided over to the dresses, wondering if there were a space behind where she could hide, and found what she was looking for—a low half-door opening into a box room, where trunks and portmanteaus were stored.

Heedless of the clouds of dust that billowed wherever she moved, Caro lifted the lid of the largest trunk she could see, and her heart bounded with joy. It was half empty, with a single layer of old-fashioned clothes smelling strongly of camphor and plenty of room for her to hide in. She wedged a fold of her skirt into the hinge to keep it open a crack, and crept inside.

Muffled by the heavy lid, the sounds of searching became immediately less threatening, though the fumes of camphor at close quarters were decidedly unpleasant. Caro disposed herself as comfortably as she could with her nose near the relatively fresh air of the unfastened hinge, and for fear of lying on the

Portland sapphires and damaging their settings, she tucked her reticule into the corner of the trunk, beneath the original layer of clothing. Gradually her heartbeat returned to normal, and with it her ability to think ahead.

The hour was by now well advanced: she judged it not far short of midnight, but still doors opened and slammed shut, feet pounded up and down the passages of the house, and from time to time she heard Tom's distant voice giving orders and urging the silent servants to further efforts. He had not given up the search yet, that was clear; but with every moment that passed in her uncomfortable hiding place, Caro began to feel more secure. She blessed the instinct that had led her upstairs rather than to make a dash for freedom outside, where her hampering skirts and lack of local knowledge would have made capture inevitable.

Tom had spoken of this as his last night in England, she reflected, and if indeed he planned to catch the Southampton packet tomorrow, all she need do was stay hidden until his departure, then make her way by public conveyance to Mrs. Furneaux's house. Though she had not the least idea where this grim hideout of Tom's was situated, it was plain that it was at some distance from London, and the likelihood of her parents tracing her route was slight. With Tom far away in France, no one would ever know of her escapade—however frightening and demoralizing it had been to discover how easy it was to misjudge a man . . . She wriggled to restore the circulation to her left foot, and the trunk rocked from side to side.

Then the heavy lid was suddenly lifted, and by the flare of an oil lamp she saw Tom, his teeth showing in a grin of triumph.

"So you went to ground up here, my fickle little vixen," he said. "I knew you hadn't broken covert." And he seized her wrist to drag her from her hiding place. Caro sank her teeth into his hand. With a string of oaths Tom lifted her bodily from the trunk, and grasping her painfully tightly, ducked out of the box room beneath the low lintel of the half-door.

"I'll teach you not to use your teeth on me," he snarled, and the brandy fumes on his breath caught at her throat.

"No, Tom. *No!*" she screamed in panic as he flung her roughly down on the lumpy bed. "I don't—I won't—I promise—"

She struggled and fought but he held her easily, letting her wear herself out before he transferred his grip on her wrists into his right hand and with his left ripped through the thin fabric of both her dress and chemise, exposing her nakedness from neck to waist.

Blood drummed in his temples as he saw her lying half naked on the bed, stunned into submission by her fear of him. Amelia had looked like that, wide-eyed and terrified, when he'd hauled that gibbering blackamoor from her lap and flung him bodily out the door before going back to set his own hands on Amelia's soft white neck. Amelia—whom, in his fury and jealousy he had meant to hurt and frighten, but never to kill.

Tom knew the sooner he quit the country, the better the chance of saving his neck. But the temptation to seduce Caro had proved too strong; her slender body and great dark eyes with their provocative tilt had fired his blood ever since he first danced with her in a waltz at Amelia's ill-fated birthday party. To crush that soft, yielding body against his and teach her love—that had been the extent of his desire; but now he needed to possess her. Excited by her protest, thrilled by her terror, the hammer in his brain was beating out: *Take her, take her, take her!*

Caro read the madness in his eyes and renewed her struggles, desperately trying to fend him off as he mauled her thighs like a wild animal. He towered above her, massive in the darkness, his wine-sodden breath coming in harsh gasps. Suddenly, he hoisted his great weight on top of her, thrusting her arms away from her sides and pinioning them in his leaden grip. He pressed his lips brutishly against her resisting ones, forcing them apart with a tongue as rude and cruel as his hands.

Caro had never endured such terror, but this was a strange, new kind of fear, mixed with soft, sharp stabs of excitement that darted from her nipples to beneath her belly, and on to every other part of her body he was invading with his monstrous touch. Caro was fighting more fiercely, more passionately, than she had ever imagined she could—yet escape seemed more unlikely as the seconds passed.

When at last Tom bent over her to ravage her breasts, she saw her chance. She screamed, a scream of fear swiftly cut off as his palm clapped over her mouth, and it was then that her straining ears heard it, above Tom's grunts and her own gasping breath, the crunch of wheels on gravel, the distant slam of a door, men's voices . . .

Tom jumped from the bed, and moving softly, opened the bedroom door and stole out on the landing, but in an instant he was back, leaning against the door, his eyes wildly searching the small, bare room.

"Trapped," he muttered, and Caro's heart leaped at the certainty of rescue. Boots clumped over the thin carpet and doors were flung back on protesting hinges.

"Open in the name of the law!" A heavy battering followed but the well-made door, with Tom's powerful shoulder against it, withstood the assault.

There was a shout: "Captain Steel, sir! This way. He's in here, for a monkey!"

Then a new voice; clear, incisive. "Out of the way, men. I'll blow out the lock. Stand clear now."

The blast of an explosion shook the room and the door buckled on its frame. Before the smoke cleared Tom darted over to the bed and hauled Caro from it, holding her half-naked body like a shield in front of him, as the police with drawn truncheons and an army captain at their head, poured pell-mell through the smashed door.

They halted abruptly and their leader gave a ringing laugh. "He's here, it's Hamilton all right, sheltering behind his whore!"

Caro gave an audible gasp of indignation.

"Seize him, boys!"

"One move from any of you," said Tom softly, "and she dies."

Again the men halted, uncertainly.

"Don't be a fool, Hamilton," said the captain urgently. "How will it help you to kill the poor wench? Come quietly with us now and you may yet save your neck. Kill her, and you'll swing for certain."

Tom made no reply, merely letting the tip of his short sword prick Caro's naked back so that she gasped in pain.

"Give up, man," urged the officer but Tom paid no heed.

"Stand away from the door," he ordered his pursuers, and like automatons the men obeyed. He shuffled sideways, keeping Caro between him and his pursuers, his sword steady on her flesh, and held by the mute appeal in her eyes, Captain Rowland Steel stood motionless.

One step to the door, another... they were through it and backing slowly toward the first flight of stairs when Tom caught his foot on the loose carpet and tripped.

"Get down, girl!"

Even before Steel shouted his warning, Caro had felt Tom's grip slacken as he tripped, and instead of straining away from him, deliberately pushed backward to knock him further off balance. They rolled together to the floor, and in an instant Rowland Steel was beside them, his hand grasping Caro's arm and jerking her behind him. Then he and Tom were grappling on the landing, locked in mortal combat, while the policemen stood uncertainly, unable to risk shooting into the melee of flailing limbs and thudding fists.

"Help them!" pleaded Caro, clutching her torn bodice, as the two men rolled toward the steep stairs. "They'll be killed!" But there was no way to intervene. Tom was fighting like a madman, raining blow after blow on Rowland's head and shoulders, while Rowland clung grimly, striving to pin his arms behind him. Though tall and well made, Rowland had not Tom's bull-like breadth of shoulder and heavy-muscled legs, but despite his lesser brawn, Caro realized, her rescuer's whipcord frame would outlast her attacker's brute strength. Slowly the force behind Tom's blows diminished and his breath labored in rasping grunts. Inch by laborious inch, Rowland forced his opponent's hands behind him until Tom at length lay still, his chest heaving, totally spent.

"All right, men, take him away," said Rowland Steel, getting slowly to his feet and flexing his hands as if they ached. Three police constables hauled Tom's unresisting hulk upright, and manacles clicked sharply as they shackled his wrists.

"Now, my girl, what shall we do with you?" said Rowland, turning his attention to Caro. "Your lover's bound for the courts of justice to stand trial for the murder of his wife, my sister Amelia—"

Seeing him for the first time since she had been a child, Caro realized how like Amelia he was. The same wide-set gray eyes beneath winged dark eyebrows, the same thick dark hair waving strongly back from a pronounced peak, the same generous, laughing mouth. But there the resemblance ended, for whereas Amelia had been small and neat, all curves and softness in her fashionable bustled gowns with their deep décolleté necklines, her laces and furs, Rowland Steel was long of limb and light of frame—six foot two of lean, hard muscle; a cavalry officer tailor made. When last they had met, she had been a gawky child, too shy to laugh or speak, especially to a dashing young cavalry officer. Now she was a woman, and she knew that Rowland Steel would never recognize her as that awkward little girl of long ago. Abruptly she switched her attention back to what he was telling her. "—You cannot accompany him there, and neither can you remain here to affront my uncle, Lord Tyndale, on his return from his sojourn abroad. His mouth twitched in a smile. "I cannot guess what his reaction would be to discovering Tom Hamilton's tart in residence, but I wager it would not be a favorable one."

Caro's face burned and she drew the edges of her ruined dress more closely together. "I am no tart," she cried. "I am Lady Caroline March and you should treat me with more—more respect!"

Rowland bowed gravely, though she suspected him of a strong desire to laugh at her. "A thousand apologies, my lady; I must confess I mistook you for a female of a very different kind. Allow me to present myself: Captain Rowland Steel, at your service!"

Suddenly acutely aware of her disheveled appearance, Caro brushed at the cobwebs on her skirt and ran an ineffectual hand through her hair, which had escaped from its comb and pins and hung down her back in a shining, tangled cascade.

"It was no wish of mine to come here, Captain Steel, I assure you," she said in a passable imitation of her mother's high-nosed tones. "I am on my way to visit friends in Hampshire, and I should be obliged if you would convey me to some hostelry, where tomorrow I may obtain transport to my destination.

Rowland's eyes narrowed. "Traveling alone to Hampshire? Then how came you to be in Hamilton's company?"

Caro was ready for that. "Captain Hamilton was bound for Southampton, sir, and offered to set me down at my friends' house as he passed near. But he deceived me, and brought me here; where, as you see, he used me abominably. Indeed, but for your arrival I fear he might have killed me." She shuddered at the memory.

"March, March...Caroline March...I think I knew you as a child...but how you've changed...," murmured Rowland thoughtfully. "Are you sister, then, to Lady Philippa Thynne, wife of my comrade-in-arms, Captain Andrew Thynne?"

"And friend of *your* poor sister," cried Caro eagerly, feeling that the more Captain Steel knew of her impeccable lineage the more likely he was to comply with her request to be taken to Hampshire. She did not, however, wish him to know too precisely where she was going, or all her efforts at secrecy would be worthless. She wondered, fleetingly, if she should take him into her confidence. If he were to give her his word of honor that he would tell no one of her whereabouts...

Her reflections were interrupted by the arrival of the sergeant of police, who clumped up to tell Rowland they were ready to depart, and inquire what arrangements he wished made for the conveyance of the young person?

"The young person reveals herself to be Lady Caroline March," said Rowland, "and she wishes us to convey her into Hampshire."

The sergeant cast a quick, shrewd glance at Caro. "Then that's two birds with one stone, as they say, sir. Her parents reported this young lady missing from home this very afternoon, and a boy they brought in off the streets that claimed to see her leave said she'd gone off in company with a bloke in a fast chaise. I might ha' guessed the two matters were linked."

Rowland looked sternly at Caro, who had gone white. "So you *are* associated with Tom Hamilton. What was your purpose then in lying to me? Did you think to give us all the slip again? No matter: you shall return to your parents forthwith. No doubt they know best how to deal with you. Get your baggage; we leave at once."

"You are wrong, utterly wrong!" cried Caro, stamping her foot with frustration. "It was as I said: Captain Hamilton brought me here when I wished to go to Hampshire. I won't go back to London with you. You cannot make me!"

"We'll see about that," said Rowland grimly, and scooping one hand beneath her knees and the other around her shoulders, he lifted her effortlessly from the ground, while the sergeant turned away to hide a smile. Caro kicked and fought, hampered by her torn dress, sobbing wildly, "You can't. I won't. Put me down at once!" Then her voice rose to a shriek. "My jewels! I've left my jewels."

This had the effect of arresting Rowland's progress down the stairs. "Jewels? What folly is this?"

"I hid my reticule in—in a trunk in the box room. I was afraid Tom would steal them from me, as indeed he was about to, had he not heard you coming and sought to escape." She saw the disbelief written plainly on his face, and pleaded, "I swear it is true: come and I will show you. Never fear that I will escape!"

He set her down, but watched her closely as she hurried back to the box room and lifted the lid of an enormous cabin trunk. Dawn light was filtering through the dusty attic window as he watched her throw back a layer of musty-smelling clothes and pounce with a cry of relief on a small bag that lay at the bottom of the trunk.

"What have you there?" he inquired. "Am I to believe that whatever that bag contains belongs to you, and not my esteemed uncle Tyndale, though it lies in what is undoubtedly his cabin trunk in his attic?"

He spoke in jest, and was sorry when he saw her most-charmingly pale face turn a shade whiter beneath the attic grime and the bruises of Tom's rough handling. She raised enormous eyes to his. "Indeed, Captain, they are mine," she said with a quiet dignity that left him in no doubt that this time she was telling the plain truth. "See, it's the Portland sapphires. Are they not superb? My grandmother Portland left them to me in her will." Gently she lifted the necklace with its magnificent pendant drop, and blue fire flashed in the dawn light.

"I congratulate you on possessing such a treasure. Now come, the police are waiting for us. We must make haste back to London."

He extended his arm to escort her out of the attic, but she hung back nevertheless. "Captain, will you not release me to go on my way? I dare not return to my parents. If you let me go"—she spoke with an obvious effort—"I will give you my sapphires. Here..." She thrust the reticule into his hands.

Rowland was angry, particularly since he now regretted his hasty decision to restore her to her family, who would undoubtedly punish the dark-eyed beauty severely for this escapade. But since the police knew her identity, there was no help for it.

"Little fool," he said roughly. "Don't try to bribe me. Keep your jewels: you may have need of them! Now, come."

She saw there was no moving him, and let out a sigh

of defeat. Meekly she allowed him to wrap her in a blanket to cover her torn clothes, and accompany her to the waiting coach.

While Rowland and Caro lingered in the attic, the party of police with Tom in fetters had gone on before them, and when Rowland halted his horses before Marchmain House he realized that any attempt to keep Caro's adventure secret was useless. That the butler already knew at least some of the circumstances of her flight was clear from his voice of doom as he informed Rowland that Lady Caroline was to go directly to his lordship's study, where the earl desired to speak with her.

Caro turned a look of mute appeal on Rowland, who in response merely said bracingly, "Come, better get it over with," and attempted unsuccessfully to take her arm.

"His Lordship desires to see Lady Caroline alone," said the butler firmly. "It was his express wish." He added in an undertone that his lordship was in a rare temper, and it would be prudent to respect his orders.

"And—and my mother?" whispered Caro.

"Her ladyship, it appeared, was in her boudoir, trying to regain her composure after an early-morning interview with Sir Robert Anderton.

"Then, Captain Steel, I must thank you for your escort and wish you a good day," said Caro in a high, haughty voice. She coldly gave him her hand, which he pressed encouragingly, though he was greatly troubled at the thought of leaving this lovely, brave little creature to face her father's fury alone. Lord Marchmain's temper was notoriously volatile, and Rowland would not have put it past him to take a whip to his erring daughter.

"I wish I could come with you," he said in a gentle voice.

"I fear it would only enrage him further," she replied icily. "I shall do better alone."

The butler steered him firmly toward the front door, but before it closed behind him, Rowland turned to see Caro, head high, follow the footman into Lord Marchmain's study.

The two little boys pattered across the bedroom and perched one either side of Caro's bed. She opened her tear-swollen eyes and managed a watery smile.

"Did it hurt very much? Did you cry?" asked Jamie anxiously.

She shook her head. "Only afterward."

"I try not to cry when Miss Thimbleby whips me," said Georgie. "But if it were Papa ..." He shuddered.

Caro shut her eyes, trying to blot out the memory of the odious scene in Papa's study; her father shouting, the long ash-plant lashing her shoulders. Georgie and his brother exchanged solemn looks.

"What will happen now?" whispered Jamie. "Betsy told us you are to be married, and we should be your pageboys. Will Papa stop you being married?"

"No, that is all changed." She brightened. At least one good result of yesterday's events was that, to her mother's mortification and her father's fury, Sir Robert Anderton had revealed immediately that he knew she had been discovered in Tom Hamilton's company. More than half the stripes she had received at his hands she owed to the withdrawal of Sir Robert's offer of marriage. She said, "Sir Robert told Papa he would not accept damaged goods."

The little boys peered closely at their sister. "You do not look greatly damaged to me," said kind-hearted Jamie. "Only your lip is swollen and there is a big bruise on your cheek. But if you cannot marry, what will you do?"

"I am to be sent away to live with Philippa, in India,

37

until everyone has forgotten that I was naughty," said Caro slowly. "I think I will like that."

The boys looked at her in dismay, and Jamie burst into noisy sobs.

"Papa mustn't send you away! We shall never see you again!"

Caro put an arm around each of her brothers. "Oh, yes indeed, you will. I shall come home riding on an elephant and make you both into Nawabs with turbans and lots of jewels."

"Will you shoot a tiger?" asked Georgie hopefully, but the mention of riding had reminded Jamie of another matter.

"Captain Steel came to call on Mama today," he said, "but she told Sampson to say she wasn't at home to him. So he took us for a ride all the way down the avenue and back again on his great black horse. He wanted me to give you a letter, but Mama took it from me and threw it on the fire. I'm sorry I didn't hide it in time." His lips quivered ominously.

"It doesn't signify in the least," said Caro quickly. I have no wish to receive letters from Captain Steel. Odious man, she thought. If it hadn't been for him, I might now be safe in Hampshire with dear Mrs. Furneaux instead of lying on my face, in the deepest disgrace of my life. "I am glad you enjoyed your ride, but speaking for myself, I never wish to see Captain Steel again. It is largely on his account that I am being sent to India."

Sadly, Jamie let flicker and die the flame of hero worship he'd been harboring since his meeting with Captain Steel. "Then I don't like him either," he asserted stoutly. "It was only his horse that we liked, wasn't it, Georgie?"

Chapter Two

SIX WEEKS LATER, in a mood far superior to her recent
London humors, Caro leaned on the rail of the fast
packet boat *India Star* as she bucked and plunged
through the white-capped waves of the Bay of Biscay.
The strong headwind blew smoke straight out behind
the steamer like a black plume, and occasional flurries
of spray dashed over the bows to sting Caro's eyes with
salty tears, but she still clung to the rail, laughing;
joyful in the discovery that dirty weather at sea had no
terrors for her: she was a born sailor.

She had never felt so free. True, she was nominally
in the care of Lady Marvell, an old friend of the
Marchmains who was going to India to stay with her
daughter and son-in-law during the "cold weather,"
but Lady Marvell was as different from Lady
Marchmain as chalk from cheese. Fat, cheerful,
untidy, Lady Marvell promised to be an excellent
traveling companion once she recovered from the bout
of seasickness that had confined her and her trim maid,
Martha, to their respective cabins since the present
storm blew up. Lady Marvell had a passion for cards
and a fund of interesting stories about the Indian
subcontinent, where, when she was first married, her
subsequently deceased husband had served as a district
officer in the Indian Civil Service.

"I must have made the journey a dozen times," she
said ruefully to Caro just before being obliged to take
to her bed, "but I have never seen the famous Bay of

Biscay from anything but a prone position. I hoped that advancing years would make my stomach less susceptible to the movement of the waves, but I fear it is not to be."

"I am sorry you don't feel well," said Caro, who thought the increased rolling of the ship very agreeable. "Is there anything I can do to help you?"

"Dear child," said Lady Marvell warmly, laying her hand on Caro's shoulder in a gesture too affectionate ever to have occurred to Lady Marchmain, "I am very grateful for your offer, but Martha knows my ways and she will look after me best. Amuse yourself for a day or two, and I will rejoin you when we reach calmer seas."

Supporting herself against the fixed furniture of the saloon, she made for her cabin, with Martha—looking as green-complexioned as her mistress—in close attendance. That had been the last Caro had seen of her chaperone for two days, for although she had knocked and put her head around the door of Lady Marvell's cabin morning and evening, Martha had on each occasion advised her to come no nearer. The illness would pass, she suggested reassuringly, but for the moment her ladyship was best left alone. Since the stuffy cabin smelled strongly of hartshorn and aromatic vinegar, Caro was glad to accept the maid's advice.

The dining room was nearly deserted during the storm, and so were the saloons which, at the start of the voyage, had been filled with laughing, chattering passengers. Caro found the gloom below decks as oppressive to her spirits at sea as the constant reminders of her disgrace had been at home. With relief she escaped to cling to the rail and let the wild strength of the storm buffet her, snatching at her sodden cloak and whipping her hair across her face.

Growing cold at her post, she had begun to consider returning to her cabin to sew or write letters when a

deck door slid open and a slender, fair-haired young
man stumbled out laughing as he struggled against the
wind.

"By Jove," he exclaimed, "but it's blowing a gale out
here! I didn't expect to find a lady with a taste for air as
fresh as this."

"I love it," said Caro, turning toward him shyly.
"The sea's so beautiful when it's angry like this; I like
watching it better than sitting in those stuffy rooms . . ."

"You'll like it even better when we get into warmer
waters." he promised. "Then you can see great trails of
phosporescence on the waves, and flying fish follow the
boat just as sea gulls follow a plow on land."

Caro looked at him with new interest. "You have
made the journey before?"

"Yes, although the first time I went out to India I
took a boat that rounded the Cape, which made the
voyage far too long. So this time I determined to try the
new overland route from Alexandria to Suez—and I'm
glad I did so, since it has given me the opportunity of
meeting you."

Caro felt the color rise to her cheeks. "Thank you,
sir." She clutched the rail harder as a sudden squall
buffeted the ship, and they ducked instinctively as a
heavy shower of spray washed over the rail, drenching
them both.

The fair young man put a firm hand on Caro's
elbow. "Sea water may be good for the complexion,"
he shouted above the wail of the wind, "but I'd be
neglecting my duty if I didn't take you indoors.
Another wave like that and we'll both be overboard."

Together they fought their way to the sliding door,
clinging to every handhold they could find, bending
their heads against the stinging rain and spray. Caro's
companion pulled open the door and they almost fell
inside, laughing at their soaked garments and dripping
hair.

"Allow me, sir." Caro turned over the collar of the young man's coat, and a rivulet of water that had collected there ran down to form a lake on the polished boards. She began to tug at the fastening of her cloak with half-numbed fingers.

"And allow me." Deftly he unfastened the sodden cloak and hung it on a convenient door catch. "I feel it is time we introduced ourselves: my name is Brook Vyner, and I am returning for my second tour of duty with the Indian Civil Service."

Caro held out her hand. "Thank you for your assistance. I am Caroline March, and I am going to visit my sister, Lady Philippa Thynne, whose husband is stationed at Baburpore."

The young man stared, then his almost too-handsome face broke into a beam of delight. "Not Andrew Thynne of the Seventy-second Foot? Oh, by all that is famous, this is a rare chance! I was Andrew Thynne's groomsman on his marriage to your sister. Do you think that gives me the excuse to invite you to dine at my table?"

"Since we are likely to be the only two passengers dining tonight, I should be delighted to join you," she assured him gravely. "In truth, I am tired of my own company! Lady Marvell was taken ill two days ago, and since she retired to her cabin the rest of the ship's company seems to have followed her. I had no idea that so many people were poor sailors."

"Yes, you and I are among the fortunate few," he agreed. "For myself, the rougher the weather the more I enjoy it, and had not my uncle offered to use his influence for me with the East India Company, I think I might have become a sailor."

Caro wondered how well he would have done in that role. With his fair hair, exquisite features and porcelain complexion whipped into color by the sea breeze, he seemed almost too fragile to sustain the rigors of a sailing life. She judged him to be twenty-four or -five, well made in his tobacco-brown broadcloth coat and narrow trousers. She warmed to the admiration in his glance; it seemed so long since she had been able to engage in casual conversation with a personable gentleman.

"Then I'll see you at dinner!" she bade him good-bye and hurried below to change into dry clothes and rearrange her tousled hair, determined to be in her best looks for the evening.

During the next few days their friendship flourished as the steamship steadied its course in the calmer waters of the Mediterranean and other passengers began cautiously to reappear from their cabins. Caro learned that Vyner, for all his youth, was already appointed to the responsible position of Assistant Collector in the District of Vanyasi.

When Lady Marvell recovered her health and spirits, Brook developed the habit of sitting with her and Caro every evening, declaring that Lady Marvell's stories on life upcountry twenty years ago would be of more practical help to him in his new appointment than reading half a dozen dusty tomes. Privately, Lady Marvell considered his manners more than a trifle fawning, but, mindful of her promise to Lady Marchmain to put Caro in the way of eligible bachelors, she tolerated Brook's attendance upon them.

"We used to call the Civil Servants three-hundred-a-year-dead-or-alive men. For their pay when they joined was three hundred pounds a year," she explained to Caro. "That is the sum their widows were entitled to draw every year should the husband die in the Service.

"Civil Servants are held in far more esteem than the military, you know, and it is rare to find an Assistant Collector as young as Mr. Vyner. In my day, they were all fat and fifty before they attained any position of responsibility, and we used to say that the only verb they knew how to conjugate was the verb "to collect." If you listened to their conversation you heard nothing but "I am a Collector; He was a Collector; we shall be Collectors; you ought to be a Collector; they would have been Collectors.'"

"A subject of limited appeal," observed Caro.

"Oh no, my dear, far from it. They were absolutely fascinated by their work and could think of nothing else. But one must admit that it was hard on the women. Now, I believe, it is much more the fashion for wives to accompany their husbands wherever they go, into even the wildest regions, and this I consider an excellent notion, since long separation never helps a marriage."

Caro sensed that the old lady was in a reminiscent mood, and encouraged her to tell stories of camp life among high hills and jungles alive with wild beasts, of balls and *burra-khana*s and questions of precedence among different ranks of ladies, of the Indians themselves, their myths and mysteries. This was the land she was traveling to, the exotic Orient in all its many-splendored hues. At length, Lady Marvel laid down her fruit knife and delicately pressed her napkin to her lips.

"How I do run on, to be sure," she exclaimed. "I hope you will have the good sense to stop me before I become a dead bore. Ah, here is Mr. Vyner approaching. Shall we invite him to take tea with us in the saloon?"

The pattern of their evenings had become drinking tea together, followed by Lady Marvell's and white-haired Mrs. Merryweather's beseeching Caro to play the piano for them while Brook Vyner sang. He had a pleasant, light tenor voice, and would sing such favorites as "Those Evening Bells" and "Drink to Me

Only," leaning romantically on the warped upright piano while Caro coaxed an accompaniment from its stiff, yellowing keys.

As they ended on a high note to a chorus of "Bravos" from their fellow passengers, the French Captain, smiling benignly in his crumpled uniform, entered and begged silence for an announcement.

He had come to bid them farewell, he explained, since the vessel had made good time from the Strait of Gibraltar, and would reach Alexandria at dawn tomorrow. Although most of the passengers had already worked out their position and reached this conclusion, they were glad to have it confirmed, and greeted the Captain's words with a hearty cheer. Passengers for India would travel by gharry as far as Cairo and thence in strong vans to Suez, where a steamer of the East India Company awaited them.

The sea voyage from England had already seemed long enough, and the Captain's little speech heralded a buzz of excitement. Even the old India hands caught the general atmosphere of anticipation, and when they disembarked in the pearly dawn next morning, Caro stared about wide-eyed, struck silent by the beauty and strangeness of her first glimpse of the East.

Gilded domes of temples and palaces caught the first rays of the sun, and the towers seemed almost to float above the morning mist. Jabbering bare-footed natives pulled at their clothes, pressing them to buy curios of wood and stone, pungent flat cakes and sticky sweetmeats already buzzing with flies. Emaciated porters, their robes tucked up above their knees, humped cabin trunks heavier than themselves, bullocks lowed and horses neighed above the general clamor, and all was bustle and confusion.

Caro could have gazed for hours, drinking in the colorful scene, but Lady Marvell needed her help as well as Martha's to assist her across to the first of a score of horse gharries drawn up in a long line near the docking bay.

"What do you think of it all?" asked Brook Vyner, laughing at Caro's bewilderment as the natives, screaming abuse at one another, shoved and pushed to be first to carry the passengers' baggage.

"Oh, it is wonderful—far beyond anything I had imagined."

"Wait until we reach Cairo; I promise you it quite puts Alexandria in the shade. I will take you to see the Sphinx and the Pasha's Palace, since we have not the time to make a journey to the Pyramids."

But these plans were thwarted when, on arrival at Shepheard's Hotel after a long hot dusty journey in the springless gharry, Caro's hands and feet felt icy cold and her head hummed with fever. Lady Marvell, coming to bid her good night, cast one glance at her as she huddled, flushed and shivering, in a chair, unable to make the effort to ease or undress herself, and summoned Martha to the room. "The poor girl's taken a fever, I believe. Ask for Mahomet Ali's special posset." Together they got Caro into bed with hot bricks wrapped in flannel at her stomach and feet and compelled her to drink a bitter-tasting compound brewed in the hotel kitchen.

"I'm sure it will be exceedingly nasty," said Lady Marvell frankly, "but I am equally certain that it will do you good. The natives have their own remedies for the fevers that are prevalent here, and I have always found them most efficacious. Just one more sip, my dear, and it will all be gone."

Caro grimaced, but obediently drank the unpleasant mixture to the last drop and soon began to drift in a haze of sleep. She was aware that Martha remained in her room all night, and once or twice the mists clouding her brain cleared sufficiently for her to protest that this was unnecessary, but Martha only smiled.

"Go you'm back to sleep, my lady," she said in her comforting Somerset burr. "I'm quite easy here, and you'll be right as rain come morning, shouldn't wonder."

But when morning broke, Caro felt as weak as a newborn kitten, though the fever had left her, and reluctantly she had to give up her plans for sightseeing in Cairo. She drifted in and out of a doze all day, hearing the faraway wail of the *muezzin* and cries of the street peddlers hawking their wares up and down the narrow alleys. Lady Marvell had engaged a boy to work a fan, so the air in her bedroom was not oppressive, and from time to time Martha turned her pillows and brought her fruit juice deliciously flavored with sherbet. By evening, Caro was feeling much better, and her cure was completed by a smiling Martha who entered with a bouquet of roses and camellias.

Fever forgotten, Caro tore open the note. *The Sphinx has lost her mystery and the Pasha's Palace its splendor,* she read. *Even the desert cannot bloom today since you are not with me to see it. I pray that your recovery will be speedy and complete. Brook Vyner.*

"I declare you have made a conquest, Caro!" cried Lady Marvell in high delight, reading the note over Caro's shoulder. "How enraged the rest of the Fishing Fleet will be if you bewitch Delhi's most presentable Civilian before you even arrive in India!"

"The 'Fishing Fleet'?"

"Oh, that's what they call the English girls who come husband-hunting in the 'cold weather,'" said Lady Marvell gaily. "When you live in India, it's the greatest excitement of the year to see new faces and new fashions after you have been shut away from civilization for months. Never fear, with your looks you will cast them all in the shade."

Caro smiled weakly at the compliment, but did not entirely like the picture Lady Marvell painted of eager girls who had failed to capture a husband at home vying with one another for the favors of these high-nosed Civilians, nor the implication that the new arrivals were assessed and discussed like cattle in a market. Inwardly she resolved that she would never compete in such a market: it was because she had wished to *escape* marriage to a self-important old tyrant that she was now traveling to India. It would be too absurd to allow herself to be maneuvered a second time into the same trap.

Next morning their baggage was stowed in the horse-drawn vans that were to convey them across the desert to Suez—a sixteen-hour journey, Lady Marvell warned, and she obliged Caro to take one final drink of the fever-quenching bitter posset—to which she attributed Caro's swift recovery—before they embarked on the long trek. "It contains opium, the great Oriental curative," she explained. "I am never clear in my mind whether opium really works a cure, or whether it merely gives the sufferer freedom from pain so that his body can cure itself. Either way, I have the greatest faith in it: no other treatment would have made you fit to travel today."

Caro clenched her jaw and hid as well as she could the waves of nausea that engulfed her as she swallowed the acid brew. However, its effect, which would last through the hot, jolting journey across the desert, was immediately beneficial, imparting a levity to the mind as well as to the body so that the exotic sights around her took on the wondrous familiarity of remembered dreams.

At first Caro gazed intently at the landscape with its unending hills of sand and gray boulders, in whose shade sat small boys in striped pajamas and ragged cloaks, watching their sheep and goats under the intense, shimmering blue sky, that she hardly noticed the discomforts of their vehicle. This was a boxlike van with wooden wheels on a strong axle, and windows with shutters hinged at the top to form shades against the fierce sun.

An ebony-faced, turbaned driver in tight, striped trousers and short jacket cracked his whip incessantly over the backs of his four horses, who had strong but different ideas about speed and direction. A second native wearing a skullcap, barefoot and with his loose robe caught up at the knees, perched on the shaft and encouraged the team with hoarse cries. Frequent violent collisions with rocks and ruts threw Caro first against Lady Marvell and then against Martha. It was stiflingly hot, and the dust that rose in choking clouds from the convoy penetrated even the netted windows of the van and covered their hair, skin, and clothes with a gritty gray film.

Lady Marvell was unfailingly cheerful, and her spirits seemed to improve with every step they took further east. She told of other journeys, other places she had visited to while away the long hours with her much-traveled husband, and when she saw that Caro was tired, she invited the girl to rest her head on her own well-padded shoulder.

"For we must not forget you are a recent invalid," she gently chided her, and although this new overland route saves a great distance at sea, and I prefer it to the voyage round the Cape, there is no doubt that this stage of the journey is excessively wearisome."

Every twelve miles or so, a huddle of buildings would break the featureless wastes of desert, and the bony horses that pulled the vans would quicken their steps toward a walled courtyard filled with travelers, merchants, nomads with animals for sale—a noisy, colorful, jostling throng that ate and drank, bartered and slept within the encircling walls.

While the fresh team was put to, Caro longed to wander amongst the crowd, but Lady Marvell preferred to keep her close at hand, drinking the thick, sweet mint tea which their Egyptian guide procured for them, and watching the scene from a careful distance.

Martha, too, had a firm way with the natives, Caro was amused to note. Instantly sensing the unapproachability of Lady Marvell, the peddlers and hawkers attached themselves to her maid, Martha, who, for all her quiet, civil manners toward her mistress, proved a forceful—even strident—haggler when dealing with those she considered her inferiors. Examining their wares with a fine show of British contempt, she offered in sign language a tenth of the price asked for them, and frequently obtained what she wanted.

"That's all I'm giving, and you can take it or leave it," she would cry, flapping her hands at the crowding peddlers like a farmwife shooing away chickens. "*Imshi*! Be off with you!" She would then return in triumph to Lady Marvell's side with a few ripe persimmons, delicate crescent-shape pastries filled with spiced meat, or a twist of hot, salted nuts for her ladies to crunch on the next stage of the long, hot journey.

At the end of sixteen hours, when dark had long fallen, they were all glad when a chorus of shouts ahead at the front of the convoy told them they had arrived at last at the port of Suez. Stiffly they clambered out of the vans for the last time, and stumbled up the torch-lit gangway of the East India Company's steamship *Malabar Star*.

"Please take me, Brook," pleaded Caro.

"No."

"But you promised!"

"I promised to show you around Cairo, but that is a very different matter."

"Then I'll never speak to you again."

"It is not that I don't wish to take you with me," said Brook, goaded, "but you don't realize how different things are in the East. A port like Suez is not a fit place for an English female to visit. Besides, Lady Marvell would never consent to it."

"She has already given me permission to go ashore," said Caro slyly, "provided that you engage to escort me. She thinks it better for me to take gentle exercise ashore today, since our departure is delayed, and says I shall have plenty of opportunity to sit on deck and survey the ocean in the next few weeks. She also says she is sure no harm can come to me in your company," she added mischievously, "so please do not lose this opportunity of proving her right!"

Brook shrugged. "I see I am outwitted and outranked and shall have to give in to your wishes. But I warn you, it will be very dull. Suez cannot compare with Alexandria or Cairo for monuments and splendors. There is little of interest here."

Caro lifted her chin. "Very well, Mr. Vyner. Since you seem so averse to my company, I shall not trouble you with it, nor hold you to your promise to show me the sights of Egypt. Perhaps some other gentleman will be more willing to accompany me ashore."

"Come, Caro, you need not take that pouting tone with me," said Brook in a more conciliatory manner. "The fact is, you misunderstand the reason for my reluctance to escort you." He hesitated, then went on in a low voice. "I would not wish it to go to Lady Marvell's ears that I had taken a girl who was in her charge in search of opium supplies for . . . for a friend of mine, but the truth is that while in Cairo I was given the address of a merchant here who will sell me what my friend needs, and I planned to visit the man today. If I could trust your discretion, I should be delighted to take you with me."

Caro sensed adventure, and her eagerness to

explore the port redoubled.

"Of course you may trust me," she exclaimed. "Why did you not explain your reticence at once? Though truly you have no need to fear Lady Marvell's disapproval, for she told me herself she has the greatest faith in opium as a cure for all ills from toothache to simple fatigue. I am already a convert to it, since it was the opium in the posset she gave me that cured my recent fever in Cairo."

Privately Brook doubted if Lady Marvell would approve so wholeheartedly of the use he planned to make of the drug, but there was no need to express his doubts to Caro. He was glad enough to have her smiling sunnily on him again, her pique forgotten, and he pressed her hand and said he hadn't really doubted her, but some people fresh out from England were inclined to have prejudices and misconceptions about opium smoking. Since she was evidently not one of these opinionated killjoys, he'd be very willing to take her to see the town provided she didn't object to returning to the ship while he went to seek his opium merchant.

Caro was more than a little dejected that Brook refused to take her on his opium mission, but she swallowed her disappointment and thanked him prettily, agreeing to his terms for the tour. They arranged to meet at noon.

As the midday gun sounded from the quay, and the thin wail of the *muezzin* began to penetrate every sun-filled square and alleyway of the old town, Brook Vyner leaned against a bollard and fought down his impatience as he waited for Caro. Where was the girl? He was already beginning to doubt the wisdom of telling her the truth about his opium-buying errand; what if she ingenuously blurted it out to someone aboard ship? He must urgently impress on her the need for silence. Besides, if she did not soon make an appearance, he would not be here to meet her. The ship was due to sail at five, and he had no idea how far he would have to penetrate into the dark recesses of the *suq* to find the merchant he sought. Four hours might be ample time to transact his business, and then again it might not. But first there was Caro, for whom he must drag around to the fort, the mosque, the few European-style shops, and appear to enjoy it so that the chit and her shrewd old duenna would continue to regard him with favor. He wished now that he'd been firmer in his refusal to the girl this morning, or thought up a more convincing story as to why he couldn't escort her, but somehow, when Caro turned those big dark eyes on a man, good resolutions were apt to vanish . . . He pulled a cigar from his case, lit it, then stubbed it out against the bollard with an angry exclamation. Even smoking lost its appeal in this heat. Where was Caro? Two minutes more and he'd be off, and let her find some other fool to escort her about the evil-smelling port of Suez. There was no one approaching who looked even remotely like Caro, no one at all, in fact, except a youth in a Norfolk suit, with open-neck nankeen shirt and cap pulled well over his hair, who, to Brook's surprise, was about to address him.

"Please, sir, be so good as to direct me to the house of one Mohammed Ahmet, the tailor."

Brook turned to him, impatience barely concealed. "My good lad, there must be at least a hundred tailors in Suez by the name of Mohammed Ahmet. Have you no further address for him?"

To his surprise and anger, this answer caused the boy to break into peals of laughter.

"I fail to see why you should find it so entertaining . . . ," Brook was beginning stiffly, when the boy took his arm and said in a voice that was now unmistakably familiar, "Admit, Brook, that I had you fairly then! Did you really not know me?"

"Caro!" Brook Vyner was deeply shocked, as much by her attire as by the fact that he had been about to deliver a stinging rebuke to the impertinent boy in words quite unsuited to a lady's ears. "Why are you dressed like that? I cannot take you on a tour of Suez wearing a boy's clothes. Whose are they?"

"They are mine—that is to say, they belonged to one of my brothers," said Caro. "You said this morning that you could not take a lady around a town like Suez, so to put your mind at rest, I have adopted this garb. You cannot now turn around and refuse to take a boy with you, especially since you yourself have proved to me how effective a disguise it is. Come! I would have joined you sooner only I wished to slip away without being obliged to explain my clothes to Lady Marvell's maid, who was in my cabin doing some mending."

Brook felt at a distinct disadvantage. He did not in the least approve of ladies going about Eastern towns in disguise, but saw no way of making this clear to Caro without throwing her into tears or a tantrum, both of which would draw unwelcome attention to them. He had no choice. Without another word, he led her off in the direction of the mosque, the first stop in his proposed tour, intending to walk her off her feet and return her to the ship with all possible speed.

Neither the grilling heat, which beat down on Caro's tweed-covered head with relentless force, nor Brook's perfunctory attempts to translate the guide's broken English had the effect of dimming the girl's enthusiasm for the tour. At the end of two hours, when Brook suggested they return to the ship, Caro pleaded, "Oh, please do not send me back yet. We have seen nothing—that is to say, nothing of any consequence— and I did so wish for an adventure! Can I not stay with you just a little longer? There are such pretty little stalls over there, and I should like to find a present for Lady

Marvell, who has been so kind to me, and for Martha, too."

Unnerved by the lengthening delay, yet unwilling to disappoint her, Brook allowed himself to be persuaded into examining the stalls at the entrance of the *suq*. Caro bought beads and other small trinkets, bargaining briskly in imitation of Martha's methods, and leading the reluctant Brook ever deeper into the heart of the old town. Beggars tugged at their clothes, whining for alms, but Caro paid them no attention as she darted from stall to stall using Brook to admire and advise, and he followed helplessly in her quicksilver wake. Suddenly he came to a decision. If he delayed his visit to the opium merchant any longer, he would be unable to go there at all, since this ship sailed at five and all passengers were bidden to be aboard by four o'clock. There was no longer time to return Caro to Lady Marvell's company: she would have to go with him, but since her clothes had attracted no attention from either the fellow Europeans they had met wandering about the town, nor from the natives, Brook felt reasonably confident they would occasion no comment in the opium den. Hailing a passing rickshaw he inquired the whereabout of Ahmet Mustafa's Almond Blossom House.

The boy nodded vigorously. "I take you there."

Caro looked up from the array of stone curios she was examining. "Ask him how much it will cost to go there," she said, but Brook disdained to accept advice from someone so new to the East.

"I'll settle all that when we get there," he said loftily. "Are you coming with me?"

"Oh, yes, please," she exclaimed, and sprang nimbly up beside him.

"You gentlemen cannot imagine how delightful it is to be able to move without being hampered by a heavy skirt," she told him.

Brook looked down at her neat legs in their tweed knickerbockers, and then removed his gaze in some embarrassment, unsure whether to laugh at this artless confidence or register disapproval.

"It would perhaps be wise if you stayed in this rickshaw while I make my purchases," he said in a low voice. "I would rather you remained in the background, in case of being recognized as a female."

Caro was disappointed, but nodded. "I will do just as you say."

Their conveyance made good speed, the strong horses clipping along through winding, ever-narrower streets with their pungent smell of spices mingled with open drains. Brook held his silk handkerchief to his mouth as they threaded past bullock carts and laden donkeys, women with huge baskets on their heads or hips, crowds of men strolling arm in arm, and myriad children, their dark eyes ringed with kohl, who ran along beside the carriage holding out their hands and shouting, "*Baksheesh! Baksheesh!*"

"Don't give them anything," said Brook, as Caro made an involuntary gesture toward her pocket. "They will bring all their cousins and friends if you give one so much as a *paise*, and we will never be rid of them."

At last the vehicle halted in front of a house set about with handsome shrubs in gaily painted tubs. On the open veranda several men were taking their ease, stretched at length or cross-legged on heaps of cushions with *hookah*s before them while white-robed attendants squatted ready to kindle the pipes or offer refreshment.

A portly middle-age Egyptian with long mustaches drooping on either side of his mouth and a flat-top *tarboosh* on the back of his head waddled down the steps and bowed in greeting.

"I have business with Ahmet Mustafa," Brook told him, "but I am pressed for time. My ship sails tonight."

The Egyptian smiled. "I am Ahmet Mustafa," he said in excellent English, "and I shall be glad to hear what brings you to my humble home. Were you, perhaps, recommended to me by an acquaintance? I have a number of friends among your countrymen." He waved a hand, as soft and smooth as his voice, toward the somnolent figures on the veranda, but Caro thought the company looked Orientals to a man. "Will you honor me by accepting a little refreshment while we talk?"

Brook jumped down from the *tonga*. "I should be glad to, Mr. Mustafa, but my young friend will remain in the carriage. As I said, we can spare only a few moments." He turned to Caro and whispered, "I shall not be gone long, but on no account wander away and get lost, or we shall miss the boat." He followed the Egyptian up the steps of the veranda and they vanished through a bead curtain.

Resigned to waiting, the driver of the *tonga* dropped the reins on the back of his skinny horse and squatted in the shade of the veranda. The horse stood hipshot, resting one hindleg, its long ears flicking idly at the flies. Dust settled, the smokers turned their attention back to their pipes, and peace descended once more on the quiet scene.

Time passed and Caro began to fidget. She had no means of telling how long she'd waited, but shadows were lengthening where the sun's rays managed to slant into the narrow alley, and the town was beginning to wake from its afternoon torpor. Faintly the cries of street traders in and around the main *suq* came to her ears, and a smell of hot oil and spices—more suggestive of an evening than a midday meal—wafted above the general odors of dirt and decay. The patient horse shifted its weight to the other hindleg, and one of the pipe smokers on the veranda slowly rose from his cushion, helped by his servant, and drifted away down the alley to vanish into the shadows.

Caro turned her head to watch him go, and at that instant she seemed to hear a faraway shout which sounded as if it came from a European throat. She started, and looked back at the bead curtain where she'd last seen Brook, wondering if anyone else had heard or if she'd imagined the shout. It had been so faint...

There was a little ripple of movement, a flurry of activity among the white-robed servants, but the smokers remained deep in their drug-induced dreams, and no figure appeared in the bead-curtain doorway.

Caro stood up uncertainly, then stiffly climbed down from the *tonga*. She told herself that she was imagining things. Time always seemed to drag if you were waiting for someone. But she could not rid herself of her unease. Perhaps she ought to go in search of Brook? She had not for one moment believed his clumsy story of buying the opium for a friend, and guessed it was for his own use; in view of Lady Marvell's warm approval of its powers, she found nothing shocking in Brook's wish to secure his own supply, and failed to understand why he wanted to keep the expedition secret. However, seeing the trancelike state to which their pipes had reduced the smokers on the veranda, she was beginning to fear that Brook had given in to the temptation to sample the wares and fallen asleep, the narcotic dulling him into forgetfulness both of Caro and the ship's time of departure.

Decidedly it was up to her to rouse him. She squared her shoulders, pulled her tweed cap well down on her forehead, and strode with the longest, most manly step she could assume up the steps and pushed through the crowd of servants thronging the veranda. No one attempted to stop her; indeed the packed bodies

seemed to melt before her as she moved toward the
bead curtain, though a glance over her shoulder told
her that the gap closed behind her as she passed,
barring her way out.

Inside the house it was dark, compared to the sunlit
alleyway, and she paused on the threshold to get her
bearings. A cool, high-ceiling room, with a flapping
punkah stirring the air, more heaps of cushions and
brass jugs and vessels on the floor, but no one in sight.
Nevertheless, Caro had the feeling that she was
watched as she strode with all the boldness she could
muster to the doorway at the far end of the room. This
led to a passage, pervaded by a strong, sickly smell of
incense, and Caro hesitated, attracted by the splash of
water ahead at the end of the passage, which indicated
a courtyard or garden of some kind. But should she
first explore the many rooms leading off the passage?
The first door she tried swung open easily and she
started back with a stifled scream as the man who had
been squatting on the threshold rose to face her.

"Come in, young master, come in," he said silkily,
and she recognized the portly Egyptian who had led
Brook away. "I wondered when your curiosity would
impel you to search for your companion. See, there he
lies."

He waved a hand toward a figure lying crumpled on
a heap of cushions. Caro ran forward.

"Brook! Wake up! What have they done to you?"

She shook his shoulder and his arm moved without
resistance. His eyes were open, unfocused, and bending
closer she saw that their pupils were shrunk to
pinpricks in the center of the dilated irises.

She turned on the smiling Egyptian. "You have
poisoned him!" she cried, but he shook his head gently.

"No, no, young master. He will wake none the worse
for a little rough handling by my servants. He is too old

to be of interest to my customers, so we will turn out his pockets and let him go. But you . . . that is another matter."

He signed to someone in the doorway; before she could move Caro's arms were grasped and held behind her in a firm grip. She sensed the futility of struggling, and stood still while the Egyptian moved so near that she could smell the heavy, throat-catching scent of *patchouli* that hung about him. He raised a hand and ran it lightly over her cheek.

"A beardless boy with a skin like a peach," he said in tones of admiration. "My friends will pay well for an hour or two in your company, young master. Had you but golden hair as well, you would be a treasure beyond price, but in this world one must not find fault with what the stars provide. It was indeed a happy hour when your purse-proud friend brought you to my humble house."

Caro did not fully understand the import of his remarks, since although his English was fluent, he spoke with a nasal, singsong intonation that fell unpleasantly on her ears, but as his hand moved leisurely to caress her flanks, she fully realized that he intended to detain her for some misbegotten purpose of his own.

"Let me go at once," she cried, tugging now at the arms that held her prisoner. "I warn you that our whereabouts are known to the British authorities, and great trouble will befall you if you keep us here against our will."

"His voice is sweet as a maiden's," marveled Ahmet Mustafa. His glittering black eyes, creased in rolls of fat, roamed assessingly over Caro, and she felt with a chill of horror that in an instant he would see through her disguise. "See, his lashes are thick as feathers on a raven's wing, and his eyes dark as the pool where the gazelle kneels to drink. Truly the gods have sent us a pearl of great price who outshines all our fair Circassian boys."

Behind him, Caro saw Brook Vyner stir, and the movement gave her fresh hope.

"Please let me go," she said steadily, holding his eyes with her own. "If you tell your men to release us at once, and not to hinder our going, I promise I will not report you to the authorities, but if you keep us here a moment longer—"

Out of the corner of her eye she saw a flash of movement as Brook staggered to his feet and stood, fighting to keep his balance as the fumes of opium cleared from his brain.

"Caro! What are you doing here?" It was a wail of anguish, and then as realization of their situation came to him, his hand dropped to where his pistol should have been, realized its loss, and snatched up his swordstick instead. "Unhand her, you black son of Belial," he snarled, and lunged at the servant holding Caro.

The attack was so sudden that Caro's guard was taken by surprise and threw up his hands, releasing her. She grabbed for a weapon, any weapon, and her fingers closed on the stem of the *hookah* pipe which had lain beside the senseless Brook. The long, flexible tube that attached the stem to the mouthpiece flew up with it, and whirling it around her head, Caro struck Ahmet Mustafa such a blow that he slumped to the floor. His servant fled from the room, and Caro seized Brook by the hand.

"Quick!" she gasped. "We must get away at once, for I am sure that man has gone to fetch help. Can you move?"

"I think so," he answered rather unsteadily, for the room seemed to be heaving under his feet, and objects shrank and enlarged dizzily as he tried to focus his eyes. "I feel a trifle foxed, still, but you're right: there's no time to lose. My pistol's gone, and so's my purse, but they've left me my swordstick, at least."

He grasped the stick, and clinging to Caro for support, opened the door. The passage outside was deserted, and the fountain still tinkled enticingly from the inner courtyard, but when Brook and Caro tried to push through the bead curtain into the outer room, they found their way barred by a crowd of Ahmet Mustafa's servants, brandishing cudgels and long, glinting knives.

Heedless of anything but the need to escape, Brook charged the man with the thin blade of his swordstick, and they fell back, moving around behind so that Brook and Caro were once more encircled.

"Look out—behind you!" cried Caro as Brook lunged at a black-bearded fellow in white robes girt with a heavy, ornate belt; too late Brook swung around to face the blow, and a cudgel cracked against his skull. He staggered, but managed to keep his feet, still holding Caro's arm as she swung the *hookah* wildly, clearing a larger circle around them, and their assailants dodged back from the whirling tube with its heavy brass mouthpiece.

The shouts of their attackers rose to a crescendo as they urged one another on, and seeing Brook's evident weakness, they began to press in again with new ferocity. Their cries broke like waves over Caro's head as she swung her weapon with all her strength, her breath coming in panting sobs, her arm aching where Brook clung to it in a desperate effort to stay upright.

Then suddenly another arm wielding a cudgel was was thumping and cracking against the heads of their attackers, while a voice Caro could not mistake thundered, "Stop! Stop, I say! Put up your weapons at once. What is the meaning of this affray?"

Those firm British tones had a magical effect on the

dark-faced assailants, who drew back in startled dismay then, to a man, turned and fled. Caro, panting, turned toward their rescuer and could scarcely believe her eyes: standing before her was the one person she had hoped never to have to meet again. Rowland Steel was wearing a loose, striped robe over his English clothes and his gray eyes sparkled with the pleasure of the fight.

"Pity they couldn't stay for a little more of that medicine," he bellowed cheerfully. "It might have taught them not to molest the island race in future! Well done, boy. You certainly gave as good as you got in that little skirmish, though I'm afraid your companion's fared worse than you."

Between them, Caro and Rowland walked Brook to the veranda steps and propped him against the rail.

"Thanks," he muttered dazedly. "Thought we were...done for just then. Who—what happened? Whom do I thank for rescuing us?"

"No thanks needed. It was sheer luck that I was there in the inner room, enjoying a quiet pipe, and heard the shindig. Brook Vyner, isn't it? I believe we're fellow passengers on the *Malabar Star*. You put up a grand fight against that crowd of blackguards, and so did the youngster."

He patted Caro on her Norfolk-jacketed shoulder, and she lowered her head to hide her face. She was torn between amusement and consternation. There was no one in the wide world she would so much dislike to discover her in this disguise as Captain Steel, yet after the fear and strain of the past half hour it was so inexpressibly cheering and delightful to hear his strong, authoritative tones, and feel his warm hand against her shoulder, that she could have laughed aloud with relief.

He was explaining how he had chanced to come to

their rescue. "I'd called on that old rogue Ahmet Mustafa for a smoke and a chat before my ship sailed . . ."

Brook gave a strangled cry: "The ship! My watch! Devil take it—we'll miss our passage!"

"Calm yourself," Rowland advised. "We've time enough to reach the docks if you will ride in my carriage. There's half an hour yet before we sail. As I was saying, I'd finished my pipe and was thinking of leaving when I chanced to stumble over Mustafa lying like a sack across his own doorway, dead to the world. I shook him back to consciousness, and he mumbled something uncomplimentary about an Englishman who'd struck him. I guessed he'd been up to some villainy and received his just deserts, and was going to leave him to sleep it off when I heard the clamor on the veranda. But tell me, how did you come to be in such a situation?"

Brook's eyes darted to and fro, but he saw no escape. He blurted, "I had business with Ahmet Mustafa, too. A friend supplied me with his address. But I did not know—I had no idea what kind of house he kept."

"Oh, he's a well-known rogue with a finger in every villainous pie that this port can offer," said Rowland lightly. "Your friend should have warned you. He deals in opium and . . . slave boys. No doubt if you'd known that, you'd have been careful to leave your young friend at the ship."

Vyner flared up at the implied rebuke. "I told Caro to wait outside . . ."

"Caro?"

"Carlo," Brook amended hastily. "My young cousin Charles—we call him Carlo. The boy was with me to see the town, and there was no time to send him back to the ship."

Rowland took no notice but pulled Caro around to face him. She saw astonished recognition in his eyes and tried to shrink away, but he held her firmly.

"So... it is you again, *Lady Caroline*." She flinched before the harshness in his voice. "I little thought to meet you engaged in another mad escapade of this kind, but clearly you were misled by whoever induced you to put on that absurd disguise." He rounded angrily on Brook. "Have you no sense, Vyner? Can't you see that it was the height of dangerous folly to bring a lady with you to such a place? You both could well have been killed by that crowd of cutthroats, whereupon your bodies would have been weighted with bricks and thrown into the Nile, and no one would ever have known your fate. Even we military are advised not to come here alone, and I was smoking in company with a Frenchman of my acquaintance. But for a Civilian and a lady...! I am astounded that you should be lost to all sense of propriety, Vyner. Upon my word I am."

Brook muttered that Caro had insisted: he hadn't wanted to bring her, and Caro cried defiantly, "It is true, Captain Steel, you cannot blame Mr. Vyner. I made him bring me here, because I missed seeing the sights of Cairo. Mr. Vyner promised to escort me at the express wish of Lady Marvell, with whom I am traveling, so there is nothing in the least surreptitious about our tour of Suez."

"Your chaperone knows you are here?"

"Certainly," responded Caro stoutly.

"Then we had better return you to her care at once, or your absence from shipboard when the gangplank is pulled up may shake even her complacency. Besides, Mr. Vyner's head requires attention. Does it hurt much?"

Relieved that Captain Steel's lecture appeared to be over, Brook placed a cautious hand on his wound and pronounced it to be "deuced sore and swollen up like a turkey's egg."

In disagreeable silence, Caro followed the two men

to Rowland's waiting carriage, and they were driven as fast as possible back to the harbor.

Captain Steel's rebuke for their adventure had done nothing but inflame Caro's smoldering resentment toward him, but when she saw the state of agitation into which poor Lady Marvell had fallen by the time the ship's hooter had blown three times without the return of her protégée, Caro felt deep remorse for causing her kind guardian such anxiety. Her first idea of slipping down to her cabin to change her clothes was instantly discarded when she saw the poor lady white and shaking by the rail as their small party hurried aboard to the accompaniment of good-natured banter from the sailors standing by to haul up the gangplank. She ran forward and grasped her by the arm.

"Here I am, dear Lady Marvell, safe and sound. I am so very sorry to have caused a fuss, and I hope you were not too worried."

Relief at seeing her charge alive caused the blood to rush back into Lady Marvell's plump cheeks, and she gave rein to her feelings: "You naughty child! What have you been doing? Why are you wearing those dreadful clothes? I have been so anxious... I thought you must have been injured or lost to have delayed so long. Where is Mr. Vyner? I shall certainly speak my mind to him for causing me so much concern!"

"No, please do not blame him, Lady Marvell. Indeed, he wished to bring me back sooner. The truth is, we have had a kind of adventure, and were delayed, but then..." She gritted her teeth and went on. "...Captain Steel rescued us. May I present Captain Rowland Steel to you, ma'am? He has saved us from a difficult situation this afternoon, and is now to be our traveling companion as far as Bombay."

Lady Marvell automatically extended her hand and Rowland bowed over it, but she was still far from satisfied with Caro's explanation of the afternoon's events.

"Rescued? Adventure? I wish to know a great deal more of what you have been doing, child. Really, it is singularly tiresome of you to cause me so much trouble, and why Mr. Vyner permitted it I cannot imagine. I thought your mama had done you an injustice when she advised me to keep a strict control on you at all times, but now I see she was quite right. Go to your cabin at once; I am very much displeased with both you and Mr. Vyner."

Brook Vyner was swaying on his feet, chalk-white, clearly in no fit state to defend his reputation to Lady Marvell.

Rowland, taking pity on him, added expansively, "Indeed, ma'am, no one was to blame for the delay. I am sure you know how difficult it is to instill the least idea of punctuality into Egyptian servants, and the streets of the old town are uncommonly confusing. Poor Vyner had the misfortune to sustain a nasty blow to the head, and if you will permit me, I will take him below and get his man to attend to the wound, for I shouldn't wonder if he has a touch of concussion."

Lady Marvell's anger, which had been caused more by fright than rancor, melted at once when she heard of Brook's injury.

"Poor fellow; it will be a lesson to him," she decided, and then added, "I should be greatly obliged if you, sir, and you, Caro, would have the goodness never to refer to this unfortunate escapade again. Summon Mr. Vyner's valet to attend him." She put out her hand to Rowland with a warm smile. "I am truly grateful for your help, Captain Steel, and hope you will join us for a hand of cards after supper."

When Caro presently made her escape below to her cabin, Rowland and Lady Marvell were still chatting on the best of terms.

The ship's doctor, who dressed Brook's head wound, confirmed that the blow had caused a mild concussion, prescribed opium for the pain, and ordered him to rest in his cabin for several days, during which Caro would have to make do without her unwilling accomplice in adventure.

In low spirits the next evening, after a day of behaving in an impeccably ladylike fashion in order to reassure Lady Marvell that yesterday's lapse from grace had been an isolated incident, which merited no reversion to the strick surveillance that Lady Marchmain had recommended, Caro pleaded a headache after supper and escaped early from the stuffy saloon where her chaperone and Mrs. Merryweather were preparing to settle down to a game of piquet.

She felt restless and dissatisfied, in need of company but without the inclination to make herself agreeable. The thought of returning to her hot, airless cabin held no allure, and on a sudden impulse she climbed a companionway and slipped out onto the moonlit deck.

Stars blazed in the indigo night sky, like diamonds against deep blue velvet. Caro leaned on the rail, idly watching the porpoises trail phosphorescence through the water, as she tried to dispel her gloomy thoughts.

Was that island they'd passed at sunset a pirate hideout, or a Portuguese adventurers' lair? She sighed: all this beauty and strangeness—a whole world inviting her to exploration—and all she was allowed to do was sit in a stifling saloon with two elderly women, speaking when she was spoken to and changing her dress three times a day.

Would it be the same when they arrived in India— with Philippa taking the place of Lady Marvell and issuing her a long list of things a young lady might and might not do? If so, she would rather have stayed at home, married that horrible old miser and sought the freedom her soul yearned for by raising his brood of children. For undoubtedly married ladies were permitted more freedom than unmarried ones. But she had no wish to marry. Tom Hamilton had deceived her, not to speak of Rowland Steel, who had possessed the power to set her free and had instead returned her to the confines of her home.

A hand falling lightly on her shoulder caused her to spin around.

"Oh ... Captain Steel. You startled me."

"As you did me, standing there like a ghost in the moonlight. I was afraid if you leaned any further over that rail, you would pitch straight into the waves. Homesick?" he asked, correctly guessing the cause of her dejection.

"Home seems very far away," she admitted, unsure whether she wanted his sympathy, but comforted by it nevertheless.

"For me it is just the opposite," he told her. "Every hour brings me closer home."

"You look upon *India* as your home?" She was astonished. How could one belong by blood to one country yet feel most at home in another? She could not imagine an Englishman like Brook Vyner ever calling India his home.

"Certainly. I was born in India, and apart from my schooling, I've lived there all my life."

His hand still rested on her shoulder, and she moved just enough to force him to remove it. The warm, strong grip had disturbed her, had made it more difficult to regard him as the enemy, who had betrayed her once and might do so again. "I should always regard England as my home, though I were to live fifty years in foreign lands," she announced firmly. "But then, I had no wish to leave England. I am here against my will, and largely by your doing."

"My doing!" He laughed. "Oh, Caro, I would not

have expected you to deceive yourself on that score. But never mind, one day you will thank me for widening your horizon. Come, you must be cold in that thin dress, without so much as a shawl. We will take a stroll around the deck before I see you to your cabin."

Will we, thought Caro, quick to resent his easy dismissal of her grudge against him. She turned away from him, and he stopped in surprise.

"You'd rather stay here? Oh, I see: you are waiting for someone."

"What if I am?"

"Oh, I agree, none of my business, of course. But if the fellow hasn't the manners to keep his...assignation, you are well within your rights in walking the deck with me instead."

"How dare you suggest such a thing?" she cried, whipping herself into a fury. "There's no question of an assignation. I came here to seek solitude, and if you were any sort of a gentleman you would leave me in peace."

Even in the dusk, she could see his gray eyes sparkle with mischief, but he bowed and said formally, "In that case there is nothing more for me to do than bid you good night."

Before she was aware of his intentions, his arms were firmly around her, easing the length of her against his hard, fine body. Then, releasing one hand, he lifted her chin as he bent over her and lightly grazed her lips with his own. Without thinking, conscious only of a sudden weakness and the unfortunate rolling of the deck beneath her, she reached out for him, as if to break her fall. Now, when he caught her up in his arms, he drew her mouth to his, lovingly stroking her tongue with his own, then powerfully plunging it deeper so that their mouths became as one.

Gently, very gently, he raised his head and loosened his embrace, and as her palms slipped down his muscled back, so beautifully different from her own, he set his tongue and mouth to exploring the small pulsing hollow at the base of her neck, the perfect curve of her shoulder, the deep, soft globes framed by her gown.

For a moment, she responded eagerly, overwhelmed by the strong, sweet craving to be possessed. Tom Hamilton had forced his desire upon her, but now it was she herself who sought surrender.

"Caro," Rowland murmured, and somehow the evocation of her name brought her back to her senses. Mingled rage at his impertinence and horror at her own reaction, caused her to break away with a violence that brought her staggering to the rail.

"Captain Steel!" she exclaimed in a trembling voice.

"Gently does it," he said coolly, drawing her back toward him as if nothing had happened. "I would not trust that rail too far. No, do not fight me," he added in a lower tone, "for I see we are observed, and for the sake of your reputation, if nothing else, I will now escort you to your cabin as if we were the best of friends."

Pray heaven it is not dear Lady Marvell, or one of her cronies, thought Caro, obeying the pressure of his arm and walking demurely toward the door she had come out through.

"Who was it?" she whispered.

"I don't know. I saw only the silhouette of a figure in the doorway, but whoever it was could not have observed anything untoward, I assure you. Just two friends bidding one another good night."

The amusement in his tone made Caro's blood boil, but for the benefit of any hidden watcher she concealed her feelings until he left her at the door of her own cabin. Then she drummed her fists on the bed in helpless rage.

How dare he treat her like a common trollop, kissing her in so casual, so cavalier a fashion—as if he owned her. Not unlike Tom Hamilton, albeit in a different fashion, he had taken cruel advantage of her inexperience! Oh, if she only were a man! She would call him out, horsewhip him, teach him not to molest respectable young females with his hateful kisses. The memory of that burning touch, and the dark, sinful pleasure it had stirred in her, roused her to fresh paroxysms of anger. He thought she was easy: no doubt he had misread her character at their very first encounter, and the scene in the Suez opium house had confirmed his opinion. Well, she would show him how wrong he was. She would be correct, serious-minded, full of polite affectations. She would encourage his advances yet hold him at a distance until he was mad for love of her. Then she would turn him down in favor of another man—a real gentleman who'd never dream of pulling a lady into his arms without her permission.

Caro laughed softly, her temper restored by the picture of Captain Steel on bended knee in an elegant parlor, begging her to marry him, and herself turning coldly away, hand outstretched to a shadowy figure waiting behind her as she spurned the Captain's love.

Brook Vyner was still confined to his cabin as Caro put her plan into operation. For three whole days, she comported herself with an elegance that would have astonished her mother, and it did not escape Lady Marvell's notice that the performance was directed at impressing Captain Steel. After the scene in the moonlight she had taken care not to be left alone with him, but he appeared perfectly content to play the part she seemed to require of him, dancing with her, joining in earnest discussions of Indian matters and customs, strolling with the ladies around the deck, or sipping lemonade in the shade of the awning.

But when Brook emerged from his sickbed with a bandage around his head, Rowland gave him every opportunity to reestablish himself in Caro's favor.

"Questions like that are more in Mr. Vyner's line than mine," he said when Caro begged him prettily to explain to her the judiciary system of British India. "He's one of the Heaven-Born, while I'm only a poor cavalryman. He knows all the legal technicalities."

Caro pouted. Brook Vyner's explanations were inclined to be long-winded. It was proving more of a strain than she had anticipated to pretend an interest in matters that held not the least hint of frivolity. She tried again. "And their marriage customs? Is it true that Mussulmans are allowed four wives?"

"Caro dear," said Lady Marvell gently, "you will tire Captain Steel with all your questions. When I was a girl, such matters were never spoken of, and you will find such information of very little relevance to your life in India."

"On the contrary," said Rowland quickly, "I find it admirable that an English lady should wish to know how Indians live. I had no wish to discourage her interest, but thought Mr. Vyner's opinion of more value than my own."

Caro glanced shrewdly at him from beneath lowered lashes. You mean you can't be troubled to launch into a long and tedious explanation, she silently railed at him, when you haven't an ounce of hope that I will understand what you say. Very well, I'll leave you to your game of cards and see if a bit of competition will sharpen your attention.

Caro's perfect opportunity occurred a day or so later when Brook finally voiced his discontent. He had asked her to accompany his singing, as she had frequently done before reaching Alexandria, and Caro had refused on the grounds that she was engaged to partner Captain Steel in a game of whist.

Brook flushed red, and then his face paled and his mouth took on an ugly line. "You were glad enough to play for me before Captain Steel came on the scene," he said crudely. "Now all I hear is 'Rowland this' and 'Rowland that.' I tell you I'm sick to death of it. I can't bear to see you being taken in by a fellow like that. Someone ought to warn you what kind of a man he is, and if the ladies won't do it, then I'll have to."

"What can you mean?"

"All that nonsense about his hearing our cries and rushing to our rescue in Suez," he said bitterly. "It's nothing but a pack of lies. Your precious Rowland Steel is hand-in-glove with that villain Ahmet Mustafa, and keeps him supplied with customers from every British ship that docks at Suez. Takes his share of the profits, too; no one could live in the style *he* does on a captain's pay!"

"But he did come to our aid," objected Caro, undaunted by his jealous fabrication. "And we would have done poorly if he had not been at hand. I suppose selling opium is a trade like any other, and as long as people wish to buy it there is no stigma attached to taking their money."

"Of course you would defend him. It's clear as daylight that you're in love with the fellow, but I can't help taking it hard because before he joined the ship I thought—I hoped—you cared for me."

"I do—I don't!" cried Caro, thoroughly confused by this abrupt declaration. "Of course I care for you—a little," she added cautiously as Brook's transparent face lit up with joy.

"Then I am not sorry I spoke as I did. Believe me, Caro," he said earnestly, "I have no wish to rush you into saying anything you will regret. But if you will just allow me to hope a little...?"

This seemed to Caro a modest enough ambition, and she agreed readily, though the memory of Rowland's embrace still caused her a degree of uneasiness. Beside the Captain's dark good looks,

Brook Vyner's blonde prettiness appeared so tame, and his personality so easily bent to her wishes, that she couldn't grudge him the small concession of being allowed to hope.

Brook, satisfied that he had gained a little ground in her favor, pressed her hand and said no more on the subject. His uncle, on whom his career depended, had made it all too clear that he would tolerate no more rumors questioning the quality of his nephew's morals: "Get yourself respectably married," he ordered curtly, "and have done with this pack of native boys around your quarters. I don't deny they're decorative, but they do your reputation no good at all, and that's bad for the Service."

Ordered to marry! Brook's face burned as he remembered that humiliating interview. He had admitted to nothing, of course, but he suspected that his uncle had a shrewd idea how the land lay in Brook's relations with the female sex. He could feel at ease with old ladies like Mrs. Merryweather and Lady Marvell, or exert himself to amuse and instruct small girls. It was the corseted, voluptuous creatures in between, with their scented ringlets and air of mystery, who frightened and revolted him. But Caro was different. The moment he had seen her leaning on the ship's rail, her hair blowing in the gale, he had sensed that she was not like the hothouse blooms whose overemphasized femininity repelled him, and when she appeared beside him in her boy's disguise, he had felt a shameful and familiar leaping of desire.

"Come, let us stretch our legs a little," he suggested, taking Caro's arm.

Stifling a yawn, she accompanied him around the deck for the twentieth time, trying to listen to his views on government, which seemed to her exceedingly tedious. Now and again she could not help stealing a glance at the wide shoulders and muscular back of

Rowland Steel, as he leaned back, laughing at some joke of Lady Marvell's, or lent an ear to Mrs. Merryweather's never-ending recital of the talents of her grandchildren. He's just as happy with those two old ladies as he is with me, she thought aggrievedly, and took care to smile brilliantly at Brook Vyner as their walk took them past Lady Marvell's little group.

Poor devil, thought Rowland, he's head-over-heels in love with that pretty little minx, and much good may it do him. When she reaches Delhi she'll bewitch a Collector, at least, with those looks, and poor Vyner won't have a hope of marrying her, no matter how hard he works to please her.

Lady Marvell thought much the same, and made no attempt to discourage the friendship as the *Malabar Star* steamed through calm, warm waters toward the Port of Bombay.

Chapter Three

FOR CARO THE most surprising thing about reaching India at last was how familiar everything seemed. From the gently waving palms against the splendid vivid blue of sky and sea to the elaborate carriages drawn up to watch the passengers disembark; from the native porters and coolies, naked except for a brief loincloth, to the bright yellow mounds of cereals, spices, baskets of salt fish and wicker panniers full of oranges, limes, jackfruit and plantains, all looked exactly as she had known it would. It was like finding herself back in a well-loved, half-remembered dream. Little girls carried bundles of freshly cut grass, carefully balancing their loads on their heads, and bent old men wove their way through the crowds with long rolls of bamboo matting. Even the smell seemed familiar: garlic and dung, sweat, coriander and hot oil, cumin and turmeric. Caro had a strange feeling of having come home.

This was reinforced the moment she caught sight of Philippa, resplendent in a green silk bonnet, hanging on her husband's arm, smiling and waving. Laughing and crying at once, the sisters hugged one another, uttering little cries of welcome and pleasure, oblivious to the crowds around them, while Andrew Thynne and Lady Marvell, who were old friends, exchanged bows and gossip.

At last Philippa drew back and patted her bonnet into place again. Her bright eyes, which always reminded Caro of a shrewd, eager dormouse, surveyed her sister with approval.

"Dear Caro, you are just the same as ever," she said fondly. "I was afraid you would have changed: it is so long since we saw each other, and I am pining to hear about your London season. Mama's letters are sadly lacking in descriptive detail; she cannot know how we in India long for news from home. Imagine: she announced that she was was sending you to stay with us for the 'cold weather' just as undramatically as if you were to pay a visit to an aunt at Harrogate or Bath. No word of explanation, beyond the fact that you'd had a tiring season in London and were quite 'done up,' as she put it. Of course I am delighted, and Andrew too, and so fortunate that he is at present on leave from his regiment so we might travel to Bombay to meet you. But I think it too bad of Mama to give us so little time to look forward to your coming!"

As her sister's words tumbled out, Caro glanced at Lady Marvell to see if she thought a fuller explanation for her sudden visit to India should be given, and saw that lady give a slight but definite shake of the head, cautioning her to hold her tongue.

But although Philippa, while delighted to see Caro, was puzzled and a little offended by her abrupt arrival, no such considerations troubled her husband. Andrew Thynne, large, fair, and uncomplicated, enveloped his sister-in-law in a hearty bearhug and said Philippa was quite wrong in saying she hadn't changed: she was prettier than ever. Although he had gained considerable weight since his marriage to Philippa, and his fair complexion was becoming florid, he was still a handsome figure in his well-cut pearl-gray suit and high, stiff collar. It was easy to see in him the echo of the dashing, hard-riding subaltern who had captured Philippa's heart. He was quick and efficient, too, at organizing the collection and disposal of their baggage,

and in no time, it seemed, Caro was taking leave of
Lady Marvell, whose son and daughter-in-law had
come to meet her, bringing her new grandson in the
arms of his *ayah*.

"Dear ma'am, I cannot thank you enough for all
your care and help," she said, smiling. "I hope we may
meet again soon."

Lady Marvell kissed her briskly, saying no thanks
were needed, she had much enjoyed Caro's companionship, and waved her white-gloved hand as she was
whirled away behind her son's team of spirited Arab
horses.

Andrew handed his wife and sister-in-law into a
hired carriage. Leaving his bearer to arrange the
transport of Caro's luggage, they drove to the Orient
Hotel, where they spent the night before embarking on
the long train journey toward Delhi.

Although she disliked keeping anything from her
sister, Caro soon realized that Lady Marvell was right
when she warned her to conceal the circumstances that
had led her to India. In her new environment, Philippa
was deeply—and to Caro surprisingly—concerned
with keeping up position, doing the right thing at all
times, and maintaining her dignity and that of her
husband. Since Andrew Thynne was on leave, they
were accompanied on their journey by only a small
part of their household: Andrew's bearer, cook, and
two porters, a *dhobi* and two *ayah*s—one of whom
looked after Philippa's clothes and the other acting as
lady's maid, brushing her hair, setting out her jewels,
and seeing that washing water was provided in the
brass *lotah*s—and a diminutive page boy, whose task
seemed to be solely that of keeping his mistress up to
date with all the household gossip.

But when they arrived at the cool, high-ceiling
house Andrew had rented for the duration of his leave,

in Shah Jehan Bagh, near Delhi race course, Caro was astonished by the number of servants needed to insure a simple captain's domestic comfort, as well as by the wide range of their duties. It seemed to her that her sister had very little to do with the running of her household.

"I never go near the kitchen," Philippa admitted, "because Andrew says it would upset the servants." She giggled. "It would probably upset me, too, if I knew exactly how some of our food is prepared. Thick black smoke everywhere and the vegetables chopped on mother earth. But I keep an eye on the accounts, of course, and order the dishes when we give a dinner because, left to himself, the *khansamah* would serve us nothing but clear soup and tough fowl. As it is, he often tries to slip one of his favorite dishes into a menu I have devised. Then, of course, I arrange the flowers ..."

"With a great heap of cut blooms laid ready to your hand by your faithful *malee*," teased Caro, who had been quick to pick up the names of the gardeners, washermen, cooks, and coolies who peopled Philippa's domain.

"Yes, I know you think me very indolent," said her sister, smiling, "but you must understand that Andrew's servants were with him before he married, and they would deeply resent too much interference by a new memsahib. Yet I assure you I keep busy, what with paying calls and entertaining our friends I have plenty to do, and when we have a family ..." Her face clouded. It was a source of worry to Philippa that although she and Andrew had been married for over a year, there was still no sign of a baby. She sighed, picturing for a moment a little Andrew with sun-bleached hair and white cotton coat, toddling about the well-tended rosebeds with his *ayah* in close attendance. Doctor McPhail had assured her there was nothing wrong; it was only a matter of waiting, getting used to the climate; she must not give up hope. Perhaps this "cold weather," when she felt less tired, the miracle would happen.

She pushed these thoughts away, saying briskly, "Now you are here, dear Caro, we shall have more than enough to do. First, I must give a ball."

"Do you think," said Caro diffidently, "that I might take lessons in Hindustani? I should so much like to. I find it most provoking to be unable to understand what the people are saying."

Philippa laughed. "I assure you that what they are saying is very dull. Really, Caro, there is no need to learn to speak their language. The servants understand English when they wish to, and any rajah you may meet at dinner is certain to have an interpreter, if he cannot speak English himself. I suppose we *could* find you a *munshi*, like that fat rascal Chaturvedi, who has helped every officer I know through his exams. I'll see what Andrew suggests."

Philippa's ball was a grand affair, to which fashionable Delhi flocked to meet the newcomer whom rumor had already declared to be the prettiest addition to the Fishing Fleet for many a year. Caro's ball gown—a dream of silver gauze over sea-green taffeta, with a daringly low neckline that showed her white bosom—caused a sensation among the ladies, whose fashions—to a Londoner's eye—looked decidedly out of date.

"I wonder her sister allows her to wear such a dress," murmured Miss Isabelle Waller to her friend, Miss Margaret Fyne. "It is almost—almost fast."

Together they gazed enviously at Caro as she glided past the line of straight-back gold chairs on which they sat fanning themselves while hoping for a partner to invite them to dance. But all the spare men seemed to be clustered round Caro, clamoring for the waltz, the quadrille, the schottische, the polka, while she laughingly scribbled their names in her gilt-edge programme.

"She certainly is a beauty," said fair-minded Miss Fyne, "and the dress is exceedingly becoming, even if it is a little fast."

"Handsome is as handsome does," snorted Miss Waller, annoyed to see gray-haired Mr. Kincaid, whom she considered her steady beau, join the group surrounding Caro. "Do you know what my *ayah* told me tonight as I was dressing? She said that Andrew Thynne has engaged a *munshi* to teach Lady Caroline to speak Hindustani! Did you ever hear of such a thing?"

Miss Fyne was startled out of her customary calm. She said incredulously, "Learn Hindustani? You must be mistaken. No lady would do such a thing."

"I assure you it is true." Miss Waller's attention was diverted from this fascinating topic by the arrival of Mr. Kincaid, come to claim her for the supper waltz. She placed her hand on his arm, saying teasingly, "So you had no success in the lists for Lady Caro's favor?"

He shook his head. "I was not the only one to be disappointed, I assure you. The ball would have to be twice as long for all Lady Caro's suitors to be satisfied."

The receiving line of Andrew, Philippa, and Caro had long broken ranks and dispersed to look after their guests by the time Rowland Steel arrived. Only the week past an urgent summons had come from the Nawab of Bhaipat, an old friend of Rowland's father, speaking of confidential information he wished to entrust to no one but the son of his old comrade. This request had resulted in a week's hard riding and some disturbing news about unrest among the sepoys, stirred up by the unseated Nana Sahib—news that Rowland had delivered into the hands of native regiments in the recently annexed Kingdom of Oudh and which now formed the basis of a dispatch to the newly appointed

Governor-General, Lord Canning.

Had Philippa's ball been given by anyone else, Rowland would have no hesitation in sending a message of regret and going straight to bed. But he was curious to see how Caro was adapting to her new surroundings, and after a bath, a bumper of champagne, and a pipe of *charrah* to shake off the effects of his long ride, he allowed his bearer to garb him in full-dress uniform and made his way to the Thynnes's flower-decked, lantern-blazing house on Siakot Avenue.

Pausing inside the doorway to survey the crowd, Rowland watched the British Civil Servants go through their customary high paces. They continue to act, Rowland thought, no matter how long they've been posted here, as if they could walk out of their houses and be constantly in England. India, glorious India, wise long before their beefy Saxon ancestors even lived in houses, was something to be avoided, worse, ignored, at all costs. They were all the same, from the rugged old collectors, who for thirty years had lived like rajáhs on the spoils of their office, to the arrogant young twits like Brook Vyner.

Rowland's revery was broken by the sight of Brook Vyner himself, waltzing across the dance floor with an exquisite creature in sea green. Caro! But a new Caro. Gone was the stuttering child he barely remembered; gone both the terrified maiden and the fiery *hookah*-wielding youth in Suez. Here was Caro the woman, all alabaster shoulders and ebony hair perfectly enhanced by the radiant green of her gown. The couple's extraordinary sensual grace as they moved across the floor had captured the attention of not a few of the guests. Vyner was not a half-bad dancer, Rowland had to admit, but what man could fail to shine with such a partner?

"Rowland!" exclaimed his host, spotting the

resplendent figure the moment he paused in the doorway to the ballroom. "You look devilish fine tonight, old fellow, but I hope you ain't countin' on a dance with my sister-in-law. Her programme's been full since nine o'clock, and there are still scores of fellows clamoring to dance with her. Better share a bottle with me, instead; you won't be able to get near her, I promise you. What's the news from Bhaipat?"

While his eyes followed Caro's every movement on the dance floor, jealousy mixing with desire, Rowland coolly gave Andrew a carefully edited account of his meetings with the old Nawab. Andrew whistled. "Thinks the sepoys will rise against us? Don't expect me to believe that! Why, the Army of Bengal's been given all kinds of perks and privileges they wouldn't dream of getting in Bombay."

"Oddly enough, that's part of the Nawab's reasoning," said Rowland watching Caro move gracefully through the figures of the quadrille on the arm of Brook Vyner. "He thinks we're too soft with 'em, and the absurd system of seniority, whereby long service is the only means to promotion, has given us no able native officers who could control the men, but merely a pack of old imbeciles. I'll tell you someone who agrees with him—and that's James Outram. No one can call *him* a fool or a scaremonger."

"All the same, it seems a trifle far-fetched," said Andrew.

"I agree. Here in your ballroom one can't imagine any kind of trouble. Ah, Lady Philippa," he said, rising to his feet as his hostess, flushed and breathless, approached from the dance floor. "What a delightful party, ma'am. I'm glad the Nawab gave me my *congé* in time to be able to attend it. Will you give me the honor of a dance?"

Half an hour later, after executing a few more duty dances, he gave up all hope of claiming Caro's hand.

She was unquestionably the belle of the ball. Rowland's every attempt to engage her for a dance was met with an enticing lowering of the lashes, which clearly signified a delicious but definite dismissal.

Disheartened, he made his way to the relative coolness of the conservatory. Tall ferns and trailing vines made a miniature forest lit only by paper lanterns that shed a soft glow over glossy leaves and petals. Rowland yawned deeply, glad of a moment's respite from the chattering throng, and sank into a basket-work chair behind a potted palm. The long hours in the saddle were telling even on his strong constitution, and he sank into a light doze.

Low voices whispering urgently at the far end of the conservatory roused him a few minutes later, and he was about to rise and make his presence known when the unmistakable sound of a ringing slap froze him in his chair. It was followed by a yelp of pain and soft scuffling.

"By God," growled a voice that he recognized as Brook Vyner's, "you shall not treat me like that. You promised me..."

"I promised you nothing, Brook." Caro's voice was cool and amused. "You have imagined it all, and your absurd jealousy gives me no alternative than to speak frankly."

Rowland grinned. If that slap was Lady Caro's notion of frank speaking, she was a girl after his own heart. No doubt young Vyner richly deserved it, but the poor fool would feel doubly humiliated if he knew his punishment had been observed. Better keep quiet and allow the combatants to sort it out for themselves. In any case, Caro appeared in control of the situation, and Vyner, however angry, would surely draw the line at causing her bodily harm at her own ball.

A moment later he was less sure of his decision not to intervene. The scuffling sounds ended in a little gasp from Caro, whether of fear or pain Rowland had no means of telling. He heard her breathless whisper: "Let me go. You're hurting me. I tell you, I don't want to marry anyone—not yet. I will not be bullied and threatened."

"Do you wish me to tell all Delhi why you were banished from your parents' house, then? I can make sure that the story of your elopement with the notorious Captain Hamilton is all around British India in a week."

"You—you know about that?" Caro gasped.

"Of course I do." Brook chortled. "The London clubs were talking of nothing else. But I won't say a word as long as you promise..."

Rowland cursed roundly and rose to his feet, spurs jingling.

"What the devil...?" exclaimed Brook, releasing Caro as if she were red-hot.

"Your manner of conversing with a lady leaves a great deal to be desired, Mr. Vyner," drawled Rowland, striding over to the couple. "Neither threats nor bodily violence should have any place in a tête-à-tête of this nature, and were I not so confoundedly deaf in my right ear, I would feel obliged to call you out for it."

"Oh, please do not," said Caro in a trembling voice.

"No," he agreed. "That would improve none of our reputations. But let me tell you, Vyner: if the name of Tom Hamilton is so much as mentioned in connection with Lady Caroline's, I shall have no compunction in telling your uncle exactly what I have seen and heard here tonight. I fancy that would do little to enhance your hopes of promotion." He turned to Caro, who stood fiery-faced, rubbing her wrist where Vyner's fingers had bruised it. Gently Rowland placed her hand on his own arm. "I believe you promised me this dance, Lady Caroline..."

Vyner's face contorted with rage and hatred as he

watched them thread their way between the chattering, laughing groups of revelers. His uncle, Sir Hope Vyner, to whom he owned his rapid rise in the Indian Civil Service, was also the one man whose disapproval he feared. Damn Steel! Cursed, interfering blockhead of a cavalryman—how dared he speak so to one of the Heaven-Born? As for Caro, her beauty tantalized him and jealousy, when he saw her distributing favors among her many admirers, drove him frantic. She should be his—he was utterly determined to make her his own, and to that end vowed to lie and dissemble, flatter and plead until he obtained her promise to marry him.

After the ball, invitations flowed in thick and fast. Captain Connell invited Philippa and Caro to a picnic at the Qutab Minar, the ancient tower of victory dominating the countryside south of the city. Mr. Moon, the choleric, red-faced magistrate on leave from Captainganj, countered by hiring an elephant to take them to a display of fireworks at the Old Fort.

Caro, quite won over by Brook's impassioned apology, the day after her ball, blamed the champagne, forgave him, and allowed him the privilege of escorting her around the greatest wonder of all, the Taj Mahal by moonlight. Adrian Grant, son of one of the richest British indigo planters, begged to be allowed to lead her into supper at the Governor-General's Ball.

Still, Caro felt most herself when Rowland Steel was at her side, but since he was frequently absent on mysterious military business, she fell into the idle habit of judging every new companion against her memory of him.

"I mustn't pine for a mere captain," she lectured herself, only half in jest. "Whatever would Mother say?" Even Philippa never ceased to impress on her the wisdom of encouraging suitors from the ranks of the Indian Civil Service.

"They call them the Heaven-Born," her sister had

explained at the Governor-General's Ball, "and small
wonder. They live like kings of their districts in the
mofussil—that's to say, upcountry: hundreds of miles
from Calcutta, Bombay, and Delhi. 'Delhi *dur ast*,'
they say—I expect you can translate that after all your
lessons."

"'Delhi is far away.' Yes, I can see that the collector
of a remote district would have little reason to fear
interference from Delhi. But to me they *do* seem rather
old and solemn..."

She broke off. They were sitting under a potted
palm tree where the breeze from a row of well-
disciplined *punkah*s could fan their faces without
disturbing Philippa's high-piled hair. Supper had just
been announced and earlier Andrew had claimed—
even demanded—the honor of escorting his sister-in-
law to the supper room.

"I never see you nowadays, you minx," he'd
declared. "You're here, there, and everywhere; a poor
soldier can't keep up with you at all. So save me the
supper dance, like a good girl, and I'll stop regretting
that I gave you that pony instead of keeping her to race
myself."

Caro had laughed, scrawling his name across her
elegant gilt-edge programme, and true to her promise,
she asked Brook Vyner to bring her back in good time
to the Thynnes' table. Brook, feeling put out, had gone
off to seek his own supper partner, though neither
Adrian Grant nor Andrew had yet appeared to escort
the ladies.

Just then, Caro caught sight of Andrew approaching, and with him a tall, familiar figure who caused her
heart to leap and then start beating faster than usual.

"Adrian sends his apologies, Caro," said Andrew,
smiling down at her, "but he has been suddenly recalled
to duty. Dashed inconvenient for a fellow partnering
the prettiest girl at the Governor-General's Ball, and he

was quite cut up about it, I can tell you. But he's a good chap, Adrian, and he sent the rascal who brought him the bad news to take his place. You can hardly beat that for turning the other cheek, can you? I believe you are already acquainted: Captain Steel, Lady Caroline March."

Caro gave Rowland her hand, and suddenly the room, which had been till then just another overheated ballroom—larger and more splendid than most with its banks of flowers and glittering chandeliers—became an enchanted palace. The music was sweeter, the dresses more lovely, the scent of flowers overpowered her with delight. Absurd, thought Caro. I seem to be in danger of falling in love with my mere captain. Philippa will never forgive me.

But Philippa was too busy organizing their retreat to the supper room to notice her sister's confusion, and by the time they had partaken of champagne, turkey and ham, followed by a profusion of ices and sweetmeats, Caro was in command of herself once more.

"Why have you been neglecting us?" she complained. "It must be fully ten days since you told me you were going pig-sticking a day's ride from here, and I have not set eyes on you since. I want to show you the paragon of a pony kind Andrew has given me. She is a gray Arab, the prettiest you ever saw, and Andrew thinks she can outpace any horse in Delhi—even your Chinatown, for whom he has the liveliest admiration."

"Nothing can outpace Chinatown," declared Rowland with conviction. "Sometimes I wonder if he is a horse at all, and not Nimrod in disguise. You know the Hindu belief in the transmigration of souls. I am convinced that in some previous incarnation poor Chinatown was a noble rajah, dedicated to hunting wild pig, and though for his sin he has now descended into the body of a horse, his love of the chase has not altered one whit. At the cry '*Woh jata*,' which signals that a boar is afoot, I can feel his heart thumping enough to shake his whole frame, and as soon as the beast has been singled out, he follows him as a greyhound does a hare."

"I should love to see it," said Caro, wide-eyed, "but I am sure he'd not beat my Nuri."

Brook Vyner, who had joined their party, took Caro's part, declaring that he had ridden Nuri himself when the pony belonged to Nasr-ud-Dowlah, who had bred her, and believed she had no rival at hog-hunting.

"Three boar in one morning to my spear alone," he claimed, "and the temperature well over ninety. The pony's a marvel, Steel, say what you like, though much depends on the rider, of course. I don't say she'd perform quite as well for a griff."

Caro saw a small smile play about Rowland's mouth, but he said nothing. She sensed that Brook was trying to rile him, but if so, he was disappointed. Even the reference to a "griff"—a newcomer to India—did not appear to annoy him. Andrew and Philippa seemed worried that the obvious antipathy between Brook and Rowland would imminently break into open warfare.

"There's only one thing to be done to settle the question," said Andrew judicially, "and that's to set up a match between you—all fair and square—and may the best horse win! You both belong to the Tent Club, ain't that right? Well, then! We're arranging a meet at Oodabad to drive some of the boar out of the cane crops. Vyner can ride Caro's mare, and Steel his own horse, and we'll see who comes out tops."

"Oodabad? That's rough country," observed Rowland.

"Too rough for you?" sneered Brook Vyner.

"Of course not."

So it was arranged, and the rest of the ball passed in

a happy haze for Caro, as Rowland took the opportunity to claim the dances that would have been Adrian Grant's, causing Brook to set his teeth and take his leave rather earlier than he would otherwise have done.

"You don't mind that fellow Vyner riding your pony?" Rowland asked, as the whirling gallop changed to a more sedate waltz. "It's a risky business, you know, hog-hunting, and sometimes horses get hurt. I'll willingly pull out of the match if you don't care to risk your mare."

"Then Brook will say you were afraid to accept his challenge." Caro glanced at him sideways, afraid to discover him a coward prepared to withdraw from a bet at the hint of opposition.

He laughed. "Brook Vyner may say what he pleases, and no doubt he'll find plenty of people to listen. It won't bother me. But I don't want you blaming me for any injury to your little animal."

She was more than a little annoyed by his lack of competitive spirit as much as by his assumption that it was her mare that would come off worst.

"I have perfect faith in Nuri's ability to win the match," she said shortly, "and I've heard nothing but praise for Mr. Vyner's horsemanship. If you wish to withdraw, it will be at your own request, not mine."

There was an angry glint in Rowland's gray eyes, but he answered carelessly, "Oh yes, he can ride a bit. If you want to go on with it, I'm quite agreeable. Just don't say I didn't warn you: it's not quite like fox-hunting, you know." As he took her arm to lead her back to Philippa's side, Caro was forced to consider the unpleasant possibility that Captain Rowland Steel was far less a man than he seemed. Had his reticence really stemmed from a cowardice she would never have suspected? Well, be that as it may, Brook Vyner would ride her beloved Nuri; it was Brook who would be carrying her favor into the lists when the contest commenced.

The site chosen for the meet lay some twenty miles outside Delhi. Philippa and Caro traveled there in Andrew's carriage and pair, while *syces* led the dancing, excited Nuri and Andrew's chestnut, Cis. Tents had been erected on the flat maidan in front of the village of Oodabad, and they spent the night in the open beneath a star-filled sky.

At daybreak the beaters assembled, swarthy men of the Kanjar and Aheria tribes, cheerful, feckless nomads who made their living weaving grass and purloining their neighbors' chickens. Barefoot, naked except for a loincloth, and armed only with stout poles, a hundred or more of them lined out at the direction of Bhopa Ram, the head *shikari*, and began to beat rhythmically through the head-high grass, uttering soft grunts of "Wah! Wah!" as the line moved forward.

From her perch on the back of the elephant which Andrew had decided was the safest conveyance for her and Philippa, Caro looked with pride at Nuri, coat gleaming silver in the early sun, mane and tail brushed to floating perfection. She curvetted and side-stepped as her *syce* tried to soothe her, fretting to be off and well aware of the business of the day.

In contrast, Rowland's mount Chinatown, looked old and phlegmatic, a dark bay country-bred, long and low, with a plain head and ears that flopped as he moved. He stood quietly by his *syce*, eyes half closed, resting a hind leg as he waited for his master to mount.

Brook Vyner swaggered out of the breakfast tent, pulling on his velvet-covered jockey cap. He called to Caro, not troubling to keep his voice down: "Don't you think that"—he indicated Chinatown—"would look happier between the shafts of a cart?"

Andrew frowned, overhearing the remark, but Rowland grinned and said, as he swung into the saddle, "It was where I found him."

His *syce* handed him his spear—a shaft of solid male bamboo some six and a half feet long, with a diamond-shape head balanced by a lead weight on the butt. Chinatown woke from his doze and tossed his plain head as they trotted quietly away to their station midway across the line of beaters.

Brook had quite a tussle before the plunging, overexcited Nuri allowed him to mount, and Caro could not help admiring the way he handled the spirited little mare. For a mile or two they rode in silence, swaying to the elephant's stride, alert for any movement in the long grass, watching the large red flags at each end of the line of beaters, and Bhopa Ram on his camel who would signal the start of the chase. Satisfied at last that the waiting was over, Nuri stopped plunging and trotted demurely through the dense undergrowth.

"*Woh jata! Woh jata!*"

Caro's heart raced and she clutched Philippa's arm. "Where? I don't see anything. Oh, look—over there on the right. Nuri's side!"

A black shape broke away in front of the central line of beaters, and Bhopa Ram's camel lumbered into a gallop as her rider waved his flag. Simultaneously, Brook and Rowland clapped spurs to their horses' sides and their mounts surged forward, outstripping Andrew's chestnut in a dozen strides.

"They're catching it!" gasped Caro. "Nuri's leading!"

Then, unaccountably, she saw Brook check Nuri's gallop. His arm extended sideways, holding his spear horizontally, and Rowland also dropped back to a walk. The waving grasses marked the pig's passage until it disappeared into a ravine.

"Too small," remarked Philippa.

"It was enormous!" The force of Rowland's remark about hog-hunting being different from fox-hunting struck her like a blow. A quarry like this was dangerous—really dangerous. These wild pig, fifteen stone or more of fighting fury, had little in common with the peaceful grunters of English farmyards. One slash from the glistening tusks she had just seen could disembowel a horse, and Nuri—her Nuri...

"I didn't realize it would be like this," she said unhappily, once more seeking the shelter of their *mahout*'s umbrella.

Philippa glanced sideways at her. "It's too late to change your mind about letting Nuri compete, but don't worry; they may not start a ridable pig all morning, and then you can be easy."

But hardly had she spoken before the cry of "*Woh jata!*" rose once more and the horsemen spurred forward. Caro held her breath. She could not see the quarry, which was on the left of the line, but Rowland evidently decided it was ridable, for he kept up speed, shouting "On-on-on!", and he and Brook, pursued at a slower pace by Andrew, rode flat out after the fleeing boar. Neck and neck, they vanished from Caro's sight.

Chinatown's mouth had been deadened by his youthful spell in the shafts, and the faster he galloped the harder he pulled. Rowland knew it was useless to try to guide him with the bit and sat balanced in the saddle, ready for the sudden check and swerve that would tell him the boar had turned to fight. Hard at his heels followed Nuri, combating her rider every inch of the way as she struggled to free her head from Brook's iron grip. Rowland could see her white-rimmed eye and the foam dropping in frothy blobs from her long-cheeked bit, and longed to shout to Brook to give the mare her head, let her run free, but he knew it would make no difference. Brook believed in mastering his horses and making them do as he dictated.

A *nullah* loomed ahead—a wide dry ditch, its crumbling edges half hidden in a tangle of undergrowth. Without checking his stride, Chinatown floated over the obstacle, finding an extra leg as he landed on loose rocks and galloped on. Nuri, unable to see her way, took off too close and stumbled badly on landing, shooting Brook Vyner up her neck. For a moment he lost his grip on the reins, and with her head free at last and the pain in her mouth gone, the little Arab took the bit in her teeth and bolted. In a few bounds she passed Chinatown and Rowland saw Brook's set white face as he leaned back, one foot kicking convulsively in search of the stirrup he had lost. They were gaining on the boar, which was now in plain view, a black hulk of rage and muscle hurtling over the rough ground.

It was making for a ravine where the horses would be unable to follow. Rowland applied his left heel leather to Chinatown's side and the bay horse wheeled obediently to gallop at an angle which would cut off the boar from his retreat. The ground was broken and treacherous, with sudden dips and humps hidden in the long grass.

Feeling himself pressed, the pig veered away from Nuri and squatted motionless for an instant. Foam ran from his tusks and his little eyes blazed red. Nuri had met this maneuver before, and before Brook even had time to signal his wishes to her, she swung to follow the pig's line. He was a big boar still full of running, and with instinctive cunning he chose a zigzag route through the thick tamarisk bushes and clumps of thorn, still heading for the ravine.

Nuri was gaining on him, despite his swerves, and seeing his chance, Brook lowered his spear to the horizontal. As Nuri thundered past the pig, Brook stabbed down with all his strength, but though the spearhead grazed the boar's shoulder, a final lightning veer saved him from the full impact. Instead the razor-sharp blade embedded itself in the hard-packed earth, and the shock catapulted Brook out of the saddle.

As he fell, he clung to the bridle, jerking the mare to a sudden halt, but before he could regain his feet, the wounded boar, squealing with rage and pain, charged straight at his tormentor.

Brook yelled and turned to run, dragging the quivering bamboo shaft out of the ground. Nuri leaped sideways, and the boar's tusks missed her belly by a hairsbreadth. She spun in a circle at the length of the reins while Brook, encumbered by the spear, tried vainly to vault on her back again.

Seeing the danger, Rowland wheeled Chinatown, who answered the pressure of his rider's legs like the top-class polo pony he was and galloped straight for the infuriated boar. With perfect coordination he presented his rider right-handed at the charging monster, and as Rowland leveled his spear, the horse's impetus drove the sharp head clean through the boar's heart. Its rush carried it forward another twenty yards, then it crumpled and dropped like a stone.

Rowland dismounted and looped the reins over his arm as he walked up to inspect the dead beast, giving Brook a moment to recover his self-possession. But Caro's self-proclaimed champion was burning with rage and shame at the ignominious end to the hunt, just when triumph had seemed within his grasp, and was in no mood to be grateful to his rescuer.

"Damn it, Steel, there was no need for you to charge up and kill my pig for me," he exploded. "I was first spear. I'd have run him through in another instant if you hadn't interfered."

"It looked to me more as if you were running *away* from him," observed Rowland with a grin, wiping the sweat from his forehead. "Don't think I blame you; only a fool tries conclusions with a wounded boar from his feet."

Brook was still fuming. "I'd have killed him first stroke if this cowardly mare hadn't swerved. She's yellow. And she's got a mouth like iron."

"She's nothing of the kind," said Rowland sharply. "It was the boar that swerved, not the mare. She ran straight as a die, and she's brave as they come, make no mistake about that. As to her mouth"—he glanced contemptuously at the red-flecked foam dropping from Nuri's muzzle—"I've never seen iron bleed like that."

The arrival of a breathless Andrew checked Brook's angry retort, but he was still nursing his grievance. "As first spear, I claim his tusks," he said sullenly, and turned away to remount.

Andrew exclaimed over the size of the boar. "Must be all of two hundred and fifty pounds; that's the biggest we've killed at Oodabad for many a long day." He laughed. "You fellows quite outpaced poor Cis. We couldn't come anywhere near you, and the beaters are a good half-mile behind."

But before long a flag-man appeared to mark the spot where the dead boar lay with flies gathering round its mouth and eyes, and a few minutes later four of the beaters tied its legs to a stake and swung it up to carry back to camp. They were grinning, chattering, in high delight at the prospect of a feast of pork that night.

Philippa and Caro rode up on their elephant, congratulating the pig-stickers, and Caro made much of her mare, exclaiming in concern over her bleeding mouth.

"It's only a scratch," protested Brook. "Very likely she brushed against a thorn bush." He looked defiantly at Rowland, as if daring him to deny the story. But Caro seized the excuse of the slight injury to forbid her mare to take any further part in the morning's sport.

"You have shown us splendidly what she can do," she said, bestowing a radiant smile, at Rowland's expense, on the still furious Brook. "Nuri did not win the match, but I for one am satisfied that she is fleeter of foot than your horse, Captain Steel, even though she lacks his experience. What do you say?"

Rowland agreed diplomatically that Nuri was one of the fastest mares he'd ever seen, and together Andrew's party rode back to camp while the Tent Club's three contestants for the next heat of the morning took up their places behind the line of beaters. Brook was slightly mollified when the boar's tusks proved to measure nine inches, a local record, and in a fine gesture he presented them to Caro, who promised to have them carved.

The days became hotter as January drew to a close, and Andrew's leave ended. Despite the increasing heat, Caro's energy never flagged, and she regretted the need to leave Delhi, where gaiety seemed never-ending, to face the long dusty trek down the Ganges plain to the military quarters at Baburpore, where Andrew's regiment was stationed. In particular she regretted the prospect of losing at one stroke the companionship of both Brook Vyner and Rowland Steel, her most constant beaus. She enjoyed the sense of power given her by their rivalry—as evident as it was unacknowledged—and took a naughty delight in playing off one against the other, although Captain Steel, she had to admit, could not always be counted on to run errands for her or bow to her whims. Too often he would disappear from Delhi; nor would he tell her, on his return, what his business had been. But this element of surprise was part of his attractiveness for her. The secrecy that cloaked his professional duties had for Caro the fascination of Pandora's box, which she both longed and feared to open.

The character of Brook Vyner, on the other hand, she believed she could read as clearly as a book, and so she allowed Philippa to encourage the friendship. To the scarcely veiled chagrin of the Misses Ormithwait and O'Kelly, the Hon. Emily Faber and dashing Mrs. Duvallier—whose old and ailing husband in no way curtailed her social activities—Brook seemed blind to the charms and deaf to the wiles of any but Lady Caroline March. It was too bad, agreed the ladies when Brook turned down a charming, carefully worded invitation to watch their amateur theatricals, on the grounds that he had engaged to escort Lady Caroline to the races that afternoon, nor would he be counted on to attend any party at which Caro would not be present.

"Every one of the Civils overweight and over forty except for dear Mr. Vyner," grumbled Betty Ormith-wait, who was in her third "cold weather" season, and still had had no offer of marriage, despite her Grecian profile and the handsome portion she would bring with her. "Yet he seems utterly besotted by that tiresome little creature. Thank heaven her brother-in-law's leave has expired and she will soon trouble us no more!"

But her satisfaction was short-lived, for Brook Vyner was recalled to his duties as Assistant Collector of Vanyasi before ever Caro left Delhi.

He came to take his leave of Caro and Philippa as they were finishing breakfast after an early gallop on the race course, and seemed somewhat put out to discover Captain Steel there before him.

Philippa's face fell when he explained his mission. She had so hoped that he would propose to Caro before their ways separated, and now, it seemed, all her matchmaking efforts had been in vain.

"I am sorry you are to leave us so soon," she exclaimed disappointedly. "I thought you purposed to stay a few more weeks in Delhi."

"I did, Lady Philippa, but the powers-that-be decided otherwise. Believe me, I am sorry to take my leave of you so abruptly, but I've had word of certain disturbances at Vanyasi, and the Collector has ordered me to attend him there as soon as I may. So it is farewell for the present, but I am not too downhearted because I hope I may visit you in Baburpore as soon as our troubles in Vanyasi are settled."

"What kind of disturbances?" asked Caro. He thought he had never seen her look more lovely—her cheeks faintly flushed from the gallop, and a lock of dark hair, escaping from a demure coil to lie on the leaf-green collar of her frilled muslin morning gown.

"Civil disturbances—nothing of any consequence, but my collector is the worrying kind, you know, and thinks nothing of troubling his staff and cutting short their leave at a moment's notice if he thinks he scents trouble. Of course, it's a large district, and he's not a strong man, physically. Suffers terribly from malaria, and when an attack fells him, he likes to feel that his work's in capable hands." He smiled complacently.

"I wonder if you are right to dismiss these disturbances so lightly," put in Rowland from the end of the table where he was doing full justice to a plate of deviled kidneys.

"Oh, my dear fellow." Brook spoke with the voice of authority. "They're nothing out of the common, I assure you. A mission church burned, a soldier who had been reprimanded calling out that the Colonel would soon lick the dust at his feet, minor clashes between religious factions in the wilder parts of the district. Nothing but straws in the wind."

"Yet I have the strangest notion that the total of these small incidents may add up to more than the sum of their parts," said Rowland quite seriously. How strange, Caro contemplated, that of late Brook had become almost as jolly as Rowland while Rowland was turning as stiff as Brook had been. "It dates, I believe, from our recent annexation of the kingdom of Oudh. The natives will accept British rule where we've won territory in a fair fight, but they distrust political manipulation as much as I do. Have there been reported instances of *chupatti*-carrying in your district, for example?"

Brook stared. *"Chupatti*s—wheaten cakes? What have they to do with civil disturbance?"

"Perhaps nothing, perhaps a great deal." Rowland leaned forward intently. "In certain districts, I've heard, *chupatti*s are passing from hand to hand with the whisper "All will become Red." We find it's no use to question those who carry them, for they haven't the least idea why they do it. But I admit I find it— disquieting."

Philippa listened attentively, but privately Caro thought that Captain Steel was making mountains out of molehills. But that was the new, solemn Rowland— definitely not half as amusing as Brook.

Brook laughed aloud. "Oh, come! If everything in India that's hard to explain were to cause alarm among the military, we should soon lose the natives' respect. I own that I did not think you, Steel, a prey to such fears." He turned to Caro.

"Good-bye, then, for the present; but I hope to see you again very soon." Unwilling to say more in front of the others, Brook pressed her hand meaningfully, and received the full dazzle of her smile.

"Good-bye," she murmured, and he bowed and strode out, cursing the whim of his Collector that had robbed him of the chance to bring his courtship to a happy conclusion, but confident, nonetheless, that Lady Caroline March would be his bride before the year was out.

Preparations for the removal of the Thynnes's entire household from Delhi to Baburpore kept Philippa fully occupied for the next week. Rowland was once more absent on missions for the Governor, and with the departure of Brook Vyner, Caro found herself desperately bored. She was glad when the flurry of packing and discarding, the scolding of servants and arranging of transports, was complete and the day of their own departure from Delhi dawned.

She was to ride Nuri for part of each stage of their journey, in order to vary the monotony of travel in a *dak* gharry, but Philippa was, on Doctor McPhail's orders, to be carried the whole distance in a *doolie*, despite the expense of extra coolies to carry this litter-like conveyance. The miracle had happened, and Philippa, radiant with happiness, had whispered to Caro that before the monsoon was ended, she hoped to present her with a little nephew or niece.

Thanks to the gossip of her *ayah*, Caro had already been aware of this interesting development, but tactfully pretended ignorance and heartily congratulated her sister. As for Andrew, his pride and delight were touching to see, and he urged his sister-in-law to help him insure that nothing was allowed to disturb Philippa's comfort or peace of mind.

So it was that one fine, still morning in mid-March, before the echoes of the dawn gun had signaled the end of the night's scavenging to the crows and pack dogs of Delhi, the straggling procession of horse and bullock carts containing Andrew Thynne's household moved off on the long journey to Baburpore.

Chapter Four

EARLY AS THEIR start had been, the kitchen party was ahead of them, and by the time they halted for lunch, the cook had ready a splendid meal of curried chicken and batter cakes, served with as much pomp and ceremony as if they had been at home.

"Beats me how they do it," observed Andrew, stretched full length on a string cot at the conclusion of this feast. "But the fact is, these fellows are as much at home preparing food in the open as they are in any kitchen. Even if you get them a lot of expensive equipment, they won't use it, but give them a charcoal fire and a good sharp knife and they'll cook you up as fine a meal as you'd ever find in a European hotel. It takes some of the sting out of traveling here, which is a mercy, since we do so much of it."

Caro was much impressed by the smooth efficiency of the servants in these strange surroundings. Tents were pitched, water drawn and heated, mosquito nets arranged over each charpoy or string bed, before she had so much as dismounted from her mare. The cool groves of trees with their gnarled roots and wide-spreading branches were a welcome contrast to the road's clouds of choking reddish dust, and as she, Andrew, and Philippa eased their limbs after the day's long ride, the smell of wood smoke and spiced meat wafting from the servants' camp a discreet distance from their own, the plaintive croaking of frogs and the soft snorting of the tethered ponies, came sweetly to her senses.

"It's a lovely way to travel. I wish it could go on forever," she said dreamily.

"Well, I'm thankful it can't." Philippa's voice was sharp. She looked pale and drawn after the long hours on the road, borne by relays of scrawny coolies who, amazingly, found the breath to laugh and chatter as they padded along in the dust. "It's all very well for you, cantering along on a horse, but the jolting and rocking of a *doolie* is hard to bear, hour after hour."

"Take Nuri tomorrow," offered Caro impulsively. "She has such smooth action that I'm sure she'd do you less harm than being bumped around in that coffinlike contraption."

But Andrew refused to countenance such defiance of Doctor McPhail's orders, and as the days passed, the journey took increasing toll of Philippa's health and spirits.

They rose early and marched an hour before *chota hazri*—the cook having left camp during the hours of darkness—then rode through the burning morning until the sun was near its height. A long siesta followed, though it was generally too hot to sleep, and their convoy took the road again until they caught up with the kitchen party in its chosen resting place.

In this way they made good progress, and although Caro was worried by Philippa's listlessness, she couldn't help enjoying the freedom of the open-air life with its ever-changing landscape as the dusty Ganges plain gave way to forest and jungle where monkeys dropped twigs on them and brilliantly plumaged birds screeched at the intruders. From time to time they would pass through a village, where naked brown children played in the dust and turbaned elders joined their hands and gravely bowed their salutation of "*Ram, ram*."

The servants would buy provisions—maize, rice, and salt; fruit and vegetables—and bring back the local gossip to their master.

"My bearer tells me that Captain Steel with a detachment of cavalry is no more than a day's march ahead of us," remarked Andrew one evening. "If we hurry we may overtake him, and it would be pleasant to have both his company and his escort for the last stretch of our journey."

Caro's heart suddenly lurched, as it often did at the mention of Captain Steel, but she schooled her features to express nothing but polite interest.

"How strange! I thought he was to remain at Lord Canning's beck and call," she remarked, quoting Brook Vyner, who had expressed contempt that a soldier should spend his time in such unmartial occupations as settling the order of precedence at dinners and teaching the native regiments' band to play "Rule, Britannia!"

"According to my fellow, he's been sent to Baburpore on Intelligence duties," said Andrew with a grin. He had little liking for Brook, whom he considered altogether too full of his own consequence, and not nearly good enough for Caro. Master Vyner would not, he reflected, be pleased to discover that his rival in Caro's affections was posted at the very station where she was staying. "Rowland's a clever chap," he added, "though he don't parade it like some I could mention, and he's got a wonderful way with the native troops. They used fairly to worship his father, old General Steel: he had a regiment of Irregular Horse up on the North-West Frontier, and they put the fear of God into those thieving brigands near the Khyber Pass. They say he had a regular harem of native women—"

"Andrew!" exclaimed Philippa sharply.

Andrew stopped in mid-sentence, realizing belatedly that further revelations on these lines were hardly suitable for the tender ears of his sister-in-law. Caro was disappointed, but consoled herself with the thought that during tomorrow's long ride she could probably extract more interesting details about Captain Steel from her guileless brother-in-law without her sister's knowledge.

It was as the swift-falling dusk blotted out the landscape next evening, that they saw their servants encamped in the same grove as a party of native cavalry, and as they drew nearer, Rowland himself rode to meet them. Quit of Delhi he was once again the virile, exciting captain who visited her dreams too often.

His blue uniform jacket with its gold frogging was travel-stained and his long leather boots still covered with a layer of dust, but his lean, sunburned face broke into a warm smile and against the tanned skin his gray eyes lit up with pleasure at their meeting. Caro thought approvingly that there was not a spare ounce of flesh on his tall, muscular body, in contrast to Andrew, who had put on so much weight during his leave that his neck bulged over his tight collar.

Rowland warmly greeted Andrew and Caro, and glanced questioningly at the approaching *doolie*. "I trust Lady Philippa is well?"

"Doctor's orders," said Andrew briefly. "She's breeding, and McPhail has forbidden her to ride a horse. I fear she finds the journey a sore trial, but perhaps your company may raise her spirits."

"Come and let's see if your fellows have made you comfortable," Rowland suggested, "and then we will dine together. I shot three brace of jungle fowl in Lallipat this morning, and was hoping for company to share them."

But Philippa declared herself too tired to eat, and Caro shook her head warningly at Andrew as Philippa's *ayah* helped her out of the litter and into her tent.

"She's not at all well, I fear. Could we not rest here a

few days to let her regain her strength?"

Andrew gnawed his thumbnail in perplexity. "There's little enough shelter or comfort for her here either." He appealed to Rowland. "What would you do? Stay here and let Philippa rest, or press on and put the journey behind us?"

"It's not a place I'd choose to linger," said Rowland slowly. "There've been some odd rumors about affairs in Patelbar, and this village is right on the border."

Caro joined the two men as they sat by a leaping fire, with the black trunks of the trees casting weird shadows on the close-cropped turf. From their own encampment nearby came the soft chatter of the servants as they grilled the jungle fowl over an open fire and the occasional snort and stamp of the tethered horses.

"You're bound for Baburpore, too, I hear," said Andrew.

Rowland nodded. "For my sins. The latest dispatches speak of unrest in the villages around the station, and now it seems it's spreading through the native regiments. Nothing much you can put your finger on," he added in a low tone. "Insolence here and there; an outbreak of fire-raising at Umballah, suspicion of the new Enfield rifles . . . I've been asked to make a report."

Caro shivered, aware, yet comforted by, Rowland's strangely frightening male presence beside her. Half listening to the men's quiet voices, she drifted into her own thoughts. It was so different here from the ordered life in Delhi. Here, anything might happen. Beyond the circle of firelight, who knew what wild beasts lurked, prowling silently through the shadows, red eyes agleam and teeth ready to rend and tear? Away to the right, a jackal raised its unearthly wail, and then, more distant still, she heard a muffled pounding of hoofs, a vibration of the earth on which she sat.

"Horses!" she exclaimed. "Someone's coming."

The men listened intently, then Rowland snapped an order and his native officer shouted to the sowars to stand to their arms. Bits jingled and sabers rattled as they sprang to prepare for a surprise attack, but before they were in their saddles, the thudding hoofs slowed to a trot, and a moment later the leading horseman rode into the torchlight, reining his showy Arab to a halt.

Behind him, twenty turbaned figures followed, their dark eyes flashing while the firelight glinted on heavily ornamented belts and curved scabbards, glistening silks and winking jewels.

"Greetings," cried their leader. "I come in peace. I am Prince Chandranaya of Patelbar, come to greet you on behalf of my uncle, the Rajah Jahan Bahadur Shah."

Rowland spoke softly to his *daffadar*; the native officer gave an order and the men relaxed, staring at the newcomers. This was the first Indian prince Caro had seen, and she could not take her eyes off him or his retinue.

Prince Chandranaya was small and slim, with fine-drawn, almost girlish features and brilliant, watchful, dark eyes beneath an extravagant turban. A thin mustache drooped on either side of his full mouth, and as he spoke his small, soft hands played constantly with the hilt of his sword.

Andrew greeted him civilly, and introduced the rest of their party, then begged to know if he could serve the Prince in any way.

"On the contrary," said Chandranaya smoothly, "it is I who desire to serve you. I have had word that one of your party—a lady—is sick, and my uncle the Rajah wishes to extend to you the hospitality of his palace at Patelbar until she is well enough to travel again."

News travels fast, thought Caro. But then she realized that the litter, the vigilant *ayah*s, Philippa's fretful complaints from within the *doolie,* must have told their own story to the villages they had passed through, and no item of news about the sahib-log was too small to be ignored by the Indian rulers past whose frontiers they traveled. But to stay with a rajah—in a palace! She gazed imploringly at Andrew, willing him to say yes. Just a few days' rest, and she was sure Philippa would recover, particularly if they could procure some opium with which to treat her.

The Prince, meanwhile, was waiting for Andrew's reply, his unwinking, almost lidless eyes fixed on the Englishman's face.

Andrew and Rowland conferred in low tones. "It might be for the best," said Rowland doubtfully, "though Patelbar's a bit of an unknown quantity politically. The old Rajah's all right, perfectly loyal to his treaty with us, but I've heard some rumors concerning that gentleman"—he nodded toward Chandranaya—"that suggest he's a horse of a different color. But there's no doubt your wife would be better off for a rest. I can provide an escort as far as the Rajah's palace, and do a little saber-rattling just for the look of the thing. I wish I could stay longer, but I'm ordered to Baburpore with the minimum delay, and you know what old Tiger Elliott's like when he gets on his high horse."

Andrew nodded slowly. He was worried about Philippa, who seemed to have lost all her usual vitality. It was not like her to whine and complain.

He felt a tug at his sleeve and turned impatiently. "Yes, Sher Dil. What is it?"

The gray-bearded old bearer in his starched white tunic seemed ill at ease. He had been born in Andrew's grandfather's compound, foster-brother to Andrew's father, and claimed privileges accorded to none other of the Thynnes's servants.

Now he cast agonized looks in the direction of

Prince Chandranaya and muttered rapidly, "Sahib, sahib, do not go. This prince is no friend to the Sirkar. He makes trouble and sends the bearers of *chupatti* among the native regiments."

But Andrew had been on leave and had paid scant attention to the curious stories regarding the circulation of *chupatti*. None too gently, he pushed the old man away.

"This is no time for riddles, old man. The memsahib is sick and needs rest before she travels again. Steelsahib says the Rajah is a man of honor and friend to the Sirkar; who are you to gainsay him?"

Sher Dil subsided, muttering, and Andrew addressed himself to Prince Chandranaya, thanking him for his invitation, which he gladly accepted.

The Prince's full mouth curved in a smile. "It is good. I go now to tell my uncle the glad news of your coming, but tomorrow I will come again to guide you to his palace."

"Oh, don't trouble yourself to do that," said Andrew. "Captain Steel will give us his escort that far."

Chandranaya's smile faded, and his hands fidgeted with the hilt of his sword. "The Rajah wishes me to bring you to him. He will be sad if his offer is spurned."

Andrew glanced at Rowland for guidance, and received a slight nod in reply; both of them knew better than to ignore the delicate question of "face." The Rajah would lose face with his people if his British guests arrived in charge of British troops, since it would indicate a lack of trust in the venerable Jahan Bahadur Shah.

"Very well," said Andrew slowly. "Please thank your uncle on our behalf, and say we shall be glad to accept his hospitality."

"Lucky dog," said Rowland to Andrew as the horsemen galloped away. "The old boy'll probably lay on a tiger hunt for your amusement if you play your cards right. Patelbar used to be a famous place for *shikar*—the hunt—in the old days, according to my father, but since the Company's annexation of the Kingdom of Oudh, very few British have set foot in the place. There's an Irishman, cashiered from his regiment years ago, who's gone to India and taken up residence in Patelbar as His Highness's personal physician. Completely captured the Rajah's trust. Kelly—or some such name. You might find him helpful to Lady Philippa. Otherwise, as I said, Patelbar's more or less *terra incognita* to us. No doubt the powers-that-be will be interested to hear what you make of affairs there."

"I'm not even sure just where the town lies," admitted Andrew. "Is it far from here?"

The two men bent over a map, and Caro craned over their shoulders to see the position of this little-known stronghold.

"There." Rowland placed a long brown forefinger on the spot. "I don't imagine this map is very accurate, since it's never been part of our territory, but it gives you a rough idea of the geography. I must admit, I'm sorry not to be coming with you."

He was also sorrier than he would admit, even to himself, to miss the chance of spending a few days in Caro's company, just when it had looked as if their roads lay together as far as Baburpore. When she had ridden up to meet him that evening, he had been startled by her transformation from society coquette into seasoned traveler. Startled, and delighted. So few English ladies contrived to look their best in such different worlds, and at the end of a long hot ride along Indian roads, he would have expected Caro's appearance to be as drained and exhausted as poor Philippa's. Instead, she radiated happiness and vitality. Her dark hair shone; her face was unfashionably and smoothly tanned, and she sat her gray pony with a straight-back, easy grace that gave not a hint of the dusty miles they had traveled.

Brought up in India, suckled by an Indian nurse, Rowland was, like his father before him, no great admirer of European standards of female beauty. The plump, pink-and-white belles with their careful ringlets who set their caps for Captain Steel attracted him not one whit. He despised their indolence, their perpetual preoccupation with matters of rank, precedence, and etiquette, their refusal to adapt to the ways of the country or learn its language. Though he recognized that he must one day marry, if only to satisfy his father's demands for a grandson, and realized, moreover, that the old fire-eater would not be fobbed off with an heir of mixed blood, Rowland had always trod warily among the matchmaking mamas and girls fresh from England who invaded British India every "cold weather." He continued to seek his pleasure with dusky maidens who, if they could not be presented at Government House, still offered a chance of escape from the stifling round of British social life.

But Caro was different from all of them. Against his will, Rowland had found his thoughts returning to her time and again as he rode down toward Baburpore at the head of his small detachment of cavalry. Thinking of her in the arms of that pompous young civilian Brook Vyner, whose station was conveniently close to Baburpore, was distasteful. Though no one else knew this, it was at Rowland's own suggestion that he had been seconded to Intelligence duties at Baburpore, and the presence of Caro there had more than a little to do with prompting the suggestion.

"I suppose Baburpore is as good a place as any to keep watch on developments in that area," the Chief of Staff had agreed. "It's only a small station, of course, but the two rivers make it of strategic importance and you'll be able to keep an eye on Ashokapur and Patelbar without letting the rajahs know we're interested." He frowned. "I wish I did know more about affairs in Patelbar. The only certain information that our man's been able to get through to us lately is that the Rajah, who has no son, has named as his heir, his nephew, Prince Chandranaya, who keeps company with Nana Sahib, of whom we recently deposed. Dastardly chap. A butcher from the word go. And toward the English he bears a dangerous grudge. When the old Maharajah dies, there could be serious trouble in Patelbar, so you'll be well placed to survey the area. You'd better get up there at your best pace, too, for old Tiger Elliott's been fretting for a replacement for Captain Dauncey, who died of cholera, and Tiger's not noted for his patience..." He grinned. "I wish you a happy 'hot weather,' Rowland, old boy; the blister flies in Baburpore are said to be more vicious than any outside Poona."

And now Caro, the woman for whom he had sentenced himself to a provincial powderkeg, was paying Rowland not the slightest attention. Using the excuse of her sister's delicate health, she had kept to Philippa's side, refusing his invitations to walk about the campsite. Finally, he was forced to seek out the amiable but tedious company of Andrew, who had also been banished from the women's quarters.

Sleepless at night, under the stars, Rowland was tortured by the image of Caro in his arms, a Caro yielding but fiery, as eager as he to bring to consummation what had begun that impetuous moment on the ship. Drawing his blanket close around him for company, he wondered if Caro, too, lay awake, hungering for that foppish fool Brook Vyner. Well, if she wanted Vyner, she deserved him. And yet, as sleep slowly came, it carried with it a soft, sensuous vision of a creature with ebony eyes and a touch like silk.

Rowland had correctly surmised that Caro was tossing restlessly inside the women's tent. But it was not the thought of Brook's embrace that kept her awake. Rather, overwhelmed by the conflict raging in her mind, she fought to stem her waking dreams of Rowland Steel, but they would not leave her.

Brook Vyner was continually hinting at Steel's wastrel ways, as well as his shadowy involvement in illegal enterprises. But Caro had learned to take Brook's opinions, diverting as they were, with a grain of salt. He was jealous of Rowland to begin with, and his skill as a general gossip monger had earned him both the terror and the adoration of the English Delhi matrons. Brook *was* amusing, as well as exceedingly good-looking, yet his presence entirely lacked sensuality. When it had become clear that he would never approach her romantically—behavior she attributed to his upbringing—she was somewhat relieved. Perhaps when they grew to know each other better, her attitudes for him would change.

But with Rowland, that attraction had been instantaneous and far more powerful than with Tom Hamilton. Try as she might, she could not forget that impassioned moment on the deck, could still feel Rowland's arms holding her tightly as they waltzed at the Governor-General's Ball. Knowing he lay asleep but a few yards away only served to make the memories more vivid, stirring up the deep, powerful feelings she had first experienced that night under the stars.

She wanted, more than wanted, craved some satisfaction she did not quite understand, but instinct told her Rowland Steel was the one man who could give it to her. It was that knowledge, exhilarating but somehow terrifying, which made her fear him, even dislike him—despite the fact that as she slipped into sleep, she could almost feel his touch, like velvet fire, warming her most secret places.

At seven next morning, Chandranaya was back with his flamboyant troop, and Rowland bid Andrew's party farewell, lingering as long as possible with Caro, although preoccupied with making her sister comfortable, had time to bid him a casually friendly farewell. Then he watched as it moved slowly away down the jungle path, for the benefit of Philippa in her *doolie*, and vanished among the tall trees.

Nuri was fresh, groomed, and fed to perfection, longing to buck and gallop in the cool, scented morning. She champed at her bit and tossed flecks of foam in the air as Caro made her walk sedately beside the litter. She was cheered by Philippa's assurance that she felt a trifle improved this morning, though her sister's waxen pallor and dark-shadowed eyes gave the lie to her words. Caro's spirits rose even more when Andrew suggested, after some conversation with Prince Chandranaya, that there was no need for her to remain with the slow-moving *doolie* all morning.

"That mare of yours could do with a gallop," he observed with his slow smile, watching Nuri's antics. "Go ahead if you like, and I'll send a couple of *syce*s with you to see you don't miss the way. We'll be halting to eat at mid-morning in any case, after which it'll be too hot for any of us to do any galloping."

He consulted with Chandranaya, who immediately offered one of his retainers to act as Caro's guide. Her own *syce*, Bhalat Ram, fell into step beside him. Waving gaily, she cantered away, with the two natives loping easily at her stirrup, and soon left the rest of the party well behind.

A jungle fowl rose with a flutter and screech, and Nuri swerved violently, partly from fright and partly from high spirits. Caro's instant response was to urge the mare to a faster pace, thundering down the soft dust of the jungle path, bent low over Nuri's neck, reveling in the cool rush of breeze in her face and the mare's bunched muscles beneath her. The path forked and Nuri took the right-hand branch without hesitation. Caro made no attempt to check her to verify the route, knowing that the *syce*s would follow her hoofprints and catch up with her eventually to guide her back to the main party.

She slowed Nuri to a walk, to allow the *syce*s to catch up, and soon heard the soft slap-slap of bare feet beside her.

"Miss-sahiba! Miss-sahiba!"

"Yes, what is it?"

Chandranaya's *tau syce* pointed back the way they had come. Sure enough, Nuri had chosen the wrong track.

"You lead the way," Caro said in her slow, painful Hindustani, and felt a flutter of pleasure at the surprise that flickered for a second across his guarded face.

They retraced their steps a few hundred yards and then branched off on a narrower trail. A shortcut, thought Caro, enjoying the harsh voices of the jungle birds as they rose, disturbed. Thick vines hung from the tree branches, and monkeys chattered somewhere out of sight above her head. The track twisted and turned around roots and rotted tree stumps, and from time to time it forked. She noticed the *syce*s always chose the left-hand fork, although her sense of direction told her that if they wished to regain the main trail they should bear right, not left.

"Are you sure you know the way?" she asked doubtfully, and drew Nuri to a halt. The *tau syce* stared up at her, his black eyes expressionless. Bhalat Ram shrugged helplessly. He knew no more than she did. Unbidden, phrases Rowland had used came back to her: danger . . . unrest . . . politically unknown . . . Then she had thought him overcautious; now she felt a little chill of fear.

Then she heard the screams. They were high-pitched, as of a woman or child, and they came from the jungle to her left. Forgetting her doubts, Caro nudged Nuri to a trot and set off in the direction of the cries, which had now subsided into a loud sobbing. Behind her back, the *tau syce* grinned at Bhalat Ram and set off in pursuit. In a few moments Caro, her escort at her heels, burst out of the jungle into a small clearing where a burly Sikh in turban and tunic, with a long curved sword stuck in his sash, was flogging an almost naked boy with a thick cudgel.

"Stop!" cried Caro. "I order you to stop."

The Sikh appeared astonished at her sudden appearance, and stood as if frozen, one brawny arm still upraised, gripping the *lathi*. Seizing his opportunity, the boy twisted away from his tormentor and ran to grasp Nuri's forelegs, looking up imploringly at Caro.

"All right," she said breathlessly, "I won't let him hurt you anymore." Nuri pricked her ears forward until they nearly met as she bent her head to sniff cautiously at the boy's hair, and then tossed her mane, snorting.

Caro turned to her *syce*s. "Ask him what is the matter," she said carefully. "Why is he beating this boy?"

A spate of talk followed, with a slower translation, and bit by bit Caro gathered that the boy was an orphan whom the Sikh had adopted and fed, and made part of his family. Now he had stolen from his master and must be beaten.

Grinning, the Sikh moved forward and grasped the boy's shoulder as if to tear him by force away from the mare to whom he still clung.

"No!" said Caro strongly. "Whatever the boy has done, he should not be beaten like that. I will take him to Prince Chandranaya, who will decide what is to be done with him. Go!" she commanded the Sikh. "Begone about your business and do not trouble us anymore. The boy comes with us." Though she now spoke in English, the Sikh seemed to understand her. His bearded face darkened, but he turned obediently and melted into the jungle. Caro watched him go and then turned to Chandranaya's *syce*.

"Now guide us back to the road."

An hour later they had doubled back to the small clearing. Caro's vague fears had become certainties. She was lost. For the past sixty minutes the small party had wandered in ever-decreasing circles, with the *tau syce* making less and less effort to keep up a pretense of knowing the route.

It was already eleven o'clock and Andrew's party would have halted for breakfast. Caro pushed back her hat and wiped her arm across her sticky face, as hot with anxiety as with the sun's increasing strength. Her cotton shirt clung damply to the ridge of her spine, and tendrils of escaping hair tormented her with their tickling. She summoned up her last reserves of energy and addressed the boy in Hindustani.

"We cannot find the way to the big town. The town of Patelbar. Take me there and I will reward you."

The boy's face brightened. He took the lead and pushed confidently into the jungle. After no more than ten minutes the trees thinned in front of them and Caro gave a cry of relief.

"The road!"

They were on the outskirts of a village, and despite the noon heat, a crowd of men were gathered round the gnarled roots of the peepul tree. Caro had an odd impression that they weren't in the least surprised to see her; that they had, in fact, been waiting for her to appear. Her mind leaped to the conclusion that

Andrew had been here before, perhaps asking for her. She rode into the tree's shade and stopped in front of a dignified old man who looked like the village headman.

"I am seeking Prince Chandranaya and the white sahib who is his guest," she said. "Have they been to your village?"

Slowly the old man shook his head and an excited babble of voices broke out from among the villagers. They stared intently at Caro, and moved closer, their thin brown hands stretching out to finger her clothes and the mare's saddlery. She suppressed the urge to give ground, telling herself sternly that it was ridiculous to be afraid, they meant her no harm. They were curious—and no wonder: perhaps they had never seen a white girl before, all alone on her gray mare.

"Miss-sahiba!" Chandranaya's *tau syce* plucked at her sleeve.

The villagers were inviting her to rest and refresh herself, and they would send messengers in search of Prince Chandranaya. Caro had to recognize the sense of this plan. She was hot, dirty, and tired; she could think of nothing pleasanter than to slip from Nuri's back and lie down for a while in a darkened room.

"Yes, thank you," she said gratefully, and followed the *tau syce* toward a hut that was larger than the other thatched dwellings grouped about the peepul tree. She dismounted, and her Bhalat Ram led Nuri away toward the well. The Prince's *syce* threw open the door of the hut and she saw a dim, cool interior with a basin and a string cot in one corner.

As she stepped forward there was a flash of movement behind her and she turned sharply. Too late: the door slammed behind her and she heard the creak of a rusty key in the lock.

"Let me out!" She hammered on the stout wooden door with her clenched fists, but all she could hear was the soft slap of bare feet retreating, then a subdued babble of voices from beneath the peepul tree. She strained her ears, her heart pounding with a mixture of rage and fright. Why had they done this to her? On whose order had she been led into this trap—for trap it was, she now realized. Ever since the *tau syce* had first deflected her from the main path she had felt a vague unease, engendered partly by her own sense of direction, which told her they were straying even farther from the road they were meant to be looking for, and partly by an indefinable shiftiness—a veiled insolence—in the man's behavior. He was Chandranaya's man: could it be Chandranaya who had arranged her capture?

No she reasoned, for since Andrew was his guest, suspicion for the miss-sahiba's disappearance would too readily fall on the man whose servant was escorting her. But it was equally unlikely that an ignorant *syce* would commit so grave a crime as the abduction of an English lady without orders from someone far more powerful than himself.

Baffled, Caro splashed water from the brass *lotah* onto her face and hands and cast herself down on the string cot. She was tired, and there was nothing she could do for the moment. The cot was comfortable and presently, in spite of her fears, she drifted off to sleep.

When she woke it was dark, but otherwise nothing had changed. Sitting up on the cot, she called for a light, and the door opened swiftly, as if someone had been close outside.

"Bring me a light," she repeated.

The hulking figure in the doorway clapped his hands and shouted, and a boy entered, carrying a smoking torch floating in a dish of water. By its light, Caro recognized the burly Sikh she had met in the jungle and the boy he had been chastising.

They laughed at her. The Sikh motioned to the boy

to bring the light closer, and stared insolently into Caro's face. She drew back but he reached out a strong hand and pulled her toward him, then ran his cupped palm over her breasts, her stomach, her thighs like a butcher assessing the quality of a joint of meat.

"Feringhee bitch," he said contemptuously. "What does the Presence want with such milk-face trash? Though we paint her eyes with kohl and rub her lips with the juice of betel nut for his delight, though we feed her on *ghee* for a year she would never become one of the beauties of Hind. But who are we to question the tastes of the Presence?"

Through her mingled rage and fear, Caro understood little of what was said, but she realized all too clearly that someone had bribed Prince Chandranaya's *tau syce* to isolate her from her friends.

After the Sikh went out, leaving the candle behind him, Caro thought back over every stage of her ride since the moment she had galloped Nuri ahead of the convoy. The Prince's *syce* had deflected her from the path Nuri had chosen, and which she instinctively had felt was the right direction. Looking at Rowland's map the previous evening, she'd gained a rough idea of where the town lay in relation to their camp, and through that weary jungle ride she had become increasingly certain the *syce*s were leading her astray. But now she realized that her twisted *syce*, Bhalat Ram, had followed blindly, because he had no more knowledge of the country than she had: less, because he had not seen Rowland's map. She thought in sudden hope: perhaps Bhalat Ram is loyal after all. He was a *syce* of no great intelligence, but surely he would wish no harm to Nuri, to whom he was devoted, even if he cared little what became of her rider.

Caro explored the hut with care, running her hands over its rough wooden walls, and at length discovered a knothole through which she could see a glimmer of torchlight. The hole was low down, near the door, but by kneeling and putting her eye to it she gained a restricted view of the open space outside where she had spoken to the village headman. Feverishly she sought for some sharp-pointed instrument with which to enlarge the hole, and was finally forced to resort to one of her hairpins. Poking and chipping industriously at the edges of the knothole, she improved the view until she could see most of what happened outside. The headman still sat beneath the peepul tree, a group of village elders around him. Women crossed the line of Caro's vision from time to time on their way to and from the well, and her heart bounded with pleasure as she saw Nuri led past the hut—pleasure that quickly turned to indignation when she saw how the mare was dressed. Caro's English saddle had been exchanged for an elaborate Indian contraption glinting with gold and silver thread. Nuri's mane and tail were dyed red, as were her hoofs, and a long-cheek, curling bit replaced her plain snaffle.

It was all Caro could do to prevent herself from shouting out as she watched the burly Sikh spring on her pony's back, and with his boy running beside him, canter out of the circle of torchlight.

She called softly, pitching her voice too low to reach the group under the peepul tree: "Ho, Bhalat Ram? Are you there!"

There was a rustle outside as of a watcher suddenly started to full attention. "I am coming," came a whisper as low as her own.

Caro let out her breath on a long sigh of relief. She'd been afraid the *tau syce* would have been set to guard her door.

"Where is Prince Chandranaya's *syce?*"

"I do not know."

"Why am I a prisoner?"

"I do not know."

Caro bit her lip in helpless fury. Bhalat Ram might be loyal, but he was not the stalwart man she would have chosen to help her out of a tight corner.

"They have stolen my pony."

That touched a chord. "Aie!" He sighed. "I tried to stop the Sikh, but he laughed in my face. He said the Presence had need of her."

Caro puzzled over this. "What Presence?" she asked at last, but of course Bhalat Ram did not know.

"The Presence who keeps us here," he whined.

Caro saw it was hopeless to question him further on that score. Somehow she must persuade him to release her from this prison by a mixture of threat and bribery. She tried the threat first.

"Thynne-sahib will be angry when he cannot find me."

Silence outside.

"Are you there, Bhalat Ram?"

"I am here, miss-sahiba."

"If you unlock the door, and let me out, Thynne-sahib will be pleased with you."

"But the Presence will be angry," he said unhappily. "Besides, there is no key."

She thought he could probably find the key if he wanted to. She went on coaxingly, "Thynne-sahib will reward you richly with gold and jewels if you set me free. His camp cannot be many miles distant, and already no doubt he is searching for me, asking in all the villages if they have seen a memsahib on a gray pony. He will not rest till he finds me," she added, hoping it was true, and paused to see if her words were having any effect.

A moment later she heard the rusty squeak of the key, and her heart leaped with hope. He was going to let her out!

"Bhalat Ram," she whispered into the dark, "you will be well rewarded for this."

"Rewarded with a broken head," growled a voice that did not belong to Bhalat Ram, and Caro stepped back sharply as the *tau syce* pushed his way into the hut. Roughly he seized her hands and forced them behind her back as he twisted a length of cord tightly round her wrists.

"Stop it! You are hurting me," she cried, trying hard to keep her hands braced a little apart so that he could not tighten the cord.

Her captor chuckled gutturally and pulled hard on the knot, tightening it too much for Caro to slip her hands out. Then he slipped an evil-smelling rag over her mouth and knotted it behind her head, tied her ankles together, and picking her up bodily, dumped her on the charpoy. He glanced round the hut and went out without another word.

Caro's heart pounded as she lay on the cot. Something was about to happen; she could feel it in the air—in the unnatural silence that had fallen on the village. Did it herald the arrival of the sinister Presence of whom Bhalat Ram had spoken? On the other hand the fact that she had been trussed and gagged could only mean that her jailers were afraid—not that she would escape, but that she would cry out and attract attention to her prison. Which meant...

Dogs barked outside, their voices rising to a shrill crescendo. Then the ground inside the hut vibrated to the thud of horses' hoofs and the jingle of bits and swords. Rolling off the bed, Caro hobbled across the uneven floor, knelt down, and put her eye to her knothole. Behind the gag she gave a smothered exclamation of relief as she recognized Rowland with Lieutenant Henry Forbes and a detachment of troopers riding into the village and halting, as she herself had halted, under the wide branches of the peepul tree.

Chapter Five

CALLING FOR WATER, Rowland dismounted and spoke courteously to the old headman, who was obviously angry—and dismayed—by the sudden arrival of the British officer at the head of twenty-odd sowars.

No wonder, thought Rowland. The poor old boy probably thinks we're going to billet ourselves on him for the night and wolf down his entire stock of attar and maize. In the princely states, he knew, it was customary for the rajah's army to live off the land, and between soldiers, tax collectors, and moneylenders, villagers had a thin time. They would hide their corn and cattle and flee into the jungle if given warning of the approach of troops, and cavalry were always more feared than infantry, owing to their greater mobility.

"We are sorry to trouble you, sirdar-ji, but we are seeking one of our party who has strayed from the road to Patelbar. A white girl, riding a gray mare."

The headman's eyes remained shuttered; his expression hostile. Rowland knew he was treading on delicate ground, for although the British had a treaty of friendship with the Rajah of Patelbar, British soldiers had no authority to enter his territory, and it was only the urgent summons that Andrew had sent to inform him of Caro's disappearance and beg for his help that had swayed him into bringing his troopers, and young Henry Forbes, who was traveling with him, to join in the search.

Andrew and Prince Chandranaya—whose agitation at the discovery of the girl's absence had every appearance of being genuine—were together making a wide sweep through the jungle to the left of the main track, but in their hasty conference Rowland had learned that the hoofprints of Caro's pony came to a sudden end without appearing to leave the road, which could only mean that someone had taken care to obliterate any indication of the direction she had taken. This in itself was suspicious, and negated the theory that the pony had bolted and thrown her. Mare and girl had vanished as if spirited into thin air, and Rowland cursed Andrew's delay in admitting his sister-in-law's disappearance.

Now it was dark, and the trail was still cold.

He asked again, with greater emphasis, "Has a white girl on a gray pony been seen in your village *sirdar-ji?*"

The headman hawked and spat contemptuously. "Why should a white woman come here, sahib? This is not the land of the sahib-log." He looked pointedly at Rowland's troopers. "By what right do you bring armed men into the domain of Jahan Bahadur Shah?"

"By no right, *sirdar-ji,* but with the authority of Prince Chandranaya, who has sought my help in finding the white girl."

"There is no white girl here," said the headman flatly, and closed his eyes, as if when he opened them he expected Rowland and his men to be gone.

Rowland was puzzled by the man's hostility. He looked slowly around the village, taking in the layout: the well, the group of thatched huts with one larger, better-built dwelling slightly apart from the others, probably the home of this surly headman, the pen of sheep and goats, chickens roosting in the low branches covering the animals' pens; dogs prowling on the edge of the circle of light, the air heavy with spice and hot oil. All seemed normal, yet something nagged at the edge of his consciousness. Was it a face he had recognized among the crowd? He scanned the silent brown features around him, but they told him nothing.

At the back of the huts, a horse neighed shrilly, and Chinatown, who stood with his rein looped through Rowland's arm, raised his head and whinnied in reply. Nuri!

Rowland turned to his *daffadar*. "Search the village. Make a thorough search of every hut and report to me."

Kneeling at her peephole, Caro saw the troopers dismount to tie up their horses, and again heard Nuri's neigh. They were going to make a search, she realized, and a great wave of relief washed over her. She had been so afraid that the headman would refuse to allow it, and that the troopers would ride on their way never knowing how close they had been to the object of their search. Her relief was short-lived, however, as a sinewy hand jerked her away from her vantage point, and she realized that the Sikh had entered silently through a back door.

He swung her across his shoulder as easily as if she had been a sack of gram, and picking up the tallow light he pushed aside a heavy curtain that partitioned off one corner of the hut. It was, she guessed, the purdah area, where the headman's womenfolk normally ate and slept. Two or three rough earthenware vessels stood on the packed earth floor, and the remains of a fire between two bricks showed where the cooking was done, but of inhabitants there was no sign. The Sikh placed Caro on the floor and drew a finger across his throat. Gagged as she was, there was no chance of calling out, though perhaps she could bang on the walls to attract attention. Her hope of rescue flickered and died. Neither Hindu nor Mussulman, she knew, would permit the searching of his women's quarters, and Rowland had no authority to enforce such a search.

The Sikh placed the tallow candle beside her and

stood close beside her while the outer door crashed open and she heard the searching sowars stamp into the room she had just left. With the Sikh's knife pricking her throat, she dared make neither sound nor movement, and a few moments later she heard the door thump shut once more.

They had gone.

Tears stung Caro's eyes and she blinked them away. The Sikh wiped his knife on his sleeve and replaced it in his sash. He silently went out to stand at his post in front of the hut. Caro wriggled into a kneeling position, then leaning her shoulders against the wall, she levered herself upright. Shuffling cautiously on her bound ankles, she edged her way to the curtain and pushed a corner of it aside. The larger area of the hut, where she had first been imprisoned, was empty, with the charpoy still pushed back against the wall but, mindful of the throat-slitting gesture, she dared not return to her peephole. Instead, she shuffled back to where the tallow dip was flickering ever lower in its pool of water. It was risky, but her only chance.

To reach the peephole now, with her hands bound, she had to lie on the floor, propping her shoulder against the wall as she put her eye to the crack. Soldiers marched to and fro across her vision, examining the huts and animals' pens, and the few poor sheds where grain was stored. They shook their heads as they made their reports: nothing.

Still Rowland sat beneath the tree's wide-spread branches, with the silent, sullen headman at his side. Caro strained her eyes, searching each torchlit face. Her wrists were swelling where the thin cord cut into her flesh, and gradually the ache in her hands and feet was giving way to a far more dangerous numbness.

When Rowland rose, and paced out of her line of vision, Caro grew weak with a sudden panic. He was going. He would mount and muster his troop, then disappear into the night, leaving her to heaven knew what fate.

Setting her teeth against the pain of her wrists, she maneuvered herself on hip and elbow across the packed earth floor, gasping as the movement made the blood in her bound feet start pounding again. Inch by inch she stretched out her fingers toward the guttering candle, grasped it, and screamed silently into her gag as the liquid tallow splashed across the back of her hands. With a great effort, she managed not to drop the earthen dish, but she knew at once that she could never burn through the cord without scorching all the skin off her wrists.

Outside, horses stamped and saddlery jingled as the troopers finished their search and formed into a column ready to depart. Caro heard Henry Forbes's gruff orders, followed by the *havildar's* high-pitched echo. In another moment they would be gone, and with them her last chance of escape.

She gathered every ounce of strength and wriggled back across the floor, carrying the candle behind her. Wrists and elbows were banged and scraped in her hurry, and she glanced fearfully over her shoulder at the tiny flame, willing it not to flicker out. As she stopped her frantic crawl, the flame steadied, and carefully she backed with it against the wall, resting it on a ledge where the flame touched an overhanging lip of wood. Once it was lodged, she turned around and studied it anxiously.

The flame smoked higher, drawn up by the tinder-dry wood above it, then suddenly eddied as a cross-draft from a crack between the timbers nearly blew it out. It retreated into a mere pinprick of light and Caro's heart sank. But a moment later, as if drawing strength from the narrow escape, the point of the flame reared higher and touched the wood. A spark clung on the door frame itself, then another, and suddenly the flame ran six inches up the door post and fell smoking to the floor. Another followed, and another: a moment later the post was blazing fiercely and Caro shuffled back as the flames lit up the whole interior of the hut.

The smoke, she thought. I shall suffocate if I breathe the smoke. Apart from the knothole she had enlarged, there was no other aperture in the whole hut, and as the fire gained strength, great billows of smoke rolled across the floor, driving her still farther into the interior. Her eyes stung, and blindly she cannoned into the hanging that partitioned the purdah area from the main room, tearing it down from the rod that supported it. For a moment the folds of coarse material kept away the smoke that was creeping into her lungs, and she drew in breath with a grateful gasp. The heat was becoming intense but the door showed no sign of disintegrating, although, under the frantic movement of her jaws the filthy rag that bound her mouth was starting to come to pieces. With a shudder of revulsion she spat it out and tried to call for help, but her voice was no more than a croak, muffled by the purdah hanging and drowned in the crackle of now-fiercely burning timbers. Surely they must hear it outside, she hoped desperately. Surely someone would smell the smoke and raise the alarm? The heat was making her senses reel and every breath she drew scorched her lungs. She could bear it no longer... But the frame around the door was going—buckling with the greedy flames eating away its support, and a fire-filled hole appeared in the wall beside it. Just as the timbers collapsed in a shower of sparks that lit up the whole interior, Caro's knees gave way under her and she fell senseless beneath the billowing pall of smoke.

Rowland surveyed his troop, awaiting the order to move off. The sowars' faces were closed, studiously ignoring the jibes and taunts of the villagers, whose hostility had increased to a marked degree since the order to search their huts.

The search had turned up neither the pony nor Caro, but something still nagged at Rowland's memory—a face, seen in very different circumstances. Yes, that was it: the big Sikh who had emerged from the headman's hut. Surely he had seen him before? Rowland chased the recollection down the winding corridors of memory. Not here: no. In Cawnpore. That was it: at the entertainment given by Chandranaya's ally, Nana Sahib, then Rajah of Bithoor, to the British stationed there. He could swear he had seen this man among Nana Sahib's bodyguard.

Rowland's gaze sharpened as he stared at the bearded face. The Sikh was hovering on the edge of the crowd, his attention apparently divided between Rowland's talk with the headman, and listening to something behind him.

Automatically Rowland followed the direction of his eyes, and heard it too: the crackle of burning timber.

"Fire!" he exclaimed.

A column of smoke rose lazily from the rear of the headman's hut, followed by a shower of sparks. The thatch caught, and in a moment the roof was well ablaze, the leaping flames casting a lurid light over the whole scene. With a crash, the door collapsed, exposing the interior of the hut as a raging inferno.

"What the devil," snapped Rowland, "is anyone in there?"

"N—no..." stammered the headman, but already Rowland was running forward, calling out orders to his men to fetch water and put out the fire. In the first bright flash of flames he had seen a movement inside the hut, the dark outline of a human body move toward the opening left by the door, then sway back as if overpowered by the heat.

Ten yards from the hut he halted, feeling the furnace-blast in his face. It must have been imagination—a falling beam, a stick of furniture crumbling into embers. Nothing human could have been moving in that fierce blaze.

He became aware of the Sikh at his elbow, tugging at his arm.

"Sahib! Sahib! Do not go further! There is nothing in the hut. *Nothing.*"

But even as he spoke, the smoke cleared and Rowland saw the huddled shape again, lying near the door. He shook off the man's hand and knotted a handkerchief swiftly across his mouth. Then, holding his breath, he plunged through the burning doorway.

Sparks showered down from the blazing timbers as he seized the inert bundle wrapped in a coarse rug that lay in the middle of the hut. Crouching to keep beneath the lever of the pall of smoke, Rowland dragged his burden toward the door, but before he could reach it the frame collapsed, bringing down part of the roof as it fell. A beam struck Rowland a heavy blow on the shoulder, momentarily paralyzing his arm, but he gritted his teeth and managed not to drop the body. His lungs were bursting in the heat, his clothes sprouting little patches of flame as he struggled over the red-hot timbers and collapsed just outside the hut.

Willing brown hands dragged him and his burden clear of the blaze, and directed by Lieutenant Forbes, the troopers soused their captain's head and uniform with *chatti* after *chatti* of cool well-water before turning their attention to the object he had pulled from the burning hut.

Gingerly Henry Forbes turned back the thick folds of curtain that enveloped it, and his fingers touched long dark hair, frizzed and charred by the flames.

"The deuce!" he exclaimed in shocked tones. "It's—it's a woman. Trussed like a chicken on a spit, poor creature! Those devils would have left her there to die. *Daffadar*! Arrest that man at once."

He pointed to the burly Sikh, whom he had spotted edging his way out of the crowd with the clear intention of making good his escape. But before the native officer could make a move, Rowland opened his eyes and propped himself up on an elbow.

"Steady on, Henry," he drawled. "You can't go arresting the Rajah of Patelbar's loyal subjects, y'know. Whatever would His Highness say?"

"But he—he said there was no one in the hut," stuttered the young man excitedly. "He must have known she was there, and he'd have left the poor creature to die in the blaze. He deserves to swing for it."

"I agree with you entirely, but alas, justice is not ours to administer here—though there's no reason we shouldn't report his villainy to Prince Chandranaya. No doubt he can devise some subtle punishment which you and I would shrink from enforcing, Henry, and that fellow may long for plain British justice before he's done.

"You say it's a woman I pulled out of there? Is it—is she alive?" He rose swiftly, and bent over the sodden form in its blackened wrappings. For a long moment he stared intently, the amusement dying out of his face.

"Caro!" he exclaimed sharply. "Good God! Quick, unlace her corsets. Give her air. By heaven, whoever is responsible for this day's work shall pay for it. I should have known, have guessed, when they swore the hut was empty that that must be where they had hidden her."

As he spoke his hands moved rapidly, peeling away the purdah hanging in which Caro had wrapped herself, cutting the cords that bound her hands and feet, and unbuttoning her riding habit. Forbes, very pink-faced, began to protest as Rowland eased the material away from Caro's naked shoulders, which looked startlingly white in contrast to her smoke-grimed face.

"Dash it, Steel, you can hardly undress her here, with all these fellows looking on..."

Rowland turned on him savagely. "I can—and will—do *anything* to save her, so spare me your moralizing and do something to help. My flask's over there with my horse, and we need a bed of some kind—a charpoy will do..." He loosened the drawstrings of Caro's corset and she sighed with relief. Rowland lifted one eyelid, which flickered at his touch, and taking the flask that Forbes held out to him, he said, rather unsteadily, "She'll pull through. Forgive me, Henry, if I was a trifle sharp, but I thought for a moment that we were too late."

He propped Caro up against his shoulder and carefully poured a little brandy down her throat. She choked and then swallowed, and to Rowland's great relief her eyes fluttered fully open and fixed on his.

"Oh... Rowland!" she said weakly. "I was so afraid you would not find me. I put the candle to the door frame, but the fire took hold so suddenly that I could not escape." She laid her hand upon Rowland's. "Thank you for coming to my rescue once more, for I truly thought I was going to die just then."

"No, thank God; we spotted you just in time," said Rowland cheerfully, gently caressing her grimy cheek. "You had a close shave, it's true, but you are safe enough now. What I can't understand is how you came to be separated from your party in the first place."

Bit by bit, with many pauses for sips of brandy and water, Caro told how she had been lured into the jungle by the screaming child, and what had befallen her since, and in return Rowland explained how Andrew's summons had reached him just as he was about to set off on the final sixty-mile *dak* for Baburpore.

"But Caro," he said. "Surely Thynne wasn't fool

enough to let you ride off on your own?"

"Of course not." Caro sprang to her brother-in-law's defense. "He sent two servants with me: my own *syce*, Bhalat Ram, and one of Prince Chandranaya's men. I was adequately escorted, I assure you, and Andrew couldn't know that the Prince's man was not to be trusted."

"He should have known, for I warned him myself," said Rowland rather grimly. "It was reckless and irresponsible of him to let you out of his sight in unsettled territory like this, and I shall tell him so."

"I beg you do not." Caro was adamant.

"I must." Rowland was equally firm. "If only to insure he takes better care of you in the future. Two *syce*s—one a fool and the other a stranger! I certainly wouldn't allow one of my womenfolk to ride here with so little protection."

"Then I must be thankful that I am not one of your womenfolk," she fumed, "ladies veiled and kept at home like the wives of Eastern potentates. Well, fortunately Andrew has more sense than to imagine danger in every inch of the subcontinent not subject to British rule, and I am sure he will continue to encourage me to ride where I like."

"Encourage you!" Rowland raised his eyes to heaven. "Of course you consider yourself a great expert on Indian affairs, having lived in the country all of two months, and naturally you resent any advice that's offered you. However, I would ask you to bear in mind that the country hereabouts is in a highly dangerous state and you would be foolish to ignore the warning signs."

But already the horror and bewilderment at finding herself lost and imprisoned was dwindling from Caro's memory, as her resentment at Rowland returned. "I am sure that what happened today can be explained as soon as we reach Patelbar. Prince Chandranaya's man was probably confused and failed to understand his instructions—at all events, he did me no harm, and the only danger was in the fire which I myself started. Philippa tells me that Indian servants always pretend they understand what you ask them, even if they haven't the least idea what you want."

Rowland was certain that the whole affair had been deliberate, and not caused by a simple misunderstanding, but he realized that it would be fruitless to argue the point further. He could not help admiring the resilience of Caro's spirits, although her determination to pay no heed to any warning and to believe that every man, woman, and child in India was her friend both annoyed and worried him.

Abruptly he rose, and ordered the headman to provide some clean clothes for the memsahib. Washed and refreshed, Caro was delighted with the freedom of a boy's loose tunic and long wrinkled trousers, which they handed her, and even Henry Forbes had to admit they became her very well.

"Now I must braid my hair Indian-fashion," she cried, "and Andrew will not know me!"

Bhalat Ram had been industriously washing the gaudy dye from Nuri's mane and tail, and had retrieved her own saddle and bridge from the bushes into which they had been flung.

Caro looked wistfully at the gold-encrusted horse trappings that lay on the ground. "Do you not think," she asked Rowland demurely, "that I might keep those as a memento of my adventure?" But this he refused to permit, saying that the villagers might even accuse his soldiers of theft if objects so clearly valuable were removed.

"You do not realize how careful we are obliged to be to avoid the least taint of corruption. If even a single member of the Sirkar, as they call us—the British Administration—gives way to bribery, our reputation will vanish as if it had never been, and long years of work will be utterly destroyed."

Caro thought this another exaggeration, but not wanting to be accused again of lack of experience in Indian affairs, she had the sense to hold her tongue and allowed him to help her to mount. She could not understand Rowland's parting speech to the headman, for he spoke too rapidly for her to follow, but from his tone she deduced that he was warning him severely to be more circumspect in his future dealings with white ladies. The troopers grinned and slapped their sabers against their horses' flanks in semithreatening gestures, and one grizzled veteran murmured *"Shabash!"* beneath his mustache as they rode away down the jungle path.

The nervous strain of Caro's disappearance had been too much for Philippa, and she burst into tears of relief when Caro entered her marble-floor room in the Rajah's palace.

"I thought they had killed you," she said, sobbing. "I was afraid we'd never see you again."

Her tears and dark-ringed eyes in her drawn face had far more effect on Caro than Rowland's scolding.

"I am so sorry, Phil," she said, hugging her sister. "I promise you I didn't mean to give you such a fright, especially when you weren't well."

But Philippa's attention was quickly diverted to Caro's clothes. "Where in the world did you get those dreadful garments?" she exclaimed with shuddering distaste. "Take them off at once and put on something more seemly. No English lady should ever dress like that. Give those rags to your *ayah* and tell her to be sure that they are burned."

"I shall do nothing of the kind: I like them. They are far better suited to the climate than the clothes we wear."

"Oh, don't say anything so terrible! The natives will lose all respect for you if you insist not only on learning their language but wearing their dreadful rags as well. We are bidden to dine with the Rajah himself tonight; it will be a great banquet, I know, and although I don't feel at all up to it, Andrew says it will be considered uncivil if I decline."

"Poor Phil." Caro looked around the room with interest. Although nearly every object of furniture in it was of Western origin or copied from its Western counterpart—bed, chairs, dressing table, even the fire screen painted with English fox-hunting scenes—they were so positioned as to present an entirely Oriental appearance. The rugs were not on the floor, but flung over chairs. The dressing table had no stool, and the looking glass faced the wall. The china basin and ewer stood not on the commode, but on the floor, and the pictures were not only upside down, but festooned with paper streamers and a profusion of flowers.

She caught Philippa's eye and they began to giggle. "So kind of His Highness," said Philippa weakly. "He is determined to make me feel at home and Andrew insists it would be discourteous to allow my *ayah* to rearrange anything. I only wonder where he can have acquired such a miscellany of furniture. None of the chairs match, and yet I believe the small table by the window is by Chippendale, and I am almost certain this patch box derives from the court of Madame Pompadour. Do you think he expects us to wear beauty spots, like the heroines of old romances? Oh, Caro, do go and change your clothes: I cannot help thinking how Mama would fall into a fit if she saw you dressed like an Indian person."

For the banquet, Caro chose her best gown, a simple green velvet with a narrow flounce around her bare shoulders and another at the hem. She tied back her hair with a ribbon of the same color and clasped a single string of pearls—her eighteenth-birthday present from her father—around her neck. Satisfied that she looked conventional enough to please her sister, she joined Andrew and Philippa where they waited, in a large, pillared room hung with glowing tapestries, for the entry of the Rajah of Patelbar.

Rowland had already departed with his troop of horse to rejoin his company on the road to Baburpore, and Caro felt an obscure pang of regret that he had not waited to bid her good-bye. Perhaps he was angry because she had mocked at his caution; perhaps he really believed her foolish, obstinate, and vain. Perhaps he was simply in a hurry to rejoin his regiment and had already forgotten she even existed.

Caro pushed aside these unwelcome thoughts and accepted a small rolled leaf from an attendant in spotless white tunic and turban.

"Careful," warned Philippa in a whisper. "It is betel leaf. It will stain your teeth red."

Caro made a pretense of searching her reticule and inconspicuously dropped the leaf into it. It seemed impolite to keep refusing the sweetmeats offered her, but the two she tried were not at all to her taste, being strongly flavored with aromatic spice and some sort of confection of roses which she found curiously difficult to swallow. Before she had disposed of it, the door at the end of the long room opened, and the Rajah entered, escorted by Prince Chandranaya and a crowd of attendants.

Jahan Bahadur Shah, Rajah of Patelbar, was a wizened old man a little more than five foot tall, who seemed bowed beneath the weight of his elaborate turban. His eyes, set in deep, hollowed-out sockets, had the sad, surprised look of a langur monkey, and the brown irises were almost completely overlaid with a milky blue film. Caro was somewhat disappointed in his appearance, having expected a more magnificent figure to dominate such a palace. The Rajah wore a simple tunic of blue silk, sashed with gold, long loose trousers caught in below the knee, and slippers with modestly curling toes. He climbed the five steps to his throne—a huge silken cushion—and seated himself cross-legged, smiling dimly at his visitors.

Andrew bowed respectfully, Caro and Philippa curtsied, and silence settled on the company once more.

Presently the Rajah spoke to Prince Chandranaya, who sat on a lower step, resplendent in a brocade surcoat and snowy jodhpurs, and a moment later the Prince beckoned Andrew to join them. The three men talked quietly, and as if this were the signal for general conversation, an answering buzz rose throughout the room. No one approached Caro and Philippa, however, and they were obliged to whisper to one another, unsure whether the men seated near them could understand what they were saying.

"Do look: I saw a movement behind the screen," exclaimed Caro raising her eyes to the delicate, carved-marble gallery that ran round the top of the audience chamber. "I'm sure the ladies are watching us."

"I expect they are: I only wish we were permitted to join them on these occasions," said Philippa. "It is such a strain to be treated as if one were invisible; I think I should prefer to be invisible in reality."

Caro knew what she meant. It was a strange and uncomfortable feeling to be present at a party and yet ignored by everyone there. She was thankful when Andrew, sensing his wife's difficulty, bowed and retreated from the steps to the throne. He brought with him a short, stout Indian dressed in a pink silk frockcoat and cream brocade waistcoat, wearing on his head a turban of pink corded silk adorned with an immense ruby. He had thick, arched eyebrows over small eyes with heavy, hooded lids; a plump, round face with a cupid-bow mouth beneath upturning mustaches. His nose was short and somewhat broad, his expression placid to the point of stupidity, making it difficult to believe Rowland's stories of his reptilian malevolence.

Andrew said, "My dear, I wish to present to you His Highness the Nana Sahib, Rajah of Bithoor. My wife, Lady Philippa Thynne, and her sister, Lady Caroline March."

The deposed Rajah, Caro thought, as Nana Sahib bowed and smiled at the ladies in turn, but his eyes lingered on Caro long enough to make her uneasy: they reminded her of a cobra's eyes beneath its hood, unwinking and malevolent.

"This is the lady who was lost in the jungle?" he remarked through his interpreter. "I am happy she has returned to grace our feast. My cousin Chandranaya would not like any accident to befall his English guests, for whom he wishes only joy. Pleasure and joy..."

His gaze continued to strip Caro of her clothes and she shivered involuntarily, wishing she had chosen the high-neck gown of tucked muslin instead of the décolleté green velvet. To her relief, the old Rajah rose just then from his cross-legged position on the cushions, and the whole company moved to the banquet hall.

"Sure and you've taken the eye of our noble guest, Lady Caroline," murmured a lazy, half-mocking voice at her elbow. "'Tis not a bite nor a sup of dinner he's had for watching you, and he's a great man for his vittles in the usual way."

Caro turned in surprise to her neighbor, for the lilt of the voice was unmistakably Irish, despite its owner's tunic and turban. She met twinkling hazel eyes in a still-boyish face tanned dark as any Indian's.

"Indeed, I wish he would pay more attention to his

food and less to me," she responded with spirit. "I find his staring quite puts me off eating, for whenever I look up I meet his glance. Noble he may be, but such behavior seems to me excessively ill-bred."

Her neighbor smothered a laugh.

"Do you know, I find myself in complete agreement with you, ma'am. You have hit the mark exactly. Dondhu Pant really has no breeding at all—he is the son of a village priest who had the good fortune to be adopted by Bajirao, the last Peshwa of the Mahrattas, rest his soul. That is your stout admirer's only claim to nobility."

Caro avoided looking across the table into those unwinking eyes. "But you, sir," she asked, eager to turn the subject away from the Rajah of Bithoor, "surely you are from Ireland?"

He nodded. "My family live in County Cork, and Fionn Kelly is my name. At your service," he added gallantly. "But it's been fifteen years since I saw the Old Country." Caro was suddenly aware of the sadness masked by the twinkle of his eyes. "I'm a physician by profession, and"—he nodded toward the wizened old Rajah on his heap of silken cushions—"I ply my trade as personal physician to His Highness."

"Oh, of course, *you're* the Irishman Captain Steel told us about!" Caro exclaimed, remembering Rowland's reference at the campsite. Kelly's only response to her words was to stiffen, almost imperceptibly. "Captain Rowland Steel," she persisted, "of the—"

"Yes," he cut in tersely, "Captain Steel."

"You know Captain Steel? Imagine that!" Caro persevered, thrilled at the opportunity to discover more about the enigmatic Rowland. "From where do you know him?"

"Enough said, Lady Caroline." Kelly's tone communicated an intensity that silenced her. "Quite enough," he repeated, then lightly brought their conversation back to the old Rajah. "He's been a good friend to me, and though he's a sick man and not long for this world, I'll stay and see him out of it."

"Will you not remain with his successor?" she asked hesitantly. "Surely a trained physician is a treasure in such a remote place as this?"

"Oh, there's no lack of work to be done." Fionn Kelly's voice held more than a trace of bitterness. "They're eager enough to make use of my skills—such as they are—but all the same they'd prefer me blind, deaf, and dumb if I could practice in that condition. Do you know, I have to be blindfolded before I'm allowed to examine one of the Court ladies?"

"That must make your work very difficult," she agreed. She gazed down the table to where Philippa sat, pale and drawn before a plate of untouched food.

"Your sister?" said Fionn, following her glance. "Is she unwell?"

"We are worried about her health," Caro confided. "She finds it hard to sleep and feels so tired all the time. I expect it is the heat. Can you—would you be able to help her?"

Fionn shrugged. "I can try. She's breeding, I suppose?" He added, as if to himself, "They always are in hot weather. Tell her I'll come to her room when the banquet is over and bring something that will make her sleep."

At the far end of the twenty-foot table, once the property of a cavalry mess, but now adorned with an astonishing array of plates and dishes ranging from pure silver trenchers to chipped enamel bowls. Andrew Thynne was drinking heavily, his face flushed and his fair hair damp with sweat under the erratically flapping *punkah*.

He had had a worrying day: First Philippa's illness, and then Caro's disappearance, and to crown it all he had had to put up with a sharp lecture from Rowland

Steel on the folly of letting women ride unattended in an unsettled territory. He would be glad to get back to his regiment and live among men again. Now he intended to drown his sorrows.

Women! he thought blearily. God bless 'em and all that, but they were a damned nuisance at times. Philippa, for instance: feeling the heat a trifle this year, and rambling on about danger and unrest, and heaven knows what, and begging him to leave Patelbar as soon as possible. Well, he wouldn't. He'd pandered to her whims and fancies quite enough during his two-months' furlough—now it was time he showed her he was master in his own house. He'd stay here for a week, as planned, and be hanged to Philippa's fads and fancies.

"Another glass of wine, Captain Thynne," said Prince Chandranaya's smooth voice beside him. "Tomorrow we will have a great hunt together. Tell me, is yours the only regiment now stationed at Baburpore?"

Avoiding Philippa's eye, Andrew unhooked the collar of his tunic while his goblet was refilled. Taking a long cool drink, he sat back, glad to be in male company once again, and began to explain to that pleasant fellow Chandranaya the deposition of British troops in Oudh.

Chapter Six

A SINEWY BROWN hand gripped Caro's forearm and she started at the touch, wishing Indians set less store by physical contact. With an effort, she stopped herself from jerking her arm away.

"Tell me, Lady Caroline," said the slimy Azimullah Khan in the slow, singsong English which he had learned as a servant in a British household before his high elevation as adviser to the Nana Sahib, Rajah of Bithoor, "my master wishes to know: in England, can you dance?"

"Dance?" she repeated, puzzled. "Yes, I can dance. Not the sort of dances your . . . ladies"—she hesitated over the word, for the sooty-eye, half-clad nymphs swaying in front of them to the crude music of viol and tom-tom were so clearly not ladies at all—"perform, but our own dances: waltz, polka, schottische . . . I can dance those. Why do you ask?"

"My master would like to see you dance."

"Oh!" She cast down her eyes, a little embarrassed. "I'm afraid I can't dance alone, you know. In England we always have someone to dance with. What we call a partner."

"The partner is a man, yes? You dance with men? Yes, I have seen it in London. My master would like to see you dance with a man."

Caro was flustered, sensing some darker meaning behind his question, something that hinted at impropriety, though the words were innocuous enough. She

145

said: "I'm afraid I don't—I mean, I couldn't..."

Philippa rescued her, asking what she thought of the *nautch* girls' performance, and Caro turned gratefully toward her sister, glad to be distracted from Azimullah Khan's insidious interrogation.

"I think it is quite the most tedious dance I have ever seen in my life," she said softly. "The same movements endlessly repeated; I am surprised they do not fall asleep from sheer ennui!"

"The Rajah of Bithoor is enjoying it," said Philippa.

Nana Sahib sat cross-legged, his paunch supported on his short fat thighs, his flat black eyes feasting on the undulating limbs of the girls. From time to time he put an arm around the shoulders of Andrew, who sat beside him, drowsy with wine and outdoor exercise, pulling Andrew's fair head close to his own dark one as he whispered some private joke.

Philippa watched her husband with a worried frown on her face. Why could neither he nor Caro feel the tension in the atmosphere of this decaying palace that jarred so strongly on her own senses? She was not normally fanciful, she knew; was it her pregnancy that made her sensitive to the least hint of danger? And there was danger near at hand, she was sure of it. She could sense it in the muttered conversations of the two princes, and their pressing attention to Andrew, urging him to talk long and drink deeply, while they smiled, and applauded, and encouraged him to tell them more.

They had now been here four days, and since the first evening had not set eyes on the Rajah of Patelbar. Fionn Kelly had expressed uneasiness about the old man's condition, and spent most of the day in the Royal apartments.

Every morning the princes went hunting, taking Andrew with them, and returned at dusk with deer and pig tied to poles, behind which their great spotted hunting cats in jeweled collars stalked proudly with their attendants. Every night there was an interminable banquet, at which the food made Philippa queasy and the heat giddy. Then followed an hour or more cross-legged on cushions, with the squealing viol piercing her ears, making conversation impossible even if there had been anyone except Caro to talk to, for Andrew and the other men sat apart, swaying gently and patting time to the tom-tom.

Philippa felt they were all treading on the edge of a dark pit, and one slip would pitch them all in headlong. She envied Caro her insatiable appetite for adventure, her delight in anything strange and new—above all, she envied her perfect health. As one who faced the increasing burden of pregnancy during the warmest weather of the year, a slim body and resilient digestion were attributes she could not help coveting.

She made one more effort at escaping the next morning as, together with a morose and sore-headed Andrew, they strolled around the Rajah's well-stocked menagerie amid the raucous screeches of peacocks and the whining of caged wolves.

"Can we not leave tomorrow, and go on our way to Baburpore?" she urged. "We would be there in three or four days' time. I am so much better, you see; I feel quite strong enough to travel again."

Andrew groaned and put a hand to his head. "Well, I certainly don't. I find the idea of traveling too horrible to be borne. No, we'll stay on a bit—I promised Chandranaya he could try my rifle tomorrow when we go after tiger." He turned to stare at his wife in petulant surprise. "Why are you in such an almighty hurry to get to Baburpore? You know you don't like it when you're there. You don't seem to realize what luck we're in to be here at all. We're the first Europeans to visit Patelbar for donkey's years—not counting Kelly, of course; I don't count Kelly because he's gone native anyway. But you can't turn down an invitation to this kind of *shikar*—it's unique. I'd have gone with them again today if you hadn't complained I was neglecting you. And I've got this beastly head."

"Captain-sahib drink too much simkin," cried Caro, saucily wagging her head in parody of Andrew's old retainer, Sher Dil.

Andrew gave a reluctant grin. "It wasn't champagne, you minx, it was Rhine wine, but I believe I did drink too much. Never again."

"Don't you see how they encourage you to take too much to drink?" said Philippa earnestly. "The princes forever filling your glass, watching you like a pair of wolves waiting for their moment to attack. I am convinced they are bent on treachery."

"What, Chandranaya and the Nana Sahib?" cried Andrew. "What utter nonsense. They are good fellows, both of them, and as to comparing them with wolves— I never heard such foolishness." His pride was hurt by Philippa's implication that he could not hold his wine, and he spoke more sharply than he intended.

"I see your mind is made up and it is useless for me to protest," said Philippa, closing her mouth with a snap that was almost audible. She could not help adding, "But the attention your boon companion the fat, greasy Rajah of Bithoor pays to Caro is most improper, and I wish you would tell him so. The poor girl is quite put out of countenance by the way he dotes on her."

Andrew's peevish expression softened as he looked after Caro, who had wandered away to inspect a pair of magnificent cheetahs.

"She's a devilish pretty girl, that's why," he said frankly. "And the Rajah's always on the alert for another beauty for his household. Not that he means to add Caro to it," he added hastily, "but he can't help wishing he could."

"Oh . . . you are impossible!" exclaimed his outraged wife.

148

It was one of Andrew's nicest characteristics that he could never sustain a quarrel for any length of time. He put an arm round Philippa's stiff shoulders, and after a moment she relaxed in his embrace. "Don't be angry with me, Phil," he said softly. "It's something I've always dreamed of: living in a Rajah's palace and hunting in the old style. Don't grudge me this chance; I may never get it again. I know it's not so much fun for you as it is for me, but after all, you have Caro for company, and we shall be here only a few more days." He smiled. "As regards the Nana Sahib, I know he's not to everyone's taste, but I have it on good authority that he's leaving Patelbar tomorrow. Think of it, Phil, after today neither you nor Caro will ever again be troubled by Nana Sahib."

In the cool freshness of dawn, the Rajah of Bithoor's retinue waited for the signal to depart. Horses whinnied and champed at their bits, elephants stamped, and camels gave vent to cavernous groans as they knelt under their unwieldy loads. But still the Rajah tarried, conversing softly with his host under the striped silk awning that shielded his *palanquin* from the sun.

"My uncle is sick and will join his fathers before many suns have set," said Prince Chandranaya confidently.

Nana Sahib sighed. "The way to heaven is hard for many old men. Hard and slow."

"There are ways of making it smooth, cousin. Smooth and quick."

"But I hear that the Irish doctor waits day and night on Jahan Bahadur Shah. He will permit none of your herbs to pass the Rajah's lips."

Chandranaya's pointed white teeth showed under the pencil-fine mustache. "Even Irish doctors must sleep at times," he murmured, "and when his eyes do close, it will be forever."

Nana Sahib looked apprehensive. "Be careful, cousin," he urged. "The Irish doctor is well loved in Patelbar. For both the Rajah and his trusted servant to die in a single night would excite suspicion."

"I will be careful," agreed Chandranaya, "but die he must. Then I will hasten to your side to help chase the Feringhee dogs far from the lands of the Mahrattas, back to the shores of the black water from whence they came, and restore the ancient glories of Hind. In return—"

"In return," Nana Sahib continued, "you shall sit on the throne of Baburpore and take back those lands and revenues the British stole from your uncle, just as they stole my birthright." The Rajah of Bithoor had conveniently forgotten that his adopted father's pension, which he so resented forfeiting, had never been his by right of birth. "But do not strike until I am beyond your borders, for there must be no hint of complicity between us until the Red Wind blows all before it."

They smiled at one another. "All shall become Red," said Chandranaya softly, "when that wind blows, and the Feringhee dogs and their spawn will rue the day they set foot in Oudh. They shall all die: men, women and children—"

"But not my dancer," interjected Nana Sahib.

"No, cousin," responded the Prince. "Never your dancer."

Caro burst into the cool, shady room where Andrew and Philippa were sitting at breakfast, their servants in attendance behind their chairs. Her face was flushed, her breast heaved, and her eyes were wide and frightened.

"Why, Caro!" cried her sister, rising from her chair in alarm. "Whatever is the matter?"

"I saw him again!" gasped Caro.

"Whom did you see?" Philippa's glance took in the wild, disheveled hair, and torn, filthy clothes. Caro was barefoot, her clothes were soaked through, and greenish slime dripped on the marble floor.

"Let her get her breath first," Andrew advised. "Sit down, Caro. You're quite safe. Get your breath and then tell us what you saw." He waved to the servant to bring her a cup of tea. "Now then, begin at the beginning. What happened?"

"It was the Sikh," said Caro in the same high, frightened tone. "The one who held me prisoner in that horrible hut after I was lost in the jungle. I just saw him again, and he turned his horse and rode after me, crashing through the jungle—and I ran and ran—it was like a nightmare."

Fearing that her sister was about to fall into hysterics, Philippa groped for her smelling-bottle and held it under Caro's nose. The strong fumes made her cough, but they cleared her head, and after a moment she said in a more normal voice, "I awakened early this morning, and it was so fresh and beautiful that I decided to take a walk to the little temple we saw yesterday, on the edge of the lake."

"Alone? Oh, Caro!"

"I did not think you would care to be awakened at that hour," she said defensively. "Anyway, I was not alone, for I took Tiger. Poor Tiger!" The brindled terror she called Tiger had been a parting gift from Brook Vyner. For a moment she struggled with tears, then went on. "It was lovely by the lake; all kinds of birds were wading and swimming, and I sat and watched them. By the temple the water was so clear I could see great fat carp beneath the surface. Then I heard the beat of drums and shouting in the distance, so I followed a little path through the jungle, and came at last to the road..."

Laden carts were bumping two abreast down the

narrow track, pulled by white buffalo and camels that swayed like ships as they shambled along on their soft, padded feet. Elephants followed, their gold embroidered *howdah* glinting in the early sun.

Caro stood in the shadow of an overhanging tree, enjoying the rich confusion of the procession, the curiously ordered turmoil of men and beasts on the march. Where had they come from? Whither were they bound? Then she recognized faces among the marchers and realized she knew the answer to the first part of her question: this was the retinue of the Nana Sahib, Rajah of Bithoor, leaving Patelbar before the heat of the day made travel wearisome.

Remembering his sly interest in her, the placid black gaze that followed her every movement and seemed to bore beneath her clothes to the naked flesh beneath, she shrank still further back into the concealing shade. It would not do to be observed here, alone and far from the palace. But she was reluctant to leave the colorful scene and lingered as rank after rank of the Rajah's retainers, his kitchen workers, baggage wagons, and hunting dogs filed past her.

It was the dogs that attracted Tiger's interest. He had been pursuing some small game, and was returning to his mistress's side, when the tall, leashed deer hounds, happened to pass.

Before Caro could restrain him, he leaped into the road, growling threats and defiance at his better-bred compatriots. Neither they nor the men who led them took any notice of him, but a horseman from the rank behind spurred forward, and leaning far down from his saddle, made a sudden cut with his curved saber, slicing Tiger cleanly in two.

"No!" shrieked Caro, rushing to her pet's defense. "You devil! You . . ." The words died on her lips as she looked up and met the eyes of her past enemy, the Sikh.

He was as stunned as she, and for a moment they

held their positions as if carved from stone: Caro with her hands clasped against her mouth, the Sikh with saber raised for a second cut.

Then Caro whirled to flee down the path she had come by, and with a bloodcurdling screech the Sikh set spurs to his horse and galloped across the line of marchers in pursuit of her.

Long-armed vines threatened to trip her, thorns ripped at her clothes—Caro paid them no heed as she pelted down the twisting path as fast as her hampering skirts would allow, the blood pounding in her throat as she heard the thunder of hoofs close behind her. The ground was in her favor, since low branches forced the Sikh to stoop uncomfortably in the saddle, but she knew that before long he would ride her down. She could not keep up this pace. Her lungs were bursting and sweat poured into her eyes, but still terror spurred her on.

She continued to run, though she had ceased to direct her legs. Hours of riding and slow promenades with Philippa had not improved her fleetness of foot, and although she dared not turn to look, for fear of tripping over some unexpected obstacle, she sensed that her pursuer was gaining.

Then she saw the lake ahead. Swerving off the path that led to the temple—for she knew that on the open expanse of turf that surrounded the small building she would lose her advantage—Caro pushed blindly through the thicket of tangled undergrowth. She splashed into the shallows, and birds rose from the water in a startled and indignant cloud of feathers. She was sobbing, partly with terror and partly for the death of poor Tiger, the image of whose severed and writhing body seemed indelibly burned on the retinas of her eyes, just as his last agonized yelp still rang in her ears.

A dozen floundering strides from the bank, she sank into deep slime that sucked off her flimsy shoes. For a panic-stricken moment she thought the stagnant water in which she was rooted would close over her head. Then her desperately searching feet struck firmer bottom, and she moved forward no more than waist-deep in the lake.

Behind her sounded a yell of frustration as the Sikh's horse balked at the water's edge. Caro looked back.

Her pursuer was flailing at his mount with the flat of his sword, and after a moment's hesitation, the horse crouched down and then sprang over the shallows with a long leap, as if to cross the lake in a single bound. He landed in the deep slime that had so nearly dragged Caro under, and the lurch as he fought to regain his footing unseated the Sikh. Horse and rider disappeared in an enveloping cloud of spray.

Caro waded on, praying that no snakes or crocodiles lurked in the murky water. Her skirts billowed round her, twining themselves clammily against her legs and hampering every move she made. Stones and rubble cut her feet, while masses of floating weed made wading slow and difficult, but at last she gained the far bank, and flopped down on the grass.

Across the narrow, elongated oval of the lake, she could see the Sikh's horse still floundering in the channel of deeper water where she herself had nearly gone under. As she watched, its repeated plunges carried it onto firmer footing near the bank. With a heave it got its forelegs up the steep incline and stood resting, head hanging, too tired to make the last effort that would bring its hind legs out of the clinging mud.

Then Caro noticed a long, V-shape ripple surging through the water toward the bogged horse, and her heart skipped a beat. A crocodile, she thought, watching in helpless fascination. It must have been alerted by the splashes.

Where was the Sikh? Had the monster killed him

before turning its attention to the horse? It seemed too good to be true, and Caro could move neither hand nor foot as she sat, hypnotized, in her dripping clothes, mud oozing from her ruined stockings and spreading into a pool about her unshod feet.

The horse saw the ripple too, and renewed its struggles. The long, thin upper jaw with its wicked teeth rose in the water, bending back until it could encompass its prey with a single snap. Just before it crunched down on the horse's hindquarters, the intended victim wrenched itself free and leaped up the bank in a single bound, to disappear with a crash into the tangled thicket.

Caro was shaking in reaction, despite the sun, which struck hot on her shoulders and bare head. Her sunbonnet had been plucked from her head by the first thornbush she pushed through. Ruefully she took stock of the other damage: lost shoes, stockings torn to shreds, her dress ripped in a dozen places and sodden to the waist, sundry cuts and bruises beginning to make themselves felt, her hair a mass of twigs, leaves, and slime. Still, she was alive, unlike poor Tiger. A sob caught in her throat and she rose unsteadily, trying to control her quivering limbs.

Then a movement on the edge of the lake attracted her eye. The Sikh was running around from the temple in a path that would cut off her retreat to the palace.

Fear raced through Caro's veins, giving her new strength. She began to run again, hitching up her sodden skirt to free her stride. Her pursuer, for all his bulk, moved as lithely as a hunting cat, and he was gaining on her...

"I remembered I was near one of those wells we saw on our walk yesterday," she later told Andrew and Philippa. "I asked you why anyone had built a well in such an isolated spot, and you said it was for the use of sweepers, so that they would not defile the water in the courtyard. So I dodged out of sight behind some low thorn trees, and ran back to the well. It had a windlass with a bucket hanging above a little low wall, where we sat and talked. Well, it came back to me suddenly that I'd noticed some steps cut in the brickwork of the well itself. I suppose they are used when the structure requires repair."

Andrew exclaimed. "Don't tell me you climbed down the well to hide? If that don't beat all! What puzzles me, though, is why the fellow should trouble to chase you so far. Prince Chandranaya swore to me he'd hanged that Sikh as high as Haman for his first attack on you. Why should the villain risk his neck by doing it again?"

"He told *me* the crows were picking his bones between dawn and sunset," said Caro with a shudder.

"Then he lied to you both," cried Philippa indignantly.

"Oh, that's in a manner of speaking," said Andrew. "Indians always tell you what they think you want to hear, and often they'll say they've done something when in truth they just wish they could do it. No, I don't lay any blame at Chandranaya's door; but all the same it's a puzzle."

His matter-of-fact tone had a calming effect on Caro, gripped as she still was by the memory of her narrow escape. She said with the ghost of a smile, "Yes, I did climb into the well, and very dark and unpleasant it was! But there were handholes let into the brickwork, and I found a sort of niche halfway down in which I could sit. I heard nothing for a long time—it seemed a long time—and was just wondering if it was safe to climb up, when I heard a clanking above me..."

She peered from her dark refuge at the circle of sunlight at the top of the well. An object was being lowered toward her, and after a moment she realized it was the wooden bucket descending toward the water that gleamed darkly at the bottom of the shaft.

Was the Sikh working the windlass, seeking refreshment after his long chase round the lake?

The thought, along with her chilly, wet clothes, made her shake as the bucket descended in jerks past the shelf on which she huddled. Then she heard soft, feminine chatter and giggles, and a feeling of relief swept over her. It must be a party of women, come to fill their water jars. While they were there, the Sikh dared not approach: she was saved.

Before the voices died into the distance, Caro began her wet and painful ascent of the crudely cut hand and foot holds. Once or twice her numbed fingers slipped, and only a sudden clutch at the rung above prevented her from falling to certain death.

At last she reached the top, and as her head and shoulders cleared the well's edge, one of the water carriers happened to look back. Her shriek as she saw the apparition emerging from the well's depths caused a flock of crows to rise squawking from the trees.

Her companions turned to see the cause of her alarm, and they, too began to scream...

Despite herself, Caro began to laugh as she related the scene. "I am sure they thought I was a ghost, at least! I tried to reassure them, but with one accord they flung down their water-jars and fled!"

"It's all very well to laugh," said Philippa severely, "but you might have been killed, and it would have been your own fault for going off on your own again. Now tell me you have learned your lesson and will stay with me in future."

"I know," said Caro sadly. "I should have paid more attention to what you said before. Poor Tiger!"

In the Rajah's darkened apartments, lit only by a lamp of cedar-scented oil, Fionn Kelly yawned and stretched. For three days and nights he had rested in snatches, ready to spring awake if the old Rajah's condition worsened. But now his patient lay propped on a mound of pillows, sleeping peacefully, and beside him the goblet of pinkish liquid that had been keeping him alive was all but empty.

Fionn stood listening for a few moments to the old man's quiet breathing, then he moved to the door and spoke softly to the servant on guard.

"I go now to rest, Sher Shah. Call me if your master wakes, but let no one else enter."

The gray-bearded warrior touched his sword hilt and nodded. "Yes, doctor-sahib. If he wakes, I myself will call you."

"*Shabash!* Sher Shah Bahadur!" murmured Fionn, and the old man grinned.

He watched the doctor's lanky form slouch wearily down the passage, then twirled his mustache and straightened his back, standing to attention outside his master's door.

To one side, out of the line of his vision, a hanging moved slightly as if a wind had stirred it, but within the thick walls of the Royal apartments, no wind could blow. Sher Shah, still standing at attention, heard nothing as a silk scarf was slipped by unseen hands around his throat. His startled grunt and instinctive movement away from the constriction instantly tightened the knot that pressed into his jugular vein. He struggled, hands clawing the air.

His sword dropped to the stone floor with a clatter; a moment later the senseless body of Sher Shah fell beside it.

The door of the Rajah's chamber swung noiselessly inward, and the old guard's killer slipped through into the dim interior.

When Fionn woke, refreshed, from his first uninterrupted sleep for a week, he looked at his clock in amazement. Seven in the morning—and he had lain down on his charpoy at ten! Why had Sher Shah not awakened him? Where was Sher Shah? It was inconceivable that his patient would have slept as long as this unless... unless... The distant sound of keening that came to his ears was from the direction of the Royal apartments, and Fionn sprang up with an oath.

He hurried down the stone passage, afraid of what he would find, and pushed open the Rajah's door. An old *ayah* stood by the bed, her shawl pulled over her head, uttering a long wail of distress. Jahan Shah Bahadur's eyes were open, but he had not moved on the pillows. His clawlike hands were clenched, and a thin trickle of pink liquid from the goblet beside his bed was dripping into a pool on the floor.

Fionn picked up the cold wrist, and sought for a pulse; there was none and he laid the dead arm gently on the bed again.

"Good-bye, old friend," he murmured, and closed the staring eyes.

He stood gazing down at the still figure, remembering the days after his court-martial, fifteen long years ago, when other young officers of the Company would cross the road sooner than meet him. He'd talked about quitting India, going home to face his disgrace in Ireland; then Jahan Shah Bahadur had spoken to him.

"Your people have cast you out, and they have stolen one-half of the kingdom my fathers left me. You and I have no cause to love the Sirkar. Come with me and together we will free my people from the ignorance and disease that blight their lives from their first breath to their last. Be my man..."

He had gone, with never a backward look. And if they hadn't quite fulfilled that long-ago dream of the Rajah's, at least they had improved conditions in Patelbar, giving the people justice, teaching, and medical care without the help, or the taint, of British money or British methods. With the recent failing of the Rajah's eyesight, his reforming zeal had flagged, and now Fionn Kelly struggled on alone, uneasily aware of the growth of Prince Chandranaya's influence, and knowing, too, that the Prince could undo in months what had taken years of patient work to achieve.

Now the blow had fallen: his patron—his protector and friend—was dead, and Chandranaya would take his place.

Fionn looked slowly round the room, and then more sharply at the body on the bed. Puzzlement became suspicion, which hardened into certainty as he noticed the marks on the thin wrists—the bluish lips and blue-tinted fingernails. Jahan Bahadur Shah had not joined his fathers of his own accord: Fionn was sure of it. The fever had been on the wane. He had left his patient sleeping quietly, the crisis past. Something—someone—had given the old Rajah the small push that could send him into eternity. His wrists had been held while something—a pillow?—was gently pressed against his face.

The *who* was not far to seek. "Chandranaya," he murmured. No one else would dare. No one else would benefit—and who but Chandranaya could force his way past old Sher Shah? Where *was* Sher Shah?

Methodically, Fionn examined the room, noting the undisturbed jewel box and carved jade ornaments that the old man had loved to caress. No thief could have ignored those. He was putting them back in their carved ivory box when Prince Chandranaya's soft voice startled him.

"So you steal my uncle's jewels even before his last rites are observed!"

Fionn turned, his Irish temper flaring. "So you enter

the Royal apartments without the leave of the Rajah's physician."

"I need no permission from you, dog of a Feringhee; and my uncle has no more need of a physician. No doubt your vile potions helped to hasten his death—who can say? Stay"—he held up a slim, beringed hand as Fionn started to protest—"I know your grief takes the guard from your tongue, but reflect: it is not wise to offer offense to a rajah, and I am the heir to Patelbar."

The eyes of the two men met and locked: Fionn's hard and angry; Chandranaya's blandly devoid of expression, yet the Prince was the first to lower his gaze.

He turned on his heel. "I go to arrange my uncle's funeral rites," he murmured, and left the room.

"A toast to our departing guests," said Prince Chandranaya. "May you return many times to Patelbar." He lowered his voice and leaned toward Andrew. "It is truly a misfortune that my uncle's death has robbed you of your last days of sport, but in these traditional matters we must do all things in the old ways. The Ranees will make *suttee*, and it is better you do not see this."

"Of course," muttered Andrew, sickened at the thought of the beautiful doe-eyed wives of the late Rajah casting themselves on their lord's funeral pyre. A barbarous custom, and one the British sought to check within British India, but with poor success. Here, in a princely state, he could do nothing to prevent the Ranees' fate and the Prince was right: the less he knew of it the better.

He cleared his throat and said with more firmness, "We understand and wish to thank you again for your hospitality, which has cured my wife of her sickness, and given me memories I shall treasure forever. Now we must depart, and you must do your duty for your uncle."

Behind him in the courtyard, old Sher Dil nodded approvingly. As soon as the news of the Rajah's death had spread through the palace, the old bearer had begun to urge his master to depart as swiftly as possible, knowing that the presence of Europeans would aggravate any trouble that might arise over the succession. There was bound to be a certain amount of rumor and unrest amongst the population, and for the new Rajah to be seen openly consorting with the Feringhees his uncle had detested might even give rise to speculation that the British had had a hand in the old Rajah's death.

Andrew had been allowed to pay his respects to the body of Jahan Shah Bahadur, lying on the floor which was covered with gold coins with Kusha grass spread over them. Four vessels filled with water, sesame, and money were placed in the four corners of the room, and lamps on these water vessels as well as other large lampstands with numerous wicks illuminated the dark path his soul must tread to the Preta Loka—the world of the departed.

While he expressed his condolences to Prince Chandranaya and observed with interest the elaborate ceremony surrounding the death of a Hindu prince, Philippa and Caro were busy overseeing the packing of trunks and loading of carts ready for their dawn departure from the road to Baburpore.

"I shall be glad to shake the dust of the place from my shoes," declared Philippa, resting from her labors on the lid of a large cabin trunk. "Andrew dotes on it, of course, but I cannot feel easy here, especially since the attack on you."

Caro's feelings were more mixed. Like Andrew, she reveled in the strange, exotic atmosphere of Patelbar, where matters were still conducted in the way that had been ever since the first Aryans swept down from the north to drive the small, dark Dravidians back into the forests and jungles. Such places, she sensed, would soon be nothing but a memory, and she wanted to drink her fill of this one. She regretted that she had been deprived by the Rajah's illness of the company of Doctor Kelly. He had seemed a charming man, forty at most, and would have been the perfect companion with whom to tour the treasures. And, best of all, she could certainly have charmed him into telling her about Rowland. Still, the days of rest had given her a chance to recover from her recent fright. She had been badly scared by her second encounter with the Sikh, but she felt sure that he was now far away.

But despite her vague desire to stay longer, she recognized that Prince Chandranaya needed peace to establish his rule in Patelbar, and the presence of British visitors would not help in this respect. Perhaps one day she would return, she thought, as she waited for her turn to bid the Prince good-bye, watching the carts and pack animals that carried their possessions move slowly onto the red dusty road. As usual, the kitchen party had left before it was light, and only Sher Dil, Philippa's *ayah* and page, and the three *syce*s, waited to accompany their master and mistress.

A white-robed servant held a double-handle goblet, which he gave to the Prince as Andrew approached to shake his hand.

"A toast of friendship," he repeated, and Andrew obediently sipped the dark, herb-scented wine. He pushed forward the reluctant Philippa to take her turn with the goblet.

"Good-bye, Highness," she said hurriedly. "We have greatly enjoyed our stay. Most kind. I trust you will visit us when your travels bring you to Baburpore."

Chandranaya nodded gravely, his dark eyes watching her. Philippa stiffened: why was he staring at her like that? Had she a smut on her nose... a tear in her dress? She brushed an invisible cobweb from her face; really, the heat was intolerable. Not seven o'clock in the morning, and already she felt quite giddy with it. She swayed slightly, and caught at Caro's arm to steady herself.

"I'm sorry," she said faintly. "I feel... feel unwell. I will have to sit down a moment..." Her voice died away, and she sank to the ground. Andrew bent over her in quick concern, but he, too, was immediately overcome by wave after wave of giddiness.

"The wine," he mumbled, his voice thick and slurred. "It's poisoned. Don't touch it, Caro. That blackguard has... poisoned the wine..."

He reeled and lurched forward a few paces before collapsing, nearly pulling Sher Dil, who had sprung to his assistance, down to the ground with him.

In helpless horror, Caro looked round the hostile ring of dark faces. The next moment she was seized; her arms pinioned behind her.

"What have you done?" she cried. "You have killed them! Philippa!" She fought to free herself, to go to her sister, but her captors held her easily. "Why have you done this to us?" she sobbed. "We have done you no harm."

"Harm!" A sudden light blazed in Prince Chandranaya's flat eyes, then he laughed. "You don't know what you speak about, little English miss. No harm! When your people have defiled my land and taken away my birthright; when the Sirkar rules where once my fathers ruled, and the people know me no more. I am a prince of Hindustan, and all that is left me is this poor corner of it. Baburpore is mine, and the rich lands where the sahibs hunt pig among the sugar-cane plantations as if the whole of Hind belonged to them alone. White children play in our palaces, and on the *guddee* sits a boy who is none of our blood, chosen and placed there by the Sirkar. Feringhee spawn!" he hissed, and she shrank from the hatred in his voice. Gone was the smooth, urbane exterior, the civilized, cultivated sportsman whose company Andrew had enjoyed.

"I knew none of this. Let me go," pleaded Caro tremulously, and Chandranaya's laugh made her blood run cold.

He walked forward and stirred the prostrate form of Philippa with the long, pointed toe of his slipper, lifting her arm a few inches and letting it flop back to the stones.

"Sher Dil," called Caro. "Go to the memsahib."

But Sher Dil was himself held by a dozen hands and could do nothing but roll his eyes in despair. As their master toppled to the earth, *ayah*, page, and *syce*s had fled, taking the horses with them. She was alone and knew not whether Andrew and Philippa lived or died.

Prince Chandranaya moved closer to her and ran his hands lightly over her hair, laughing softly as she tugged at the men who held her. Seeing that her struggles were only feeding his amusement, she stood rigid and silent as his hands explored her body, making her skin crawl beneath her thin muslin dress.

"So soft," he purred, sliding his fingers into the crevice between her breasts, then cupping one in his hand. "So soft and white."

He stepped away abruptly with an exclamation of disgust. "Faugh! She smells of English lavender like every memsahib that defiles our land. Take her away and cleanse her of the smell of the Sirkar. As for the old one"—he nodded toward Sher Dil—"blind him and cut out his tongue and leave him to tend his masters!"

The last sound that Caro heard before she was dragged away by her captors was a long wail from Sher Dil as he took in this command, followed by a torrent of pleas. She twisted her head around and saw, to her surprise, that Prince Chandranaya appeared to be listening to something Sher Dil had to say.

Hot sun beating on his unprotected head roused Andrew from his stupor, and he twisted in a futile attempt to escape its fierce rays. With difficulty he opened his eyes and focused them, taking in the rough wooden planks on which he lay, among sacks of gram and bundles of dried grass. From the slow, jolting pace, he realized he was in a bullock cart, rocking across a track pitted with potholes. Bit by bit, memory came back to him, and with it a mounting sense of indignation. The scene in the courtyard—the loving cup—Prince Chandranaya's treachery. What had happened since then? Why was he bundled up among the fodder in a forage cart? Where was Philippa?

Panic struck at him and he sat up quickly, clutching his head as the change of position caused a piercing pain to shoot behind his eyes. The world swam, then slowly steadied again. Moving more cautiously he clambered to the top of the pile of sacks that formed a sort of well about him, and looked out at the driver.

"Sher Dil!" he croaked, recognizing with relief mixed with astonishment the bent back and snowy hair escaping beneath the turban of his bearer. "Where are we? Why am I at the bottom of this confounded cart? Where is the memsahib?"

The old man looked around, and when he saw his master peering down on him from the top of the load, he pulled up his oxen and climbed up beside Andrew.

"Sahib, stay hidden; here are very bad mens. The memsahib is safe; she is behind in next cart. I tell you there is much danger is Patelbar."

"And the\ miss-sahiba, Lady Caroline?"

A shutter seemed to fall over Sher Dil's face, hiding all expression. He had bargained long and hard for the lives of his masters, and willingly traded their safety for

Miss-sahiba Caroline. He was not going to have his efforts to save Andrew and Philippa put in jeopardy by any attempt to rescue the miss-sahiba.

"Lady Caroline is dead," he said firmly. "You cannot help her sahib. When she would not drink the wine, the Prince of Patelbar was angry and his servants struck her down with swords. Alas, I saw her die. When the Prince saw what they had done, he told me to get out of his sight forever. So I hid you in the cart and drove away at all speed."

"You saw her die," said Andrew slowly. His splitting head could hardly take in the catastrophe. "But why? Why should he kill little Caro? Why try to poison us?"

Sher Dil was not prepared to answer any more questions. "You must hide until we leave Patelbar, sahib," he insisted. "Tonight we shall reach the great road and be safe."

By then, he thought, he would have perfected his description of the miss-sahiba's last moments, and would add to it such a wealth of detail that the sahib would believe every word he said, and count himself lucky to have escaped from Patelbar with the loss of only a single life.

Chapter Seven

THROUGH THE MISTS of grief and shock that threatened to overwhelm her as she was dragged away from the courtyard by the Prince's guards in their distinctive green-and-gold turbans, leaving her sister and brother-in-law lying in the dust with dogs creeping up to sniff at their clothes, one corner of Caro's brain took note of where they went.

Somehow, sometime, she would escape, and then she would need to know her way to the outside world again.

They passed through a side gate in the wall of the outer palace and crossed a garden bright with flowers and fountains. A high wall confronted them, its only portal guarded by more of the Prince's followers who, after a word from Caro's escort, swung open the heavy iron gate and let them through. Within lay another smaller courtyard, paved with azure and jade tiles, and windows above the pillar cloisters were latticed with grilles of fretted ivory.

Another greeting to the slippered graybeard who guarded the entrance and they entered a long, winding corridor, dimly lit with tiny lamps, the oil from which gave off a heavy scent of roses. The dull red walls gleamed softly and all about them, unseen, were the patter of soft feet and rustle of silks and muslins.

At the third portal Caro's guards halted, and her spirits sank lower. Could she ever escape from such a labyrinth? Walls within walls, gates within gates; she had never imagined such a complexity of barriers to guard the Royal ladies from unauthorized eyes. For that, she realized, was where they were taking her. They were drawing ever nearer to an entirely feminine world where no man except the Rajah and the palace eunuchs who served the Ranees was ever permitted to pass.

Even the guards who escorted her must stop at the third portal, and hand her over to the slim, gray-haired lady in a sari of violet silk with a deep gold border sewn with pearls, who met them there.

For all her grief and bewilderment, curiosity was beginning to stir in Caro again, and she went with her guide willingly enough, glad to be free of the guards' remorseless grip on her muslin-covered arms. As she looked about her in wonder, she found it hard to believe that she had not stumbled into a dream.

Even the *deorhi*—the gracefully arched doorway—that led to the innermost courtyard was of marble, inlaid with red and green stones in an intricate, winding pattern of long-stemmed flowers and jewel-bright birds. Beyond it, like the pearl gleaming in the secret recesses of an oyster, the marble colonnade with blue mosaic pillars rising from a snowy white floor presented a spectacle so dazzling that Caro involuntarily shielded her eyes.

She had no time, though, to stand and stare. Like a flock of brilliantly colored birds of paradise the ladies of the *zenana* crowded round her, stroking her hair and face with little, fluttering hands, laughing and chattering shrilly as they examined her clothes from the pearls in her ears to the shoes on her feet.

Most of them wore jewels to make even the Portland sapphires appear trifling by comparison. Pigeon-blood rubies and square-cut emeralds swung around their slender necks, while their high-piled black hair was wreathed in ropes of pearls. Beside their delicately perfumed loveliness Caro felt as dowdy and unkempt as a bedraggled sparrow that had hopped into a cage of exotic finches.

A sudden hush fell on the chattering crowd that surrounded her, and Caro became aware of a new figure, a man so fat that his smooth face appeared completely round, dressed in a flowing gown of yellow silk and matching turban. His tiny eyes, creased in rolls of puffy flesh, surveyed her coldly, and she felt a chill run up her spine. This, then, must be the Nazir, the keeper of the Rajah's women, old in evil, skilled in intrigue—a castrated male who compensated for his lack of virility by the use of other powers. That he was feared as well as respected by the ladies he guarded was evident from their confused silence under his gaze. His small, wicked eyes reminded Caro of a tusker contemplating mischief, as they rested first on one flowerlike face and then another before he turned his attention back to Caro.

He spoke in English, and the thin, high-pitched timbre of his voice was as shocking as his physique.

"You make clean. Dance for Rajah tonight."

He stretched out a puffy hand from the hanging silk sleeve, and though she flinched away he gripped her firmly, dragging her after him down a passage to a bathhouse patterned from floor to ceiling in blue mosaic, where two shaven-headed assistants, bare to the waist, began to strip Caro of her clothes...

She opened her eyes hours later to find Prince Chandranaya looking down on her, a smile curving his full mouth.

"You sleep well, English miss? You enjoy Rajah's hos-pit-al-it-ee!" he mocked, mimicking Philippa's words of farewell with cruel delight. "'We are so grateful for your hos-pit-al-it-ee.' Bah! No more of sahibs with red faces and memsahibs in clean white dresses.

They are gone—blown away by the wind that begins to
sweep through the land of Hind, bringing back the
ancient glories, making my people clean again. *All will
become Red!*"

"Gone?" she faltered, uncertain of his meaning but
realizing from the note of suppressed triumph in his
voice that the devilment that had led him to launch this
attack against his guests had been more than a passing
madness. It had been calculated: carefully planned and
timed to coincide with the moment that he assumed the
reins of power in his adopted princedom. What had he
said about Baburpore belonging to him by right? Caro
shook her head, still heavy with the drugged drink she
had been forced to swallow after the eunuchs had
dressed and painted her to their satisfaction.

"Where have they gone?" she repeated. "You mean
they are dead?" A sob choked her throat. They *could*
not be dead—not gentle, brown-eyed Philippa, and
Andrew with his bluff, hearty kindness.

"Dead for you." His keen eyes took in every detail of
her costume. He leaned down and deftly twitched a
lock of hair forward across her bosom.

Swiftly she struck at his hand—only to find her own
as quickly imprisoned.

"No, no: you have much to learn. Indian ladies are
for their lord's pleasure. They must be gentle and obey;
and never, never seek to harm their lord."

Caro's eyes flashed. "I am English, and you are *not*
my lord! I would never obey you."

Chandranaya laughed delightedly, languidly stroking her hair, suddenly grasping it so tightly that her
head jerked back. "Not I, little viper. You are destined
for one higher than me. The Presence seeks English fire
that he can quench: English spirit he can break to his
will. What he has suffered at the hands of the Sirkar
will be forgotten when he holds you in his arms and
sees you dance to his bidding. When first his servants

brought word of their clumsy attempts to capture you, I told him to wait in patience, for I would lime the twig and set the snare. I did so—and *lo!* the bird is taken."

Unwillingly Caro realized what had happened. He had deliberately lured her to Patelbar; baited the lure with sport for Andrew, rest and recovery for Philippa. All his friendliness and good fellowship had been a mask assumed to lull his guests into false security. But who was this Presence who desired an English captive on which to wreak his spite? Caro shivered. The words stirred a memory she would rather have forgotten. The burly Sikh, too, had spoken of "Huzoor"—the Presence. And he had been part of the Rajah of Bithoor's retinue. Was it the Nana Sahib himself who sought to add her to his household? After Chandran-aya left her, that conviction grew, and she waited in an agony of fear, remembering the heavy-lidded eyes that had followed her every movement at that first banquet in Patelbar, the soft, slurred voice that seemed to hint of obscene pleasures, the fat hands with their pointed fingers absently stroking the shoulder of a *nautch* girl as he conversed with Andrew about the day's sport.

Caro's knees shook and her palms felt clammy despite the afternoon heat. She crouched back into the heap of barrel-shape cushions like a small captive animal, dreading the fall of night.

Hot, tired, dusty, and inexpressibly saddened by the loss of his pretty sister-in-law, Andrew Thynne's spirits nonetheless lifted a little as he saw the familiar outline of the Baburpore quarters take wavering shape in the heat-haze. It was nearly eleven o'clock, and they had been traveling since dawn, having caught up with their own advance party the previous night on the outskirts of Patelbar.

He touched his wife's hand. "Cheer up, Phil," he said softly. "We're there."

Philippa's eyelids were still red and swollen from a storm of weeping. "But Caro—" she said in a choked voice.

Andrew's hand tightened on hers. "Tiger Elliott will see she is avenged," he promised with a confidence he was far from feeling. "As soon as he hears our story he'll send a strong force to smoke that two-faced villain Chandranaya from his lair and teach him a lesson he'll not forget. I blame myself, utterly. If only I'd listened to you—" He broke off. "Hallo, what's this?"

A small party of horsemen were galloping toward them, bent low over their saddles. The dust kicked up by the galloping hoofs completely obscured the riders' faces, and it was not until they pulled up and surrounded the Thynnes' hackerie that Andrew recognized young Henry Forbes at the head of half a dozen native cavalrymen.

"Hallo, Henry," he said, summoning a smile. "Is this the kind of welcome you give travelers nowadays?"

The young man saluted. "Sorry, sir. We took you for the mail *dak*. Your servant, Lady Philippa."

"And why should the mail *dak* cause such burning interest? Are you waiting for a letter from your latest conquest?"

Henry Forbes's large blue eyes bulged slightly, and his troopers shifted uneasily in their saddles. "You mean to say you don't know, sir? You haven't heard the news?"

"Don't talk in riddles, man!" Andrew's throat ached from the dust. "I've been traveling close on a month. What is this great news I'm supposed to have heard?"

Henry edged his horse close to the hackerie and said quietly, "Bad news, I'm afraid, sir. It's mutiny. The sepoys at Meerut killed their officers outside the church on May the tenth, and now Delhi itself has fallen. The mutineers have proclaimed old Bahadur

Shah Emperor of Delhi and the last we heard from Cawnpore was that General Wheeler is boxed up tight in the Lal Koorti Ka hospital—the old Dragoon hospital—with provisions for twenty-five days."

"May the tenth!" Andrew was dumbfounded. He looked around quickly but Philippa was still sunk in her private grief; she had heard nothing. "God's bones, man; that's over three weeks ago! Why haven't they brought up troops from Calcutta to set things right? What's the Governor-General doing?"

"That's all we've heard, sir," repeated Forbes stolidly. "General Lawrence is besieged at Lucknow and General Wheeler at Cawnpore. Troops are being mobilized but they can't reach us before July..."

"Reach us?" This time Andrew had difficulty in keeping his voice low. "You can't believe our men capable of mutiny? It's inconceivable."

"That's what I say," agreed Forbes. "Utterly inconceivable. Although some sources swear Baburpore is in imminent danger. But our General Elliott's taking no chances, though it's my belief he'll do more harm than good by listening to Captain Steel and disarming the native infantry here..."

"My men?" exclaimed Andrew indignantly. "Well, if that don't beat all. You say Steel recommends it? I suppose his sowars are above suspicion! I'd have thought Steel would be the last man to panic, but—"

"Panic?" asked Philippa, catching a word at last. "What cause is there for panic?" Her face paled another shade as she saw Forbes's solemn expression. "Why are we waiting here? Is something wrong?"

Neither of the men answered her, but as Andrew shouted to the driver to move on, he saw his hopes of a punitive expedition against Patelbar disappear as completely as the mirage of a lake on the dusty road behind them.

"Well, cousin?" said the Nana Sahib. He belched gently and sought between his teeth for an elusive strand of chicken. "You wanted me?"

Prince Chandranaya smiled mysteriously and held up a hand. From the floor in front of the *guddee*, tom-toms began to throb. The Nana Sahib shrugged and sighed. He would hear nothing until Chandranaya's accursed musicians had finished playing. Really, it was too bad; to be dragged all the way back to Patelbar with an urgent summons and then him—the Rajah of Bithoor—to be made to listen to inferior musicians for an hour before having the reason for his visit explained to him. Did the Prince not know that Cawnpore was besieged not forty miles to the south, and the sepoy mutineers had begged him to lead them? Once they had triumphed over the flimsy defenses of the Lal Koorti Ka hospital, they would sweep on in victorious unison to Lucknow, the capital of Oudh, mopping up such minor nests of Feringhees as Baburpore and Shahgani on the way. Who could resist them?

He glanced sideways at Chandranaya, but the other sat apparently wrapped in the music, swaying gently, his eyes fixed on the undulating half-naked forms of the *nautch* girls, with their sooty eyes and garishly painted lips.

The Rajah of Bithoor contained his impatience with an effort. It would not do to antagonize Prince Chandranaya at this delicate stage of affairs. By and large, the chiefs and princes he had approached had been disappointingly unenthusiastic about Nana Sahib's dream of a new Mahratta empire. One and all had thanked him for his offer of power and riches but had preferred to honor their treaties of friendship with the British. Only the dispossessed, like Chandranaya of Baburpore, and habitual malcontents like Tantia Topee showed any eagerness to throw in their lot with the rebellious sepoys under the grand leadership of Nana Sahib. Chandranaya had promised twenty thousand men, so perhaps it was worth listening to a little music, though it was neither as loud nor as lively as he was accustomed to.

Nor were the girls such skilled dancers. Nana Sahib reckoned himself a connoisseur of *nautch*, but he would not have paid these performers to entertain his guests. The girl in the middle did not even appear to be properly trained. She was waving her arms in vague imitation of the others, but no one could have called her movements graceful or correct.

A fair-skinned girl—possibly a Pathan—and a pretty little thing, now he came to look at her carefully. But there was something odd about her...

"My dancer!" exclaimed the Rajah of Bithoor, setting down his goblet with such a crash that the delicate crystal shattered.

Prince Chandranaya's lips curved upward in a smile.

Caro heard the crash of glass and knew she was discovered. It was a dreadful moment. For the past half hour she had been trying to convince herself that this monotonous waving of arms and gyration of the trunk was all her captors required of her. If the gossip of Philippa and her friends were true, she knew that Indians had strange, often perverted tastes in erotic pleasure, and that lovemaking as Europeans understood it was scorned by Orientals as lacking in subtlety.

But even as she sought to persuade herself that the Rajah of Bithoor enjoyed the spectacle of a gently nurtured English girl degrading herself by dancing at his command even more than he would enjoy the physical act of ravishing her, one glance at the heavy, coarse features and slack lips beneath the drooping mustache told her that he intended the second pleasure to follow the first.

All too soon he raised a hand and beckoned her to kneel before him. She approached, trembling, acutely aware of the sweat running down between her breasts, which molded the filmy bodice against her nipples, the heavy rows of bangles about her ankles that threatened to trip her at every step, and worst of all the voluminous gauze skirt slashed in panels to give tantalizing glimpses of pale thighs as she moved. Her face felt stiff from the unaccustomed paint, while the diamond pendant bound tight to her forehead felt as hot and heavy as a branding iron.

She bowed her head to hide the fiery blush that rose to her cheeks as she felt the fat, ring-loaded hand squeeze and knead the flesh of her upper arm. A violent shivering shook her from head to foot, but the hand held her firmly.

"She is not defiled?" asked the Rajah of Bithoor, turning to his host with a slow, satisfied smile. He had long craved to run his fingers over the white skin of a memsahib while she trembled before him, to look on her nakedness and see the proud, complacent smile of the race he hated turn into a grimace of terror.

Prince Chandranaya frowned. The creature's virginity was a matter he had failed to verify. "She is young, cousin, and carefully reared in the manner of English ladies," he temporized. "Assuredly you need not fear that she has been defiled."

Seated on a cushion on the step below his master, Azimullah Khan had been following the conversation with keen interest. Now he spoke, framing his words to draw attention to this travels and knowledge of the world beyond the forbidden Black Water. "It is true, O, Prince, that English ladies are carefully reared and guarded from the sight of men when they live in the land of Hind. But in England it is another matter. There boys and girls are allowed to swim naked together in the lakes and rivers, and ride horses about the countryside without attendants." He leaned forward importantly. "I have seen unmarried girls visit men alone, and it is common for married women to take lovers. This I know."

The smile faded from Nana Sahib's face and his hand ceased its circular stroking movement. "Then she must be examined," he said firmly.

Chandranaya clapped his hands and gave an order. Wondering but thankful, Caro felt herself hustled away.

Fionn Kelly had been confined to his own apartments since the death of the old Rajah, with a silent guard outside his bedroom door, and knew nothing of Chandranaya's treachery toward his guests. Philosophically he accepted his loss of liberty, but he was conscious of a grim amusement. Despite the death of his old protector, he was still called by the honorific title, doctor-sahib. Doctor-sahib could still be a power in the state of Patelbar—perhaps even complete the building of the hospital he needed so badly—if he played his cards right. But these first weeks of the new reign were bound to be full of pitfalls. He must walk warily, arousing no suspicions, giving no offense— make himself as indispensable to the new regime as he had been to the old. And if that milky blue spot in the Prince's left eye were to worsen . . . Until that occasion arose, Fionn was happy enough to lose himself in the many books that lined the walls of his room, to sit in his small courtyard with its tinkling fountain and chisel delicate tracery in the fur of an ivory tiger he was carving, to smoke his opium pipe and dream old dreams until he fell into a deeply peaceful slumber, to sleep the clock around as he made up the rest he had lost while tending Jahan Bahadur.

He had just been drifting off into a heavy opium sleep when the Prince's messenger roused him with the news that his services were needed at once.

"Tell him it'll keep till morning," he growled fuzzily at the messenger, and picked up a slipper to throw as the man stood hesitating by his charpoy.

"No, no, doctor-sahib!" gabbled the miserable envoy. "You must come at once. The Prince commands."

"Oh, very well." Resignedly, Fionn forced himself alert, rose and gathered up the bag that held the tools of his trade. "What's the trouble this time?"

But the messenger either could not or would not tell him. Through the courtyards they hurried, with the heavy doors of the guarded portals swinging open instantly on hearing that they were about the Prince's business. "One of the Ranees ill," diagnosed Fionn as they came to the third *deorhi* and he was obliged to wait while a blindfold was tied over his eyes. "Hope it's not an outbreak of cholera. It's about the time of year for it." By tensing his jaw and raising his eyebrows during this operation, he had learned from years of experience he could cause the blindfold to slip a fraction and leave him a limited vision down the side of his high-bridged nose.

He had, however, no intention of giving away the trick, which had helped him diagnose many an illness that baffled more effectively blindfolded physicians, so he staggered and leaned heavily on the arm of his guide as they passed the last door and entered the ladies' apartments.

As usual, he was led to the silk-screened cubicle through which he was to make a pretense of "examining" his patient, without either seeing or speaking to her, but when the fat Nazir explained the Prince's wishes, Fionn laughed aloud.

"Faith, you never had a Christian awakened from his night's sleep to tell you that!" he exclaimed, torn between anger and amusement. "It's a wet-nurse or a marriage broker His Highness is wanting more than a physician. Just give me a look at the wench and I'll soon tell you if she's a virgin or not. If she's plain she may be, but if she's a handsome piece, His Highness had better resign himself to the fact that he won't be the first." He began to pull at the knot of the blindfold, but the Nazir restrained him.

"That will not be possible, doctor-sahib," he said with a disapproving cough. "The Prince cannot permit you to look on the lady. She is a gift to the Nana Sahib, Rajah of Bithoor, from His Highness."

"Lot of damned nonsense," grumbled Fionn, but he knelt down and inserted his hands through the slit cut in the screen for this purpose. His fingers touched warm, soft skin, and with the skill born of long practice he quickly discovered the answer to the Nazir's question. What to tell him, though, remained a problem. With his face carefully blank of expression, his hands still out of sight behind the screen, Fionn considered.

If he were to give this poor girl a clean bill of health, he would condemn her to spend the best years of her youth satisfying the perverted sexual whims of that sadistic monster, the Rajah of Bithoor. If, on the other hand, he declared her to be no virgin, what would be her fate? Would she be cast out of the palace, returned to her parents in disgrace? Would she end up as an outcast, a public woman? And when she grew too old to sell herself, what then?

As he was debating with his conscience, Fionn felt his arm gripped hard by the hand of the girl behind the screen. With difficulty he smothered a smile. The old Rajah had been impotent for years, and frustrated ladies were inclined to take every chance they could of feigning illness simply for the pleasure of being visited and examined by a doctor—the only man allowed to touch their bodies, albeit through a screen. But wait;

this wasn't a frustrated Ranee. This was a girl, a genuine virgin, as he had just ascertained. If she felt as anxious as that for a man's hand on her skin, perhaps he would be doing her no favor by saving her from the Rajah of Bithoor. Perhaps she was longing to become a Royal concubine, and this was her way of telling him so. Fionn waited for the gentle pressure on his fingers, the soft giggle that would tell him that his patient was enjoying the situation, but the only sound from behind the screen was a rather muffled breathing.

The pressure on his arm grew stronger and he tried unsuccessfully to disengage it. Something was digging into the thin skin of the inside of his forearm— something sharp and pointed. The smile faded from his face: the little vixen was scratching him.

"Hell's teeth!" he exclaimed, jerking his hands back through the slit in the screen. Her nails were as sharp as claws; she had almost drawn blood.

"Well, doctor-sahib?" said the Nazir. He was suspicious as a cat, sensing that Fionn had taken too long over a simple examination, scenting some communication between him and the girl. Automatically Fionn began to wash his hands in the rose-scented water brought him by an old serving maid. The scratches the little hellcat had gouged in his skin stung sharply, reminding him of his immediate problem. How should he answer the old eunuch? Send the girl home, or sentence her to a life of vicious luxury? He rubbed absently at his arm, squinting down his nose beneath the blindfold but unable to get a clear view of the damage. She had held his arm with one little hand, while the other had inflicted these deep, deliberate scratches, almost as if she were drawing on his skin. He must make haste to disinfect the wounds—heaven only knew what filth might be in her nails.

Fionn felt very tired all at once. His doctor's instincts urged him to protect the girl behind the screen, but the rules that governed his secret life commanded otherwise. If he declared her no virgin, he would disappoint the Prince, thereby jeopardizing his own vital position at Court—and that, above all, must never happen.

"She is a virgin," he admitted heavily.

The Nazir relaxed and became expansive at the excellent news. He offered betel nut from a silver box, which Fionn declined, and then presented the doctor with a handsome cabochon emerald—a turban jewel—as a mark of favor from Prince Chandranaya. Fionn strolled back through the two inner courtyards feeling satisfied, at least, that he had made a promising start with his new master. At the second gate he was divested of his blindfold, and had the opportunity to admire the emerald as he made his way back to his own apartments. The guard was still at his door, but he was confident that a request for greater liberty tomorrow would be granted, and from there he would ease himself back into the position of trust he had held under the old Rajah.

Perhaps Prince Chandranaya, now that he held the reins of power, could be encouraged to turn over a new leaf and seek to improve the lot of his people, though the less he saw of his old crony, the Rajah of Bithoor the better, thought Fionn, peering by the light of an oil lamp at his scratched arm as he dabbed it with disinfectant.

Deep red lines showed on the skin—some straight, some curved, some crossing others. A pattern? No, he thought, and his heart began a slow, heavy pounding:—not a pattern, letters. The girl had scratched letters on his arm—large, wobbly Roman capitals. But no Indian girl could read or write the characters of her own language, let alone Roman letters. There was a C, no mistaking that deeply gouged crescent; followed by something that could be an H, or an A with the apex badly joined; then came a P. No, not a P—he could see a small leg drawn to join the loop. An R. C—A—R, and the last letter was clearly an O, scratched with desperate haste as he tried to drag his arm away. C-A-R-O...

The truth burst on him then, but his brain refused to accept it. Andrew Thynne, the bluff, hearty English officer Fionn had disliked at first sight, had left Patelbar two days ago, just after the Rajah's death, taking with him his sickly wife and his enchanting sister-in-law. By no stretch of the imagination could Fionn visualize Andrew Thynne leaving *without* Lady Caroline; handing her over to the care of eunuchs in the Royal apartments. That would be beyond belief, behavior unimaginable for a British officer no matter how thick he had become with an Indian prince. Yet those letters...

Then a new thought struck him. What if Andrew and his party had been attacked, Thynne and his wife killed, perhaps, and Lady Caroline brought back alone? The more he thought about it, the more possible—even probable—it seemed. He remembered the way Nana Sahib's eyes had followed the girl throughout that first banquet, before old Jahan Shah Bahadur took to his bed, and visualized again the heaps of food left untasted by the scoundrel as his gaze devoured Lady Caroline. If ever he'd seen lust on a man's face, it had been written then on those heavy features; and he, Fionn, like a fool, had joked about it with the girl herself.

He must save her. In his heart he was sure of what his brain still rejected: that Lady Caroline—lovely little Caro, whose soft dark eyes and slender arms had reminded him of the adored wife he lost so long ago— was in the clutches of those devils. He ran to the door and pulled it open, but the guard outside pointed his sword menacingly at the doctor's throat when Fionn tried to cross the threshold. Back, he gestured. The Prince has no further need of you tonight.

Slowly Fionn closed the door and sat down on the charpoy, staring unseeingly at the flickering oil lamp; A moth was dancing around the flame, its delicate wings drawing it irresistibly to the tempting, destructive light. As the flame destroyed the moth, the Rajah of Bithoor would destroy Caro, and she would have no more idea than the moth had why she had been chosen to endure this pain; why she must pay for all the real and imagined grievances the Rajah nursed against the British.

Abruptly Fionn stretched out his cupped hands and captured the moth. Its furry body fluttered against his palms as he carried it to the window and released it, before dousing the light and stretching himself on the string cot. He could not help Caro now, but tomorrow he would devise a plan to see her unless—a sudden chill struck him—unless she was spirited away before daylight in the Rajah's train. Fionn groaned and with a sudden gesture flung the emerald Chandranaya had given him into the furthest corner of the room. The wages of sin, he thought bitterly. They had duped and tricked him, and then contemptuously tossed him this bauble: he could never bear to touch it again, knowing that he, who had hesitated to give even an unknown Indian concubine into the arms of that monster, had himself condemned Lady Caroline March to that horrible fate.

Like a bloated spider gloating over the delicate creature trapped in his web, the Nana Sahib, Rajah of Bithoor, stared down at Lady Caroline March as she lay spread-eagled on a great bed heaped high with cushions. The brightly colored silken cords that bound her wrists trailed to the bed legs, around which they were firmly knotted. And though Caro still wore the voluminous gauze skirt of a *nautch* dancer, her bodice had been ripped brutally from her shoulders, leaving her naked to the waist.

Gingerly the Rajah stretched out a pudgy hand to caress her breast. Caro's teeth clenched and eyes closed; she shuddered but made no sound. She had given up all hope of rescue at the instant when Fionn Kelly's arm, on which she was trying to trace the letters of her name in a desperate effort to communicate, was pulled roughly from her grasp. With anguish, she heard his voice, its Irish brogue distinguishable even though he spoke a language she could only barely follow, grow gradually fainter as he was escorted out of the ladies' apartments. There had been no further hope of salvation.

Too late the muslin scarf wound tight across her mouth for the examination had been removed, only to be replaced by the cords that now restrained her limbs and a creamy rose-scented substance had been applied to her inner thighs and up into her body. She was a sacrifice to the Rajah's vile desire, and could do nothing to save herself or her pride, nothing except deny him the satisfaction of her tormented response. She would fight back, as she had never fought, but later, not while the hands of Nana Sahib violated her body.

The Rajah was growing bolder, biting her nipples till she thought they would bleed, poking and pummeling her body in a ghastly pantomime of desire so painful that she could barely restrain her screams. But she refused to cry out or struggle vainly to force him away.

You will not scream. You will not struggle, she recited over and over. You will not close your eyes. You will detach you mind from what is being done to you, but you will watch and remember every moment, for when all this is ended, you will savor the memory of pain and humiliation as you take your revenge.

"A body made for love," gloated the Nana Sahib. He turned to Prince Chandranaya, who was observing the proceedings with a faint, supercilious smile on his thin lips.

"My trusted cousin," continued the Nana Sahib. "Your gift of this woman moved me deeply at the time, but now, seeing her like this, I realize there is no sufficient way to express my gratitude. She is the apogee of female perfection of which the Kamasutra speaks: A face as pleasing as the full moon; her body soft, her skin tender and fair as the yellow lotus, eyes bright as the orbs of a fawn; she possesses a firm, high bosom, the neck of a peacock, a straight nose, and a love place which resembles nothing so much as a lotus bud. She is a goddess."

Chandranaya laughed, "Ah, but, cousin, the Kamasutra speaks also of that soft body as well padded with flesh and with a bosom full as the moon. This one has a waist like a needle, the hips of a youth, and the breasts of a child. I am infinitely joyed that this little English nightingale has so delighted my cousin, but for myself, I cannot see the fascination of these pale English boy-women."

"Ah, yes," exclaimed the Nana Sahib, his gaze never leaving the unmoving, open-eyed treasure on the bed. "A proud memsahib. See how she lies there silent, defiant, clinging uselessly to her pride. Before I have done with her, she will scream for mercy—the first of all of them to scream and beg on their knees—when the Red Wind blows through Hind."

"Enough of this." Prince Chandranaya yawned, but Nana Sahib laid a hand on his arm to detain him. "Do you think," he suggested, "we could allow her a little more freedom of movement? I want her to kneel before me but, bound as she is, she cannot do all I require."

Chandranaya considered, then shook his head

firmly. "I do not advise it. Wait until you have had your will of her, and taught her to obey you. Her English pride will not be broken until she calls you Master, and until then she may be dangerous, like the snake that lies quiet in the dust the better to strike your heel."

He bowed with joined palms and padded softly from the chamber.

The Rajah unwound his turban, and with slow, deliberate movements pulled at the fastenings of his pantaloons, exposing his desire. Involuntarily, terror blinding her will, Caro strained against her bonds, trying desperately to shield herself with her hands. A small whimper escaped her as his fingers probed between her legs, and up into her at the sensitive flesh. Now the Rajah's slack mouth twisted into a smile. This was his triumph. This was what he wanted to hear—the proud memsahib crying and pleading for mercy. Savagely he forced her legs apart.

Caro gasped with pain and tears of fury filled her eyes, but though his hands were digging into her flesh with ever-increasing brutality she made no further sound. The Rajah drew back, baffled and angry. What was wrong with her? Why did she deny him the ultimate pleasure of watching her writhe? She lay as limp and passive as a dying flower, her face betraying revulsion but not the terror he craved. The haughty memsahib was arrogant and that English arrogance must be broken, broken with brutality.

Biting her lips till she could taste her own blood, she let him thrust into her. Although the perfumed ointment helped ease the pain of entry, Caro thought of nothing but revenge, of debasing the Rajah as he was joyfully debasing her. And then suddenly came the agony, shooting up her loins to spread throughout her body. It was an agony comprised of hideous wrenching and the knowledge of irreparable loss, and although she somehow knew she would never feel this torture again, the memory would haunt her always. He pounded into her, sensing her pain and reveling in it, digging his fingers deep into her breast, spearing her with rapid, powerful lunges until he moaned and immediately withdrew.

Angrily he fumbled with the cords that bound her to the bed, jerking the knots undone and freeing Caro's hands and then her feet.

"Kneel," he commanded her, dragging her bleeding off the couch. Caro collapsed in a heap at his feet, with life returning painfully back through her numbed limbs.

The Rajah seized a handful of her long, thick hair, pulling her head back with spiteful force, and at this last small pinprick of discomfort, something exploded inside Caro. Suddenly she ceased to care if they tortured or killed her, and a new strength surged into her. Like a baited wildcat that turns on its tormentors, she sprang at the Rajah with a scream of fury, her nails raking for his eyes, and a single thought in her mind: to hurt him as much as she possibly could. She missed his eyes, but four parallel trails of blood coursed down the Rajah's heavy jowls, and as he stumbled backward with a bleat of alarm, fumbling in his sash for the dagger he'd never dreamed of using, Caro snatched up a brass *lotah* that stood in a corner and flung it at her assailant's head, striking him on the temple.

The room was suddenly, totally quiet. Caro held her breath, backing slowly away from the fallen figure of her enemy, staring as if hypnotized at the slackly open mouth, the jumbled necklaces and pendants heaped in a glittering tangle on the great mound of stomach, to which the short fat legs seemed ridiculous appendages. The seconds stretched out. Still he did not move. Caro breathed again, and a wild elation swept over her. He was dead! She had killed him. A few moments ago he had debased her—and now he had paid for it. She forgot her nakedness, her bruised and violated body, and every childhood precept that had predisposed her against physical violence. She forgot that an English gentlewoman should never, never raise her hand in anger against another human being, and that murder—even in self-defense—was a mortal sin. All she could feel was an unreasoning exhilaration, different from any emotion she had ever experienced. Her knees shook and her pulses hammered, but her heart was singing in triumph.

Gradually her senses returned, and with it fear for the consequences of her action. She snatched up the bodice and skirt so recently torn from her, and dressed as fast as her trembling hands would allow, wiping the blood from her thigh with one of the silken scarves. A glance through the lattice showed a sixty-foot drop to the marble-floor courtyard, but beneath the arched window of this room there was a narrow ledge, perhaps eighteen inches wide, which jutted out sufficiently to give shade to the room below.

Without considering the danger, Caro slipped through the window and sidled onto the ledge. After the cool interior, the sun struck hot on her head and shoulders as she began to move carefully sideways, praying that the red sandstone would not crumble beneath her weight. Vertigo was the main peril, she knew. The ledge she stood on was quite wide enough to support her as long as she did not panic, did not look down.

Palms clammy with sweat, mouth growing ever drier, she shuffled sideways, her eyes fixed at roof level, and her outstretched arms feeling along the wall for the next window. The temptation to glance at the ground was almost overwhelming, but she resisted it grimly, concentrating on a steady rhythm of movement: feel with left foot, place weight on left foot, move right to join left foot, feel along wall with left hand—*don't look down*...

Her left hand felt empty space behind her: she had reached the next window. At the same time her left foot, ready to make its next step sideways, hovered in empty air. Slowly, stiffly, she turned her head and twisted her gaze downward until she could see her left foot—and the gap in the ledge over which it was poised. It was a small gap, no more than six inches before the ledge began again, but she would have to step across it before she could reach the window. The panic that she had been keeping so firmly in check threatened to engulf her, and she stood transfixed against the sunny wall. unable to move either hand or foot.

She had no idea how long she stood there, fighting the waves of vertigo that tried to make her sway forward until she lost her balance and plummeted to the marble floor far below, but it seemed an eternity. "Give up," a treacherous voice in her brain insisted. "Let yourself go. A second or two of conscious fear while you drop—then oblivion. No more struggle; let yourself go..." She swayed dizzily and tried to move, but her limbs refused to obey. She was set fast, as if crippled by sudden cramp, and her brain had lost the power to direct her muscles.

A scream from far below broke the spell; someone had seen her braced against the red wall and raised the alarm. The shock of discovery brought Caro back to her senses. She raised her left foot without difficulty and stepped delicately over the yawning gap in the ledge. Two more shuffling paces and she was level with the window embrasure. Hitching up her skirt, she swung a leg over the sill and stepped into darkness and safety.

But the hunt was up: she could have no doubt about

that. The quiet of the old building, honeycombed with rooms and passages, suddenly erupted into activity, like a beehive when the top covering is lifted.

She opened the door, peered out, and began to run down the dark passage hung with silken tapestries that brushed softly against her arms as she fled. Down steps, around corners, the passage twisted and turned until she lost her bearings entirely. Breathing hard, she stopped to listen for footsteps, but all she could hear was the drumming of blood in her own ears. She rounded another corner and sunlight beckoned at the end of the passage. She gazed longingly at the courtyard, bright with mosaic and colored birds, fountains and flowers, where two or three ladies in gold-spangled saris trailed idle fingers in the carved marble basin of water. They looked so sweet and gentle that for a wild moment she considered asking their help and stood there, irresolute.

Then a heavy hand fell on her shoulder and her heart gave a sickening lurch of fear. Her panic-stricken flight was over.

Nana Sahib had lost his immediate appetite for his English dancer, but his spite against the whey-faced Feringhees had increased fifty-fold since Caro struck him down. The violet ointment with which Prince Chandranaya's physician had anointed his wounds gave him a terrifying aspect as he consulted with his cousin on how best to punish the white girl.

"Put her in the cage with my tigers," suggested Chandranaya wearily. "Or see how she dances tied to an elephant's foot."

Nana Sahib shook his head. "Death is too good for her. I want to hear her scream—not one day but many days. A scream that continues for years; how may we contrive this?" He frowned in concentration; it had been a long and unsatisfactory night. His temple ached, and the long weals raised by Caro's nails would mark him for life. "She had scorned to dance for a prince and yield to a rajah; we will make her lie with the vilest of men in the temple of love..."

Chandranaya's face cleared. Here was an easy solution to his problem. It would make a new attraction in the Joyhouse of Kali to have an English *devadasi*, and demonstrate to any doubters among his people that the British had lost their grip on India. The English girl who had caused him so much trouble and grievously wounded his honored guest would get her just deserts, and he could make political capital out of her debasement.

"Excellent!" he agreed. "We will send her to the Joyhouse of Kali, and there she will serve any man who pays a few *paise* to the black goddess." He clapped his hands and gave an order. "Take the white girl to the temple and leave her there as a present to Bulbul."

Chapter Eight

THE JOYHOUSE OF Kali was no ordinary brothel, nor was its presiding angel, Bulbul, any ordinary courtesan, as Caro was soon to discover.

Although long years of good living had allowed cushions of fat to creep around her frame, Bulbul had at one time been a dancer, slim and pliable as a reed, and possessed of a voice which as her name indicated, had rivaled the nightingale's. It had attracted many men from many races and faiths, but none so powerfully or for as long as Lieutenant Jimmy—later to become General Sir James Steel—terror of the North-West Frontier and the Punjab, lover of many women and father—among dozens of semiacknowledged children born to his native loves—of Captain Rowland Steel.

Promotion came slowly in the Army of Bengal where Jimmy Steel started his military career, and he had been forty-five years old and still a captain before he felt his finances secure enough, and the need for a legitimate son urgent enough, to embark on the tiresome and costly business of procuring an English wife.

For two or three years his eagle eye scanned the faces and figures of the fresh-complexioned simpering misses in each "cold-weather" Fishing Fleet without finding a single girl to his taste. Pallid, giggling, stiffly corseted little ninnies he considered them, with shrill voices and innocent eyes that entirely failed to stir a man who had known Bulbul's slim, sari-clad grace, her fathomless dark eyes and hands skilled in caresses. At length, with a bad grace and a retinue of Indian servants to protect him from the rigors of English society and climate, the newly promoted major set sail for the native land in search of a bride.

He was nearly fifty by then, but still handsome and erect, a fine figure of a military man, with frosty blue eyes, bristling mustache, and crisp dark hair only lightly sprinkled with gray. A splendid catch—he thought himself—for one of the society chits to whom he intended to offer his heart and hand; but inexplicably the young English ladies to whom he chose to pay his addresses saw him in a totally different light.

Stiff-necked, old-fashioned, conceited: to the dashing girls his fancy lighted on, the "Nawab"—as they called him with a fine disregard for the great gulf fixed between Indian civil and military—was a figure of fun, and his abrupt proposals of marriage after the shortest of acquaintances to girls twenty-five and thirty years his junior caused the ladies in question to turn their heads away to conceal their mirth. One and all they answered no.

The Major was not a patient man, nor did he regard the search for a suitable wife as more than a wearisome duty. Tiring rapidly of balls where the dances were not those of his youth, and dinners where smothered yawns greeted his reminiscences of the Sikh wars, he lowered his sights from the duke's daughter, who had been his first choice; down past the eldest child of a belted earl; the ward of a great landowner; the youngest of seven daughters of a sporting parson; and married instead Miss Emily Jones, governess to his cousin's large brood of children: a thin, plain, sallow girl, so shy and retiring that she had not the courage to refuse the Major's curt proposal.

It was a marriage of convenience which made neither of them particularly happy; but since Emily had very little idea of what it meant to be happy, and never expected happiness from life anyway, she was not disappointed and they lived amicably enough together. They sailed for India immediately after the wedding ceremony, and with very little delay, Emily presented her husband first with a daughter, Amelia, and then with Rowland, the son and heir for whose sake the Major had gone to the trouble and expense of matrimony. He was delighted with both children and, in the manner of elderly fathers, could deny them nothing.

Her duty done, Emily contracted cholera soon after Rowland's birth, and died as quietly as she had lived, with her last breath commending her children to the care of God and their *ayah*, Bulbul, for both of whom she entertained the liveliest respect.

The Major—recently promoted to colonel—grieved perfunctorily, then returned with undisguised relief to the welcoming bed and undemanding arms of Bulbul, his Indian nightingale, whom Amelia and Rowland also adored. Life in Colonel Steel's bungalow resumed its tranquil pace as though the memsahib had never existed.

They might, indeed, have lived happily ever after, had it not been for the tireless appetite for philanthropy of Sarah Ramsbotham, sister of one of Colonel Steel's brother officers, who saw in the widower and his motherless children a field ripe for good works. Unfortunately, the brother for whom Sarah kept house when she was not improving the lot of others less fortunate than herself lived in a bungalow adjacent to Colonel Steel's, and as soon as the mourning period was over, Sarah was always in and out on some pretext or other. She fussed over the children's clothes, bullied the cook, oversaw the household accounts, and generally meddled in every domestic pie.

The Colonel, whose approach to household matters was lazy as well as fatalistic, didn't resent Sarah's interference nearly as heartily as did Bulbul, who saw in the domineering, sharp-eyed, sharp-tongued memsahib a very real threat to her own position. Her attempts to warn the Colonel against this determined woman fell on deaf ears. Sarah was a handsome, square-jawed, deep-bosomed lady approaching forty years of age, with snapping black eyes and a commanding manner. She was well endowed with worldly goods and accustomed to getting her own way. One fatal evening as she and the Colonel strolled back from evensong in Baburpore's small whitewashed church, with the frogs croaking a serenade and Sarah in a particularly fetching bonnet, the Colonel made a mistake he was to regret for the rest of his life.

He asked Sarah to marry him.

On their return from a honeymoon in the hills, the installation of the new memsahib caused as much disruption in the household as if a typhoon had struck it.

Servants who had loyally worked for the Colonel for years were dismissed on petty charges and new ones engaged. Furniture was shifted from room to room as if the bungalow were inhabited by a swarm of poltergeists. Sarah ordered a new carriage—the grandest in the station—and bought a pair of matched grays. The garden burgeoned with new plants brought from England, and Rowland and Amelia were obliged to wear sun hats and frilled white collars, instead of romping naked with their half-brothers and half-sisters in the dusty compound.

In vain did the Colonel protest that he *liked* his study littered with papers and thick with dust: Sarah herself supervised its restoration to order and cleanliness.

Worst of all, she soon guessed correctly the relationship between her husband and her stepchildren's *ayah*.

"Bulbul must go," she decreed.

The Colonel was now nearing sixty, and the fire to resist his wife was burning low, but at this it flickered to life again.

"Bulbul stays," he countered. "'Pon my word, Sarah, you can't do a thing like that. Damn it, she's all my children know in the way of a mother, and they're both devoted to her. Besides"—he coughed and would not meet her eyes—"she's in a delicate condition. You can't dismiss her when she's in that state."

"Your child, I assume," said Sarah tartly, and as usual she was right. This would be the fourth child Bulbul had borne to her master.

"She may remain until after her confinement," Sarah conceded. "If the baby is a boy, he can serve as Rowland's bearer; if it is a girl, she can attend Amelia." With this the Colonel had to be content.

The baby—a boy named Sita Ram—was born, and Bulbul went, but not very far.

Reacting to the situation as his father would have, the Colonel installed Bulbul in a pretty little bungalow on the far edge of the dwellings, near the native town, a ten-minute ride from his own house, and continued to visit her there whenever life with his Sarah seemed oppressive. His visits became more and more frequent.

Sarah was perfectly well aware of this strategem as, indeed, was every other European in Baburpore. She waited until her husband's regiment was sent far away on maneuvers, then drove herself behind her matched grays to visit Bulbul.

The former dancer squatted gracefully on her veranda, her violet sari spangled with gold stars arranged around her in sculptured folds. The chubby toddler, Sita Ram, stared at his mother's visitor out of black eyes that, like his father's, pulled down a little at the outer corners.

"He is a fine boy," said Sarah, who disliked children and was thankful she had none of her own. "You should be proud of him." She pulled her shawl tightly around her as Sita Ram reached small fingers to touch the pretty material. Bulbul admonished him softly in their own tongue.

"Do not touch the memsahib, *baba* mine. She is made of ice and will freeze your fingers."

The child drew back hastily, staring all the more, and popped his fingers into his mouth for safety.

Bulbul laughed softly. "How may I serve the memsahib?"

The slightly mocking edge to her voice was not lost on Sarah, but she chose to disregard it.

"You may oblige me by removing to some other house in some other town and ceasing to lure my husband here night after night," she said crisply.

Bulbul feigned astonishment. "How can this be? I live here where the Colonel-sahib told me to, in the house he bought for me and his sons from Lall Gopal the durzee, and nightly the Colonel-sahib come to talk and see his sons' progress. Why do you now tell me to leave this house and live without a roof to shelter the Colonel-sahib's children?"

"The money with which the Colonel-sahib bought this house was not his to spend," said Sarah calmly. "It was, and is, mine. So the house is mine also, and I have the right to tell you to go. But I am not vindictive, and I wish you no ill. It is not your fault that the Colonel-sahib has placed you in this position—I realize that quite well. But I, too, have my pride, and I am not prepared to see my husband leave me night after night for the bed of an Indian woman. You see, I am speaking plainly, for I want you to understand that I am not angry either with my husband or with you, but I am determined that this—this liaison should cease once and for all. Therefore I will give you, Bulbul, two thousand rupees if you will leave Baburpore secretly, taking your children, before the regiment returns from maneuvers, and promise me you will never return to awaken my husband's love again."

Two thousand rupees! Bulbul's pretty mouth fell open and she gazed dumbly at the memsahib. She was not a greedy woman, and had never imagined possessing such wealth. To be free—free of her elderly lover, of whom she had long tired, free forever of the need to work, the fear of poverty in her old age. The memsahib must be made of gold, she thought, to offer her so much money for such a little service. She had no knowledge of European law, and believed the memsahib when she claimed the money that had bought the bungalow was hers, for had not everything new and costly appeared at the Colonel-sahib's bungalow as soon as he married the new memsahib? Of a certainty her family must be rajahs, thought Bulbul, for who else possessed such wealth?

Sarah, who had deliberately worn her finest jewels for the interview saw the ex-dancer's large eyes travel wonderingly over the diamond spray at her breast; the ruby rings, and the three strands of graded pearls round her throat.

"You will go tomorrow, and tell no one where you have gone," she instructed, and slowly Bulbul nodded. Alone in this bungalow with her children, she missed the cheerful bustle of compound life—missed, too, the attentions of the Colonel's *syce*, who had been used to console her when his master was too occupied to visit her hut. A condition of the tenancy of this bungalow had been that she should entertain no other men there, and for one of Bulbul's passionate nature, this was a deprivation that irked her greatly. However, partly from fear of being found out, and partly from natural honesty, she had held to her promise. It would be nice to be released from it; to see whom she chose when she chose.

Here in Baburpore, a white man's mistress was between two worlds. She would go to Patelbar, the native state, outside the bounds of British India, where she had been born and trained as a dancer, and there she would be her own mistress. With so much money she could buy anything she wanted, live anywhere she pleased. Her sons would be princes, and her daughter marry a maharajah.

Yet she hesitated.

"What is it?" asked Sarah, impatient to be gone from the bungalow with its heavy scents of turmeric and jasmine, hair oil and *ghee*.

"It is about Sita Ram," said Bulbul in a rush. "I have promised that Sita Ram will be the *baba*-sahib's bearer. I cannot break my word."

Sarah frowned, then she said, "Oh...that! Very well: When Sita Ram is old enough to leave you, send him to the Colonel-sahib, and I will see that he is trained as Rowland's bearer. That is the only time in the future that I wish to hear from you. Is it agreed? Come to the compound tomorrow when you are ready to leave, and I will give you the money."

Thus Bulbul left Baburpore never to return, and traveled by *dak* gharry to Patelbar to join her brothers there. She was a rich woman now, and had no further need to follow her profession, but idleness, she found, did not suit her. Years of childbearing had thickened the waist which the Colonel had once been able to span with his strong, sinewy hands, and dancing made her short of breath, but she could still sing, and she still loved the company of men.

With her brothers' warm approval, Bulbul bought the Joyhouse of Kali, and under her expert teaching the girls there soon became the most sought-after in the state of Patelbar.

Her long association with the sahib-log made Bulbul's manner of entertaining her clients rather different from that in the usual run of houses of pleasure. She gave value for money, and she was a first-class business woman. Frowned on at first by the traditionalists, Bulbul continued in her own way and soon established a virtual monopoly in her trade. To her house flocked every kind of traveler in need of rest and refreshment, sex and music, and as a clearinghouse for gossip and information, the Joyhouse of Kali was soon unrivaled.

All this Caro was to piece together, bit by bit, during the weeks she spent under Bulbul's tutelage. But now, as the bead curtain swished shut behind the yellow-clad Nazir who had brought her to the tall, narrow house with the gaily striped awning, Caro—disheveled, wretched, and finally bereft of hope—raised her eyes from the floor on which she crouched.

Some six inches from her face stood a pair of doll-size embroidered slippers with elegantly curled toes on each of which was coiled a dragon, spiny tail erect and claw lifted in heraldic fashion. Above the slippers an emerald green sari, of silk so fine it was almost transparent, hung in graceful folds around its owner's short, stout body. Bangles clinked gently on her ankles and wrists as she moved, placing her hand on Caro's shoulder in a gesture that was at once friendly and protective.

Looking up still further, Caro saw a face from which beauty had not quite vanished, although it was blurred by surplus flesh, with a delicate straight nose and short upper lip, though the mouth was seamed with wrinkles that spread into layer upon layer of chins. A winking turquoise was set in the curve of either nostril, and a red beauty spot decorated the wide forehead. But it was her eyes that held Caro's attention. Large, dark, and heavily rimmed with kohl, they were both gentle and shrewd, and dominated the whole once-lovely face.

Bulbul smiled and hesitantly, tentatively, Caro's anxious expression relaxed in an answering smile. A moment later she was convinced that she had fallen into a dream, when the soft, singsong voice above her said in strongly accented English, "All right now, bad mens gone and Bulbul take care of you. No more bad mens. Don' cry, memsahib."

Caro's eyes widened. "Help me," she whispered. "They want to kill me. Oh, please help me."

The tiny, glittering figure bent lower. "I help you. Old Bulbul help you hide, but there is danger. Evil comes to the land of the Sirkar, and many will die when the Red Wind blows. You must be brave, *baba*, and trust no one, tell no one who you are or whence you come. You safe here. Not leave Joyhouse of Kali or you get killed. Many bad mens in Patelbar gone to kill sahibs and memsahibs; make all red with blood. You stay here."

"You mean—I'm a prisoner?" said Caro, dismayed.

Bulbul's fat face creased in a smile. Her thickly painted lips parted, revealing small, white, beautifully even teeth, unstained by betel nut. "Yes, you are prisoner. But I love you, miss-sahiba. I keep you safe. You Bulbul's *happy* prisoner. Now—"

She drew the tousled hair back over Caro's shoulder. Head on one side, eyes twinkling bright as a bird's, she considered the effect. She bustled away and fetched a length of spangled gauze; then she gently pushed Caro down on a rug beside a brass tray loaded with jars and bottles.

"Now we make you beautiful," said Bulbul.

*   *   *

In a land of many tongues and races, it was less hard than Caro had feared to conceal her identity from the rest of Bulbul's girls. They were beauties one and all—apple-cheek, slant-eyed girls from Kashmir, bird-boned girls with blue-black hair from Goa, sallow willowy beauties with strongly marked brows from Bombay—and they spoke a mixed language in which Hindi and Urdu predominated. They accepted Caro as the kind of silent, scared newcomer each of them had once been, and treated her with casual kindness, pulling her hair into a sleek, oiled braid and supplying her with bits of cast-off finery for which she gave stammering thanks.

She tried hard to blend into the background as Bulbul had commanded, and though the days that followed her initiation into the Joyhouse of Kali were strange and frightening ones, she worked hard. Bulbul feared to show her any preferential treatment, and trembled nightly lest the Prince should come to see how the English *devadasi* was faring. But Chandran-aya had ridden off in the Nana Sahib's train, to ferment more trouble in Oudh, and as the days went by with no trouble from the palace, Bulbul breathed more easily and concentrated on teaching Caro her trade.

Under Bulbul's expert tutelage, Caro soon became one of the most sought-after pleasures in the Joyhouse of Kali. Every stage of lovemaking she performed with grace and charm, first offering her guests refreshment, music, or dancing girls, then washing the men's bodies in an especially arousing manner, her hands and fingertips strong but sinuous, floating over the flesh like silk or massaging the private parts with a firm, supple stroke that dizzied the spirit. The act of union, she performed with a woman's submissiveness coupled with a directness that was almost exhilaratingly male. She was skilled in the use of devices, if desired, and in the myriad erotic positions, bites, scratches, and kisses set down in the great love book of Vatsyayana.

Unlike most of the other *devadasis*, she was clearly a *ganika*, a cultured courtesan skilled in the arts of the mind, as well as the body. She did not, like women of her rank, indulge in sophisticated conversation with her guests, turning her head away shyly when the opportunity arose. That she spoke so seldom so enhanced her air of exotic mystery that Caro came to be known to the Joyhouse of Kali as the "Silent One."

For Bulbul's sake, Caro had at first pretended relative contentment, burying the sense of shame and degradation that had not left her. After her duties were completed, she would creep away from the snoring, sweating merchant or soldier who had just possessed her, and wash frenziedly at the well before lying down on her own pallet, in a torment of fear and disgust. Still, as the weeks wore on, as her life wove itself into a pattern, she found her terror and her loathing diminishing. Most of the men were crude but few were violent and rarely did anyone force her to perform a disrespectful act. Often, they brought her garlands of flowers, betel nuts, and perfumed ointments as a token of appreciation for her artistry.

In the beginning, lovemaking was still somewhat painful, but that had quickly passed. Due to the scented creams with which she massaged her clients' members, penetration was rarely uncomfortable, and though she derived little actual feeling from the union, it generally passed quickly. Sometimes she tried to picture Rowland's face before her closed eyes, attempting to imagine he was here with her, but somehow, the need for fulfillment he aroused in her seemed worlds away from her present circumstance.

Before long, she found it hard to remember who she was: that long ago, far away, there had been an English girl called Caroline March, who wore clean muslin dresses with wide sashes, carried a frilled parasol, and was addressed as "my lady" by the servants.

Lady Caroline March: she seemed a faint, dim, distant creature now. Had she ever existed? Could it be only two months—three months—four months ago that Lady Caroline had waltzed with the Governor-General, flirted with Captain Steel, fended off half a dozen proposals of marriage from hopeful Civils and subalterns? What would Brook Vyner say if he could see her now?

This thought struck Caro as she dressed before Bulbul's mirror for the evening's entertainment one evening in July when the monsoons were emptying their heavy hot burden of rain over Patelbar. For the first time for days she felt like laughing. Brook Vyner, so correct: how his jaw would drop and his eyes bulge from his head if he saw Lady Caroline March in this preposterous rig! He had disapproved of her wearing Harry's clothes at Suez: how much more he would feel she was letting the side down if he were to glimpse the gauzy silver *choli* with no undergarment, the jewel in her navel, and voluminous trousers of semitransparent silver tissue, caught in at the ankle above the bangles and bare feet. With her hair oiled flat to her skull, parted in the middle, and weaved into a single heavy braid down her back, she looked wholly Indian, and her eyes appeared twice their normal size when outlined with lampblack by Bulbul's skilled hand. A bright red spot adorned either cheek, and her mouth was dark with heavy red salve.

No, she would not find favor in Brook Vyner's eyes.

Captain Steel, on the other hand: Rowland . . . Suddenly she had the oddest sensation that he was there, behind her, his eyes alight with laughter, complimenting her: "By Jove, Caro, those garments certainly become you. You should wear them more often . . ." He had a trick of turning up lately in the oddest places; not only had he begun to haunt her dreams, but even wide awake she could almost believe she heard his voice. Caro swung around suddenly, and Bulbul, who had been adjusting the folds of Caro's headdress, clicked her tongue in disapproval and barked in her peculiar pidgin English used for reprimands, "Why you laugh? Why you not stand still?"

Why laugh indeed? The smile faded from Caro's lips. It had been months since she had even heard good English spoken or seen a British face. Rowland was far away, and she was Lady Caroline no longer. She was just Caro, the Silent One, who might at any moment be plucked from this small refuge and put to death at the whim of a cruel prince. No, she had no reason to laugh.

But, curiously, the thought of Rowland had given her courage, and reestablished her identity in her own mind. Strange men might paw and penetrate her unresisting body, but they could not touch her spirit. As long as she remained mistress of her thoughts, she could still hope to escape back to her old, happy life.

Business was brisk that night, and the tall house with its many latticed windows filled quickly with an enthusiastic crowd.

The Joyhouse's main room was on the ground floor—a single high-ceiling chamber decorated with a strange mixture of traditional Indian murals and mosaics which blended oddly with furnishings supplied by Bulbul's vague memories of illustrations in *La Vie Parisienne* and similar saucy periodicals which had come her way during her long association with the dashing bachelor officer that James Steel had been when first she knew him—red velvet curtains and cushions with gold tassels, quantities of chipped crystal goblets and a great silver bowl on a long mahogany table that had once belonged to the officers' mess of a crack cavalry regiment. The table had lost a castor, and leaned enough to cause dishes to slide off the edge, and its once brilliant polish was scratched and smeared, but Bulbul considered it an added cosmopolitan touch to her salon, and though it impeded the progress of the servants as they padded to and fro with steaming bowls of rice, curry, and *dal*, she refused to move it from the center of the room.

Caro squatted unobtrusively on her mat in the corner, observing the noisy, bustling throng. Her head ached with the din, the wail and thump of viol and sitar, the air thick with tobacco, sandalwood, hemp and the all-pervading smell of hot human bodies. Bulbul's eye was upon her, and much as she wanted to, Caro dared not slip out to breathe the slightly fresher air in the courtyard.

Listlessly she listened to the men squatting next to her, sucking at the water pipes and occasionally caressing her as they talked. She had no difficulty now in following a conversation in Hindustani and had ceased to be surprised at how quickly understanding of another tongue had come to her.

"You travel far, brother?" asked her nearest neighbor, a sturdy, splendidly mustachioed young sepoy, his gold-frogged red uniform jacket unbuttoned and slung carelessly round his shoulders.

The fat, clean-shaven *babu* next to her, dressed in a violet sashed tunic and skullcap above wrinkled white cotton jodhpurs, coughed importantly. "I follow the Red Wind," he said.

The phrase caught Caro's attention. She listened more carefully.

"What wind is that?" inquired a boy with a handsome, effeminate face, sitting not far away. He was richly dressed in a high-collar silk coat, with jewels about his neck and wrists.

"A wind of madness," grunted the soldier. "I have

eaten the Sirkar's salt for all my years and I follow no
red wind."

Caro's interest sharpened. Rowland had been right.
That trouble which Brook Vyner, even Andrew, called
rubbish, was real. She, Caro, now knew it for certain,
and she was powerless to convey it to the British.

"If you do not follow the Red Wind, you betray
your caste and care naught for your religion," the man
in the violet skullcap was insisting heatedly. "For know
you not that the cartridges you tear open with your
teeth are greased with the fat of kine? What manner of
Hindu are you that you can eat the flesh of cows
without defilement?"

The soldier shifted uneasily. "My captain has
spoken of this," he muttered. "He told us there was no
truth in that saying. Neither the fat of cows nor of
swine is used for greasing the cartridge of the new rifle.
It will not break our caste or defile our Mussulman
brethren."

"And you believe his words?" jeered the man in the
violet skullcap. "O, brother, you are deaf as the serpent
and foolish as the gray ape! Know you not that the
sahibs want one thing above all else: to make you
forget your gods and worship the God of the sahib-log?
Truly they are wise to give you cartridges to break your
caste, for so they may more easily draw you to their
God."

At a loss for an answer to this, the sepoy turned half
away, and beckoned Caro to move closer to him. He
slid an arm firmly around her waist and with his strong
fingers kneaded her buttocks. A month ago, Caro
would have wanted to flinch and pull away, but now
she was inured, indifferent to the touch of strange
hands invading her body.

Not quite indifferent, though. Against her will, she
began to feel her body respond to the soldier's
exploring fingers. Her pulse beat faster, and every

nerve seemed to tingle; she felt a pang of disappointment when the sepoy released her as suddenly as he had embraced her—disappointment followed by a feeling of horror at her own behavior.

She drew a long, shuddering breath. What was happening to her? How could she enjoy—almost invite—the touch of a man's hand on her breast, and crave the pressure of his hard, angular body against her? Not a man she knew and loved, even—just an Indian soldier to whom she had never even spoken. How could such a man awaken these dark longings in her blood? Loose women, she knew from her mother's lectures, were the only creatures who took pleasure in such things. Could a few weeks of captivity and abuse turn a gently nurtured English girl into a loose woman?

Attempting to still her self-doubt and calm her mind as well as her body, Caro turned her attention again to the argumentative *babu*.

"Woe to the men that have land in Oudh!" he was proclaiming, while his little piggy eyes roamed over the faces of his audience, "for their sons will never inherit their fields."

The richly dressed youngster stopped picking his teeth and looked up keenly. "How can that be, when the Sirkar has promised justice for landlord and peasant alike?"

"Thy father has lands in Oudh?" said the *babu* happily, scenting a fertile field for the suspicions he wished to plant. "O, wretched youth! When the Sirkar annexed the kingdom of Oudh, it stole the very heart of Hindustan and with it *your* inheritance. The Nawab was banished to exile..."

"And thou art his man," said the sepoy suddenly, as light broke in on him. "The mouth of the Nawab of Oudh blows the Red Wind, and thou followest it with thy tales of cow grease. I have heard enough. Come, my gazelle—"

He tried to rise, pulling Caro with him, but she hung back. While dressing that evening she had imagined Rowland's voice. Now, when she heard the *babu* talk of the sahib-log—her own people—she felt a sharp nostalgia, a sudden awakening from the unthinking, uncaring apathy in which she had so meekly accepted her fate. She was not a chattel or slave to be pawed and used by every man who wanted her. She was part of this same sahib-log—this proud race that had conquered and now ruled Hindustan. With this revival of pride came an acute repugnance for the dark sinewy fingers now tugging at her arm. What right had he to treat her so? Angrily she raised a hand to strike him, then stood aghast, aware once more of the extreme vulnerability of her position.

The sepoy had noticed nothing amiss. He laughed at her reluctance to move. "Do not waste our moments of pleasure, little lotus, for when the sun rises I must depart from Patelbar and rejoin the regiment. I shall not come back to the Joyhouse of Kali for many moons. Who knows? Phillip-sahib may be ordered to the snows of the high Himal, or away to the burning plains of the Deccan, and where he goes, I go. I may never see you again. But tonight is ours, and I have no wish to spend it listening to the lies of yonder fat *babu*."

Disregarding custom, he swung her bodily into his arms and ran up the wide, shallow steps. Through her thin garments, Caro could feel the pounding of his heart against her side. Though the stairway was dark, smoky lanterns in wall embrasures illuminated through the open doorways couples with arms and legs entwined as they writhed and sprawled on the piled rugs and cushions. The air was heavy with the smell of burning sandalwood, the mingled tangs of smoke, sweat, and opium.

As soon as they entered their love room, the soldier, ignoring the usual ritual on which most clients insisted, stepped unhesitatingly over to Caro, picked her up, carried her over to the couch, and gently laid her down. He fumbled with his clothes, pulling off the tight, heavy jacket and white trousers.

Caro was completely disarmed by the eager young soldier's ardor. Night after night she had plied her trade, giving and taking according to the laws of love. But this man's lovemaking respected no rules but the commands of his own body. Although he was not, like Tom Hamilton, brutally forcing his desires upon her, it was clear that what he wanted, he intended to have. In the face of such impulsive desire, Caro's new-found worldliness crumbled. As he stood before her, boldly presenting himself, she shrank away.

"No . . . n-no . . ." she pleaded, trembling, shutting her eyes against the sight of her would-be lover's stocky, muscular body silhouetted in the lamplight.

The sepoy, who had been about to enfold her in his arms, stopped in surprise. This was not the usual way in which Bulbul's beauties welcomed their customers. The girl was a treasure, all right; there was a defenseless, fawnlike air about her that had attracted him the moment he saw her. But also, like a deer, she was wild and wary, poised for flight. The sepoy had no taste for the bold brassy wenches, glittering with tinsel and colored glass who swooped down like birds of prey on any sepoy newly arrived in Patelbar with pay in his money belt. Such girls knew instinctively when a man's leave was over—as his was—and his money gone, and he'd been allowed to choose the Silent One for his pleasure without interference from those experienced and aggressive damsels.

He gazed speculatively at Caro, wondering if he'd made a bad bargain after all. The slender resisting body quivering on the couch gave little promise of sensual delight.

The sepoy sighed. He was a patient man, and came

of farming stock. He knew how to soothe a frightened animal. Carefully restraining himself from any sudden advance that might alarm her further, he laid a hand on Caro's shoulder and began quietly, reassuringly, to stroke the smooth skin.

"Do not be afraid, little one," he murmured. "You have nothing to fear from Manda Lao. Come, lie back in my arms and be happy. No one sees you. No one will hurt you. There is no need to be frightened." The soothing, cheerful voice and gentle hands had their effect. Caro slowly began to relax, her skin warming at his touch, her breath quickening, her body reaching out for his without her even knowing it. This stranger, this farmboy, had no sophistication about his lovemaking, but his boundless enjoyment and passion more than compensated for what he lacked in manners.

So many delicious sensations blended together into the sweetest pleasure as Caro felt him fondle her breasts, then gradually loosen and remove her garments. When at last, they embraced in their nakedness, she arched firmly to him, moving her body in voluptuous rhythm against his enormous hardness. He stroked her flanks, her hair, the length of her back, and then, gathering her up in his arms and cradling her like a child, he murmured words she did not know but understood, and they inflamed her.

It was she who moved her body to lie under his, she who clung to him, unable to remember who she was or what was being done to her.

Locked in her arms, the sepoy smiled. He had been right after all. This was going to be worth the time and trouble, well worth waiting for.

"Now, my lotus," he whispered, as he entered her and the golden fire swept over both of them...

In what seemed much too short a time, the sepoy rose and dressed, and kissing Caro heartily, made his farewells. After he had gone, she didn't return directly to the downstairs chamber. The hum of voices and steady thump of tom-toms beaten with the bare hands throbbed through her head, and she felt hot and exhausted, though she knew sleep would be impossible for many hours. No breath of breeze stirred the chain curtains, and inside the house the air was thick, heavy, and still. She could almost feel its weight pressing down on her.

Languidly she made her way to the courtyard, where a thin trickle of tepid water ran into a stone basin. She was about to kneel down to wash when she became aware of the figure of a man moving silently toward her through the dusk.

Caro started back, hands pressed to her mouth to stifle a scream. Men were not allowed to enter this courtyard. The side gate was guarded by a burly Punjabi, an ex-wrestler, who had strict orders to repel any overbold reveler who sought to pursue the woman of his choice within the walls of the courtyard.

Therefore, the newcomer could only be one of whom Bulbul herself had admitted from the house—one of whom she was afraid—and that meant one of Prince Chandranaya's servants. Had the Prince sent for her at last? Caro's legs shook with fear, and she sank down helplessly on the rim of the stone basin, staring hypnotized at the approaching figure in its vee-neck tunic with a wicked, curved sword stuck through the sash. She stretched out her hands as if to prevent him from coming any closer.

"Go—go away!" she faltered. "You cannot come here. It is forbidden to enter the courtyard."

The newcomer spoke in English, in a soft, urgent whisper. "Caro! Lady Caro! Hush, do not scream or make a noise and alarm the *chokidar*. I am—Fionn Kelly."

"Doctor Kelly!" Caro let out sigh of relief. "Oh . . . I was so afraid. Have you come to rescue me? How did you find me?"

"I came as soon as I heard where they had hidden you, but up till now I thought you had been taken away in the Nana Sahib's train. Alas, I have not the power to rescue you. I am as closely guarded as you are, and indeed, have come to ask you for your assistance."

Her disappointment was so great that tears formed in her eyes as his words sank in. She blinked them away and asked in a voice which she forced herself to steady, "What can we do? Why have they treated me so?"

"Ah, that's a long story, and I know but the half of it myself. Take me somewhere where we may be private in this rabbit warren of a house, and tell me how you come to be separated from Captain Thynne and his wife."

"But Bulbul—" she began.

"You can be easy about Bulbul," he reassured her, with a ghost of his old smile. "She is the protector of us both, good lady: and the only soul we can trust in this whole God-forsaken town since my rajah died. I am watched wherever I go, and two of the Prince's spies are with me now, playing dice within. It is only through Bulbul's aid that I am able to speak with you, and I have much to impart."

He moved closer, lowering his voice until she had to strain her ears to hear. "A great rebellion is spreading through the land, headed by the sepoys of Oudh's native infantry, with the Nawab of Oudh and that scoundrel the Nana Sahib fanning the flames of mutiny. Patelbar is used as the meetingplace between their faction and that of the King of Delhi."

"Yes, I have heard such talk in the Joyhouse. But the price? What of Chandranaya?"

"In it up to his neck. But this is too public a place to

discuss it—we may be interrupted at any moment. Where can we speak in private?"

"Upstairs," she said uncertainly. "There are the rooms..."

"I understand. That will do very well." He followed her across the courtyard and into the stifling house, where he grabbed her round the waist as the sepoy had done, nuzzling her neck as they traversed the opening to the main chamber. Caro was thankful for this piece of play-acting when she saw two men in Chandranaya's yellow uniform catch sight of the doctor—and look up alertly—but when they saw where he was heading, their vigilance relaxed and, they turned back to their game of dice.

Caro was relieved that Fionn Kelly appeared to know at least part of her story and that she had no need to explain her strange costume or her presence in this house of ill fame. We are both in disguise, she told herself, and have been forced to it by circumstances beyond our control. There is no need to be ashamed. The doctor's tacit assumption that they were together in their trouble set her at ease, and sitting on the string cot of an upper chamber, while he leaned against the closed door to prevent any sudden interruption, she poured out the story of Chandranaya's treachery, the poisoning of Andrew and Philippa, and her own capture.

"I do not know yet if they are alive or dead," she ended disconsolately, "for I never saw them again, and have been here ever since."

Fionn was able to reassure her on this point. "I had word from Baburpore that they arrived in the troop quarters precisely three weeks after Delhi fell."

"Delhi fell!" Caro stared at him open-mouthed. "You cannot be serious!"

"I was never more serious."

"You mean there has been a rebellion?"

"Worse than that. It is the sepoys themselves who have mutinied against their officers. The Army of Bengal has been rotten to the core for years and now it is falling apart."

Mutiny! The words crystallized all Caro's vague fears, though even now she found it hard to believe. It had really happened—the terror against which Rowland Steel had warned so long ago, while Brook Vyner mocked him as a "croaker," one who foretold evil. The threat that had seemed so remote while she whirled and spun at "cold weather" balls in the arms of handsome, confident, debonair British officers and Civils, was now even more frighteningly immediate than she had suspected.

The doctor was looking at her curiously. "Of course, you could not know most of it," he said, "unless you had some hint from Bulbul or her customers."

"How—how did it begin?"

"As far as I can establish, the first outbreak of mutiny was at Meerut, where the Third Bengal Light Cavalry broke into the jail and set free eighty-five of their comrades who had refused to receive cartridges for their new Enfield rifles. They believed these cartridges to be greased with cow and pig fat, and nothing would persuade them that they were not. Whereupon they butchered their British officers and set off for Delhi, where they proclaimed old Bahadur Shah, the Nawab of Oudh, the last King of the Mughals. That was in May. Since then, I have had no certain news, but I fear the disturbances have spread throughout the Ganges Valley."

Caro licked her dry lips. She could hardly bring herself to frame her next question, but ask she must. "And Baburpore. Has that escaped?"

Fionn nodded. "I think the trouble is unlikely to reach Baburpore. It is a remote station, although strategically important because of the river crossing, and they are fortunate in having Captain Steel and his native cavalry among the garrison there. Most of his troops are Sikhs from the Punjab who do not share the grievances of the men of Oudh, and moreover, there is a strong tradition of personal loyalty to members of Steel's family, which has served in India for four generations. His father, you know, became something of a hero during the Sikh wars, a decade since. Bulbul was for many years attached to his household and, I believe, bore him several children."

Caro was somewhat shocked by this casual reference to a history she assumed was never spoken of, but managed to check the words of disapproval which Philippa would have felt obliged to utter. After all, who was she to judge a man's morals? Nevertheless, it was reassuring to hear that because of Rowland's close connection with India and its peoples, her sister was in no immediate danger.

"Yes," went on Fionn. "As long as Steel remains in Baburpore, I think General Elliott need have no fear that the Red Wind will reach the town."

Caro caught at the phrase. "So this is the Red Wind," she murmured, almost to herself. "Oh, I have been blind!"

"You have heard them speak of it? I, too, but I never dreamed it would fan such a holocaust. As to your blindness, I assure you that it cannot compare with the stubborn, blind inflexibility of British officers in the Army of Bengal. This trouble has been brewing thirty years and more, and they have consistently refused to see it—refused to acknowledge even the possibility of their trusted sepoys and sowars turning. The trouble is, where firm handling was called for, the Army of Bengal has been too soft, and bowed to prejudices of caste and religion that would never have been tolerated in the Armies of Madras and Bombay. Add to that Lord

Dalhousie's absurd decision to annex the Kingdom of Oudh instead of merely setting its affairs straight and leaving the Nawab ruler in name, at least..."

Since Lord Dalhousie was a good friend of Caro's father, she felt obliged to protest indignantly, "It was not his decision. Lord Dalhousie recommended the course you approve, but he was overruled by the India Board in London. I know, for I have heard him speak of it."

Fionn looked at her with new respect. "Well, well; so you know more than I thought about our politics," he remarked. "Be that as it may, whoever took the decision must bear largely the responsibility for the present state of affairs, which I greatly fear will result in a bloodbath such as India has never known. It is our duty to prevent it as far as possible, and that is why I have come to ask your help."

"Mine? Of course I will help you in any way I can, but there is a thing that greatly puzzles me. Why should you trouble to work for a people who have treated you so ill? When first we met, you remember, you told me you had been a Company soldier, court-martialed for a crime you had not committed. You said you had come to live among Indians, since they would not betray you as your own people had done. Yet now you speak of saving the very sahibs and memsahibs you declared were your enemies—or so Andrew told me."

A mischievous smile lit up Fionn's thin face. "For many years I've been obliged to maintain that fiction, and it has served its purpose well, but now I think it is outdated."

"It was not true? Oh, I am so glad!" said Caro simply. "For I did not quite know if I should trust you or not."

"Yes, you may trust me. Since the rule of law looks certain to collapse before the monsoon, you and I should have no secrets from one another. As to the court-martial, it was engineered by the authorities when they wished to plant an agent here in Patelbar, for the old Rajah steadfastly refused to allow a political advisor within his territory. Since it was known that his eye condition required specialist treatment if he was not to join his fathers prematurely, leaving the state in the grasping hands of a regent, the notion was conceived of introducing an agent who was also a physician, and their choice fell upon me."

"They dishonored you publicly in order to mislead the Rajah?" cried Caro indignantly. "Oh, it was ignoble! How could you agree to such a trick?"

This time Fionn laughed aloud. "My dear Caro—I may call you that?—do not take it so much to heart. Honor in the abstract never meant much to me. My wife was dead and my family far away in Ireland—who could be hurt by the story of my disgrace? I grant you it was disagreeable when ladies cut me dead, and gentlemen crossed the street in order to avoid meeting me, but I saw it as a means to an end: the opportunity to study Indian life at close quarters without the stigma of being known to be attached to the East India Company and with no responsibility beyond guiding the Rajah in the way Britain wished him to go."

A strange world of trickery and treachery, isolation and manipulation seemed to open before Caro's eyes as she listened to the slim, turbaned figure. Was nothing in India what it first appeared to be?

Fionn said briskly, "We must look forward now, Caro; not back. We must do all in our power to prevent the rebellion spreading toward Nepal, for if that country were to set aside its treaties and throw in its lot with the mutineers as the Prince of Patelbar has done, British chances of regaining control of the siutation would be poor indeed. This very city of Patelbar is the key to containing the trouble, which we must see extends no farther."

It sounded an impossible task. "How can I help?" Caro asked doubtfully.

Fionn grasped her hands, trying to instill in her his own enthusiasm. "You can help a great deal. You understand Hindustani?" She nodded. "Then you are a jewel beyond price. I want you to watch and listen, and report to me all you hear in this house, for this is where travelers to Patelbar foregather and information is to be gleaned. I myself am too well known"—he grimaced—"and notoriously in disfavor at the palace, to hear much of interest, so you must be my eyes and ears. No one will suspect a *devadasi* of understanding the workings of sedition, and they will speak freely in your presence as they never would in mine. Can you do it?"

She nodded again, sensing he was about to leave her, pleading with her eyes for him to stay. "Will you come here often? See me often? I feel so much— stronger now. Before you came I had nearly given up hope; I felt so alone."

"I'll come every night," he promised, then held up a silencing hand. In the hush they heard a soft scratching at the door.

"You must come, doctor-sahib," Bulbul urgently whispered. "You have stayed long, and the *badmash*es grow impatient. Come quickly now."

Fionn pressed Caro's hands and released them. "Farewell—and courage!"

The door hinge squeaked, and he was gone as softly as in a dream.

Chapter Nine

PHILIPPA LEANED ON the rail of the veranda, gazing toward the Baburpore parade ground across the burned-up beds of marigolds and zinnias, and the brown oblong of lawn that never, except at the height of the monsoon, looked lush or green.

Faint shouts, made musical by distance, floated to her ears, and from time to time the imperious note of a bugle sounded.

It was so hot. She leaned her burning forehead against the rail, but the wood was just as hot as her own skin, although it was barely eight in the morning.

Why had the Colonel ordered an extra parade, she wondered with weak irritability. At this time of year parades should be kept to a minimum. She had hardly had a wink of sleep last night, what with Andrew being called out twice to fires in the native lines, and Trixie, his fox terrier, whining with fever as she lay beneath the dining-room table, showing an alarming tendency to growl and snap at anyone who lifted the folds of tablecloth to look at her. She had never behaved like this before, and refused to take even a teaspoonful of the brandy-and-egg mixture that Philippa had offered her. Indeed, she hardly seemed to know her mistress at all, and blundered round in circles in her chosen refuge with a rim of foam dripping from her sharp little muzzle. Most of the servants were wary of Trixie at the best of times, and now they wouldn't go near her at all.

Toward gunfire, with Andrew at last returned from

his fire-fighting activities, Philippa had eventually drifted off, to dream of a ship with sails limp, becalmed in the torrid doldrums.

Unfortunately, the *punkah-wallah* on the veranda outside their bedroom must have chosen that moment to fall asleep too, and Philippa had been rudely aroused by a volley of curses from her husband, followed by a crash of glass as the boot he flung in the *punkah-wallah* direction collided instead with the gilt-framed mirror on Philippa's dressing table beside the window.

Seven years' bad luck for breaking a mirror, she thought despondently, watching the boy sweep up the glittering fragments. Why couldn't Andrew improve his marksmanship?

He, too, looked heavy-eyed as he ate his *chota hazree* on the veranda, and announced that the Colonel, Tiger Elliott, had ordered an extra parade.

"Surely he's not still worried about the new rifles?" said Philippa. "He spoke to the entire garrison on church parade, and the men seemed to accept what he said. What good will it do to say it all again?"

"You forget that when he addressed the troops on Sunday, Rowland Steel was at his elbow to back him up," grunted Andrew. "Steel's got a lot of pull with the native troops, you know, and most of his own fellows are Sikhs—a good deal more reliable than my high-caste Hindus, for all that the Sikhs smell to high heaven."

"Really, Andrew!"

"They do, and Rowland would be the first to admit it," insisted Andrew with a grin. "It comes of washing all that long hair of theirs in curds. Still, they're grand fighters, and loyal to the backbone. I wish they were still with us to calm the hotheads in the rest of the garrison. Tiger Elliott must have been insane to send them off on a punitive expedition when they're the only reliable native troops in Baburpore, but then I suppose he was afraid of what Rowland would do if he wasn't allowed any action. I was half afraid of him myself," he admitted, "when he heard the news about poor Caro. No, Phil, don't start crying again..."

With an effort, Philippa mastered her ready tears at the mention of her sister. "When will he come back?" she quavered.

"It can't be too soon, as far as I'm concerned, but I'm afraid we won't be seeing him for a week or two. It all depends on the reliability of the reports by spies who said they'd seen the Rajah of Bithoor with Chandranaya in his train on their way to assist the mutineers at Cawnpore. If we once get clear proof that Patelbar's joined the rebels, we can scotch that nest of vipers without worrying about violating any treaties. As it is, we sit here with fresh reports of trouble arriving with every *dak*..."

"Do they?" Philippa turned very white, and Andrew laid a reassuring hand on her arm.

"I'm sorry, my dear. I don't mean to alarm you, but it's no use hiding our heads in the sand like a lot of ostriches. What we should be doing is preparing our own defenses in case the trouble strikes here too, but every time I say as much, I get called a 'croaker' for my pains."

"Where would we be safe?" asked Philippa in a trembling voice. "There are so few British soldiers here, and think of all the women and children who cannot bear arms!"

"It's the same throughout India, more's the pity. Twenty-one thousand British troops, or thereabouts, compared with two hundred and seventy thousand natives. It's out of all proportion, and damned unsafe, though I wouldn't say it to anyone but you, my love."

"You're no croaker," she reassured him with a smile. "But where could we go if there was—trouble?"

"I'd vote for the Judge's house," said Andrew without hesitation. "It's a choice between that and the church, and I for one don't mean to be besieged where there's nothing to drink but Communion wine."

"How you can joke about it!" exclaimed Philippa primly, but she smiled and waved as he allowed the bearer to pull on his boots, mounted the bay charger that was standing with his *syce* by the veranda rail, and cantered away.

With a sigh, Philippa turned her attention to household matters, pushing to the back of her mind the gnawing anxiety which their conversation had aroused. She visited Trixie, whose condition remained the same, and summoned the cook and Rhitmatgan, who served at table, to discuss the day's menus. Then she inspected the household accounts, and queried the price the cook claimed to have paid for melons the previous day, feeling the usual small shock of indignation when he promised blandly to adjust the amount. *Really, they cheat us all the time*, she thought, but it was too hot to read him a moral lecture on the evils of embezzlement, and she knew he was no worse in this respect than any other cook she might choose to replace him.

She relieved her feelings by ordering him sternly to buy no more fish in the bazaar, since the weather was now too hot for fish to reach the table in a safe condition, and the *khansamah* was wont to disguise the taint of decay by the liberal use of hot spices.

When she had dismissed the cook, Philippa selected a few of the already wilting blooms which the *mali* had cut before dawn, and stuck them in a vase. They looked limp and tired, and refused to fall into a pleasing design, but Philippa did not much care. She had little artistic sense, and with this morning's conversation fresh in her mind, she found it harder than ever to concentrate on matters so trivial as flower arrangement. Also, she knew that Andrew, who had an unexpected talent for decoration and a good eye for color, would very likely rearrange the whole vase to better advantage when he returned for luncheon.

Surely the parade was taking a long time?

She was tempted to go back to her post on the veranda, but instead seated herself at the pretty bureau of ebony inlaid with mother-of-pearl which Andrew had given her for their first wedding anniversary, and began to dash off notes inviting Major and Mrs. Dowell, Captain Mackenzie and his shy young bride, and the German missionary couple, Herman and Gertrude Bocker, to a small supper party on the Thursday of next week.

After all, she thought almost defiantly, life must go on, in spite of these alarms. In another month I shall be too stout and ungainly to enjoy the company of friends for supper, and anyway it will be too hot. We will serve melon à l'Indienne and ices, and I will take good care that the gentlemen do not linger too long over their port or ply Herr Bocker with such quantities of liquors that he is unable to play the piano for us afterward.

Andrew was justly proud of his wife's clear, high soprano, and always urged her to sing when they had company. The new duets that she and Caro had practiced in Delhi would have delighted their friends in Baburpore. Oh, thought Philippa, pausing in her writing, if only Caro were here! If only I had not asked Andrew to turn aside to Patelbar!

Tears filled her eyes and she brushed them away before they could spoil the envelope she was addressing. She must not start crying again. She had wept day and night after her sister's disappearance, until Andrew, at his wits' end how to calm her, had called in grim old Doctor Brownstone, whom the children called Doctor Brimstone, to attend her.

He had examined her, clicked his tongue and tapped

his teeth, and spoken sternly. "I know it is hard for you, Lady Philippa," he had said in his abrupt, jerky voice, which still betrayed his Lowland origin, "but you must stop this weeping for it does you no good and may harm your child. Try not to brood on the loss of your sister; keep busy and see plenty of company to distract you. Above all, do not allow yourself to become dehydrated in the hot weather, and look forward to the birth of your baby."

He had prescribed laudanum to help her sleep, and she tried her best to obey his instructions. The main improvement in her spirits, though, occurred a few days later when, for the first time, she felt the soft fluttering movement of the baby within her.

"High time it was stirring, too," said Doctor Brownstone, "for it must be all of six months!"

She was so pleased by this direct evidence of the baby's existence that she failed to catch the hint of apprehension behind his words.

Philippa finished her notes and sent them to be delivered by the *chuprassi*, Andrew's red-coated messenger, but before he was well on his way she heard wheels outside, and a moment later, Mrs. Mackenzie was announced.

"Melissa, my dear," cried Philippa, "what a charming surprise! Come in and sit down a moment. The heat outside is dreadful, and I was about to order tea and ices. By an odd chance, I have just finished writing to you."

Melissa Mackenzie was a tall, somewhat ungainly dark-haired girl with a creamy white skin and a fluttering, indecisive manner. She lived in a bungalow, isolated from its neighbors, on the edge of the quarters. Unkind people wondered aloud why Angus Mackenzie had married such a poor-spirited creature, afraid of her own shadow, who seldom ventured to take part in the life of the station. She reminded Philippa of one of those large, furry moths that blunder into lamps as soon as they are lit, and brush your face with their soft wings as if they find it hard to judge their own span in confined spaces.

Now she stumbled over a footstool as she moved to clasp Philippa's hands. "Please forgive me for disturbing you without sending a note, but I am so worried," she said in a soft, breathless voice. "Angus went to the parade this morning and I have not seen him since, and now all my servants have run away. The house is deserted. I did not know what was best to do, so I drove over to ask your advice."

"You drove here?" asked Philippa, staring. She had not supposed Melissa Mackenzie capable of controlling even the quietest horse, since she always declared herself terrified of animals.

"Yes, for the *syce* has gone with them; *ayah*, cook, bearer, *chokidar*—all vanished as silently as if they had never existed. Oh, what does it mean?" She seemed to gulp, and then controlled herself. "I called and rang, and when no one answered I went out in the garden but found not a soul, although I had the horridest sensation of eyes watching me wherever I went. So I hurried down to the stable, where there was only one old pony left. Angus's carriage horses have disappeared, and the polo ponies, But I suppose this last horse was too old for anyone to wish to steal.

"I found some harness and fastened it on as best I could. Fortunately, the pony stood quite quietly, and at length I was able to back him into the wicker chaise, and so drive here."

Philippa was astonished by this recital: not so much by the servants' defection—Indian servants were always running away for some trivial reason or another, generally returning to collect their wages— but by the spirit shown by Melissa.

She said warmly, "It was most courageous of you,

my dear; and now you must stay here until Angus returns from the parade. I'm sure he would not wish you to go back to an empty house. Your servants will come back—you can depend on it—but it may take a little time for them to come to their senses."

She ordered tea and ices, but barely had the two ladies taken up their spoons, before the clatter of hoofs outside announced Andrew's return.

"Such a queer-looking rig is hitched to our veranda," he exclaimed, striding in and kissing Philippa boisterously before he saw Melissa standing uncertainly behind her. "It's a pony about a hundred years old, with its harness half upside-down, traces crossed, girth undone... Why, Melissa, this is an unexpected pleasure! Don't tell me that's your equipage without? Angus would die of shame if he knew. You'll have to get him to speak sharply to your *syce*, if that's the best he can do. Why, it's hardly safe to drive like that, even if the pony's dead-quiet."

Melissa blushed and Philippa hurried to her defense.

"Hush, Andrew; you must not criticize Melissa's turnout, for she harnessed the pony all by herself, since her servants have run away and deserted her."

"Then I withdraw my comments unreservedly and most humbly beg pardon, ma'am," said Andrew, laughing. "Run away, have they, the black rascals? Well, they'll be back soon enough when they hear the news."

"What news?" exclaimed the ladies simultaneously.

"Why, that our gallant native fellows have today accepted their cartridges and we may sleep easy in our beds again. Is it not splendid news? That was why the parade took so long—the General wished to test each man's loyalty. By Jove, it was worth it! Send for a *burra-peg*, will you, my love, for I'm parched to death and can hardly speak."

Philippa hastened to set the servants scurrying to and fro to wait on him, and when Andrew's boots had been removed and a long cool drink was in his hand, he told them of the morning's happenings.

The troops had been drawn up in companies under the pitiless sun on the dusty *maidan*, in full parade order, native infantry on one side of the square and Irregular Cavalry on the other, and the General, bluff old Tiger Elliott, had addressed them in their own language.

"I thought he'd never cease," said Andrew. "There we were, grilling in the heat, with the glitter of weapons enough to dazzle you and the horses fidgeting, poor brutes, and the men with that damned sullen, closed look to their faces that tells you they mean trouble..."

Philippa felt, rather than saw, Melissa flinch at Andrew's language, but she was too eager to hear his tale to reprove him for swearing.

He went on. "Elliott's a brave man, for all his faults, and he stood there like a ramrod and harangued them like a lot of troublesome children. He took them through a hundred years of the East India Company's history—treaties, battles, the lot—and then asked them if they had ever found the Sirkar untrue to its word. At that, old Gulab Singh, the color-sergeant of the Forty-first, shouted 'Never,' and more and more of them took it up until they were all shouting. You never heard such a din."

"All of them?" asked Philippa, sensing he was holding something back.

"I was coming to that," said Andrew reluctantly. "The only company that stood silent was Captain Haldane's, and when the shouting died down, the General turned that cold eye of his on this company and said, 'Captain Haldane, I shall first ask your men to accept the new cartridges.'

"Poor Haldane looked sick as a dog, but he gave the

order to step forward and receive them. Not a man moved. Haldane swayed as if he'd been struck in the face. Then he repeated the order, but his men just stared at the ground and would not move."

"How dreadful," whispered Melissa. "What happened then?"

Andrew tugged unhappily at his collar. "I believe the General expected something of the kind," he admitted, "for he showed not the least surprise. He immediately ordered Haldane's company to be stripped of their arms and marched away to the jail. It was a sad sight, I can tell you, to see men with fifteen and twenty years' loyal service so dishonored. Some were weeping and some threw their weapons in a heap. I never wish to see such a scene again."

He sat silent, overcome by the memory.

"But the others?" prompted Philippa.

"After that example, they took the cartridges like lambs. There was no further trouble, not even from the cavalry. I can't help feeling sorry for Haldane, for it seemed almost that the General made him the scapegoat—"

"You mean his men might have taken the cartridges if they had not been asked first?"

Andrew nodded. "But at least when the native infantry saw that Tiger Elliott would stand no nonsense, they pulled themselves together and forgot their grumblings. I have just been down to the lines, and there is a better feeling abroad than we've known since the news of Delhi's fall." He sighed. "Steel was right, you know; firm handling's the key to control of native troops, and for too long we've given in to their fads and fancies. At least we'll sleep sound in our beds tonight..."

But despite the parade's satisfactory outcome, Andrew did not get the rest his tired body craved.

Trixie's condition suddenly worsened and they could do little to ease her pain.

At lunch, Andrew managed to coax her into lapping a few spoonfuls of egg mixed with buffalo milk, after which she lay comatose for several hours, stretched flat on her side with eyes glazed and only the quick flutter of her heart to show that she still lived.

Andrew took a last look at her at ten that evening, before preparing for bed, and found her awake and whining piteously, her flanks heaving as she rushed blindly around and around the central leg of the table. As she snapped at the hanging folds of tablecloth, flecks of blood-stained foam flew from her jaws.

"Hush now, Trixie; hush, good dog." He knelt and tried to stroke her, but she turned on his hand, and he had to pull it back quickly to avoid her teeth. Never in her life had she snapped at him before.

"She doesn't know me," he said sadly to Philippa, who was watching from a safe distance. "I fear she's suffering so much it has affected her reason. There's only one thing I can do for her." He raised his voice. "Sher Dil! Bring my gun, *ek dum*."

"Oh no," wailed Philippa, who well knew how he valued the little dog. "You can't shoot her. Let Sher Dil do it."

"She's *my* dog," said Andrew so stonily that she dared argue no more. She turned and went quickly away, muffling her ears against the sound of the shot.

When Trixie saw the gun, which she associated with so many happy days of *shikar* with her master, she seemed to regain her senses for an instant—pricked her ears and feebly wagged her stumpy tail.

Andrew held her eyes with his own as he put the muzzle to her head.

"Good bitch," he said. "Good hunting!"

He squeezed the trigger and the echoes of the

explosion rolled like thunder around the confined space. It was followed by a series of other explosions, but Andrew did not hear them as he sat staring at the limp little bundle of black, white, and tan, remembering the good times they had shared.

His father had given him Trixie when he left school; she had lived fourteen years and been a mighty hunter for all her small size. She had killed her first rat when she was a mere puppy, and thereafter bolted many a gone-to-ground fox for the pack of fell hounds hunted by Robert Thynne, Andrew's father.

He had brought her to India when he got his commission, and Trixie had quickly learned the difference between English rat and Indian musk-rat, English fox and Indian jackal. She was wise in the ways of the slinking mongoose, and learned to bark at snakes without coming within range of their deadly tongues. And now she had fallen victim to the dreaded hydrophobia, the scourge of the canine tribe in India . . . Andrew felt a sudden wave of hate for this cruel country, with its thousand and one diseases and dangers that attacked innocents like Trixie—and Caro.

He rose abruptly, laying the gun on the table, and was about to call Sher Dil to take away Trixie's body for burial when there was a thunderous knock at the front door.

At the same time he heard Philippa scream. "Andrew! Andrew! There are guns in the street and the sepoys have set fire to the General's house. We are betrayed!"

Bulbul peered over the edge of the veranda and rearranged the folds of her gold sari with precise, finicky fingers.

"Certainly not!" she said decidedly. "Certainly not."

"Why not?" asked Fionn.

"I am old woman now. I cannot bound over the land like a scared gazelle, bearing messages to sahibs. You ask too much of me. There is great danger and I am much afraid."

"You, old?" scoffed Fionn, marshaling his considerable Irish charm. "You, scared? Loveliest of singing birds, thy voice alone can entreat the son of Steel-sahib. He will listen to thy words as to none others', for is he not the son of thy heart?"

Bulbul's expression, which had been set in lines of dramatic refusal, softened at this, and she giggled like a young girl, drawing a fold of her sari to hide her laughing mouth.

"You talk, what I think they call in your language, 'blarney,' doctor-sahib. Though you flatter me, you will not persuade me to do your bidding. Rowland may be the son of my heart, but he must fight his battle alone as he did when he was only the *baba*-sahib. He will not listen to me. Too often has he laughed at old Bulbul's warnings, and gone his own way. It is for you, doctor-sahib, to bear this message."

Caro squatted comfortably on the cool veranda, enjoying the night breeze and the spirited company. She had come to look forward to Fionn's nightly visits, to his serious but good-natured harangues with Bulbul, and especially to the time afterward when, pretending to be a customer, he would accompany her to a chamber to hear the information she had garnered that day. These private meetings had instantly become the basis for a warm friendship. Fionn was affectionate and indulgent, kissing her cheek or idly throwing an arm around her with the amiable indifference of an older brother. Alone among the men who frequented the Joyhouse of Kali, Fionn Kelly sought information and companionship from Caro, never even alluding to physical desire.

"But how," Caro had asked him a few nights after

his visits had commenced, "... how do you manage to come here, night after night, through the front gate, without arousing the suspicion of the guards?"

Fionn grinned broadly. "Ah, that part was easy. By now, all Patelbar must know that the doctor-sahib is crazed with love for the Silent One at the Joyhouse of Kali. They say he cannot bear to be parted from her, that he must lie with her every night. They whisper that he loves her better than his hospital and his opium!" He laughed heartily.

Caro feigned annoyance. "I do not understand what strikes you as so humorous about the idea of someone loving me."

Fionn chucked her affectionately under the chin. "Ah, little Caro, it was me I was laughing at, not you. I cannot see how any man in his senses could fail to fall in love with you."

She had pulled back. "Fionn, you vile flatterer! You're absolutely shameless."

Over the nights, their meetings in the love room had taken on a pleasant pattern. After Caro provided Fionn with intelligence he would sit back, smoking a pipe of opium or *charrah*, growing dreamy and whimsical. Then he would tell her wondrous tales of maharajahs richer than any Englishman's dreams of avarice, of magnificent tiger hunts and splendrous royal outings. He adored seeing her pleasure at his fables, and embroidered them more and more, until she had to beg him to stop before she died of delight.

Some evenings, the drugs made him melancholy, and then he spoke of his old life and of his adopted country and its sufferings. Trapped between the greed and corruption of the rajahs and the imperial incursions of the British, the people of India lived in a misery unimaginable to the European mind. Fionn told Caro of his dream to build a hospital, to relieve at least a modicum of that suffering, but he sadly spoke of how that dream had grown daily more faint and had most probably died with the old Rajah.

"I have come to love this land very deeply, Caro," he had told her, "but she is like a patient with a grave sickness whose cure might kill her. Were the Company to disappear, conditions would most likely be as they are here in the native states, where the poor are even more abject than in the districts under British rule. So, ordered by my conscience to prescribe for the patient, I struggle and choose England." He was silent a moment, then brightened and asked her, "Isn't it about time for you to ask me more about Captain Steel?"

Early on, Caro had drawn out from Fionn the story of his association with Rowland, first in Kelly's youth, when he had served under Rowland's father, now, more recently, in secret, daring affairs of espionage.

Fionn's view of Rowland contradicted the poor portrait Brook Vyner had painted of him, and Caro could never hear enough of Rowland's bravery, his honor, his admirable sympathy for the Indian predicament. Once the source of Caro's interest became obvious, Fionn would gently gibe her about her schoolgirl infatuation with the dashing captain, but he never hesitated to tell her more stories of Rowland's daring, often making her exclaim aloud and sometimes giggle.

"Never!" A sharp bark from Bulbul brought her thoughts back to the altercation still raging on the veranda.

Fionn wanted Bulbul to leave Patelbar immediately and travel in the direction of Baburpore, picking up information as best she could about the movements of the Nana Sahib and trying to ascertain if the mutiny were spreading.

Baburpore was strategically important, although a relatively small military station, where only about a hundred mixed British officers and men of the East

India Company Bengal Army and two native regiments, numbering about a couple of thousand sepoys, their noncommissioned officers, and forty-odd native officers, were commanded by one-eyed, sixty-five-year-old Major-General Sir William Elliott, nicknamed after the tiger which had torn out his left eye some forty years before. There were, besides, a squadron of regular native cavalry, and a small detachment composed mainly of Punjabi Sikhs, the latter being Irregular cavalry under the command of Captain Rowland Steel.

Positioned as it was on a confluence of two fast-flowing rivers, Baburpore possessed the only safe crossing for thirty miles upstream and down and had been, in the past, a well-known haunt of *dacoits*—thieves and brigands of all types—besides providing a refuge and convenient meetingplace for Thugs, professional stranglers devoted to the worship of the cruel goddess, Kali, a sect against which the British had waged bitter war a decade before.

Each year at the end of the traveling season, Thugs from both sides of the rivers had met at Baburpore to dispose of their spoils, and the money they paid to the Rajah, Adeen Rao, for his protection, had filled the palace coffers to overflowing with *lakhs* of rupees and jewels beyond price. Adeen Rao had been Prince Chandranaya's father.

With the downfall of the Thugs came the downfall of Adeen Rao. British soldiers had set fire to his palace when he fought to defend his gains, and while her husband died in the smoking rubble, Chandranaya's mother, a Mahratta princess famed for her beauty, fled with her young son from the blazing ruins, and sought refuge with her brother, the Rajah of neighboring Patelbar.

The East India Company promptly applied the

Doctrine of Lapse, a favorite device for gaining control of disputed territory. They claimed that as no direct heir was available to succeed Adeen Rao, who had, moreover, been guilty of the grossest maladministration and crimes against British property, they had no alternative but to annex his domain. So Baburpore became another bastion of British India, while the Mahratta princess who was Chandranaya's mother devoted the rest of her life to implanting in her son's mind an implacable hatred against the Company, which had dispossessed him.

Not everyone was satisfied with the arrival of law and order in Baburpore, and in particular those who had grown fat on the old days of corruption and vice smarted under the new, strict, impartial administration by the sahibs, which robbed them of opportunities for plunder. Discontent seethed just below the surface, but to outward appearances Baburpore seemed a typical small upcountry military station, with its white-painted church and tidy quarters well separated from the native town and bazaar; its mall, where the British could drive, gossip, and take the cooler evening air in their open carriages; its polo ground and clubhouse where white-coated natives served gimlets and whisky-sodas to sweating, red-faced sahibs.

Bulbul had not seen Baburpore since the early days of its annexation, and part of her longed to return and relive her memories of the Colonel-sahib and his easygoing household. But whenever she felt herself drawn toward agreeing to Fionn's request, another memory—that of the high-nosed, stern new memsahib who had told Bulbul she must never again set foot in Baburpore—caused her to shy away like a frightened horse, and give the doctor-sahib yet another spurious reason why she could not take his message.

She was too old—too busy—too scared.

She could not leave her business—her children—her new lover, who would surely creep away into other, younger, arms.

It was too hot to travel; she would be set on and robbed; her gharry needed a new wheel and her horses were lame.

Fionn persisted patiently, night after night on the flower-scented veranda, seated crossed-legged on a mat smoking his water pipe while he quietly disposed of Bulbul's excuses. He sensed she would give in in the end, and the worst thing he could do would be to hurry her, to press her into a straight refusal from which she could not retreat without losing face. So he joked and gently bullied, laughed at her fears and promised to lend her his two best horses.

When at length he rose, Bulbul was on the verge of capitulating, and Fionn winked at Caro.

"Tomorrow night she'll agree to go and take you with her. You'll see," he whispered.

Caro clasped her hands to her heart as it gave a sudden bound. She could hardly believe it. To leave the degradation of working as a *devadasi*, to put off her tawdry finery and once more feel cool, fresh, British linen against her skin, to eat good English food again...

"Now," Fionn proclaimed, "escort me upstairs to your chambers, Silent One, and make my love dreams come alive!" They all laughed at his play-acting, then Bulbul returned to the main room as Fionn and Caro, assuming their public roles, proceeded upstairs to her chamber.

Fionn smoked the pipe of *charrah* Caro had prepared for him, then lay back among the pillows as she poured refreshment for both of them and came to join him. As he took the cup from her, Caro noticed that a sudden sadness had overtaken him, much in contrast to his high spirits of only moments earlier.

"Fionn," she asked, "why so sad?"

He set the cup down on a low lacquered table and ran his palm across his eyes as if he were exhausted.

"So many things, Caro," he answered at last, taking her hand, "so many things, not the least of which is your imminent departure. Not only do I worry for your well-being, but before you're even gone, I miss you."

"I will miss you, too, Fionn," Caro replied, realizing for the first time how much she would. "I wish more than anything that you could come with us."

"Quite impossible, my not-so-silent one." He squeezed her hand. "I doubt that I will ever leave Patelbar. But you! Think of what lies ahead in Baburpore—your family, your people, and of course, Captain Steel."

"Of course," she replied, lowering her lashes half in embarrassment.

Fionn had reached for the *charrah* pipe and was smoking languidly, saying nothing, still holding her hand. After a moment, as if bolstered by the *charrah*, he spoke. "Caro, I have told you of my wife, of how I loved her and lost her and how that loss had become a chronic pain undulled by the years. And now, tomorrow or the next day or the day after that you'll be leaving Patelbar. It seems my destiny always to lose the women I love."

Caro stared at him in surprise, thinking she had mistaken his meaning.

"You see, little Caro," he continued gravely, "it is true what they say in Patelbar. The doctor-sahib *has* fallen madly, passionately in love with the silent girl from the Joyhouse."

"But you never spoke of it, never intimated!" Strange feelings sprang to life and warred with each other inside Caro's head.

"How could I speak of it," Fionn countered, "after you had declared your love for Rowland Steel? I am

not\the sort of man to force a woman against her will."
He dropped her hand.

Caro gazed at the still-boyish face, the lean, lanky
body of her friend, realizing that he had grown so
familiar to her that she had stopped seeing him. Now,
all at once, the ever-present charm coupled with
melancholy, the gentleness and loneliness all came
together for her in a rush of feelings very soft and
warm. She knew what she must do, what she wanted to
do.

Bending toward him, she said simply, "I would like
to offer a gift to my most constant patron. If he so
desires it."

"Caro—" he began to protest, but she silenced him
with her kiss as she lay down beside Fionn and drew
him to her.

Next evening, buoyed up with hope and warmed by
the memories of Fionn's tender lovemaking, she found
it hard to sit meekly on her usual mat, with downcast
eyes, listening to the men's talk as they lounged at their
ease amid the acrid fumes of tobacco and *bhang*.

Near her were two soldiers, high-caste Brahmans, as
she could tell by the thread about their wrists. The
younger was dissatisfied with the wife he had returned
to his village to marry on this furlough.

"Her *araya* swore she was lovely as the moon," he
grumbled, "but no moon I have ever seen has a face
pitted with smallpox. Her voice is harsh as the
kingcrow's, and her dowry is of small worth since it is
mostly property settled on herself. I shall be glad to
return to the regiment and ride once more at the side of
Steel-sahib."

One of Rowland's men! Caro listened eagerly,
careful to let no expression show on her face as she
stared at the floor.

The other soldier seemed surprised. "Do you, a Brahman, ride with Sikhs?"

The young man shrugged. "It is the will of the Sirkar..."

Oh, thought Caro, if only they would go on talking about Rowland and not begin one of those interminable discussions of Army matters, or squabble about petty differences of caste. Hearing them speak of Rowland seemed to bring him closer; she could almost conjure up the feel of his arms about her that long-ago night on board ship, the hard demand of his lips as they sought hers. She had not known then what he wanted of her. She had been as unawakened as any schoolroom miss. But were he to make the same demand now...

Heat flooded through her at the idea and she shifted uncomfortably, wrenching her attention back with an effort to what the men were saying. Her wish was granted: Steel-sahib was still the topic of conversation.

The older man spoke quietly. "You will have to make haste if you wish to ride with your captain, for I have heard it said in the bazaar that the Rajah of Bithoor waits only for Steel-sahib to ride out from Baburpore before he strikes at the town."

Here was news indeed for Fionn! Caro wondered by what magic the bazaar learned so speedily of Nana Sahib's intentions, and whether bazaar rumor would be proof enough to convince Bulbul of the urgency of their mission.

Fionn Kelly himself could not leave Patelbar, for he was watched by palace spies, and his absence would probably be reported at once. But Bulbul frequently toured the district in search of new girls for her Joyhouse. No one would question her leaving the town.

The sepoy and sowar were whispering now, too low for her to catch their words. Then Rowland's man stood up quickly and pulled his jacket straight.

"I leave my wife with my mother: it is best when times are so uncertain," he said, as if trying to convince himself. "My place is with the Captain-sahib. And thou, brother?"

"I go to my village to help with the harvest, and I shall not return until the Red Wind has blown far away," replied the other. "Too long have I eaten the Sirkar's salt and fought its battles. I cannot raise my hand against the sahib-log, nor can I fight my own brethren. But thou are young, brother, and see thy way clear. May good fortune attend thee!"

As the young man smiled and threaded his way out of the crowded room, Caro rose with studied languor and followed. She made her way to Bulbul's veranda, where candles glowed in paper lanterns and sweet-smelling cedar sticks burned to ward off insects and evil spirits. She half expected Fionn to rise from his mat to greet her, but there was no one on the veranda.

Caro squatted on her haunches in the way that was now second nature to her, listening to the steady beat of the tom-tom, the lugubrious croaking of frogs, while her thoughts darted here and there like a shoal of scared fish.

Nana Sahib, Rajah of Bithoor, was planning to attack Baburpore: that was clear. Less certain was the temper of the native troops stationed there. Would they, like the young sowar tonight, remain loyal to the British? Or would they betray their salt and butcher their English officers, their wives and families, as had the native troops in Meerut, Delhi, and Jhansi? Large numbers, she guessed, would adopt the line of least resistance and melt away to disappear into their villages until they saw for certain which way the Red Wind was going to blow. Remove a sepoy's red uniform jacket, his black, bell-shaped shako, his crossbelts and insignia, and he was impossible to distinguish from any other peasant peaceably tilling his tiny fields.

Why didn't Fionn come?

Every night since his first visit, Caro had meticulously passed on to him every detail of the conversations she had heard from soldiers and travelers passing through Patelbar. Rumors and counter-rumors. She had reported their grumbles about the Iron Monster, in whose boiler the wily British had trapped a demon, which they fed with great sacks of coal and barrels of water. The demon shrieked and struggled to escape from its iron prison, and this sent the monster roaring across the land on its iron road. In its train were carriages, in which high-caste Brahmans and the lowliest sweepers were expected to sit side by side.

Wilder stories still concerned the British desire to convert Hindus and Moslems alike to the worship of their God—and in response, the Sirkar ground up the bones of dead sepoys and mixed the powder with Army flour; that thousands of English widows, whose men had died in the Crimean Wars, were being transported to India to become the brides of sepoys; that the new Enfield rifles had cartridges greased with the fat of cows and pigs.

Only the youngest and most credulous peasants wholly believed these fantasies, and Caro sensed that most of the data she relayed to Doctor Kelly was known to him already. What he was really interested in was news of troop movements, snippets of information concerning the mutineers' strength and what popular support they enjoyed at Cawnpore, Aligahr, and Lucknow; and on these points Caro, who had only the haziest notion of military matters, was unable to understand much of what she heard.

But now, when she had news that was undoubtedly important and, for once, free of ambiguity, Fionn was not there to hear it.

Caro fidgeted, wishing Bulbul would join her on the veranda. The sounds of revelry in the main chamber were dying away as sleep gradually overcame all but the most determined merrymakers. Soon Fionn would come.

At last Caro heard the soft shuff-shuff of Bulbul's slippers, and with it another, stranger sound: a monotonous muted wail, as from a wounded animal. Bulbul glided across the veranda and squatted beside Caro, her sari pulled over her head. She rocked to and fro, moaning.

"What is it?" said Caro, alarmed. "What's the matter?"

"*Aiee, aiee,* the Prince has returned to his palace," mourned Bulbul. "The downfall of the sahibs is at hand and nothing can save them. One hundred years has the Sirkar ruled, and now it will fall in the dust. It is written."

Cold fingers of fear clutched at Caro.

"Why do you say so? Has not the doctor-sahib shown you how the rule of the Sirkar may be saved?" she demanded, trying to shake poor Bulbul from her misery.

"Too late, too late. The Prince has returned and tomorrow we shall die. His spies have watched and listened at the Joyhouse of Kali, and now they whisper to him that I, Bulbul, am the friend of the Feringhee and must die. They have heard me speak with the doctor-sahib and my fate is sealed. *Aie,* for my children who will be motherless! *Aiee,* for old Bulbul, who will dance her last dance on the elephant's foot!"

This time Caro did shake her. She gripped the old woman by her fat shoulders, forcing her to look up.

"Bulbul," she said, speaking gently as to a child in shock. "Tell me, what have you heard? Where is the doctor-sahib?"

Fear gleamed in Bulbul's eyes, smeared with tears and kohl, but she spoke rationally. "He is dead, *baba*. That is why he did not come tonight. He is dead by the Prince's command, and the dogs lick his eyes in an alley off the Chowdri Chowk. Tomorrow will be our turn."

Panic mingled with great sorrow struck Caro like a blow over the heart. Dead—that good, loving man who had tried to carve and shape the future of Patelbar's people as secretly and patiently as he had chiseled his small ivory figures. She touched the dangling earrings of fretted ivory he had carved for her, as she remembered how he had taught her the great joy of giving—and accepting—love. Trying to remain calm, she forced herself to marshal her thoughts and bring Bulbul back to her senses.

"Tomorrow will *not* be our turn—not if we leave at once," she said.

And Bulbul echoed, "Not if we leave at once."

Chapter Ten

THE KEEPER OF the North Gate of the city of Patelbar was a man of poetic soul, and every morning as his gate swung open to greet the dawn, his heart rejoiced to see the early sunlight glinting on his city's gold towers and minarets, the blue and gilded domes, the columns, pillars, and terraced roofs in faultless perspective.

From the gate house, too, the keeper enjoyed a clear view across the plain, where this morning nothing moved except the lazy flap of a vulture's leathery wings as it pecked at a sprawled body with a green silk turban wound around his battered head—a turban as green as the emerald hills of Erin the dead man had left long ago.

The keeper turned back from surveying the plain, and focused his attention on the morning's traffic, now starting to jostle under the archway. There were the usual herdsboys, with their scrawny, half-fleeced sheep and sleek goats with knowing amber eyes; a pot-bellied child driving an ancient buffalo with blows of a knobbed stick; a party of shaven-headed priests in saffron robes, and a troupe of dancing-girls, wrapped in cloaks and heavy-eyed in the dawn light.

Nothing unusual, just the everyday crowd of travelers drifting along the dusty *sudduk* like leaves on a slow-moving stream. But wait, thought the gatekeeper, and his gaze sharpened. Here was something of interest. A wooden-wheeled gharry drawn by snow-white oxen with gilded horns—now *that* was someone who traveled in style. The driver wore a red silk tunic and turban, and the coolies who shuffled behind with empty *doolies*, their open curtains fluttering in the light breeze, wore head cloths of the same color.

The gatekeeper strained for a glimpse through the light muslin draperies surrounding the bullock cart, allowing its occupants to see out without being seen, but the flimsy barrier effectively concealed the cart's interior.

Inside it, Bulbul squawked with laughter and jerked the curtains suddenly aside, pushing her head right into the face of the startled gatekeeper.

"Better wait to stick thy long nose into my *doolies* on our return, O, guardian of the gate," she screeched in the raucous, showman's voice that contrasted so oddly with her usual gentle tones. "I go to seek new beauties for the Joyhouse of Kali." She cackled again and swished the curtains closed.

"Bulbul!" went up a delighted shout from all who had witnessed her brief appearance.

"Bring me a girl with a neck like a dove!"

"Eyes like mountain lakes!"

"Breasts like ripe melons!"

More ribald suggestions followed, and Caro, seated beside Bulbul in the swaying gharry, put a hand to her mouth to smother her laughter. How delightful it was to sit here concealed yet able to hear and understand all that went on outside! How very shocked her mother— or Philippa—would be, but she could not help savoring the earthy comments that floated more and more faintly to them as the driver applied his goad and the bullocks moved forward.

Bulbul caught her eye. "Verree noortee," she said in her Anglo-Indian singsong, and they both burst out laughing. There was a marvelous freedom about being on the move in the fresh early morning, the night's terrors behind them. Only the memory of Fionn Kelly's violent end and the Prince's wrath at finding his birds flown remained to damp Caro's spirits.

Once she had made up her mind to leave, Bulbul's preparations for departure had been carried out with astonishing speed. Her servants stayed up all night preparing the gharry, loading supply wagons, harnessing bullocks and pack ponies, repairing *doolies*—all with the minimum of fuss and a smooth efficiency Caro had not expected.

Watching the final preparations in the pearly, rose-tinted light before sunrise—as the last ropes were tightened, whips were cracked, and the little procession moved off between the high house of the Hathi Bund— Caro realized that this was a people to whom travel was a way of life as simple and natural as the air they breathed.

Europeans on the move demanded the same degree of comfort they experienced in their own homes: beds and mosquito netting, hot water to shave and wash in, clean clothes and cooked meals, to be seated at a table laid with plates, glasses, and cutlery. Hence the long preparations and days of uproar that had preceded the Thynne household's departure from Delhi.

But an Indian felt well-equipped for the road with no more than a knife, a bag of *attar*, a brass water pot, and a blanket to roll himself up in at night.

Bulbul, too, was in high spirits as Patelbar merged into the dust-haze behind them. She hummed a little tune in a minor key, full of strange half- and quarter-tones, and glanced sharply about her as she occasionally shrilled advice and encouragement to the driver.

Toward midday, when the sun was burning hot, they halted in a mango grove, where a flock of screaming parrots wheeled in circles before settling, all at once, on the topmost twigs to scold and chatter at the interruption of their feast of green fruit. In the deep shade, where a small temple stood beside a well, the servants drew water for their beasts and squatted among the giant roots to eat their noon *chupatti*s.

The slow, uneven clack-clack-clack-clop of horses' hoofs aroused Caro from a half doze. She looked up the dusty road, shading her eyes from the midday glare.

A strange conveyance was approaching the grove from the opposite direction—a battered phaeton with wobbling wheels, drawn by two handsome chestnuts, which moved as if the effort of putting one leg in front of the other was almost beyond their powers. Their fine coats were caked with dust and streaked with the white lines of dried sweat, and one was favoring a foot that had lost its shoe.

Perched up behind her tired team was a scarecrow figure of a white woman, wearing a dirty blue dress and a sunbonnet from which wisps of straw-colored hair had escaped to fall across her face. Her lips were cracked and blackened in the heat, and her eyes looked utterly dull and hopeless as she feebly flapped the reins on the chestnut rumps, urging them toward the shade.

It was so dark under the mango trees after the glare of the road that the woman did not at first see Bulbul's party, and she had half fallen from her carriage before she realized that there were others in the grove.

A cry that was more like a raven's croak broke from her parched lips, and she shrank back against the nearest horse, staring at them with a look of stark terror.

"Who—who are you?" she whispered.

Slowly she reached in the deep pocket of her stained and torn dress and drew out a long horse pistol. Her wrist could hardly hold the cumbersome weapon steady, but she rested it on the shaft of her phaeton and pointed it at the head of Bulbul's driver, who happened to be nearest to her.

She croaked, "Don't touch me or I will shoot you dead, I swear it." She spoke bad Hindustani, the mixed language of Anglo-Indian households, but her meaning was plain enough. Bulbul's driver uttered a wail of fear.

Bulbul spoke reassuringly in the same tongue: "We are travelers, memsahib. We will do you no harm. Be seated and let my servants bring you food, and water for your horses, who look tired to death."

The pistol sagged in the woman's hand, and she let it slide to the ground.

"Thank God! Oh, Thank God!" she sobbed. "I never looked to find friends again."

"Mama?" came a plaintive voice from inside the phaeton. "Who is there, Mama? Baby Jack lies so very still that I am afraid."

The woman rallied, and turned to open the door of the carriage. "Tommy, you are a good boy and you can come out now. We're among friends."

A moment later a pale child of six or seven, the white collar of his sailor suit accentuating his peaked face and dark-rimmed eyes, climbed stiffly down into the road, clutching in one arm an ominously quiet little bundle wrapped in a shawl.

Bulbul took charge at once. "Give me the *baba*-sahib." She took him gently from his brother's unresisting arms, and then began to issue a stream of directions to her servants, bidding them look to the horses and prepare food for the memsahib.

The poor woman sank down on the ground, incapable of further effort, and it was only after she had swallowed milk and a few mouthfuls of *chupatti* that she could begin to answer Bulbul's questions.

Her story confirmed Caro's fears. The mutiny was spreading eastward like a fungus through the Army of Bengal, creeping ever nearer to Baburpore.

The woman, whose name was Mrs. Evans, had been the wife of a captain in the 43rd BNI, on garrison duty at the little town of Fatiganj, the next upriver crossing from Baburpore. The day before, after a prolonged period of unrest, during which the Commandant blandly ignored the mounting disquiet of the European community, the sepoys had risen in revolt, shot their officers, and then rampaged through the Civil lines, murdering and looting before reaching the military quarters.

It had been the day of her elder son, Tommy's, birthday, she told them, and she had promised to take him for a picnic to a temple some five miles from Fatiganj, where there was a lake with a large population of waterbirds. Tommy had been given a toy musket by his father, and wished to taste the joys of *shikar*.

Captain Evans had promised to join the expedition when he came off duty, and by eight in the morning his wife and son were waiting for him in the phaeton, behind the young chestnut mares he was so proud of. Half an hour passed: an hour. Still he did not come.

At last Mrs. Evans, fearing the heat and Tommy's disappointment if she lingered any longer, decided that her husband had been delayed and she must set off without him.

She had not driven the young mares before, since they had only recently been promoted to drawing the phaeton, but there seemed nothing for it but to set off at a steady pace, instructing the bearer to tell his master where they had gone so that he might join them. They had reached the lake without mishap, and had their picnic, all the while watching and listening for the hoofbeats of Captain Evans's horse. Tommy amused himself by stealing up to the rim of the lake and pretending to fire his small gun at the flapping, splashing waterfowl, but the game would have been twice as much fun had his father been there to join in the make-believe. After a bare hour of solitary play, Tommy himself suggested that they should go home.

"If only Papa could have come," he had said sadly, and Mrs. Evans, too, felt the expedition had been a failure.

She had signalled to the *syce* to bring up the horses, and as he did so there was a sudden loud squawking, and a whirring of wings, and every bird on the lake rose in a great cloud, and flew around and around above their heads.

"Guns!" exclaimed Tommy. "Did you hear them, Mama?"

She had heard nothing, but then she'd been busy checking the horses' curb chains, which the *syce* had failed to twist until they lay flat. One had even rubbed a small sore on the corner of the animal's mouth, and she scolded the man briskly. He scowled, and did not apologize.

They had climbed into the carriage and were soon spanking along the dust road at a good pace, the mares stepping out well, eager to regain their cool stables.

When they were no more than a mile from the quarters, Tommy again exclaimed, "Guns, Mama!"— and this time she heard them loud and clear.

She had slowed the mares, puzzled, and smelled smoke in the air. A thick black column was lazily rising into the clear blue sky.

Far down the white, dusty road a figure appeared, hurrying toward her, and she flicked the whip over the mares' backs, eager for news. The figure drew nearer, and to her amazement she recognized Abdullah, their native butler, carrying in his arms the sleeping form of her younger son, Baby Jack.

Tears were running unchecked down Abdullah's lined face as he handed the baby to his mistress. "Go, memsahib! Go quickly," he had sobbed. "Sepoys kill sahibs, burn houses. Red Wind is blowing in Fatiganj. All becomes Red."

"But—but I must go home!" She could not take in

what he was saying. "My husband will think—"

"Sahibs dead," he had repeated. "Sepoy shoot all sahibs, burn house. House finished. You take *baba*s, go quickly."

He had pointed back the way they had just come, and hardly aware of what she was doing, she obeyed and turned the reluctant mares' heads, clicking them into a trot. Abdullah ran alongside, waving something, and at the last moment she reached down and took from him a small, heavy bag of chickpeas, and a canvas water bottle. She had tried to call her thanks, but the words choked in her throat as, behind them, she heard once more the crackle of muskets and the solid, dull boom of a cannon.

All through the afternoon heat and on through the night, the mares had responded gallantly to her demands, but by morning Tara, the nearside horse, had a shoe missing and soon after dawn Mrs. Evans had been obliged to halt and rest them in a village. The headman had been surly, disliking to assist her or even to sell her food. Though dropping with weariness herself, she had not thought it safe to sleep there, and as soon as the mares were fed and a little rested, she once more resumed the road for Baburpore.

"How much farther is it?" she wanted to know, but neither Bulbul nor Caro could tell her.

"We also go for Baburpore," said Bulbul. "You travel with us."

Mrs. Evans looked doubtfully at the bullock gharry and shook her head. "You are very kind, but I must make more haste than you. I fear we are sole survivors out of all the Europeans in Fatiganj, and since the electric telegraph was cut a week since, General Elliott will not know of the disaster. I must tell him with all speed so that he may prepare Baburpore's defenses." She brushed away tears with the back of her hand. "My husband had planned to bring the children and me to

Baburpore last week, but Colonel Mayhew insisted that to send families away would show a lack of confidence in our sepoys. This is how they have rewarded his trust!"

Bulbul stroked her hand with little soothing murmurs, and cast a warning look at Caro, cautioning her not to join in the conversation. It had been difficult to listen to Mrs. Evans's story without uttering a single exclamation of sorrow or indignation that would at once have told the fugitive that Caro was no Indian. But Bulbul was right, and the fewer the people who knew her true origin the safer she would be.

So Caro fought down the desire to reveal herself as a countrywoman of Mrs. Evans's, and instead said softly to Bulbul in Hindi, "Ask her if we should take the baby to Baburpore in the gharry. He would be better with us."

Mrs. Evans seemed tempted by this proposal when it was explained to her, but after thinking it over she shook her head with obvious regret.

"You must not think I do not trust him to you. Indeed, I would dearly like him to travel with you instead of in this uncomfortable phaeton. But," she said in a shaking voice, "my children are now all I have left, and we must stick together. Harry would have expected it of me."

None of Bulbul's arguments could shake her resolve. Mrs. Evans lingered with them in the grove until after sundown, when her horses were well fed and somewhat rested, then as the moon rose across the flat, open fields, she placed the two children in the phaeton under the half-open hood, and herself mounted the box.

"Farewell, and may God reward you for you kindness!" she called, and flicked her whip over the mares' backs.

"Reward!" snorted Bulbul, watching the carriage

bowl briskly down the straight white road. "*I* ask no reward. That is a brave memsahib, but she should have left the *baba* with old Bulbul. I fear she will never reach Baburpore."

Before long they were following her, at the bullocks' slower pace; the gleaming silver disk of the full moon lit the landscape as brilliantly as daylight. On this long straight stretch of white road, any object could be seen some distance away, and when they had gone but a few miles, Bulbul's driver gave an exclamation of alarm and stopped his beasts.

"Jats! *Dacoits*!"

A crowd of men were drawn up across the road several hundred yards ahead. They seemed to be armed with spears, the wicked curved *talwars*, and iron-bound clubs known as *lathis*.

"I fear no Jats," said Bulbul scornfully. "Drive on."

With reluctance the man obeyed, but as they drew nearer Bulbul's confidence proved well-founded. She stuck her head through the curtains to proclaim her identity, and the menacing mob of brigands at once fell back, laughing.

"Where are you going, Bulbul?" cried one.

"Take my sister to work in your Joyhouse," called another, "and you may have her for half the bride-price. Truly, she has eyes as sweet as almonds, but her tongue is worse than the cobra's bite!"

Their good-humored voices faded behind them, but Bulbul turned to Caro with a face from which all trace of laughter had fled. "I fear for the brave memsahib with her *babas*," she said somberly. "There are many *badmash* on the roads this night."

Soon after, they fell in with a party of Bengal Light Infantry, and at this first contact with the mutineers, Caro was more thankful than ever of Bulbul's protection. She shrank away behind the curtains while Bulbul exchanged greetings with the sepoys, who were escorting half a dozen heavily laden wagons, heaped with muskets and ammunition.

"Whither are you bound with those great guns?" asked Bulbul of their *havildar*, a tall, burly Hindu with a dirty bandage covering one eye.

"We march to join the forces of Nana Sahib, who sits before the gates of Baburpore. Bring the treasure of your Joyhouse to our camp to cheer us, O, Bulbul; for the Feringhees have built a great wall and the siege will be a hard one."

"Baburpore is besieged?"

"Aye. The officers of the Sirkar and their whey-faced spawn are caught like rats in a trap," shouted another sepoy. "When the army of Prince Chandran-aya comes to swell our ranks we will cut every white throat in Baburpore. *Sub lal hoga hi*—All will become Red!"

Within the gharry, Caro shivered, thinking of Philippa and Andrew and of Rowland Steel. Was he even now within the gates of Baburpore? "We are too late," she whispered. "The siege has already begun. What can we do?"

Bulbul shook her head. "We cannot return to Patelbar. We must go on. Sepoys are much given to boasting, and it may well be that the sahibs will yet prove too strong for them."

They met no more soldiery that night, but as day was breaking, streaking the eggshell blue of the eastern sky with soft pinks, yellows, and greens, they came to what Caro had been dreading.

Overturned on its side by a little stone bridge across a *nullah*, horses gone and one wheel badly buckled, lay Mrs. Evans's black phaeton, and some fifty yards away from it an untidy bundle of blue-and-white checked gingham sprawled lifeless in the hollow of a *kutcha*.

We must stick together, she had said, and true to her word, they found her with Tommy still clasped to her breast. A savage blow from a *talwar* had all but severed his neck, and the once-white sailor collar was stained red.

"*Aiee*, poor memsahib," mourned Bulbul. She examined the ground with close attention. "See where she tried to drive past her enemies, but they must have put a rope across the bridge, and the carriage could not pass. See, there is the end still tied to the post."

Signs of the struggle for life that Mrs. Evans had put up were clearly visible, but of her murderers there was no trace. Bulbul's servants laid the bodies in a shallow grave, and piled heavy stones on top to discourage jackals. Then, as the sun was rapidly gaining strength, Bulbul gave orders to drive on to the village they could see in the distance, to seek shade during the noonday heat.

Stunned as she was by the horror of this murder, it was not until they were about to depart that Caro realized they had buried only two bodies.

"Where is the baby?" she exclaimed.

Bulbul shrugged. "Sowars take *baba*-sahib," she suggested.

"Please wait a moment."

Caro ran back to the wrecked phaeton. Gently she pulled open the half-concertinaed hood and discovered, hidden in its folds, the tightly wrapped bundle of cashmere shawl. As the sun struck the baby's waxen face, his eyes screwed up and he uttered a faint wail of protest.

Of all the European community that had flourished at Fatiganj, Baby Jack was the sole survivor.

A thunderous frown drew Rowland Steel's thick black eyebrows into a single line as he glared at the paper which the General's galloper had just brought in.

Squatting on his haunches in a corner of the hot, lamp-lit tent, the wiry young native whom he had just been interrogating observed him with mounting anxiety, and twisted a corner of his *dhoti* between his thin, nervous fingers. What had angered the Captain-sahib? A moment ago he had been glad to hear of the pale-skinned *devadasi* at the Joyhouse of Kali, the one who conversed in English with the Feringhee doctor who came to her late at night. Had he done wrong to bring this tale to the Englishman?

As houseboy to Fionn Kelly, young Gupta Ram had been ideally placed to spy on the doctor's doings, and had carried many interesting pieces of information to Prince Chandranaya's ministers. But now the Prince had returned and ordered the death of the doctor-sahib. They no longer wanted information from Gupta Ram. The rewards he had expected from the Royal treasure house had never materialized, and dimly he realized that by bearing tales to the palace he had himself slain the goose that never again could lay golden eggs.

So, in revenge against the Prince of Patelbar, who had cheated him, Gupta Ram had brought his story to the British, and the Captain-sahib had been well pleased, until now...

What could be in that paper? Was it, perhaps, a document that told the Captain that Gupta Ram was a liar; not to be trusted? Had he better tell a different story?

Silently Rowland damned General Elliott to hell and back again. Why were all senior British officers in India well beyond the verge of senility? Blundering, vacillating old idiot, sending him here to check how matters stood on the Patelbar state border, and then chucking him back to Baburpore like a hen with a strayed chick, just when he had been given the first indication that Caro was still alive.

Return without delay, ordered the dispatch, without even the courtesy of giving him a reason for the summons. Damn it, he would not go! The thought of Caro, humiliated and bewildered, in the hands of that devil Chandranaya, with his smooth, effeminate face and cruel mouth, caused a red haze to rise in front of Rowland's eyes, and a dull rage to fill his being so completely that he was no longer wholly answerable for his actions.

Six weeks ago in Baburpore he had lost his temper entirely when Andrew Thynne haltingly explained the circumstances leading up to Caro's disappearance.

"You left her in Patelbar? You came here without her?" His shocked and incredulous voice had caused a sudden hush in the crowded mess. The waiters stopped serving drinks as they looked for the cause of the disturbance, and officers' heads turned to where Rowland and Andrew confronted each other.

"She is dead, Rowland."

"I don't believe it!"

For an instant everything had seemed to go dark around him, and then he was lashing out at Andrew in a fury of rage and grief, determined to beat to a bloody pulp the man who had abandoned Caro to her fate. A dozen officers sprang from their seats and rushed to pull them apart, but Rowland continued to fight like a madman until the padre, who happened to be passing with a bottle of claret in his hand, cracked it scientifically and impartially across the heads of the grappling figures.

"Control yourselves, for the love of God," he had entreated. "This is a poor example to the heathen."

His words had had little effect, but the claret bottle laid Rowland senseless. When he came to himself, the burning grief was still with him, but he saw he had behaved unjustly toward Andrew and forced himself to make some kind of apology.

"But you were right; I deserved it, old fellow," said Andrew humbly. "I should have gone back and insisted on bringing home poor Caro's body, but Philippa was so cut up about it that I was afraid she would lose her baby. To be honest, I didn't know what to do, but I see now I should never have left without seeing her body."

However the fact that Andrew had not seen her dead body was enough to raise in Rowland the faintest flicker of hope. A native servant seldom told the plain truth, but would twist and bend it to suit himself and render it, in his opinion, acceptable to the ears of his listener. Andrew had only the word of Sher Dil, his old bearer, who claimed to have seen Caro killed. How far could Sher Dil be trusted?

Andrew had allowed Rowland to interrogate the old man himself, but with no very satisfactory result, for Sher Dil retreated into a shell of feigned stupidity, and would only repeat the story he had given Andrew. The miss-sahiba was dead. She had refused to drink the poisoned stirrup cup and had called Prince Chandran-aya a murderer, whereupon the Prince's guards had rushed upon her and cut her to pieces with their *talwars*. When he saw what his soldiers had done, the Prince was sorry, and had allowed Sher Dil to put his master and mistress in the bullock cart and drive away.

He would not budge from this story, but Rowland was not wholly convinced he was telling the truth. Part of the truth, perhaps, but by no means all.

"Why then did the Prince not order the death of Captain Thynne and his memsahib?"

"Who can read the minds of princes? Perhaps he feared the wrath of the Sirkar," said the old man, incessantly stroking his white beard. His eyes had refused to meet Rowland's.

Unsatisfied, Rowland had gone to General Elliott and demanded permission to make a tour of the villages along the river that divided Patelbar from British India, gathering information that might determine Caro's fate.

The one-eyed General, who had heard something of the fight in the mess, and saw from Rowland's strained face and sharp, nervous movements that he was near the end of his tether, put his unease at allowing the sole troop of cavalry in whom he had complete confidence to leave the town, assented and gave the foray his blessing.

"Very well; but be sharp about it," he had grunted. "We can't have you miss the Station Ball on the twenty-first. Don't know what m'wife would do without her favorite waltzing partner."

A small, tight smile had broken the lines around Rowland's mouth. Lady Elliott was sixty years old, but she still had a child's love of parties, and her tiny neat feet far outshone younger but clumsier maidens at the station's annual ball.

"I'll be back for it," he had promised, saluting.

That had been a week ago and, even in so short a time, the fact of being on the march instead of cooped up in quarters had brought Rowland to a frame of mind which, if not exactly easy, was at least less tortured then before. His grief and fury had not disappeared, but it had abated. He could think more calmly about Caro, remembering her slim dark beauty and soft, trusting eyes with their curiously direct quality. He could even accept her dallying with Vyner as a half-conscious strategy designed to arouse his own jealousy. Caro did not simper and dissemble, like other white girls—her eyes meant what they said, and they were without fear. He remembered, too, that strange power she had to blend in with her surroundings, appearing to belong perfectly naturally in settings as varied as the drawing room of her father's London house, an opium den in Suez, or cross-legged in a tent in an Indian mango grove. Always herself and yet, in some indefinable way, she could take on the coloring— the tone, almost—of the place she happened to be in.

Like an actress—no, he thought, that was wrong. It was the very antithesis of acting, for where an actor sought to draw attention to a person who was not himself, Caro simply adjusted herself to fit in with her surroundings.

One could not, of course, compare a lady with a cat, but that was the creature of which Caro most reminded him. A cat was always recognizable as a cat and did not look out of place anywhere in the world. The same cat could bask in a filth-strewn alley or luxuriate on a silken cushion, whereas a dog could look terribly out of place in the wrong milieu. A foxhound looked as foolish in a lady's boudoir as a Pekinese would in the foxhound's kennels.

Like a cat, Caro radiated the ability to adapt—and survive. *She could not be dead!*

Rowland crumpled the General's dispatch in his fist and called softly, "Oh, Bakta Bahadur! Send Mr. Allan in to me."

Gupta Ram stirred uneasily in his corner, but when he saw that the Captain-sahib's frown had vanished, he took fresh heart. It was all right. The sahib had been angry at what the paper said, but it had not concerned Gupta Ram...

As the young lieutenant entered, wiping from his sandy mustache the iced beer which had slaked his thirst, Rowland, straight-faced, said, "Ah, Allan; good of you to drop by, but I'm afraid I have bad news for you. Your horse has gone lame."

"Lame?" The boy's pale eyebrows almost disappeared into his sandy thatch of hair. "That's dashed odd, because he was all right when I rode in."

"I know, but he's lame now, and that means you'll have to bear me company for a few days."

"Oh, look here, Steel—that's all very well, but the General insisted I should return at once to Baburpore. And bring you with me."

"You know what was in the dispatch?"

"Yes."

Rowland sat silent in thought for a moment, then he said, "How were things when you left?"

"Oh—quiet. Much the same as ever. Each new band of travelers that passes through the town seems to bring half a dozen fresh rumors, but I think even the sepoys are getting tired of them now. At all events, they accepted their cartridges on parade the very morning I left."

"Ah."

Rowland's taut shoulders relaxed a little. He smiled. "Just as I hoped. Then, whatever the General says, there is no immediate urgency for me to return?"

William Allan, who had been taught that orders were orders, no matter how unreasonable, swallowed and said nothing. Steel was a law to himself, he knew, and fellows who ran afoul of him were apt to get the cutting edge of a very rough tongue. All the same, it wouldn't be right deliberately to refuse to obey a command. The General must have his reasons for requiring Captain Steel's immediate return...

Rowland's laughter broke in on his thoughts. "Don't look so hangdog, William. Nobody's going to eat you, and any blame that results from this enterprise shall be mine entirely, I promise you. Wait till you hear *why* I want you with me."

William looked up alertly. "You have discovered something?"

"I have information that Lady Caroline March is alive—in Patelbar."

"You... *what?*"

William flushed scarlet, remembering in a flash the jasmine-scented conservatory at Lady Wilding's, the gilt-leg chairs behind the potted palm where he had offered Lady Caro his own heart and hand. She had refused, of course, telling him—so sweetly and gently that a fellow couldn't take it hard—that there was another to whom her love was promised. Naturally, he had soon understood that it was Captain Steel to whom she referred, and he thought it quite right that she should prefer a dashing captain with Steel's looks and reputation to a humble griffin like himself. There was no doubt in William Allan's mind that they were meant for one another, and they made a deuced handsome pair. In his heart he'd wished them happy.

When the word raced through Baburpore that Lady Caro was dead, Steel had been like a madman. No one dared to speak to him, and it was rumored that there were black eyes and bloody noses aplenty among his servants. His fellow officers had breathed a collective sigh of relief when General Elliott gave permission for him to leave the station, and he clattered away at the head of his bearded Sikhs on their tough little horses, which always looked workmanlike rather than smart, even on parade. Action was the best medicine for a broken heart, they all agreed, and there was no doubt that Steel's heart had taken a bad knock. Captain Steel wouldn't admit it, of course, but he hadn't been quite right ever since Andrew Thynne and his wife, with drooping shoulders and black-circled eyes, rode into Baburpore with the news.

Steel had looked like a man in the grip of a nightmare, unable to eat or sleep, with overbright eyes and skin stretched too tight over his cheekbones. There were strange tales, too, of his goings-on in the native town, dragging home traveling merchants and dancing girls for questioning—behavior decidedly unbecoming to an officer and a gentleman. But then, it was difficult to decide if Steel really was a gentleman. He had some strange ideas about the way to treat natives, and he'd had the oddest upbringing, if the old cats in Baburpore were to be believed—romping with a pack of naked half-brothers and -sisters in the dust of a ramshackle compound inhabited by his father's dusky concubines. He must have been all of twelve years old—a man, in Indian terms—before his stepmother, the present Lady Steel, an old Tartar if ever there was one, took him in hand and sent him and his sister to England for their schooling.

William Allan had heard the matrons of Baburpore whispering that the effects of such a wild, undisciplined childhood were bound to show sooner or later, and it explained to their satisfaction, at least, why he had never courted their pale, pretty daughters, but preferred copper-skinned beauties from the bazaar to warm his bed.

But there was no doubt he cared desperately for Lady Caro, thought William. Anyone with half an eye who'd seen them together in Delhi would swear to that, for all her sister's eager promotion of the suit of that pushy Civilian—Brook Vyner. Lady Caro's death had hit Rowland so hard that it was clearly up to his friends to make allowances. William stared hard at Rowland: he looked sane enough, but was it mere wishful thinking for him to believe she was still alive?

Rowland said, in a voice that vibrated with excitement, "She's here—just across the border—in Patelbar. I have it on the word of this rogue"—he indicated Gupta Ram—"who used to be houseboy to Fionn Kelly, our agent in Patelbar. Kelly's dead now, poor fellow, he was a decent sort... But Patelbar's only a morning's ride from here and I cannot—*cannot*—return to Baburpore without investigating this report. Now do you see why your horse has gone lame?"

William blushed and held out his hand. "Lend me another and I'm your man; you can count on me," he said dazedly. "When do we ride?"

Chapter Eleven

A DULL, SONOROUS *boom* shook the ground under the bullock's feet, and the beasts dug their toes in, snorting. The gharry creaked to a halt.

"What was that?" cried Caro, cradling the sleeping Baby Jack against her shoulder. She pulled aside the gauze curtains and peered ahead, trying to see where the sound had come from, but tall trees on either side of the track obscured the view.

"It was a gun," said Bulbul somberly, shaking her head. "Drive on, *ek dum!*"

With some difficulty the driver persuaded his beasts to proceed while further cannon shots resounded in front of them. They mounted a little rise and looked down across the plain at the beleaguered town of Baburpore, half encircled by its conjoined rivers, and half by the army of mutineers, reinforced by every soldier Prince Chandranaya could raise in Patelbar. The evening sun glinted on the gun carriages and bathed in soft light the brilliant hues of the Rajah's tents. Below them men moved as thickly and busily as ants in an overturned anthill, but in front of the walls of Baburpore stretched an empty expanse of dusty red earth, once the parade ground, where now nothing stirred but the crows and vultures tearing at the carcasses of dead horses. Caro and Bulbul stared in silent dismay.

Most of the town was protected only by low mud walls no more than four feet high, where an occasional

flash and spurt of flame gave away the position of a
sniper, but the walls surrounding a single large
residence, set well back from the perimeter wall, had
been piled with a triple row of sandbags to form a
formidable barrier, and this was reinforced by a wide
dry ditch protected by the iron spikes of a *cheval-de-
frise*. There could be no doubt as to where the small
British garrison of Baburpore had taken refuge, and
Caro saw that all the besiegers' guns were trained on
this single target.

"Twelve-pounders," said Bulbul, shaking her head
like an animated, highly painted wooden puppet.
Another report, followed by a puff of smoke, drifted
lazily up to their vantage point. "Steel-sahib used such
guns to force the town of Kattawar to yield. No walls
can withstand them."

Caro shivered. Jagged, blackened sections of wall
showed where shells had gone home and the defenses
been hurriedly patched up again.

"How long...," wondered Caro aloud, "....how
long have they been fighting here?" The thought of
Rowland within those walls was tantalizing beyond
bearing. Had all the regiments mutinied, and his men
with them, in spite of Fionn Kelly's prediction?
Philippa must be there, too, and Andrew. Oh, if only
she had wings to fly to them across this intervening
space! If only she knew what was happening there—if
they had food and water, ammunition and medical
supplies. Or had the attack taken them by surprise so
that weakness and hunger would soon force them to
surrender?

She tried to count the ranks of the besiegers, but the
lines of men and guns and horses, gaily colored tents
and wagons swam before and dazzled her eyes. The
besieging forces could not number less than three
thousand, while within the walls of that one building
were crowded how many? Surely less than two hundred

souls, she thought dully. The odds were too great against them—they could never fight their way to safety.

Against her shoulder, Baby Jack stirred and gave a fretful cry. Segments of sugar cane smeared with opium paste had kept him docile and sleepy for many hours, but now he needed food.

"Give me the *baba*." Bulbul's old instincts briskly reasserted themselves. "Peace, now, my princeling; soon you shall fill your belly but first we must make camp. We will not approach any nearer to those *badmash*es or their big guns may disturb your slumber..."

Scarcely were they settled around their small fire of thorn twigs, with the bullocks unhitched from their pole and the pale baby once more dozing in Caro's lap, than they heard the jingle of a horse's harness as it climbed the slope toward them. All too familiar in the fading light was the green-and-gold uniform of the horseman as he halted by their fire. Caro twitched her sari across her face and bent over the baby, but it was Bulbul whom the soldier addressed.

"The Prince of Patelbar sends you greetings," he cried in a high-pitched whine, "and bids you come quickly to speak with him in his pavilion. He has work for you."

Stretched at his ease on a bank of silken cushions, beneath the elaborately draped roof of his tent in an atmosphere thick with the scents of sandalwood and roses, Chandranaya, Prince of Patelbar, set aside his amber-stemmed *hookah* and regarded his visitor with a smile that curved his thin mouth into the semblance of the lips of a cruel idol that was nourished on human blood. An emerald winked in his flat-topped *puggree* and more jewels blazed on his smooth, plump hands. The campaign to exterminate the pale-faced rulers of

Hind was gathering momentum, and he was well content.

Yesterday the Nana Sahib himself had come with news of the surrender of General Wheeler and his tattered, half-starved garrison at Cawnpore to the south. For weeks the British had held out in the battered shell of the old Dragoon hospital, with scarcely any shelter from the death-dealing sun or the shells of the besiegers, and a single well to supply all their daily needs. Sunstroke and disease had killed more of them than the mutineers' guns.

They had agreed to negotiate at last, driven to it by their rapidly mounting numbers of sick and wounded, and tempted by the offer of boats to convey them upriver to safety.

But when they were embarked on those boats— Prince Chandranaya twisted his hands in cruel ecstasy at the thought—the mutineers and Nana Sahib's forces had opened fire on them from the banks. Mounted sowars cut down the fugitives as they floundered in the reddening shallows by the Suttee Chowra Ghat, and when not a man remained alive—except a handful who escaped upriver—the numbed and bewildered women and children had been roughly herded into carts and consigned to the Bibi Ghur—the House of the Women—to be used as hostages should the British threaten vengeance.

Aiee, it had been a mighty killing, better than anything Chandranaya could hope for at Baburpore, though he licked his lips at the thought of some sport he might yet achieve with certain haughty, well-nourished memsahibs who now cowered in the Judge's residence. Proud, they had interested him not at all, but now, humbled and desperate, the white women were beginning to excite his desire. Beneath the tight, whale-boned corsets and bustles they wore, their skin would be as soft and white as the flesh of a newly opened coconut, with pink-tipped nipples like the buds of young lotuses... Not so fine as the little English boy-girl he had scorned, but still... While he had his pleasure of the memsahibs, he would make their men look on; it would be a double shame for the race that had stolen his birthright.

Such thoughts occupied his mind as he stared over the bowed head of Bulbul, enjoying his power to keep her in suspense. No doubt she thought he had summoned her here to punish her for slipping out of Patelbar without his permission. Well, yes: he had been angry when his guard reported her missing, but his anger was long past. Now he was glad he had not ordered her death along with that meddling serpent of an Irish doctor, for she could be of use to him. Understanding English as she did, knowing the ways of the sahib-log, she was of greater value alive, as a negotiator, than lying dead outside the city walls as a warning to others who might offend the Prince of Patelbar. No one in Baburpore could yet have heard of the massacre at the Suttee Chowra Ghat: it was possible that one-eyed General Elliott might fall for the trick that had been used to lure General Wheeler from his refuge. Still, before he came to business, there was no harm in frightening fat Bulbul a little...

He said abruptly, "Why did you flee from Patelbar without asking my leave?"

Bulbul trembled so much that her tiny feet threatened to give way under her, but she answered bravely, "I left the city only to seek new girls for your delight, O Prince. I did not flee by night: I traveled openly, as is my custom. It has never been my way to spread abroad news of my quest, for then the price of virgins for my Joyhouse becomes too high, and old Rajah, your uncle, allowed me to come and go at will. Besides, I thought you were far from Patelbar, marching with the Rajah of Bithoor."

"Fighting the Feringhees you love so well," he sneered. "Can you deny that you were friend to the Irish doctor, Kelly, who ruled the mind of my uncle, and through him the State of Patelbar, for so many years? You are lucky, indeed, not to bear him company at the vultures' table today."

Bulbul knew it would be dangerous to deny any connection with Fionn Kelly, since his movements had clearly been spied on by the Prince's agents. She said with a show of indifference, "He came to the Joyhouse; he was a man, as others are. What of him?"

Chandranaya played with the amber mouthpiece of his *hookah*, his eyes narrow as a hunting cat's. "He was a spy in the pay of the Sirkar. You did not know this?"

"How should I? I am Bulbul, the nightingale; I know and care nothing for state affairs."

Chandranaya smiled, and she took heart, playing up the image of pretty helplessness that she had learned appealed so strongly to Steel-sahib and her many other lovers. Incongruously although it sat on her rolypoly figure and hair thickly streaked with gray, the expression of girlish innocence had its effect on him. "When men come to the Joyhouse of Kali, Prince Bahadur, matters of government are far from their minds. They want to forget the heat of noon and the day's toil—forget fighting and gathering the harvest in the arms of my treasures. But men are fickle, O Prince. They seek fresh faces and young bodies for their pleasure. Therefore I travel from village to village, searching out the choicest jewels of Hindustan to adorn the crown of Patelbar."

More confident now, she peeped at the Prince from behind the folds of her sari.

"Will there be fighting here, Prince Bahadur? It is rumored that the guns are speaking at Cawnpore and Lucknow. Also I have heard that under the command of Havelock-sahib tall British memsahibs in short skirts, playing wild music, are marching on Delhi to slay the old emperor, and there will be a great battle."

"Peace, old meddler!" Chandranaya frowned. Bad news always traveled fast, and he, too, had heard frightened tales of Havelock-sahib's rapid advance to Delhi, where the mob had proclaimed old Bahadur Shah, heir to the Moguls, Emperor. Shopkeepers and peasants were fleeing before the wrath of the giant male memsahibs in swinging kilts, with their outlandish pipes and grim, brick-red faces. There had been hangings and shootings without number, and even the Nana Sahib's forces were being slowly driven back from his headquarters at Bithoor. Chandranaya cared little for this. He had one aim in joining the rebellious Army of Bengal in its bid to throw off the British yoke, and one only: to regain the rich fertile lands and noble city of Baburpore from which his family had been so rudely expelled by the usurping pale-faces.

Through the flap of his tent, floating in a misty haze above the incense-laden air, he could see the rooftops of Baburpore—his city—where the eleven-year-old puppet-Rajah whom the British had placed there, lorded it over the lands that should have belonged to *him*. Chandranaya knew that Patelbar lay in the path of Havelock's advance, but this caused him no concern. They could take and keep it, for all he cared. What was Patelbar to him—a backward, crumbling walled city, half smothered by the vines of the encroaching jungle, its narrow streets and alleys crawling with dirt and disease—compared to the glittering prize that was Baburpore?

Let Nana Sahib hold back the British just a few more days, and Baburpore would fall to him. It had no defenses that could long withstand his artillery, and could he but persuade the Feringhees to step out of their refuge and meet him in open fight, his forces must triumph by sheer weight of numbers. But so far none of his overtures to General Elliott had been met with anything more promising than a charge of roundshot. Now, fired by the success of his ally's ruse at Cawnpore, Prince Chandranaya had devised a better plan.

He motioned to Bulbul to rise. "We will forget the past," he said grandly. "Since it was not your custom to inform my uncle before you left his domain, I will not blame you for doing the same now. I am ruler in Patelbar. Therefore be easy, and attend. I wish you to take a message from me to General Elliott, telling him that if he will lay down his arms and surrender the city to me, I will provide safe conduct for all his people as far as the gates of Lucknow."

"But, Highness," protested Bulbul, completely taken aback by this proposal, "Elliott-sahib will not listen to me! Why should he heed the words of an old woman—a *devadasi*—more than those of a mighty prince? He will refuse my message and turn me away from his gates—if he does not kill me first."

"Be silent," snapped Chandranaya. "Have you forgotten your years in the compound of Steel-sahib? You know the ways of the Sirkar better than anyone in this camp does, and your sweet voice, O nightingale, will tempt the British from their lair more readily than a man's gruff bark."

"Tempt?" she faltered. "My days of tempting men are long past. The guards will shoot me before I can cross the *maidan*"—she wrung her hands, pointing at the forbidding stretch of dusty ground that ended in the dry ditch with its ugly *cheval-de-frise*.

"You will carry a flag of truce. No servant of the Sirkar will fire on a woman if she bears a white flag."

Bulbul whined and raised every objection she could, but slowly it was borne on her that the Prince was in earnest. Curtly he bade her hold her tongue.

"I will ensure your swift return by taking charge of

the treasures you have collected for your Joyhouse while you speak with the sahibs," he said with a smile that showed his pointed teeth, stained black and red with betel juice.

"As yet I have none worthy of your notice, Highness," she countered hastily. "In Baburpore I was promised a dozen young virgins lovely enough to grace a palace. They shall be yours, I swear it."

"Would you have me believe you have journeyed here from Patelbar without filling a single *doolie*? Bulbul, you are getting old and your eyes lose their keenness. Who, then, sat with you by the campfire when you received my messenger?"

"None but the driver of my gharry, and other servants. Oh, and my brother's daughter, Serinda, whose child is sick of the bloody flux. She seeks a doctor-sahib who can cure him, but I fear the disease has gone too far and the child will soon die. Shall I leave *them* in your charge?" Her eyes twinkled with malice. Chandranaya was known to live in dread of the bloody flux, which had killed half his relations in a single week in 1852.

Chandranaya shifted uneasily. "Get you gone, old woman, and your stinking, disease-ridden dependents with you," he snarled. "If you find a doctor-sahib to treat the child he may take the bloody flux himself, and so much the better. Begone, and do not return until you have the General's answer! But before you leave me, hand over your gold and jewels—that necklace, and those rings—lest you be tempted to linger overlong with your friends the sahibs..."

The morning air struck chill through the thin cotton of Caro's sari as she and Bulbul set off on their exposed and lonely walk across the shell-pocked, dusty expanse of *maidan*. Half mocking, half curious, the eyes of the encamped army followed them. Sitting well-wrapped in blankets, stirring pots over their small fires from which blue wisps of woodsmoke mingled its fragrance with the all-pervading smells of ordure and putrefying flesh, the sepoys gazed after the bundled figures of the two women, one clutching a white flag, the other a sleeping child, and laid bets on how far they would progress toward the city walls before the defenders blew them to bits.

"Impossible to miss such a target," grunted Naik Hari Singh, late of the Company's 89th Bengal Native Infantry. He drew an imaginary bead on Bulbul's wobbling backside as she tottered across the rough ground, her small feet slipping and stumbling in the drifts of loose soil. "Why are they sending our nightingale to pleasure those dogs of Feringhees? We need her on our side."

"Haven't you heard? She's carrying a message to the General-sahib, telling him to surrender before we break down the walls of the city. If he does, we shall all become colonels and generals, and go home with a lakh of rupees in our pouches," said sepoy Parsenn Bakh, who was already tired of the discomforts of the campaign and worried, moreover, about the state of his crops at home. The sooner the siege of Baburpore was over, the better as far as he was concerned.

He watched moodily as Caro side-stepped to avoid the bloated corpse of a troop horse, then flinched involuntarily as a shell whistled past his head and exploded in a mushroom-shape cloud of red dust just beyond the picket lines.

"Wh...what...?" he stammered, his mouth full of dust. "They're firing at the women—at the flag of truce!"

Slowly the air cleared, and the mutineers trained their eyes to see what had become of the two women. The torn white flag now lay beside the dead troop horse, but Bulbul and Caro had risen unsteadily to their feet again, staring round in a dazed fashion.

Caro seized Bulbul's arm. "Run!"

"They will kill us." The old woman moaned, clutching the screaming baby to her shoulder. "We should not have come."

"Quick," Caro urged. "Quick, before they can fire again!" She tugged at Bulbul, but still she hung back.

"We have lost our flag of peace. We must go back."

"We can't go back."

Bulbul looked yearningly at the sepoys massed behind them, then ahead at the grim, battered rampart of Baburpore. She nodded and responded to the pressure of Caro's hand. They began to hurry forward over the rough ground, crouching and flinching as muskets cracked in all directions and the balls whined past them; slipping and stumbling in their thin slippers on the sharp stones.

"Faster!"

Even as Caro spoke, the sinister high-pitched whistle overhead made them both duck and freeze like statues. The shell from a six-pounder landed within a dozen feet of them, shaking the ground and showering them both with dust and rubble.

Bulbul's eyes rolled. She looked half crazed with fear, and the power of movement seemed to have left her. "You go, *baba*," she said faintly. "I can't run anymore—I am too old. Leave me here." She held out the child for Caro to take.

Caro forced herself to speak calmly. "Come on, we're nearly there. I won't leave you, do you understand? We'll stay together. Now try to walk again—you must try, and I'll help you. Don't worry; they'll stop shooting as soon as they know who we are."

Bulbul groaned, but to Caro's relief she obeyed. Behind them the mutineers opened fire, trying vainly to cover their messengers. The din was deafening, but at the height of it Caro and Bulbul reached the dry ditch, and dragged themselves into its depths, heedless of the sharp spikes lining the banks and the myriad shiny-back bluebottles that rose in a buzzing cloud from their feast on the dead bodies at the bottom of the ditch.

For a few moments the two women lay still, too thankful for cover even to examine their surroundings. Then, as she recovered her breath, Caro cautiously raised her head and looked up at the walls of Baburpore. There was a lull in the shooting just then, but what she saw made her duck back into the ditch with a whimper of fear.

"Keep down!" She pulled the unresisting Bulbul still deeper into their unsavory refuge.

No more than sixty paces away, she had seen the sandbagged wall of the Judge's residence bristling with muskets, and every one of them was trained directly on the ditch in which they lay.

"They're in there all right," grunted the sergeant of the 42nd Queen's rubbing his mouth with his hand in a vain attempt to rid it of the choking red dust. "With me own eyes I see'd 'em duck into that ditch like a pair of ferrets going into a burry. Keep yer eyes skinned, me lads, and we'll blow 'em to Kingdom Come the minit they shows theirselves above that rim."

Bloodshot eyes swiveled briefly toward him and then returned to their vigil. The few remaining men of the 42nd Queen's who had survived the surprise attack on the Baburpore military quarters the night that Trixie had died, and had managed to hole up in the Judge's fortified residence along with nearly fifty civilians and the handful of British officers who had escaped when their native regiments mutinied, were a grim, tattered crew, very different from the highly polished, splendidly uniformed soldiers they had been a month ago.

They had seen horrors they never would have believed before: the hideous butchery of women and children, the burning of their homes, the wanton destruction of a century's partnership and trust. They had looked on, helpless to prevent pillage and carnage, murder, arson, and wholesale looting, and now they thirsted for revenge on the natives who had shattered the secure, well-ordered world of British India in the Presidency of Bengal.

Two of those cursed blacks had blundered into the dry ditch and were trapped; the men of the 42nd Queen's needed no telling what to do about it. It was hot as hell in that ditch, and stinking with bodies that had fallen during the mutineers' first attack. No one could stay in there for long, and there was no way out. Sooner or later the black bastards would have to show themselves, and when they did, the bullets would be waiting for them.

Ten long minutes crawled by. The soldiers lounged at their posts, spitting to clear their mouths of dust, rearranging the curtains of their shakos to protect angry, sunburned patches of neck, rifles at the ready. In the dark shadow of the ditch, nothing stirred.

Corporal John Jones had learned in these past grim weeks to divorce his mind from the discomfort of his body. Now, while sweat trickled down his spine and his throat ached for water under the blazing, merciless sun, his mind was far away, beside the sparkling waters of Norton's Beck, between the steep sides of Scarfdale and Carradale.

A hand suddenly fell on his shoulder and he jumped guiltily, jerking his crumpled tunic straight and grasping his rifle more firmly. The cool, silver waters vanished and the hot, dangerous present reclaimed him.

"To your right, corporal. Something moved to your

right." The low, gritty voice of Captain Tom Hamilton brought him back to full alert. He stared, slitting his eyes against the glare.

"I can't see nothin', sir."

"Hand me your rifle."

Hamilton's hand with its strong, thick fingers gripped the stock and put the rifle to his shoulder in a smooth, easy movement. He fired, and a spurt of dust kicked up from the lip of the ditch. A piece of cloth billowed up and then sank; they heard a high-pitched, faraway scream.

"Winged him," said Hamilton with grim pleasure.

"Good shot, sir," said Corporal Jones, rather reluctantly. Captain Tom Hamilton made him uneasy; it was hard to say just why, but Jones was aware of some dark force, some barely suppressed violence that emanated from the bull-like frame with its wide shoulders and narrow hips, the face burned dark as any native's, with close-curling black hair growing low on the forehead and forward over each cheekbone. Hamilton was no stranger to India, but a comparative newcomer to the 42nd Queen's, and rumor had it that he was only with them because he'd been drummed out of his regiment back in England after standing trial for the murder of his wife. Some said he would have hanged but for the testimony of a blackamoor, who swore that Tom Hamilton had been watching a cockfight with him fifty miles away at the time of the crime.

The Captain, they said, owed his life to that native—a Mussulman named Azimullah Khan, envoy from the Rajah of Bithoor to the Honourable East India Company—but it didn't seem to have given Tom Hamilton any love for the rest of his breed. Jones had never seen an officer display such an open delight in killing: during the first attack on Baburpore he'd been knee-deep in corpses, hacking off heads and limbs with a captured *tulwar* in a perfect frenzy of blood lust. Jones had thought then that if Hamilton's wife, poor lady, had happened to throw her lord into a rage such as that, he wouldn't give two pins for her life or anyone else's. Brave Captain Hamilton undoubtedly was, and stronger than two or three other officers rolled into one, but all the same Jones preferred not to stand too near him.

Still, it had been pretty shooting to wing that native down there in the shadow of the ditch; Jones said, as he took back his gun, "I couldn't even see 'im, let alone 'it 'im from 'ere."

His words trailed away as, very faintly, they heard a shout: "Don't shoot! For God's sake don't shoot anymore. I'm *English!*"

Captain and corporal stared at one another.

"It's a trick," exclaimed Hamilton. "Give me back that rifle. How could it be an Englishman over there?"

"Dunno, I'm sure. Sounds more like a woman to me," said Jones doubtfully.

Tom Hamilton cupped his hands around his mouth and shouted, "Stand up and show yourself! If you're English you've nothing to fear. I'll count to three, and if you're not out of that trench with your hands above your head, I'll blow you straight to hell. Ready now? One—two—three!"

He raised the gun to his shoulder, cocked it, and waited.

There was a moment of silence, then slowly a figure clambered out of the ditch and stood, a small, exposed bundle of flapping rags on the dusty parade ground.

Corporal Jones felt an infinitesimal movement beside him, and saw Hamilton taking deliberate aim, his knuckles whitening as his forefinger tightened on the trigger.

"'Ere, sir; you can't do that..."

He got no further, for he saw from Tom Hamilton's

set, angry face that no words would sway him from his purpose. Corporal Jones breathed a prayer and struck the muzzle of the Enfield upward just as Hamilton fired. The ball sailed harmlessly over the head of its intended victim, and Hamilton turned on the corporal in a fury.

"By God, Jones, I'll see you flogged to a bloody pulp for that! What the hell d'you mean by it?"

"It's a woman, sir, like I said." Jones stood stolidly, his eyes still fixed on the ragged, childlike figure beside the ditch. "No—*two* women, and it looks like one's got a baby. You can't fire on women and children, sir."

"I'll fire on whom I please, you miserable scum," growled Tom Hamilton. "Sergeant, put this man in close arrest."

He raised the gun again and was taking aim when a soft voice full of authority spoke behind him.

"One moment if you please, Captain Hamilton," said General Elliott, strolling forward to lay a restraining hand on Hamilton's shoulder. He put his telescope to his eye again. "It appears that those native women wish to communicate with us. I think we should hear what they have to say." He turned toward Jones and his mouth twitched in a smile. "Be so good as to escort them in, Corporal."

Through the sandbagged window overlooking the parade ground, Brook Vyner watched with interest as the women were surrounded by redcoats and marched toward the walls of Baburpore. What could Tiger Elliott be thinking of? What possible use could the commander of the depleted Baburpore garrison find for two dirty native crones? He trained his glass on them, trying to see their faces.

The one carrying the child was certainly old, though the child looked light-skinned for a native. The other woman's head was bent, hiding her face, and she swayed as she walked. But there was something in the way she moved—a gliding lightness of step—that touched off a fleeting memory in Brook's mind. Remembrance tugged briefly at him, then faded. What did it matter?

He shook his head, and tucking the telescope beneath his pillow, he lay back with a sigh as feet outside the door warned him of the approach of Miss Emily Drinkwater, his self-appointed nurse. Though plain and inclined to plumpness, she had a kind, motherly heart and an overriding desire to catch herself a husband. These characteristics had combined to prompt her into volunteering to nurse the Englishmen wounded during the mutineers' first attack on the Judge's compound, and so skillful had she proved to be that now, ten days later, of her patients only Brook Vyner remained bedridden.

This was not wholly on account of his physical condition. The flesh wound in the upper arm which he had received from a saber cut was healing well, and the ensuing fever had well nigh abated. But the mental wounds went deeper, for Brook Vyner was thin-skinned. The bumps and bangs that are an inevitable part of childhood always seemed to hurt him far more than they did his brothers and sisters, and his old nurse used to tell him he'd been born with a skin too few. Physical violence appalled and repelled him, and to see the natives he despised turned from humble, obedient servants into ravening beasts had profoundly shocked him. He'd had a bad scare on the fateful night of Trixie's death, when Andrew Thynne and his terror-stricken wife had burst into the study where Brook had been reading, and told him that the native regiments had mutinied and killed their officers. The three of them had had to fight their way out of the bungalow through the servants' quarters, and Brook, who'd never struck a man in anger before, still shuddered at the memory of how the sword that Andrew thrust into his hand felt as it bit into dark flesh; the sickening crunch of steel against bone.

"How do you feel?" Emily bent over his bed, smoothing the single cover. Her bosom in its tight bodice swayed above him, and he suppressed a shiver. Women—always trying to touch you, to rub themselves against you! He pressed himself back against the pillow, and said in a weak voice, "A little better, thank you. What—what was that noise of firing I heard just now? Are the natives preparing another attack? If so, I must help to man the defenses."

"Oh no; that was only a guard bringing in two poor native women whom the General wishes to question. As to leaving your bed"—her voice became emphatic—"you must not dream of it, Mr. Vyner. You are still feverish, you know. A few more days of rest..."

Her eyes met his in unspoken conspiracy. No one but she must know that he had lost his nerve; had cried and pleaded, clutching her skirts with panic-stricken fingers, until she'd produced a morsel of the garrison's small stock of opium to calm him. She would not tell, but the knowledge lay between them, giving her power over him.

"You are so good to me, Miss Drinkwater." He sighed, watching her through the slits of his half-closed eyelids as she moved about the room. "It's true that I still feel a little weak, but if I am needed to fight, I will do my duty."

"No, I cannot allow it. You must let me know what is best for you for a few days yet. Wait till you are stronger." She handed him a small, dirty-gray pellet and smiled. "Your medicine, Mr. Vyner," she said softly.

His fingers closed hungrily over it. "Thank you, Miss Drinkwater. Thank you very much."

*   *   *

Scattered shots at extreme range were still spraying the small party with dust as the corporal of the escort boosted Caro roughly over the sandbagged wall into the compound. She landed on the ground beside Bulbul, who was uttering little gasps and whimpers.

"Tell them," she urged Caro in her own tongue, "tell the Lal Koorti who we are."

But Caro was too numb with shock to obey her. Ever since Fionn's violent death, she had padlocked her tongue and remained silent when English was spoken, knowing that her safety depended on it. Bulbul had impressed on her that should anyone else guess Caro's true origin, both she and her protectress would be put to death, for in the native state of Patelbar all foreigners were unwelcome and the British openly detested. Throughout their encounter with the fugitive Mrs. Evans, Caro had yearned to speak—to reassure the poor woman that she was among friends—yet she had remained silent. And now, when at last she had nerved herself to reveal her identity, the response from her fellow countrymen had been the crack of a musket, and a bullet that missed her by inches.

They had gone mad—the world had gone mad. These sweating, red-faced soldiers who used to treat the native women with rough courtesy now shoved and jostled her as if they hated her. They flung her and Bulbul to the dusty ground and then prodded them to their feet with blows from their rifle butts.

"Get up and *move*, you black bint!" yelled their sergeant, a ferocious giant with angry, bloodshot eyes. "Don't just lay there, you 'eathen bitch. Move! Go on, lads; give 'em a taste of their own physick."

Grinning, the soldiers closed in on them, and Caro cringed, trying to crawl away from the hail of blows. The ranks of redcoats in front of her thinned, and Caro's sensation of nightmare redoubled. For striding toward her, enormous in his dusty boots and crested white *topi*, his head and shoulders bent forward like a bull about to charge and his dark eyes glittering with hate, was the unmistakable figure of Tom Hamilton.

Caro swayed, and the ground seemed to tilt under her feet. The pistol in Tom's hand was pointed steadily at her head. "That's right, Sergeant," he growled, and the well-remembered voice sent prickles along Caro's spine. "Let's hear 'em squeal. Now we've got our hands on the treacherous black bastards we'll teach 'em not to play their dirty tricks on us, worming their way under our defenses by pretending they've information for us. We'll give them a lesson they'll not forget and *then* the General can question them—if they're still capable of speaking. Go to it, lads!"

He aimed a vicious blow with his pistol butt at Bulbul's head, and as she heard it crack against the old woman's skull, Caro found her voice at last.

"No, Tom *no!* It's me—Caro March. Don't you know me?"

Tom Hamilton's hand dropped to his side and his jaw sagged open.

"Caro?" he breathed. "Caro? It—it can't be. You're dead. They told me you were dead. I don't believe it." He made a futile pushing gesture as if to ward off a ghost. The soldiers fell back, staring and muttering.

"It's true, Tom," said Caro more steadily. "I was— left in Patelbar, but they didn't kill me. Bulbul saved me and hid me in her house." She laid her hand on the shivering old woman's arm. "Tom, you've hurt her. She needs a doctor."

"Fetch the surgeon," ordered Tom. Some of the color returned to his face. "And—and the child?" He shook his head as if to clear it. "Surely that's an English child?"

"Yes—his name is Jack Evans. All his family are dead; his father murdered by the sepoys at Fatiganj, and his mother killed yesterday as she tried to drive her children to safety here."

Tom swore under his breath. "Mutiny at Fatiganj? That's damned serious if you're right, Caro; but it's the first we've heard of it. Of course we've been cut off since that swine Chandranaya surrounded the place..."

He wiped his forehead and pulled himself together with a visible effort. "Come, now. The General will want to speak to you, though he'll have the shock of his life when he finds out who you are. Caro...I still can't believe it's you." He moved as if to enfold her in his arms, but the memory of their last encounter made her flinch.

"Of course," he said, too softly for the men to hear. "I forgot you'd feel like that, but I'm a free man now, Caro. I stood my trial and was acquitted. I'm trying to put the past behind me, Caro, and if you'd help me..." His eyes pleaded, but Caro knew she could never return to the old hero-worship relationship. She had grown up in the past months, since she came out to India, and now she could see Tom Hamilton for what he was: a handsome, dangerous animal who lived by impulse and would never know how to control his feelings. He meant it—*now*. He was truly sorry for trying to seduce her, for beating a defenseless native woman, probably for killing Amelia as well...Fleetingly she wondered how Rowland Steel had taken the news of his brother-in-law's acquittal. Rowland had loved his sister dearly and had been convinced of Tom's guilt. And then, what was Tom doing here, in Baburpore? What quirk of fate had sent him to the very station where the brother-in-law who believed him a murderer was garrisoned?

As if aware of her train of thought, Tom explained. "I wanted to make a fresh start, and soldiering's the only profession I know. I joined my father's old regiment, the Queen's 42nd Foot; they don't ask a fellow too many damned awkward questions out here. My company was sent from Fatiganj to escort the Rani of Baburpore and her son back to their palace after the Company had settled a lawsuit in their favor." He shrugged. "We didn't know then that General Elliott's native regiments had deserted, so we marched straight into a trap. Barely had we seen the lady home before Prince Chandranaya was beating at the gates of Baburpore, with half of General Elliott's prodigal sons at his heels. We've been here ever since."

Caro was hardly listening. She asked hesitantly, fearing what the answer might be, "Is my sister here? Philippa? And Captain Thynne? I have had no news of them since we were separated at Patelbar. I have been so anxious... And—and what of Captain Steel?"

He patted her arm and this time she did not flinch from his touch, for she saw from his smile that all was well. "You can set your mind at rest, for your sister is here; so is Andrew Thynne. They were rescued from Patelbar by their bearer, who hid them beneath a load of sacks in a bullock gharry. I heard the story of their escape when I dined with them on my first evening here, and the next night we had to remove to the Judge's compound for safety. Since then we have been living cheek by jowl, though it's fortunate the Judge keeps a good cellar!"

He frowned, the thick eyebrows drawing together until they formed an unbroken line, and his voice hardened. "As to my damned brother-in-law, I can tell you little, for he rode out from Baburpore with his Sikhs on a patrol before I arrived here, and none of us had clapped eyes on him since."

So Rowland was not here. Caro felt utterly drained of strength. Their hazardous journey had been in vain, and the hope that had buoyed her up and given her the courage to face that last frenzied dash across the corpse-strewn *maidan* vanished with Tom's words, leaving her tired and empty. With a great effort she brought her mind back to what he was saying.

"Come now, Caro. We'll talk of this later, but now the General wishes to speak to you."

Chapter Twelve

THE STEADILY FLAPPING *punkah*, billowing like an ill-reefed sail above the polished table in what had been the Judge's dining room, did no more than eddy hot air from one side of the room to the other. It was noon, and the heat pressed down like a heavy blanket, making it an effort for the men sitting around the table to breathe.

General Elliott passed his silk handkerchief across his forehead, and looked wearily at his officers.

"I see no help for it, gentlemen," he said slowly. "If our plan is to succeed, Lady Caroline and the native woman must return to Prince Chandranaya's camp. If they do not, their credibility will be destroyed, and with it our hope of staving off an attack until the return of Captain Steel and his men."

"If he *does* return," said Tom Hamilton. "Surely—if the galloper sent to recall him managed to deliver his message—he should have reached Baburpore days ago. I say we should launch a surprise attack ourselves, while we still have the strength to do so. Chandranaya's forces are nothing but an undisciplined native rabble when all's said and done. Personally, I am inclined to think that Captain Steel's men have betrayed him, and we shall wait for him in vain."

Wishful thinking, Tom Hamilton, thought Andrew Thynne savagely. What you mean is, you would *like* to know that Steel's Sikhs have risen against him and hacked him to pieces. Yes, that'd please you, I'll be bound. He glared across the table at Tom, who would not meet his eyes.

"Thank you for your opinion, Captain Hamilton," said the General frostily. "We are always glad to know your views—even before we've asked for them. You have only lately come to India, and therefore cannot know the depth of Sikh loyalty to Captain Steel's father and, by extension, to him. What you suggest is unthinkable. Now then, Major, any comments?"

Major Symington's hand, dry and yellow as a chicken's claw, shook visibly as he put down his glass of whisky-and-water, but his voice was clear and decisive. He was the longest-serving officer present, and although drink and malaria had wrecked his constitution, his opinion commanded respect. A ricocheting musketball from the first attack on Baburpore had smashed into his left leg, which now lay propped at an awkward angle on the chair beside him.

"I agree, General. The old woman must go back with your reply. Got to keep communication open— it's our only hope of staving off an attack. Can't say I'm happy about sending the girl back to that scoundrel Chandranaya, though. Suppose he were to realize who she is?"

Andrew nodded vigorously. "It's too damned dangerous," he agreed. "It's a miracle she's managed to pass as a native for so long, and I believe that was largely due to old Bulbul's influence. I've been hearing all about it, and it's the rummest story you can imagine. But my wife, sir, would be dead against sending her sister out again, no matter how important it was."

"I know. I've been trying to think of another way out. I don't like it any more than you do, but my duty must be to the garrison as a whole." Tiger Elliott twitched his mustache. "We *must* return some answer to the Prince's offer of a safe conduct to Allahabad. We can't risk another attack which would certainly overrun our defenses. Therefore we must negotiate, and if we are to avoid suspicion of our good faith, we should send back *both* messengers."

Major Symington cleared his throat. "There's a rumor going around that there has been a massacre at Cawnpore, sir. My bearer heard it from the *dhobi*, who'd got it from some native woman in the bazaar. According to the rumor, General Wheeler's entire garrison has been wiped out, and all because they trusted the Nana Sahib, Rajah of Bithoor, whose men have blown up the magazine and rifled the treasury which they'd undertaken to guard."

There was a shocked silence, broken only by the steady creak of the *punkah*.

"Betrayed by the Nana?" General Elliott shook his head. "I don't believe a word of it. He's a good chap—almost one of us. I've been to his palace a dozen times, and I'd swear he's as straight as they come."

Symington said steadily, "There's worse news than that, sir. They say that the Nana offered General Wheeler's garrison a safe conduct upriver, but just as they were embarking on the boats the sepoys opened fire on them and killed every man there."

"And the women? The children?" Elliott's voice was sharp.

"I don't know, sir. I fear they may be used as hostages."

Symington glanced around the circle of officers, assessing their capabilities. Someone must be sent to recall Rowland Steel and his Sikhs to Baburpore, but who should it be? The choice was painfully limited. The General, hunched in his chair, looked an old, sick man, shaken by the betrayal of the sepoys he regarded as his children. It was no use hoping for rational, decisive leadership from him.

Andrew Thynne, his jaw set, pale under his tan, was a good fellow and a brave officer, but had nothing much in the top story. His Hindustani was halting, while his heavy build and fair complexion made it almost impossible to disguise him as a native.

Young Cornet Wilson, on Andrew's left, had gone a queer, greenish shade. Of course, thought Major Symington, Wilson had been head over ears in love with that attractive stepdaughter of the *dak* agent at Cawnpore—Lauretta something-or-other—ever since his last leave there. He must be worrying about her, imagining her suffering... His glance moved on. That young fire-eater Tom Hamilton, of the Queen's 42nd, was dark enough, but he hadn't the right temperament for the job. Besides, he was new to the country and spoke less of the language than Andrew Thynne.

Symington's gaze rested on Brook Vyner, the only civilian present. He'd risen from his sickbed with suspicious alacrity when he heard of Lady Caroline's strange arrival. Now he was clenching his fists to stop them from shaking and staring with unseeing eyes at the portrait of a charging horseman on the wall opposite. Fellow's in a blue funk, through Symington, and trying not to show it. That's why he's been skulking in bed for so long, giving out he's too ill to move. Must be hell to be as scared as that. All the same, *he* could do it. He knows the country from here to Patelbar, speaks the language, too. Darken his face, dress him in uniform, and he'd pass as a sepoy; he's got the right build. Yes, Vyner's the obvious choice.

The General spoke slowly, as if the words were being dragged out of him one by one. "If there is any truth in that rumor, Major, and if Prince Chandranaya is employing the same tactic, we should treat his advances with the utmost caution."

"We must fight it out," said Tom Hamilton excitedly.

"We can't send Caro back to him!" Andrew Thynne protested.

"Don't trust him!" pleaded Brook.

"Gentlemen, *please*...," said the General, and the hubbub died.

Major Symington saw his chance and leaned forward. "With your leave, General," he said quietly, "I should like to propose a plan. We all know that at our present strength we cannot risk a second attack, even from an 'undisciplined rabble of natives,' as Captain Hamilton is pleased to term our adversaries. Discipline apart, the fact that they outnumber us twenty to one must weigh in their favor. It is therefore imperative that Captain Steel be located and recalled at once, since we can expect no reinforcements now from Fatiganj.

"Of our number, there are only three who could hope, given reasonable luck, to pass as natives journeying through the countryside. One, of course, is myself; but this damned leg of mine makes it impossible for me to ride a horse. The other two"—he glanced around the faces turned toward him: the General resigned, Thynne and Hamilton frankly puzzled, Wilson bewildered and Vyner frightened, his eyes darting to and fro as he saw the net closing—"are Lady Caroline March and Mr. Vyner."

A hiss of in-drawn breaths sounded around the table, but before anyone could raise an objection Symington held up his thin, yellow hand. "I have already spoken to Lady Caroline, and she has very bravely undertaken to go in search of Captain Steel. Mr. Vyner, will you accompany her?"

At sundown the next day, Bulbul and Caro walked openly back through the gates of Baburpore and across the shell-torn *maidan*. Both wore saris, the ends pulled over their heads, and in a special leather pouch Bulbul carried the General's carefully worded reply to the Prince. Baby Jack had been left in the care of

Philippa's *ayah*.

Great with child and emotionally overwrought, her wavy chestnut hair—which was her chief beauty—lank and dull on either side of her pale face, Philippa looked as wretched as she felt. The shock of Caro's resurrection followed so swiftly by the news that she must leave again was almost too much for Philippa's sensibilities, and she cried and clung to Caro, refusing to let her go.

"I can't bear to lose you a second time," she said, sobbing. "It's too cruel. They cannot send you out on such a mission."

Andrew gently disengaged her clinging fingers. Above her bent head he gave Caro the suspicion of a wink. "Hush, Phil; you'll only upset yourself. No one wants Caro to go, but you must see that it's our best chance. If she can find Steel..."

"With Bulbul's boy, Sita Ram to guide me, I'll be safe enough," said Caro cheerfully. "Don't 'cry, Philippa. It will be quite an adventure."

In truth, Caro was glad to have the chance to leave Baburpore. Just twenty-four hours in the company of her sister and the other European ladies cooped up in the Judge's compound, bewailing their losses and bickering over such small matters as the use of *chatti*s and washing water, had fretted her nerves to a surprising degree. She no longer felt at home with them—if she ever had.

She had even found it hard to be civil in response to the expressions of horror and sympathy that greeted the vague story of her own adventures and which the ladies poured over her like treacle. It was useless trying to explain her life as a prisoner in Bulbul's house: they could have no conception of the day-to-day life of a native whore, and their constant harping on the sufferings she must have undergone annoyed rather than consoled her. Resuming English clothes—a muslin gown and borrowed shift; stays, petticoats, stockings, and tight, pinching shoes—had been a torment in the humid, premonsoon heat.

Bulbul, on the other hand, had openly reveled in the attention and praise of haughty memsahibs who, in other days, would never have acknowledged her existence, and it had taken all of Caro's powers of persuasion to induce her to return to the mutineers' camp. But she had found an ally in Sita Ram, Bulbul's nineteen-year-old son, who was Rowland's bearer as well as his half-brother. He was a good-looking youth, with glowing dark eyes under delicately marked brows, lighter-skinned than his mother but with her graceful, dancer's movements. A badly cut hand had prevented him from accompanying Rowland when his company left Baburpore on patrol, and he was now eager to rejoin him.

Caro, having heard so much about him, greeted him with pleasure, and when Major Symington's plan was proposed to her, she asked if Sita Ram could act as her guide. Brook Vyner, the fourth and highly reluctant member of their mission, was less convinced of the wisdom of taking Sita Ram with them, but Caro overruled him with unusual firmness.

"For if our enterprise is to succeed," she said in her soft, clear voice, "we must put aside differences of race and station and look on one another as equals. You and I can speak Hindustani and dress ourselves as natives, but without the help of Bulbul and Sita Ram we have no hope of discovering the whereabouts of Captain Steel."

Brook stared at her for a long moment, and then nodded. Could this be the same eager, biddable girl he remembered from shipboard days? The girl whom he had been gracious enough to instruct on many aspects of Indian life and law, who had accepted his views without question? She had changed somehow. She even seemed to think that she might, on occasion, know India better than he—the Civil, the Heaven-Born. Well, let her have her way now, he thought. Time will show that I know a good deal more about this country than any flighty miss who'd been here less than a year. Since the appalling moment when Major Symington had proposed that he, Brook Vyner, should leave the relative safety of Baburpore and take to the country in a wild-goose chase after Rowland Steel, a strange fatalistic calm had overcome him. Having obtained the whole of Emily Drinkwater's supply of opium pills, and filled two pint flasks with *eau-de-vie*, he was ready to go.

"God, but I envy you, Vyner!" Tom Hamilton burst out as they all left the dining room after working out the details of the escape plan. "I'd give anything to stand in your shoes!"

And I in yours, thought Brook, managing a grin. Tom glanced back at Caro and saw with amazement that her eyes were sparkling, her teeth gleaming white between eagerly parted lips. Lord, he thought irrelevantly, she's prettier than ever. She's freer, more sure of herself than she was in London. Can it be because of the life she's lived these past months? Because of the men who've possessed that soft body without managing to conquer it? The thought that Brook, that scared, milk-and-water Civil with his damned pompous patronizing manner would spend the next week alone—or almost alone—in the jungle with Caro, tormented Tom Hamilton nearly beyond endurance.

Caro and Bulbul had reached the mutineers' lines before the firing designed to cover Brook and Sita Ram's escape broke out from the Judge's compound.

Prince Chandranaya, watching the action from the safety of his elephant's green-and-yellow silk *howdah*, received the General's red-sealed missive from Bulbul's hands and waved them impatiently away. He had changed his plans. He could not wait for a protracted negotiation with the besieged garrison of Baburpore, for he had just learned of the Nana Sahib's defeat by General Havelock and Major Renaud at Futtehpur, near Cawnpore, and he was in a fever to secure his own position before the avenging British forces turned their steps in the direction of Baburpore. But first, surely, they will march to the relief of Lucknow, he thought. They are near, too near, but they will not come here yet. I will have time to take the palace, and string the Maharanee and her usurping son by the heels from the battlements. But before that we wipe out the nest of Feringhees sheltering behind the Judge's walls. No longer can I await the Rajah of Bithoor or even Tantia Topee. I must act at once, alone, or all will be lost, and my chance to regain the *guddee* of my fathers will vanish like a dream.

Bulbul glanced at his abstracted face and speedily withdrew. Unhindered, she and Caro made their way to their own small camp as the crackle and thump of General Elliott's guns faded into the distance.

"*Aie*," sighed Bulbul, "they will waste all the roundshot that remain to them."

Spurts of orange flame brightened the rosy stone walls of the city, and the sullen barking of the three six-pounders left in the Judge's compound made the mirage over the parade ground shiver and reform after each explosion.

Caro wiggled her bare toes in the dust and pulled her sari close about her. "Is not the ammunition stored in the Judge's compound?"

Bulbul shook her head and pointed to four squat, resistance towers surrounding the white-domed mosque. "No, *baba*. That is the magazine, behind the walls of the Moti Mosque, which lies in the hands of

the Prince's men. If Elliott-sahib could but capture it
and feed his big guns, the battle would be his..."

She sighed, then resumed her usual brisk manner.
"Now you must rest, and at nightfall we will dress you
to meet your lover, Steel-sahib bahadur." She cackled,
but Caro was aware of a sudden sharp ache that had
nothing to do with her sore feet. She was overcome
with a wave of longing to see Rowland, to hear his
voice, feel his arms close around her, as she so often
had in her dreams. But when he hears how I have slept
with men and pleasured them like any casteless
devadasi, he will never want to touch me again, she
thought.

She knew enough of men now to have read the
desire in the eyes of the British officers at Baburpore
when they looked at her. Careful as she had been to
conceal the precise role she had played in the Joyhouse
of Kali, she knew that every man would question
whether her virginity could have survived so long an
absence from protection. Some had looked specula-
tive, some calculating, some had let their lust show
plainly; one and all had subtly altered their attitude
toward her. Gentlemen they might believe themselves,
but Caro saw that the civilized veneer was paper-thin,
and they regarded an unattached yet sexually experienced white woman as fair game.

Caro shivered. She was glad to be away from the
shikar, from the innuendoes veiled in supposed
sympathy, the women's hints and the men's sidelong
glances. Would Rowland be the same, she wondered.
Would her new status—or lack of it—repel him, or
draw him in wolfish pursuit of her body as it had drawn
Tom Hamilton and young Cornet Wilson?

Brook Vyner, at least, had continued to treat her
with the same respect as before, and Caro was thankful
that he, not Tom Hamilton, was the man chosen to
accompany her in search of Rowland. The mission was

dangerous enough without the added complication of holding would-be lovers at bay, and Caro was glad that Brook's attentions now seemed directed toward the plump Miss Drinkwater.

She lay down on the bedding roll as Bulbul directed and tried to sleep, but behind closed eyelids her thoughts raced on—dancing, ducking, weaving from the myriad pitfalls and dangers that lay ahead.

The rendezvous with the two men was fixed for midnight, at the ruined temple of Shiva some three miles back along the road to Patelbar. But suppose Brook and Sita Ram had been caught as they escaped through the Baburpore military quarters under the cover of General Elliott's diversionary fire? She had a shrewd idea of how little persuasion it would take to make Brook reveal all he knew to the enemy: he would talk, and she—Caro—would walk into a trap.

Suppose Sita Ram proved false? But he was Bulbul's son, and on that account alone Caro could not distrust him. Besides, he was devoted to his half-brother, Rowland. Somewhat comforted by this thought, Caro turned on her side and slept.

Bathed in silver moonlight, the marble temple of Shiva seemed to float above the gleaming mirror of water that surrounded it, insubstantial as a dream. A bad dream, thought Caro, hugging the gold-frogged sleeves of a dead sowar's jacket she was wearing across her chest to stop herself shivering. She stared at the temple with its creeper-laden walls and delicate cupola half hidden in the strangling hold of jungle vines. As she shifted her weight, the *tulwar*—the curved sword of Damascus steel that had once belonged to a Bengal Light Cavalryman—bumped against her calves, encased in long, tight topboots. It would be better when she was in the saddle, but where were the horses? Where were Brook Vyner and Sita Ram?

She had a curious, unpleasant sensation of *déjà vu,*

as if she had walked into the very situation that she had imagined behind closed eyelids in Bulbul's tent.

Beside her Abdur, her guide, touched her arm. "Sahib not coming in temple," he said out loud. His eyes gleamed with malice.

"Hush; of course he is coming. We are early, that's all." Caro wished that Abdur, with his thick, drooping lips and insolent eyes, had not been the servant chosen to accompany her. Soft-footed Abdur, Bulbul's houseboy, had brought Fionn's *hookah* and replenished his glass during those long conversations on Bulbul's veranda. He alone among Bulbul's retinue knew Caro's true identity, and she sensed that only his fear of Bulbul stopped him making capital out of the knowledge. She wondered if she should send him back now that they had reached the temple, but she feared that if he should meet with any of Chandranaya's followers on the road back to camp he might be tempted to reveal her whereabouts to them.

It would be safer to keep him with her until Brook appeared, little as she relished his company in this lonely spot.

In the jungle behind the temple a high-pitched, unearthly laugh broke the silence and Caro's heart thumped. Only a hyena, she scolded herself, annoyed at Abdur's sly smile.

"Miss-sahiba scared?"

"No, I'm not. But don't call me miss-sahiba anymore," she whispered tautly. "I am Hoseyn the sowar now, and wear his uniform. Come: we will go and wait in the temple."

"But you are the miss-sahiba—the English miss-sahiba." His voice was soft and menacing. "You have defiled the house of Kali with your white skin, and shamed my gods, but now you will pay for it."

"I? Pay?" she faltered, moving away from him toward the little bridge that spanned the water between the island and the mainland. "Abdur, what nonsense is this? Bulbul will be angry to hear you have spoken thus to me."

"She will not hear."

Caro was chilled by the certainty in his tone. Swiftly she ran across the narrow arched bridge and paused on the steps of the temple, listening. The vines swayed as a light wind caught them, and soft, groping tendrils caught at Caro's hair. With a dry rustle something—lizard or snake—slithered to hide from the intruder. Caro stifled a cry. She must make no noise: the mutineers' patrols were out in the jungle, watching and waiting. Perhaps they could see her now, silhouetted in the moonlight against the white marble walls. Quickly she flattened herself against a pillar, staring about her with wide eyes.

Just across the bridge, Abdur squatted on his haunches, a knife in his hand. He was fingering the blade, running the ball of his thumb lovingly over its bright edge. There was something intent, almost sacrificial in his attitude and Caro's breath came fast, her heart beating in slow, heavy thumps. He can't mean to use that on *me*, she thought wildly, and looked around for a way of escape.

With a single lithe movement, Abdur rose and stood grasping the rail of the little bridge in one hand; his long knife shone in the other.

He bent swiftly, picked up a stone, and tossed it into the water. Caro, frozen with fear, saw the mirrorlike surface of the lake shiver into movement as long, wedge-shaped ripples appeared under the little bridge. Muggers, she thought. He means to murder me and throw my body to the crocodiles.

"Muggers hungry, miss-sahiba," Abdur gloated. "Long time muggers not eating." The knife glinted in his hand. He moved toward her.

Caro's limbs felt heavy; her heart threatened to

suffocate her with its thumping. Slowly her hand moved, fumbling at the swordbelt, at the curved hand guard. She tugged, and the metal slid willingly from its scabbard, but when she tried to raise it to the guard position, her wrist sagged under its weight. She had never done more than spar with her brother, using the lightest of foils; this weapon was too long, too heavy for a woman.

Abdur laughed softly and came closer still, his knife weaving to and fro in patterns that threatened to hypnotize her. Impatient now, the muggers' tails threshed the water into milky foam.

Suddenly strength returned to Caro. She grasped the *tulwar* in both hands and swung it low over the top of the handrail in a scything sweep. She missed Abdur, and staggered off balance, but he was forced to leap back out of reach.

"Now you pay, miss-sahiba," he hissed. "Now!" The knife wove circles in the air.

"Stand back," she gasped. "I'll kill you if you come any closer." She swiped backhanded across the rail and though the blow wrenched her wrists it drove Abdur back once more.

How long can I keep this up, she thought desperately. Where is Brook—why doesn't he come?

Abdur's smile had vanished and his lips were drawn back in a snarl as he approached once more. He feinted to the right, drawing Caro's answering blow and then, before she could recover her balance and control the heavy sword, Abdur's blade flickered to the left. Caro saw his face above her, contorted with the desire to kill, his knife pointed at her throat. She waited for the burning pain as the blade ripped her skin, but before it could come Abdur's head jerked suddenly backward.

His mouth opened in a wordless grunt, and the knife tinkled harmlessly down on the marble steps.

Caro reeled away and grasped at a pillar for

support. Sita Ram had his foot in the small of Abdur's back, a black scarf pulled tautly about the man's neck, and he was pulling...pulling...She closed her eyes.

A moment later a splash told her that Abdur had met the fate he planned for her. Bones cracked as the muggers tore and threshed in the blood-stained water.

Running footsteps, an arm around her shoulders, and Caro buried her face in the harsh comfort of Brook Vyner's coat.

"I thought—I thought you'd never come," she whispered.

He tightened his arms around her. He had been terrified himself; when he saw Caro struggling with that villain on the bridge he'd wanted to slip straight back into the jungle, fetch the horses, and ride like hell. Who was to say there weren't half a dozen more murderers inside that little temple? It would have been a pity to leave poor Caro to her fate, but there was no sense in risking the whole mission for the sake of a single member.

Sita Ram had acted too quickly, hadn't waited to consult Brook on what he should do, but had darted forward with nothing but a silk scarf in his hand, and by Jove, he'd garrotted that black bastard on the bridge quicker than you could say knife.

Brook had had to follow, and now here was Caro snuggling up to him, dressed provocatively in her sowar uniform, with those great eyes glowing gratitude at him. Brook said curtly—honor where it was due— "Good work, Sita Ram. You took care of that devil, right enough."

"Yes, sahib."

Sita Ram's handsome brown face was impassive as he tucked away his silk scarf, and Brook felt a sudden chill. Could Sita Ram have guessed that he'd meant to leave Caro to her fate? He hadn't said a word, and yet...

Caro said softly, hurriedly, "We must get away from here. Quickly. Where are the horses?"

Sita Ram nodded. "Yes, we go now, miss-sahiba. Do not fear. The horses are close at hand."

They rode for five nights along jungle tracks, avoiding villages, resting by day in deep undergrowth while Sita Ram in his tarnished sepoy jacket and stained white trousers went to the nearest hut to buy food and gather information.

Despite the ever-present danger of discovery, Caro loved the open-air life, the blazing sun and torrential storms of the monsoon, the long hours on Nuri's back as the Arab mare's tireless trot ate up the miles between her and Rowland.

"I never thought I'd see her again," she confided to Brook as they groomed and fed their mounts in the dawn. Sita Ram had been away since long before daybreak.

"I persuaded Andrew Thynne to let me bring her," said Brook, bending the truth in an almost automatic attempt to curry favor. In fact, Andrew had pressed him to take Nuri, knowing how pleased Caro would be to ride her again. "They're eating horsemeat at Baburpore since they ran out of bullocks to kill, and I thought she'd stand a better chance with us. We ate a troop mule the other day, and deuced tough it was, believe me. Anyway, you're better off on that neat little mare than I am on my clumsy brute."

He laid a gentle hand on the raw insides to his knees. Unused to living in the rough, he was suffering the deprivations of the journey far more than Caro, and wondered enviously how she contrived to appear so fresh and blooming. True, her complexion was tanned too dark a shade for English beauty, but it suited her and assisted her disguise. With her hair hidden beneath the *puggree*, and the high-collared coat setting off her slim figure, she looked like a charming native boy wearing his big brother's uniform. Desire such as no woman ordinarily aroused in him stirred as he regarded Caro. Perhaps later on . . .

His thoughts were interrupted by Sita Ram, who slipped through the undergrowth into the clearing carrying a bag of gram and another of meal. He looked worried.

"Sahib, we must eat quickly and go. The Rajah of Bithoor's army is approaching."

"Does that mean Nana Sahib is retreating?" asked Caro eagerly. "Will Colonel Havelock turn aside to Baburpore on his march to Lucknow?"

Sita Ram shook his head. "I do not think so, miss-sahiba. For Havlook-sahib's line of march lies to the south, and Lucknow is hard-pressed."

"So is Baburpore!" she cried indignantly, thinking of Philippa, so near the time of her confinement, and the flimsy sand-bagged defenses of the Judge's residence.

Brook Vyner looked grave. "No intelligence has been sent out from Baburpore for two weeks now," he reminded her, "nor have we been able to receive any. It is possible that Colonel Havelock may not know the straits to which we are reduced. Also he may be unaware that the army of Prince Chandranaya of Patelbar is supporting the insurrectionists among our sepoys. Baburpore is only a small station: he may believe it already in enemy hands."

Caro stared at him in dismay. "You mean he will not halt his advance to discover Baburpore's fate?" she asked in a small voice.

"I did not say *will* not. I said *may* not. Consider: Lucknow is the former capital of the Kingdom of Oudh, and for it to fall into rebel hands would be an irreparable blow to the British in India. The same cannot be said about Baburpore."

Sita Ram was packing their saddlebags hastily.

"Hurry, sahib," he urged. "Here we are in danger."

Caro untied Nuri and swung on to her back without assistance, though Brook stood ready to help her. "If only we were to meet with one of Colonel Havelock's patrols," she exclaimed, "and could persuade them to return with us!"

Sita Ram spoke eagerly. "I have news of Steel-sahib. He and his Sikhs are encamped not two days' ride from this village. They say he fought a battle against the Ranees of Patelbar, and is marching to seize the city itself. If we ride hard we may soon catch him."

Not two days' ride away! Caro clapped her heels into Nuri's sides. They galloped away down the dusty track and did not draw rein until they reached the blackened remains of a village.

"Who—who has done this?" whispered Caro. Her horrified eyes took in the smoldering heaps of ashes that had once been huts, and the slowly revolving bodies surrounded by buzzing clouds of bluebottles that hung from the limbs of the great peepul tree. Nothing else stirred: pigs and chickens, goats and sheep had all been driven away.

"A village that resisted the Nana Sahib," said Sita Ram grimly. The horses shied and snorted at the smell of death that hung like a mantle over the ruins. "We must leave the road and ride across country to Patelbar. We cannot risk meeting him here."

He turned his pony and jumped the low mud wall that separated the huts from the tall thickets of sugar cane. Caro followed, sitting tightly as Nuri swerved to avoid a jackal slinking up to the village in search of carrion. Guided by Sita Ram, they made their way through a maze of small, carefully tended fields, crossed and recrossed the shining threads of irrigation channels, and stumbled down dry riverbeds, traveling always parallel to the road, yet out of sight of it.

The horses were tired when at last they camped in a field of trampled corn, but it was Brook Vyner who most resented the hardships of the day's travel.

"You may like it or not," he declared, "but I am not riding across country again tomorrow. We've far outstripped the main body of the Nana's army, and if we go carefully, we'll be able to avoid any advance patrols he may have sent out. Tomorrow we return to the road."

"Sahib, it is too dangerous," murmured Sita Ram.

"You think everything is too dangerous, confound you," Brook growled. "I tell you I've had enough of it. If you want to go across country tomorrow you go alone. The miss-sahiba and I will journey by the road."

"Brook, that's unjust!" exclaimed Caro as Sita Ram's face fell. "He's been taking far more risks than either of us. I think we should do as he says."

Brook's mouth fell open. He looked almost comically amazed at her daring to side with a servant— a native at that—against him. "You—you keep out of this, Caro. You know nothing at all about such matters."

"Yes, I do," she persisted. "It may be less comfortable to travel through the fields, but it is certainly safer. It is not the villagers who want to hunt us down, but the mutinous sepoys and deposed princes like the Nana Sahib, who believe they may gain by this uprising. If you decide to return to the road tomorrow *you* will go alone, for I ride with Sita Ram."

Plead with her as he might, Brook could not budge her from this decision, and after a time he subsided into sulky silence, swilling brandy from his hip flask until that was dry, and then, rolling a small, dirty-gray opium pellet in a wad of betel leaf, he lay chewing on it until the kindly fumes misted over his physical discomforts and he slept.

Caro, too, rolled herself in her cloak and lay

watching the stars. She listended to the gentle stamping and munching of the horses, the howl of a jackal, the faraway laugh of a hyena that cut through the steady whirring of insects and croaking of frogs. Tomorrow, she thought. Tomorrow I will see Rowland.

She pictured again the lean planes of his face, the way his dark eyes with their curled lashes crinkled at the corners when he smiled, the hard-muscled strength of him. The image she had conjured up made her stir uneasily on the dew-wet ground, as every fiber of her body cried out for physical release. Like any appetite indulged, then suddenly frustrated, her newly awakened sensuality craved a lover's arms about her, a man's sinewy body pressed to her soft skin.

The men in the Joyhouse had been faceless males, driven by a single desire, but there had been the young sepoy, who had shown her the sheer, impetuous pleasure of unabashed desire, and Fionn, dear Fionn, who had taught her the deep, abiding tenderness that came of loving surrender. She wanted a man, but more than that, she wanted Rowland Steel, the Rowland Steel who had visited her dreams so often in the Joyhouse that she had, in her sleep, grown to know him intimately, memorizing the thousand and one different shades of his expression, the unquenched fires of his embraces, the strength and ardor of his love. It was these dreams that had bolstered her resolve to return to the happy, safe existence she had so recently known.

But when she reached Baburpore and Rowland was not there, she was shaken. In her memory he had become a giant among men with the strength of Hercules, the looks of Apollo, the courage of Achilles. Now she began to doubt. The picture of her mind blurred as she heard again the whispers of the Baburpore ladies.

"Not quite a gentleman"... "Should have returned days ago"... "Either he's deliberately disobeying orders or"... The pursed lips, the shaking of heads. *Or he had been killed*. That was the other possibility— even likelihood. If his men had mutinied, Rowland must be dead or in hiding. Either way, her journey would be in vain.

Yet Sita Ram's confidence that they would find him gave Caro fresh heart. Sita Ram was their best hope of survival in this land turned suddenly hostile, and she must make Brook realize that fact. *If only* he were not so obstinate, so full of his own importance, so uncompromisingly lordly in his manner toward Sita Ram. Toward her too: in his eyes Caro was just a woman—a pretty, delicate, empty-headed toy to be petted and sheltered and deferred to in unimportant matters.

But let her display any initiative or intelligence, let her dare to challenge his male superiority, and he reacted like lightning to put her back in her place and show her her opinions were worth nothing. All this might have been bearable once, but now when she knew herself better able, both mentally and physically, to deal with their situation, it irked her beyond endurance.

Caro was sure that Sita Ram felt as she did about Brook, but the habit of obedience was too deeply ingrained for him to dream of defying a sahib. Very well, thought Caro, let Brook Vyner go his own way tomorrow, and see how he fares.

In the chill of dawn she did make one last attempt to reason with him, but he refused to listen.

"You have made it plain where your loyalties lie, my dear, and there's nothing more to be said," he informed her coldly. His voice was slightly slurred as if the effects of last night's drink and drugs were still with him, and twice he missed the stirrup before managing to haul himself onto his pony's saddle.

In silence, Caro and Sita Ram munched cold

*chupatti*s and watched Brook ride away, weaving a slow path between the fields and water channels, toward the road. *He looks as conspicuous as a beetle on a patchwork quilt, though Caro. That fool! Not to know his only chance of survival lies with us!*

He was nearly out of their sight when a group of horsemen rode out of a clump of trees, almost as if they had been waiting for him to pass. Caro clenched her fists in sudden fear. For a moment it looked as if the horsemen had merely greeted Brook and allowed him to continue on his way; then they closed in behind him. Watching closely, Caro saw the bright gleam as a sword was drawn.

"Help me, Sita Ram. Help!" The despairing shout floated to their ears and both Sita Ram and Caro were already in their saddles, riding hard, before she realized the full import of Brook's cry. *He had spoken in English.* He had given them all away.

When they reached him, Brook was fighting with a sort of desperate courage, stabbing and thrusting at the robed, turbaned figures that circled him warily, trying to attack from the rear. They were six to one, and too intent on their prey to hear Caro and Sita Ram thunder to the rescue.

Caro tugged the *tulwar* from its scabbard and felt a strange, fierce pleasure as the impact of Nuri's rush drove the springy Damascus steel through layers of cloth to flesh and bone beneath.

"Ayah!" called Sita Ram; a moment later his musket cracked beside her and another man fell.

Four to three.

Caro hit wildly at a bearded sowar with a blue *puggree* whose hand was raised to stab Brook in the neck. She succeeded in deflecting his aim before a heavy thump on the side of her head knocked her half out of the saddle. She was saved by the thick folds of her own head cloth, but swayed, sick and dizzy, seeing through swimming eyes Sita Ram produce weapons from his sash with the speed and dexterity of a conjurer.

He shot the bearded sowar at point-blank range, cut fiercely at a brown arm holding a heavy horse pistol, and then it was over as suddenly as it had begun. The two remaining attackers clapped heels to their ponies' sides and galloped away, leaving their dead where they had fallen.

"How is it with you, miss-sahiba? Can you still ride?" asked Sita Ram anxiously.

Caro nodded.

"Quickly, then. There may be more of them."

Brook seemed unhurt, but dazed. He sat his horse like a sack of meal, looking blankly about him, saying nothing.

Sita Ram took his rein and led the horse away at a fast trot, taking the first turn they came to off the main track.

From time to time during that long, hot day, Caro thought she heard hoofbeats behind them, but when at last the horses were worn out and they made camp, all was quiet.

Brook had shaken himself from his stupor, and made an attempt to apologize to Sita Ram. "... See now you were in the right of it," he muttered stiffly. "Grateful for prompt assistance ... Hope to give you an adequate reward ..."

Sita Ram's dark eyes were fathomless, nodding acceptance, but as he turned away the faint mocking movement of his fringed eyebrows made Caro catch her breath. How like Rowland he is, she thought. It must be true that they're half-brothers. She smiled warmly at him, trying to bridge the gap that Brook insisted on keeping between sahibs and servants, trying to show Sita Ram that she looked on him as a friend.

His apology delivered, however ungraciously,

Brook turned to Caro with relief. "I shall never forgive myself for putting you in such danger," he exclaimed in a tone utterly different from the brusque, staccato phrases which he had addressed to Sita Ram. "When I saw you obliged to raise that heavy sword to defend yourself..."

"Raised to defend *you*," Caro felt bound to point out.

"Miss-sahiba fight well," proclaimed Sita Ram. Caro felt warmed by his approval, and protected by his presence.

"It was terrible! Terrible. And all my fault. I should never have left you to fend for yourself with only a bearer for company. Will you ever forgive me?"

Now was the moment to upbraid him: to catalog Brook's shortcomings as an emissary in enemy-held territory; to take him to task for his stubborn pig-headedness which had endangered them all. Caro could not do it. Even while she resented the way he seemed to have twisted facts until he believed that in the morning's incident he was the rescuer and they the rescued, Caro found his self-castigation even less attractive than the arrogance preceding it.

Sita Ram padded silently away to attend the horses, and Caro said, in an effort to rebuild Brook's shattered self-esteem, "You fought well, too, for one who has not been trained as a soldier. Think how proud Miss Drinkwater will be to hear of it!"

He glanced around, grasped her hand, and said with a passion that surprised her, "I care nothing for Miss Drinkwater—*nothing!* It is you I love, Caro. There, I've said it now. It has always been you, ever since we met on shipboard, since we went ashore together at Suez, you remember? You were wearing those ridiculous clothes from your brother's wardrobe, dressed as a boy..."

As I am now, she thought, and a little chill touched her.

Brook's words spilled from him as though a long pent-up dam had suddenly given way. Fleetingly she wondered if this was the real Brook speaking, or whether a brace of the gray "toothache capsules" had loosened his tongue. He still held her hand, but to her relief made no other move to embrace her.

"I loved you then, but it was too soon; I could not be sure that you returned my feelings. In Delhi there were always others about. We could never be alone. Time and again I was on the point of declaring myself when we were interrupted. I hoped that when you were settled at Baburpore, and knew a little more of station life, my opportunity would present itself." He laughed, with more than a hint of bitterness. "Believe me, dearest Caro, I never dreamed of speaking my heart to you in a place such as this! But now I have, will you, can you give me hope?"

How could she tell him that the very touch of his hand repelled her far more than the embrace of Bulbul's most loathsome customers? That to lie in his arms would turn her sick with disgust? Back in Delhi, in the carefree days before the first rumblings of distant thunder heralded the sepoy revolt, she might have said yes. Philippa would have approved wholeheartedly: *her* respect for the Indian Civil Service knew no bounds. Indeed, every mama in British India would have reckoned that Lady Caroline March had made a considerable catch since Brook was already assistant to a district officer; he was a young man with his future assured, whom any girl, titled or not, would be lucky to marry.

But now that the sensual side of Caro's nature was awakened, she was even more sharply aware of Brook's lack of physical attraction for her. His rather prominent eyes seemed to her like the outside of a fine, fresh apple, which would fall open to expose a rotten core. For all his apparent authority, there was something wavering and insecure in his nature which sought a stronger will to lean on or, failing that, propped up its resolution with alcohol or drugs. Caro had no wish to support a weak man who would only suck her dry and smother her.

She said quickly, "Brook, you do me great honor but I confess you—surprise me! I would not be at all the kind of wife you need in your career." She swallowed, but it had to be said: "Since my recent experiences, I find—"

"Ah, do not speak of them. I know—better than anyone—what you must have suffered, but now you must put all that behind you. Memories are short, Caro, and if you were my wife I would make it my business to see that no one thought the less of you because you had lived as a native." He added magnanimously, "After all, if *I* can overlook such a lapse from grace, no one else would dare cast it up to you!"

Caro caught her breath, half angry, half amused. Why, the self-centered, conceited prig! "That was not what I was about to say," she remarked dryly. "What you regard as a 'lapse from grace' has been a turning point in my life. I cannot go back, Brook, to being the girl you knew in Delhi. It would suffocate me. Once a prisoner has tasted freedom, he is reluctant to return to his cell, you know."

Brook released her hand abruptly. "You regarded your life with that dreadful old native as *freedom?*" he asked incredulously.

"Perhaps not at the time. But I see now that it was; and I am happier here, sleeping in the rough, with danger all around, than ever I was in England—or in Delhi, either. Even if you cannot understand that, you must see that I would not be a suitable wife for a man in the position you aspire to."

Brook shook his head in a kind of despair. "I know, I know. I have told myself so a thousand times, but it makes no difference. I want you, Caro, as I've never wanted another woman, and although I cannot approve of many of the things you say and do, I persuade myself that in time you would come to realize the folly of such wildness, and would become a wife I could be proud of."

"Can't you see? The—the *wildness* you speak of is part of me. I cannot change it any more than I can change the color of my eyes. It would be the blindest folly to suppose that our differences would disappear simply because we were married. Please, Brook, do not speak of it any further."

"But I may continue to hope?"

Was there no getting through to him? Had he taken in none of the sense of what she had been saying?

Caro said tiredly, "I hardly see how I can prevent you."

Chapter Thirteen

IT SEEMED THAT Caro had barely fallen asleep before Brook was shaking her awake. It was a fine, clear morning, and in the early sunlight his face looked drawn.

"Sita Ram has gone," he whispered. "He's left us!"

"He must have gone to get us food," she said, turning and stretching on the thin bedroll.

"No—listen!"

Fully awake now, she rolled off her mattress and stood staring into the jungle toward the small path they had followed yesterday.

"Horses—coming fast! Quick: saddle and mount."

She had flung her bedding roll across the front of Nuri's saddle and was on her back before Sita Ram thundered into the clearing. White lather dripped from his pony's belly, and its nostrils flared, red-rimmed.

"*Badmash*es! Sepoys!" he gasped, and set spurs to his pony again. Caro followed, marveling at the way Nuri, dog-tired only a few hours ago, now sprang gaily forward as if she had spent the night eating oats in a stable, groomed and pampered, instead of standing tethered, fully saddled, with yesterday's sweat still caking her silvery hide.

Sita Ram's mount was in a worse state: Nuri outstripped him with ease and as they reached a branch in the path, Caro glanced back to know which road to follow. To her dismay, she saw that Sita Ram had fallen forward over his pony's neck and that a dark-brown patch, like an island, was spreading across the shoulder of the brave red jacket. She drew rein at once and whirled Nuri round.

"You're wounded!"

Sita Ram turned an ashen face toward her. "Shot—sepoys following. Leave me, miss-sahiba. Ride away quickly and save yourself. Tell Steel-sahib—" His voice died away.

"He's right, you know," said Brook in a low voice, staring at Sita Ram's back. "That wound looks bad. We'd better do as he says—they're not far behind us, and there's no sense in getting us all killed."

Caro threw him a look of angry contempt. "Never!" She took Sita Ram's rein. "Hold him in the saddle," she ordered. "We won't leave him; we'll find somewhere to hide."

"Don't be a fool, Caro," said Brook emphatically. "He's done for, can't you see?"

Indeed it looked very much as if Brook might be right, for Sita Ram had fainted, and the stain on his coat was increasing rapidly from an island to a continent, dripping off the hem to leave a blood trail in the dust.

"No, he's not," she said with more confidence than she felt. "Keep him steady." They were still trotting down the road, but the hoofbeats behind were getting louder. "Look!" exclaimed Caro. "What's that?"

It was a bungalow—a white-painted, European bungalow—long and low, set a little back from the dusty track, with sturdy white gates in a round-top archway, and trim borders of marigolds around the brownish yellow of a carefully tended lawn. It seemed to Caro like the answer to a prayer. "They'll shelter us here."

But her hope sank as she saw the gates swinging open on their hinges, the boxes and bundles dragged out and scattered in the stable yard, the desolate air of broken and half-shuttered windows.

Nuri stopped dead as Caro tried to urge her toward the entrance. She lowered her head, snorting, at an object on the ground, then backed rapidly away. Caro looked down and in horror recognized a severed white arm and hand—a child's hand with a gold bracelet around the wrist—lying right in their path. Brook saw it, too.

"The rebels have been here before us," he said shakily. "Come on, Caro, we can't stay here."

"No—can't you see, this is our only hope. Turn the horses loose, Brook." She dismounted and stamped her foot as Brook hesitated. "Go on. Do as I say."

She helped Sita Ram to slide to the ground and hastily tugged the bag with their small store of clothes and provisions from behind his saddle. Then she waved her arms at the ponies, trying to send them off, but they stood bewildered, unable to accept their sudden liberty.

"Go on—shoo! Away with you, now!"

Pulling Sita Ram's pistol from his sash, she cocked it and fired into the air. The ponies shied away at the noise and trotted down the road, shaking their heads and nipping playfully at one another. With a heavy heart Caro watched Nuri's silvery quarters vanish in the heat-haze. No mutineer would pass by the chance to acquire such a horse: this time she must have seen the last of her. But she had no time to regret the parting, for Sita Ram was losing blood quickly: they must get him into hiding without delay.

The once-pretty yellow brocade covering the sofa and the four overstuffed armchairs in the drawing room bore ominous red-brown stains, and a dead Highland terrier, its fluffy coat matted with blood and flies crowding thick on its glazed eyes, was stretched across the threshold as if denying entry to all intruders.

Caro explored on tiptoe, afraid of what she might find in the silent house. The dining-room carpet was a glittering sea of broken crystal and smashed china, to which the greasy, crusted remains of a leg of mutton and boiled rice still clung. Spilled bottles of claret on floor and table told how the occupants of the bungalow had been engaged when the mutineers burst in on them.

Upstairs, every bedroom had tumbled clothes and the contents of wardrobes lying where they had been flung, but of people there was no sign.

Perhaps they escaped, thought Caro. Perhaps they were warned in time and managed to ride to safety.

But when she and the reluctant Brook carried Sita Ram's limp body down the steps to the *tye-khana*—the underground cellar—these hopes were dashed. They were not the first to see the *tye-khana* as a possible hiding place.

Crushed up against the single barred window that gave onto the courtyard, lying in sticky pools of their own blood, a man, woman, and four small children bore mute witness to the savagery of their murderers. The smell of death in that confined space caught at Caro's throat, threatening to choke her, but remembering Baby Jack's miraculous escape she forced herself to go closer and find out if any of this family still lived.

They had been dead for hours. The man was tall, with curly graying muttonchop whiskers and a pointed beard. His plain round collar and the gold cross hanging from a chain around his neck explained his calling and his choice of such an isolated situation for his family home. Although a man of God, he must have fought bravely to defend his wife and children, for his face was a mask of blood in which only the snarling teeth retained any definition, and the great gash across his throat showed where his life had ebbed away.

They must have murdered him first, thought Caro, while his wife and children watched, then slaughtered the little ones before their mother's eyes. The pages on an open book stirred in the hot breeze from the door; Caro stooped and picked up a Bible, open at the Twenty-third Psalm, its pages spattered and stained with blood.

She turned to the flyleaf: *To my dear wife, Ada Emmeline leMesurier, from her loving husband George Michael leMesurier on the occasion of our tenth wedding anniversary.*

"What are you doing?" Brook's appalled whisper reached her from the foot of the steps. "We can't stay here!"

"Where else can we go? Listen..." The steady clop of hoofs on the dusty track warned them of the mutineers' approach. Caro strained to hear if any turned aside to the bungalow, but she thought they all went on. "We can hide here till dark," she whispered, for indeed she could see no farther ahead, "and then—then one of us must go out to try to make contact with Captain Steel's patrol, if he is still nearby."

As she spoke a feeling of hopelessness swept over her. Find Captain Steel? What hope had they of meeting with him in this hostile terrain where every man's hand seemed to be against them? Brook had passed examinations in Hindustani, Urdu, Tamil, and half a dozen dialects without being able to speak an intelligible sentence in any one of them. As soon as he opened his mouth he betrayed himself for an Englishman, while she herself, hiding her sex as well as her nationality, would be even more easily unmasked. But if she were to put on the sari that Bulbul had hidden in the saddlebag...? Posing as a native girl, as she had before, she might stand a better chance.

Caro sighed and turned back to the urgent business of tending Sita Ram's wound. Brook, for the moment, adopted a perfectly negative attitude and obeyed clumsily, but without question, her instructions to remove the wounded man's coat and shirt. She sensed the lull before the storm. Soon Brook would recover from his shock at seeing the murdered family and begin to assert himself once more. She must make the most of this period of docility.

Once exposed, the wound proved—though ugly— to be far from mortal. A ball had passed at an angle through the epaulette on Sita Ram's shoulder, torn across the muscle and lodged against the bone of his shoulder blade. His left arm hung useless, but as far as Caro could tell none of the vital organs had been touched. The immediate need was to clean the wound and apply a dressing.

Caro said tentatively, "Brook, he is in great pain. Do you suppose that one or two of your 'toothache capsules' might help him to bear it? I shall be obliged to remove the ball if I can"—she shuddered at the thought of touching the gory mess—"and I remember that Lady Marvell had the highest regard for opium to relieve pain. Your capsules are opium, are they not?"

Brook hesitated and she was afraid he would refuse. Then he shrugged, cast a look around him, and said, "Oh, very well, if you feel they would help the poor fellow," with an unselfishness that surprised her. Between them they propped up Sita Ram and forced him to swallow two of the gray pellets.

"How soon will they take effect?"

"Oh, very quickly. Perhaps in ten minutes."

"Then I will make a search for medicines and bandages while you stay here with him." She half hoped he would offer to search in place of her, but Brook only glanced uneasily at the bodies by the window.

"Hurry, then," he said. "The sepoys may return."

He had no need to remind her of *that*, listening with

her senses at full stretch before slipping out of the cellar and softly closing the door. Behind her, Brook turned the key.

All lay silent in the heavy noon heat. Caro padded through the deserted rooms, seeking Mrs. leMesurier's medicine chest. It would be locked, no doubt, and the key around the waist of that poor mutilated figure in the cellar beneath, but Caro trusted the strong knife she had taken from Sita Ram's sash to prise open the stoutest lock.

Here was the master bedroom, its sheets torn and twisted, and the *punkah* collapsed from its mooring on the ceiling, lying in a tangled heap across the bed. Small feet scurried across the floor at the approach of a human. How quickly the jungle takes over, Caro thought. Only yesterday this must have been a neat, clean, well-ordered household—frugally run, perhaps, but with every evidence of respectability; today the reptiles creep in. Tomorrow a wild pig may bring her children to feast on stolen vegetables; in a week the vines will poke tendrils through the lattices and force cracks between the brickwork. Next year no one will know that a British missionary and his family lived here. The thought depressed her. She pushed it away and began her search, finding trunks full of Bibles, clothes put away between camphor-scented sheets, a tea set of fine bone china, carefully wrapped in tissue paper—all the treasured bric-a-brac of an expatriate family, but no medicine chest.

She tried the bathroom and then the children's rooms, in one of which a small, sad-eyed monkey crouched mournfully in a cage, with its unnervingly humanlike face pressed against the bars. It chattered at her and she opened the door of its cage. It climbed out cautiously, hesitated, then with a single graceful bound he leaped out of the window and vanished, its tail streaming behind him.

Clothes, toys, samplers, more Bibles: no medicines. Where had Mrs. leMesurier, that careful housewife, kept her store of remedies for all the ills that could beset an Anglo-Indian household?

Caro imagined the lady conducting her daily affairs, interviewing the cook and bearer, issuing instructions to the *dhobi* and *durzee*, hearing her children recite their catechism, holding a surgery for accidents and ailments among her staff. An office! That must be where the medicines were kept. While the missionary was out converting the heathen, his wife might use his study for directing her household.

She crept back through the disordered drawing room to a small, book-lined cubbyhole leading off it. Sure enough, it contained not one but two desks. The Reverend George leMesurier's was a sea of scattered papers inadequately weighted down with odd objects: a veined stone, a horseshoe, an Afghan dagger, a small leather box. Christ in Majesty, His bare feet just brushing rose-tinted fluffy clouds, looked down serenely on His minister's disorderly working habits.

Mrs. leMesurier's desk was, in contrast, severe in its neatness. The highly polished top was bare, and each locked drawer—when Sita Ram's knife had done its work—proved a miracle of method, filed and cross-indexed, with every paper clipped precisely to its fellows and the piles of stationery squared up with parade-ground exactitude. There were household accounts in flowing copperplate, carefully tabulated lists of attendance at church services, and amounts of food issued to converts.

Nothing in this room appeared to have been disturbed; either the marauders had not penetrated so far, or they had felt a superstitious awe of the strange God and left His servant's work place unmolested. Caro's spirits rose as she observed this, and she attacked the lock of the big cupboard under the bookcase with renewed vigor. It must be here! Time was passing, and she thought it might be an hour since she had left the cellar. She hoped that the opium was affording Sita Ram some measure of relief.

With a final wrench, the stout blade burst the cupboard lock.

"Ah," breathed Caro.

Rolls of bandage, lint, gauze, ointment, scissors: all the medicaments she could possibly need were stacked in neat piles before her eyes. There was even a box containing razor-sharp scalpels, hooks, fine tweezers, a small saw, and other surgical instruments at whose purpose she could only guess. Mrs. leMesurier had evidently been prepared to tackle minor surgery as well as first-aid. If only her husband, too, had confined his efforts to improving the natives' bodily condition, and refrained from tampering with their souls. Caro was convinced that Bible-thumping missionaries had sown many of the seeds of the present mutiny.

Picking up a wicker tray, she made a careful selection from the shelves. Then, drawn by a sudden urge to breathe fresher air, she stepped onto the veranda that ran the length of the bungalow. After the relative cool of the study, the heat hit her like a furnace blast. The air was heavy, almost thick, and to the south great copper-tinted clouds were beginning to pile up. By four o'clock they would have blotted out the sun and then the drenching rain would begin, as it had every day for the past two weeks.

As usual before the downpour, Caro felt tired yet on edge, full of vague unease. She was unwilling to face the task ahead of her, the dressing of Sita Ram's wound, with only Brook to assist her. In yet another effort to delay her return to the *tye-khana*, Caro went back into the silent bungalow. She was hungry: in the kitchen she might find something to eat.

The ashes of the cooking fire were cold, but a great

black pot swinging from a hook above it contained a mess of *dal*—lentil porridge—and beneath a gauze flycover stood a platter of cold boiled rice. Caro dipped a bowl in the thick yellowish orange porridge and ate ravenously, rolling balls of rice in her fingers and scooping *dal* into her mouth with frenzied speed. It was ambrosia: it was the finest food she had ever tasted. Reluctantly she scraped the last morsels from the bowl and found a larger vessel to fill for Brook and Sita Ram. To this she added a jug of water from the tall earthenware pot on the floor. Carrying her load carefully, she returned to the cellar door and tapped.

There was no sound from within.

"Brook, let me in," she whispered. "It's Caro."

Silence.

Puzzled, Caro set down her tray and rattled the door handle. It was locked from the inside. Could Brook have fallen asleep?

"Brook!" she called more loudly. "Open this door. I've found some food."

There was no answer, but putting her ear to the keyhole, Caro heard a slight shuffling sound and a hiccup. What could be the matter? Seizing the handle of the door, Caro shook it vigorously and battered her fist against the planks. The sudden hammering sounded almost profane in the still house.

"Brook! Answer me! Where are you?"

She felt fear rising in her like a wave that would swamp her senses. Had there been someone hiding in that cellar—someone who had murdered Brook and was waiting for her? She was on the point of fleeing outside, running into the jungle, anywhere that would put the bungalow and its grim secrets far behind her, when a voice spoke from within the cellar.

"Whaa—what you wan'? Go 'way, I'm busy."

"Brook!" Her panic ebbed, for although slow and slurred, the voice was certainly his.

"I want to come in, Brook. I've brought you some food."

"Food, eh? That's good. Clever li'l Caro, finding food."

The shuffling steps came to the door, fumbled with the key, turned it. Caro was confronted by a swaying, giggling figure, his shirt unbuttoned and sleeves pushed up, lurching against her, a half-empty brandy decanter clutched in his fist.

"Come, in, come in, clever li'l Caro," Brook invited. "See what *I've* found." As she pushed him away she could smell his alcohol-heavy breath, coming in short, drunken grunts.

"Brook! You've been drinking."

"Wha' else can a fellow do in a cellar?" He sounded aggrieved. "You leave me here in the dark with nothing but a heap of dead bodies for company, you've only yourself to blame if I take a li'l drink..."

"But Sita Ram isn't dead! You were supposed to be looking after him." She went quickly to the side of the wounded man.

"Dead or near enough," said Brook sulkily. He gulped the brandy. "He's bleeding like a pig and that groaning's enough to drive a fellow to drink. Come on, why don' you join me?" When once again Brook staggered to Caro, his arms unsteadily grabbing for her, she caught him by the shoulders, turned him around, and maneuvered him firmly to a wooden box. "Now, Brook"—she spoke slowly and distinctly as if to a child—"I want you to sit here and stay out of my way. Is that clear?" Brook managed a befuddled yes before she continued. "A man's life is at stake, and I intend to save it."

How Caro managed to dig out the musketball and bind up Sita Ram's wound was something she never afterward remembered. Merciful forgetfulness blanked out the details of the operation. The double dose of opium combined with shock had sent Sita Ram into a deep coma, and he lay inert and unresisting as she probed with Mrs. leMesurier's shining instruments among the smashed fragments of bone and tried to stanch the blood which dripped into an ever-increasing pool on the cellar floor. She could see the flattened edge of the lead bullet that had ripped through the thick cloth of his uniform jacket; and though his heavily fringed and stiffened epaulette had taken the worst of its force, it had penetrated over an inch into the shoulder muscle before lodging against the bone.

At last she drew it free, and let out the breath she had been holding in a long sigh of relief. She bound a wad of lint over the gaping hole, eased his shirt back into place, and then wiped the film of sweat from her own forehead. She felt limp with exhaustion.

Brook had long since fallen into a drunken sleep, and though she felt uneasy at leaving the patient in his charge again, there was no help for it. The urgent need to wash overcame her fears.

Taking the cellar key with her, and carrying her small bag of clothes, she slipped into the bathroom. Although the tall water-storage vessels were often favorite lairs for snakes, Caro found that Mrs. leMesurier had contrived a kind of crude filter over the central drain, effectively barring the way to reptiles, and knew she could bathe in peace. The touch of cool water against her grimy skin was so delicious that she almost forgot the need to hurry back to the cellar.

She washed from head to foot, and wrung the water from her long dark hair. Was there time to wash her clothes? She looked doubtfully at the stained white shirt and breeches she had worn since leaving Bulbul's tent. There was nothing she could do about the sowar dark-blue tunic with its frogging and gold braid, but the thought of putting on other dirty clothes was intolerable. Hastily she wound the sari around her body and dumped the soiled garments in the hip bath. She had just begun to scrub them when the sound of hoofs outside the bungalow's gates make her leap to the window.

A glance confirmed her fears. The mutineers had returned, and hard on their heels rode more horsemen, with beards and turbans, waving long swords. They thundered through the archway into the courtyard in a jumbled melee of shouting men and wild-eyed, lathered horses. A pistol spat flame, and she saw the foremost horse rear, its rider toppling slowly backward with a bloody mess where his head had been.

For a moment Caro stood frozen, water still dripping from her hair and soap on her arms. The mutineers who had chased them were flinging themselves off their mounts, running toward the bungalow with their pursuers hot on their heels. Screams and curses echoed round the courtyard and explosions seemed to rock the bungalow.

Caro fled from the bathroom, abandoning her sowar's clothes. She'd left the cellar door locked, but any moment now some of the fugitives might burst into the house and find her. Down the passage she sped, her bare feet making no sound on the polished boards, her wet hair streaming behind her. With trembling fingers she thrust the key into the lock just as she heard the front door crash open. The key was stiff, but she turned it with a frenzied effort and almost fell down the cellar steps, slamming the lock behind her.

Another moment and she would have been too late. Spurred boots clumped in the passage and a voice shouted, "*Ko hai?* Is anyone there?" Then the steps came on toward the cellar.

Caro ran to the window, stepping over the bodies of the dead family, and peered out into the courtyard.

Against the light she could see horses' legs and the dark humps of bodies lying on the ground. A pair of tall, polished boots near the window moved to block her view: there was no way out.

We're trapped, she thought. We'll have to stand and fight.

She went over to Brook, still sitting slumped on the wooden box beside the empty brandy decanter, and shook his shoulder. "Brook," she whispered urgently. "Wake up and help me. There are soldiers outside. Where's your pistol?"

His eyes opened slowly. They stared at her without recognition and he uttered a cavernous groan.

Outside the cellar there was a sudden, startled silence, then the voice called again sharply, *"Ko hai?"* The door handle rattled vigorously.

Caro picked up Sita Ram's horse pistol and crept to the foot of the cellar steps, determined to shoot the first man who entered.

There was a sudden flash and explosion, loud in the confined space, as the intruder blew the lock to pieces. A moment later the cellar door swung inward, and Caro saw the tall figure of a man outlined against the light. She raised the pistol, cocked it and took aim.

The man on the steps spoke, his voice low and excited.

"Corporal—bring a light! It's dark down there but I swear I heard someone stirring."

Caro's fingers went limp, and the pistol clattered to the floor.

"You're English!" she cried. "Brook, they're English! We're saved!"

The soldier advanced down the steps, followed by another man, carrying a lantern. "Sweet Jesus, look at what we have here!" the first man exclaimed. "Well let me introduce myself. I am Lieutenant Lewis Allan, under the command of Captain Rowland Steel."

*　*　*

As the dull roar of the eighteen-pounder shook the ground, the body of Muzzur Ali, second-in-command to Tantia Topee of the Gwalior insurgents, who had been roped alive across the muzzle of the cannon, disintegrated in a cloud of blood.

"Good riddance!" exclaimed Captain the Hon. William Arbuthnot, as he and Rowland Steel, their duty done, turned back toward their tents. "That's one more gone to avenge the victims of Cawnpore, but it's not the same as cuttin' them down in fair fight. Are you sure you can't ride back with us to Patelbar tomorrow, Rowland? It seems such a waste: us meetin' up like this and then goin' our separate ways without the chance of a bit of scrum together. Your cavalry and my infantry could take a city the size of Patelbar with no trouble, and that'd be one in the eye for that scoundrel Chandranaya. Teach him to keep his troops at home instead of stirrin' up trouble for us. Besides"—his voice took on a pleading note—"my lads are spoilin' for a fight, you know. You can't blame 'em. They've been brought here to India instead of goin' to China for a crack at the opium barons, marched upcountry at a hell of a lick, and now what? All they've been able to do so far is blow a few mutineers sky-high while waitin' for Havelock-sahib to collect enough troops to march on Lucknow. I tell you, Rowland, they're in an ugly mood, and it'd do 'em a power of good to march on Patelbar and give the pandies hell."

Rowland looked at his cousin in amused exasperation. Willie was a good fellow, a dear fellow, but his enthusiasms could be rather overwhelming. A little of Willie Arbuthnot's company went a long way. It had been the purest chance that they had met in this tiny village near the Patelbar border: Willie and his Highlanders on patrol from Cawnpore and Rowland with his Sikhs about to return to Baburpore.

Willie's pleasure in his men's triumph at capturing

an important rebel leader, Muzzur Ali, had been doubled by being able to show the prisoner to his cousin, and he had begun there and then to urge Rowland to join him in a raid on the city of Patelbar. But Rowland had had enough of Patelbar. Every lead he had followed in his search for Caro had come to a dead end. That part of his mission had utterly failed, leaving him weary and heart-sore. He was in no mood for Willie's heroics.

So he said, "I'm sorry, Willie. I would if I could but I can't. My orders are to return to Baburpore when I've finished this patrol and I've delayed enough already. We've picked up a fair bit of information, and now I must make my report to General Elliott. You'll get your share of fighting soon enough—never fear!" He held out his hand. "I'll say good-bye now, and all the best, for we'll be making an early start and I may not see you before we leave."

"Hang it, Rowland," exclaimed Captain Arbuthnot. "That's not good enough—nowhere near! You're not escapin' as easy as that. Come on, lad, what's got into you? You can't ride off after an—an *historic* meetin' like this, without some kind of a celebration. You're goin' to dine with me tonight—no, don't shake your head—it's all arranged and I'll be mortally offended if you refuse me." He lowered his voice. "My man Mustafa has a way with jungle fowl you'd hardly believe. You'll swear you're eating young grouse. He'll see to it you have everything you like, and we'll make it a night to remember."

As she saw the lights of the picket lines glimmering through the velvety darkness, Caro, reunited with Nuri, who had been caught by Lieutenant Allan, trotted ahead of the column. She was tired after the long ride, but buoyed up on a tide of excited anticipation. The months of hoping and dreaming were almost over: she was going to see Rowland again, hear his deep, warm voice, feel his arms touch . . . Farther than that she could not think. Rowland would greet her, together they would return to Baburpore; the nightmare she had lived in so long would vanish as if it had never existed.

Impatiently she urged Nuri on, and the little mare, scenting the end of the day's weary journeying, broke into a canter. Behind them Lieutenant Allan, commanding the patrol that had rescued them, was deep in talk with Brook Vyner and did not see her go.

The camp buzzed with small, familiar sounds and aromatic smells. Men squatted round their fires, talking earnestly, smoking; horses munched and stamped, cooking pots bubbled. Somewhere behind the trees a sitar throbbed a plaintive love song.

A single large tent, placed on its own, blazed with light. From it came shouts of men's laughter, and then a pistol shot. Glass tinkled and a voice groaned, "Missed again!"

Three more shots crashed in quick succession; there was a moment's silence and then a rousing cheer.

Another voice, high-pitched and cracked with laughter, called, "Bravo, Rowland—three out of three! Now the song. Sing us *Zakhmi Dil*, and the prize is yours!"

A viol struck up a pleasant, lilting air, and Rowland's ringing baritone swung into a Pathan marching song.

Outside in the shadows, holding Nuri's rein, Caro's face burned as she listened.

"There's a boy across the river, with a bottom like a peach—

But, alas! I cannot swim—"

The guard on duty had turned to watch the sahibs at

play, laughing and stamping in time to the music. Caro ducked under his outstretched arm before he could stop her and darted into the tent.

For a moment the light dazzled her. The long table with its snowy cloth was set with a dozen candles, and the air was thick with incense and cigar smoke. White-robed servants bustled to and fro in the shadows at the back of the tent, and on a sideboard a pyramid of bottles with a playing card stuck on top—the three of hearts—provided a tempting target. The sideboard was littered with broken glass and the card had a neat hole through each pip.

Her eyes fastened on Rowland. He stood on the table in operatic pose, weight on one leg with the other's toe absurdly pointed, head flung back and both arms raised as he serenaded the brandy glass clasped in his hands as a lover might clasp a rose. His cheekbones wore a hectic flush, and his dark eyes glittered in the candlelight. He was very drunk. Like the other four officers in the tent, he had removed his coat, and the white shirt clung damply to his chest. Willie's hospitality had been lavish, and after the lean weeks on patrol the opportunity for horseplay was irresistible. He shook back his hair and delivered the last notes *rallentando*, with great emotion, holding his pose apparently oblivious of the stamping and clapping that followed his song.

Then he bowed, hand on heart, and as he straightened up his eyes fell on Caro, standing under the lamp just inside the tent flap.

"The prize!" he shouted, leaping off the table. He caught Caro up in his arms. "Willie, you dog! Where've you been hiding this little beauty? Look at those eyes! What a mouth! Who'll play me double or quits for her?"

Willie Arbuthnot was choking with laugher. "No, *no*, Rowland. You're quite mistaken," he spluttered.

"Allow me *some* morals, if you please! I've no more idea than you where that—that creature has sprung from—my oath on it. *This* is my prize." He held up a handsome silver hip flask.

Rowland swung Caro, speechless with shock, up to his shoulder. "I'll keep my prize and you keep yours," he offered, riveting his gaze on her, "for I'll have no need of a brandy flask to keep me warm tonight. Come, my gazelle, tell me your name."

Didn't he know her? Could he gaze into her face, hold her tight within the circle of his arms, and still not know her? Caro's world broke from its moorings and rushed crazily through whirling blackness. The candles, the tent, the red, glistening faces of the men around the table spun and danced before her.

Outside, like faint echoes of sanity in this lunatic world, she could hear jingling and stamping, barked orders and marching feet as the column she had outstripped rode into camp. She should have stayed with them! She had been made to think that—that Rowland would know her. The long dream that had sustained her through these weary months exploded, leaving her in a vacuum.

Rowland had lowered her to the ground, but only to let his arm tighten around her. "Your name, my pretty," he repeated in Hindustani. He stared at her and something stirred behind his brandy-glazed eyes. Some flicker of hope that he would not, could not, allow himself to admit. It was a trick of the light, a cruel deception conjured up by alcohol and wishful thinking that made this bedraggled little Mahratta drab look like—

"Caro," she whispered, clinging desperately to the last shreds of her identity. He did not seem to understand, so she said it again in Hindustani. "My name is Caro."

Rowland's face turned ashen. "You lie," he shouted,

harshly pushing her away. "Willie, what damned trick is this? Take her." Without another word, he strode angrily from the tent.

Caro felt as if a sliver of ice had pierced her heart, turning it numb. There was a roaring in her ears and she stood with head bent, unable to speak or move. As if from a great distance she heard the clink of spurs behind her as William Allan, together with Brook Vyner, ducked under the tent flap and blinked in the blaze of candlelight.

Chapter Fourteen

MUCH LATER, ROWLAND came to the tent they had given Caro. He found her sitting cross-legged on a rug, huddled in a shawl, and the forlorn droop of her head pierced his heart.

"Caro," he said softly, kneeling beside her.

She looked at him directly, without smiling. "How is Sita Ram?"

"Oh, improving steadily. But I didn't come to talk about Sita Ram."

"Why, then?"

He took her hands in his, as if to warm them. "Caro—I'm sorry. I can't tell you how sorry I am. That I should have behaved like a wild beast to you, of all people! That I should have mistaken you for one of Willie Arbuthnot's wenches! But, Caro, I was certain you were dead, and you are so different now from what you were. It was impossible to know you!"

"You didn't know me!" She cried, and the pain in her voice cut sharp as a knife through his lame excuse. "I don't care if you were drunk or not; what hurts is that you looked at me and didn't know me and now—now I don't know myself! I am lost between two worlds and I can't tell which I belong to. I thought that you, at least, would know me however I was dressed; however I spoke. I see now that I was wrong, and everything I have dreamed during these long months has been an empty lie."

"I was drunk," he murmured again, but pulling her hands free and shrinking from him, she did not seem to hear. Her words ran on, spilling from her as if only by giving them voice could she exorcise this terror that gripped her; this nothingness, this total loss of herself. "Who am I?" she cried, and he could not stop her words, which still poured out, releasing all her pent-up grief and loneliness.

"They did not know me at Baburpore," she cried. "They took me for a native woman and the soldiers beat us as if they hated us, though we had done them no harm. Even Philippa, my sister, seems a stranger," she said sadly. "I cannot understand her, or she me. Oh, Rowland, where shall I go? What shall I do? I feel that I have risen from the dead and the world I used to know has shut me out."

He tried to take her in his arms, soothing her as he would a scared child, but she resisted. "Caro, you are utterly mistaken. It is a new world that has opened to you, not an old one that's shut you out. Don't you see? The very thing you complain of—the way you can be accepted among natives and Europeans alike—is the rarest gift ever given to a mortal! It must have saved your life countless times in these dangerous months; even with old Bulbul's protection you could not have survived without it. I own, I am green with envy of you! As to the ladies of Baburpore—yes, and Philippa, too—don't let their coldness cause you a moment's distress. They are scared and overwrought, poor souls, and their tempers are on edge."

Rowland's mouth twisted bitterly. Of course, living in a native state, she could not know the depths of suspicion and hatred that now divided British India. Since the outbreak of the sepoy revolt in May, atrocities that would have been unbelievable a year ago were daily committed by both sides. English children had been skewered on meathooks hung on walls, to watch their mothers raped and mutilated. Muslims had been sewn in pigskins and blown from cannon, and Brahmins forced to lick the blood they had spilled. There was a madness in the land, and Caro had touched only the fringes of it.

She still wandered in a limbo in which nothing was secure. "Rowland," she trembled as she spoke, "you do not know what I've endured. You could not possibly imagine." Then she told of her capture, of the Rajah of Bithoor's brutal ravishment, of her escape to Bulbul's protection, and of her life at the Joyhouse.

Rowland listened quietly, appalled yet understanding her need to rid herself of the horror of the past months. This was his punishment: to know yet not to blame; to realize that the delicacy and purity of the Caro he remembered—the Caro he had searched for—had gone forever. She had been a public woman, and pleasured strangers for a few *paise*. She had endured sexual humiliation, and now she turned to him for comfort, for reassurance that her experiences would not make her an outcast for the rest of her days. This time, he thought grimly, he must not fail her.

As she spoke, a dark rage filled him that Caro should have been the one to suffer for the follies of the others: for Philippa Thynne's hypochondria and Andrew's vainglorious desire for *shikar*; for Tom Hamilton's thirst for blood and now for his own drunken rejection, which seemed the final blow that had broken her spirit.

No one else had heard the full story of how she had spent the missing months at Patelbar and, he vowed silently, from him at least no one else *should* hear it. He cursed himself with a new-found self-hatred as her quiet voice explained simply, with no attempt to disguise the implication, how he had been the rock against which she leaned during her long captivity, dreaming of him, not her countless lovers, even pretending he was there to cheer her when her spirits failed.

She told him how she had rehearsed their reunion over and over, and how those expectations had bolstered her courage through the horrors of all the previous days.

Attempting to stem the torrent of words, he laid his arm about her shoulders, which seemed indifferent to his touch. But now, when he took her hand, her fingers, twined in his, clung with desperate strength, and she fell silent.

"Caro," Rowland soothed her, "you are the bravest miss-sahiba in all of India! But I think that all these tribulations have brought you close to the heart of India. And that is why I envy you so."

Slowly her fingers relaxed, and the beginnings of a smile touched her mouth. He had struck the right chord, reawakening her self-respect, and the lost, haunted look faded from her eyes.

"Envy? You, Steel-sahib bahadur?"

"Yes, for I still cannot pass as a native," he assured her. "I am always the outsider, the sahib from whom all matters of importance must be concealed. Though I was born here and have lived most of my life under Indian skies, yet I am not accepted by them as you have been. You may not realize it, Caro, but in those clothes you *become* an Oriental—it is the strangest thing to see. I was drunk tonight, I admit, when I took you for one of Willie's native wenches, but had I been cold sober I think I still would have been deceived. Perhaps if I had looked long enough I would have seen Lady Caroline March... perhaps..."

She turned an anxious look on him. "And now that you have?"

"I wish I had not," he replied promptly, withdrawing his arm from her. "I wish I had accepted Willie's silver flask as my prize for singing that abominable song! For though I may be permitted to talk to Lady Caroline March about—oh, the weather, and the state of her mother's health, and the balls we attended in Delhi, and other tedious matters, and I may be allowed to smile at her, and possibly even to hold her hand, that is as far as matters between us can go."

As he stopped speaking, the hiss of the oil lamp seemed suddenly very loud. In the small circles of light, the warm, slightly spicy air lapped them around, like a tent within a tent, drawing them into a world of their own. Caro's eyes were downcast, the black lashes casting half-moon shadows on her cheeks. Very slowly the corners of her mouth curved outward.

"But with Caro, the dancing girl? What would you talk about with her?"

Rowland affected to consider, pushing the cushions together in a heap, fiddling with the wick of the lamp. Caro leaned closer, waiting.

He said judiciously, "With her, matters could be very different. I don't say they would be—but they *could*. You see, there would be no need to talk at all. She would know—we both would know—a language without words. I might put my arms about her, very gently—like this... and bring her mouth close to mine—like this... She would place her arms about my neck—like this—and draw me back on the cushions— *so*. Then... then I would untie the knot of her sari... Yes, things would be very different."

As his mouth touched hers, he pulled her to him, gently at first and then with increasing urgency caressing her hair, sliding his hand down her spine to the curve of her buttocks, kissing her eyes, her throat, her breasts. She shivered, feeling the hardness of his body pressed to hers, his strong hands moving everywhere, arousing a hunger greater even than the desire of her dreams.

A spark flickered and flared within her, racing along her veins, filling her body with liquid fire, setting her skin ablaze and her belly yearning with a deep craving such as she had never known before. Rowland's fingers seemed to burn wherever they touched, sliding over her shoulders and expertly unfastening the flimsy *choli* that covered her breasts, and as his mouth closed around her erect nipples her body raised itself to meet his in a torment of longing.

Suddenly she withdrew from his embrace, her eyes shining, a dazzling smile playing on her lips, as she said in Hindustani, "It would be my pleasure to assist the Captain-sahib in his disrobing."

She gently pushed him back against the heap of cushions, permitting her hands to wander down the length of his body, following her fingers with her lips, until she had positioned herself at his feet. With her back to him, she removed one of his boots, then, bracing his foot against her naked buttock, pulled off the other boot. Slowly, sinuously gliding against him, she crept back up to his shoulders and she removed his shirt, covering him with tiny, enflaming bites, her tongue flicking at his nipples, her teeth softly pulling the hairs of his chest. Now she lowered her head, and she unfastened his jodhpurs, her mouth explored, through the heavy fabric, every inch of him, mouthing his hardness, kissing his thighs.

When at last they lay naked, every muscle braced as he controlled his own hungry passion, Rowland looked down into the velvety eyes, now huge with desire, and whispered, "Tell me, lotus woman, what is your name tonight?"

She answered with a ghost of a laugh in Hindustani, "My name is Caro, but they call me the Silent One.

And what will be your pleasure, Steel-sahib?"

In response, he moved above her, his tongue exploring the corners of her mouth before sliding silkenly between her lips. With one hand he massaged her breasts with a pressure so arousing that it dizzied her, while, with the other, he caressed the burning space between her legs, his fingers journeying inside her, stroking and thrusting, readying her.

"Now, Silent One," he murmured, "now."

Then it was like nothing she had ever known or dreamed. They were born to be lovers, to move instinctively in the same ecstatic rhythm, to arch and plunge at the same moments, to feel the same, overwhelming power building and building until, together, they were hurled into the radiant depths of infinity.

Three days later Caro once again stood on the hills above Baburpore, gazing down on the besiegers' tents and pavilions, their elephant lines and the gaudy blocks of color that formed the native regiments.

"You'll get the fight you want now, right enough," murmured Rowland to Willie Arbuthnot. "Are you still game?"

Willie's blue eyes sparkled. "D'you think you've dragged me all the way in this abominable heat, without a valet, for me to croak at the first sight of the enemy?" he demanded. "Let's have at 'em, and de'il tak' the hindmost."

Between the two officers, Caro stared apprehensively at the colorful ants moving so far below. A puff of smoke, like a cottonwool ball, spurted from a toy-size cannon and seconds later the small explosion drifted to their vantage point.

"There are so many of them," she whispered.

"I'd put it at six to one," said Willie cheerfully.

"They've not breached the Judge's wall, at all

events," said Rowland, taking the telescope away from his eye. "That means the garrison's still holding out. We have only to capture the Moti Masjid, then drive the rebels back from the Sultanbagh and the Ranee's palace, and the game will be up for them. Willie, old son, this is what I want your lads to do..."

He drew Willie and the other officers aside and began to plan the attack. Caro sat watching the scene below, with fear in her heart.

Rowland and the others were so sure of themselves, so confident that they had only to bring their guns and their well-trained troops up in the rear of the besiegers for the latter to fling down their arms and flee. But Caro remembered that a large portion of those besiegers were not the "native rabble" that Tom Hamilton had so contemptuously dismissed, but well-armed and disciplined Company sepoys under their native officers, avid to settle old scores with the haughty sahibs who had ruled them for a hundred years. How could one be sure they would lapse into fawning subservience at the first whiff of British grapeshot?

Even if Willie Arbuthnot did not share this doubt, William Allan and Rowland must. Caro gazed across at Rowland's tall, whipcord figure in plain blue tunic and long top boots, the thick black hair she had so recently stroked falling forward as he bent over a map. Was it to end so soon, this new-found happiness?

She had awakened from their night of love with a delicious feeling of fulfillment—a deep content as new to her as it was delightful. Stretching and yawning like a little cat in the soft light of dawn, she'd put out a hand and found Rowland gone, though the warm dent in the cushions beside her told how recently he had left her. Otherwise I might have believed I dreamed it all, she thought, smiling. He loves me—in spite of what I have said; in spite of what I have been! He loves me!

As the company had progressed rapidly toward Baburpore, bivouacking in the open, under the stars, Caro had been deprived of further nights in Rowland's arms. Still, his attentiveness to her, even in the midst of a hurried, rugged journey, touched her heart. He always made sure she rode beside him, joking and making small talk in a charming attempt to quell her fears of what lay ahead at Baburpore.

At night, when camp had been made, he would appear at her side, suggesting she walk with him. Although to wander far from the campsite could be dangerous, they would seek what little privacy they could without jeopardy. Strolling through the darkness, the embers of the campfire glowing in the distance, they would pause for a brief kiss or a fond caress, but would soon be on their way back to camp before they were missed.

Caro knew she would always remember in vivid detail those hurried embraces, those stolen kisses in the indigo darkness. Never had she felt so serene—amidst the thousands of menaces lurking in the Oriental nights, she was safe in her lover's arms. Never had she felt so free—yet so possessed.

"You are mine," he had told her their last evening before Baburpore. "You belong to me. But in no greater measure than I belong to you. If you want me, of course," he added lightly as they strolled back to the campsite. "If you'll have me, I'm eternally yours."

"Well, Captain Steel," Caro replied, feeling a thrill of joy dance through her, "I will certainly promise to consider your argument." She fluttered her lashes in a particularly coquettish fashion, then threw her arms impetuously around him, locking her fingertips behind his back and hugging him as tightly as she could.

"Oh, Rowland," she said softly. "This is the most perfect happiness. But why must it end? Why must it end so soon?"

He ran one finger gently down her nose, then over her lips and chin, then, spreading his hand, he cupped her chin and gently raised her head. "Because of an Indian thing called *karma*. Because we are who we are and because we must go where we were meant to be."

Then he kissed her tenderly one last time before they headed back to camp and on to Baburpore.

And now came the reckoning. Were those few days and nights to be no more than an interlude of golden sunshine between the dark thunderclouds of death and destruction? She shivered, picturing the flashing saber cut, the ricocheting musketball, the cannon's explosion—all the thousand and one dangers that could claim the life of the man whose strong, gentle hands and lips had made her his.

A little apart from the officers, Brook sat his horse, his eyes fixed on Caro. He alone had chanced to see Rowland slip from her tent three dawns ago, and the jealousy that smoldered so near the surface in his nature had burst once more into raging flame. The trek to Baburpore had been made in haste, and since the rougher accommodations allowed for little privacy, Brook had been aware of Caro and Steel wandering off together in the evening when they camped.

Damn Steel! he thought. Damn him for an arrogant tomcat, forcing his attentions on defenseless women! When he had first spotted Rowland Steel leaving Caro's tent, he had nearly, but not quite, challenged him there and then. Later that same day, when he realized, from words and looks, how eagerly Caro had welcomed the tomcat's attentions, he was glad he had restrained that first impulse to drag her indiscretion into the clear light of day. Instead he cursed inwardly at the fickleness of women, and the fate that drew him to Caro with an almost magnetic attraction. No matter how often he told himself she was quite unfitted to be his wife, he could not prevent watching her, listening for her voice, longing to touch her, even if it was only by accidentally brushing his leg against hers as their horses paced side by side.

If Steel were to die in the next few hours, would she turn to me, he wondered. Or would she rather seek comfort in the arms of yet another tall, self-confident nincompoop with a handsome uniform? He could neither understand her nor predict her reactions to any situation. When he expected her to be frightened, she was not; when he corrected her, she challenged his opinion. At times she could show a practical good sense to equal his own, but at others she displayed a lack of savoir-faire and a disdain for convention that alarmed and discouraged him. The influence of Philippa, her fastidious and correct sister, had been lamentably weakened, thought Brook, by these months of separation, but it was possible they could be restored . . .

Brook roused himself from his thoughts as he heard orders to advance and unlimber the guns.

"This is where our ways must part—for the moment," said Rowland, trotting back to Caro. "My orderly, Gul Mohammed, will look after you during the attack, and should matters go against us—as Heaven forbid—you may trust him to take you to safety."

"Can't I stay with you?" pleaded Caro, but he shook his head.

"Then you will take care?" she asked him, realizing she was speaking absently. How could a man going into battle take care?

"Of course." At her desolate expression, he leaned over and caught her hand.

"Be brave, Caro—*carissima*—and all will be well."

"Can't at least tell me what you plan to do?"

Rowland hesitated, then pointed across to where the gun bullocks were lumbering away to take up their positions on the slope overlooking the red walls with towers at the four corners, surrounding a white marble dome. This was the Pearl Mosque—the Moti Masjid—which, together with the British-held Courthouse, commanded the river-crossing.

"If it will make you happier . . . Briefly, it is this. As you can see, the Judge's compound is roughly triangular in shape, with the long side fronting on the Gharti river, where the water is too deep and the current too dangerous for gun bullocks to cross. This is what has protected the British garrison so far. Should the enemy capture the Sultanbagh, however, which lies on the opposite bank, and install guns behind its walls, he could fire across the river and quickly reduce the British defenses to rubble, for the compound has no fortifications on that side.

"Chandranaya's problem, therefore, is to get his guns across, but he is reluctant to leave his present position for fear the British will break out of the Judge's compound and recapture the Moti Masjid, where the bulk of the rebel gunpowder and ammunition is stored. My guess is that he is awaiting the Nana Sahib, or another of the rebellious Gwalior contingent, with reinforcements."

Caro nodded. "But there is a bridge of boats, Philippa told me . . ."

"Precisely. The bridge of boats on the northern fork of the river is commanded by General Elliott's guns as well as those of the rebels in the Moti Masjid, so Chandranaya cannot use it to bring his artillery across the stream. In short, a stalemate."

"So you plan to capture the mosque—the Moti Masjid."

Rowland smiled at her. "What a strategist you would make! While Willie's guns attack the Moti Masjid from the northwest, and draw the enemy's fire, my Sikhs and I will cross the river by the ford above the bridge of boats and occupy the Sultanbagh. Once those two strong points are in our hands, we will be able to evacuate the garrison across the river."

Caro was thinking hard. "But what if General Elliott's guns mistake *you* for the enemy as you cross the river?"

He shrugged. "That is a risk we have to take."

"I will carry your message to the garrison!" exclaimed Caro eagerly. "I have done it before. Gul Mohammed can guide me through the native town, and you said yourself that my disguise is near perfect."

Rowland thought it over, then shook his head. "No; it would be far too dangerous," he said firmly. "Don't think I do not admire your bravery in making such an offer, but I cannot accept it. Now, I must go." He leaned across from his saddle and kissed her lightly. "Smile for me, Caro!"

Her heart was heavy, but she summoned up a smile and watched him ride away. In the distance, thunder rumbled, heralding an afternoon's storm, and the copper-tinted clouds pressed down like a low ceiling over the battle scene.

Behind her, Gul Mohammed coughed gently. He was high-cheekboned, yellow-skinned, almost Tibetan in appearance, with bright slanting eyes under winged brows.

"Miss-sahiba take message?"

Caro stared at him. It sounded like a challenge, a test of her courage. "No. Steel-sahib forbids it."

"I guide through native town. No one see."

"No," she said again. "Steel-sahib told me to wait here. We must do as he says."

The slanting eyes half closed in scorn. He thinks I'm a coward, thought Caro angrily. Can't he see how much harder it is for me to wait here in suspense, with no way of telling how the battle is going?

Gul Mohammed looked up at the sullen sky. "Rain

coming," he said accusingly, as though she were personally responsible for the humid discomfort of the monsoon.

"This I know." Caro would have liked to add "son of a pig," as the bold girls in the Joyhouse of Kali were wont to do, but such speech would be unbecoming now that she was a memsahib again. She said curtly, "It is the season," and turned Nuri's head to face away from the sneering Oriental eyes. She stared instead after the marching column of Highlanders, their kilts swinging as they vanished in the hazy distance. Rowland took Brook Vyner with him, but he would not take me, she thought; why are women always left behind? She felt a sharp sense of injustice.

For an hour Caro and Gul Mohammed sat in disagreeable silence, then the rain began.

In a few moments the heavy, oily drops had soaked them both to the skin. A wind sprang up and cut through their sodden clothes; Nuri tucked her tail in and dropped her head low, the picture of shivering misery. Caro looked longingly toward the jumble of huts about a mile away on the plain below. Surely no one would notice if they took shelter on the edge of the native town? She still wore her sowar's *puggree* and dark-blue tunic over baggy white cotton breeches, and would never be taken for a woman. Besides, any patrol from Chandranaya's army would surely have taken cover from the downpour. Rowland could not mean her to stay rooted to the spot in this deluge; it was beyond all reason.

Almost without meaning to, she urged Nuri forward, and Gul Mohammed immediately took the lead, moving confidently down the winding path. They reached the first group of huts only to find them ruined, affording no shelter from the torrential rain: no doubt they had been in the rebels' line of fire during the capture of the Moti Masjid.

The rain felt cold now and Caro's tunic had become a soggy, clinging mass of cloth across her shoulders. "We'll have to go on," she said through chattering teeth. Gul Mohammed nodded and walked on briskly with his long, hillman's stride, threading through the narrow streets of the deserted bazaar in a silence broken only by the drumming rain and the splash of Nuri's hooves as she sidled delicately past heaps of rotting fruit and vegetables in the open shopfronts, making for the river.

Behind them, to the northwest, a cannon crashed as Willie Arbuthnot's six pounders opened fire on the rebels guarding the Moti Masjid.

Some miles upstream, Rowland heard it too, and grinned. Good old Willie, how proud he was of those noisy popguns of his! Calling his men to a halt beside the dark, swift-flowing water, Rowland trotted up a rise in the ground until he could see the red towers on the southern side of the Moti Masjid. His spyglass revealed much activity on the battlements. Red-coated midgets scurried to and fro, and from within the walls a heavy gun boomed in reply. So far, so good. If Willie could contain their fire while Rowland crossed the river, all would be well. If Willie actually succeeded in storming the Moti Masjid, so much the better.

Rejoining his men, Rowland cursed the rain that dripped into his collar and trickled in muddy rivulets down his boots. He was still worried that there was no place for Caro to take shelter on the bare hillside where they had parted. I shouldn't have left her there, he thought, but where else would she be safe? One cannot take a woman into battle—even a woman like Caro. The grim line of his mouth relaxed as he recalled her wild ecstasy that night in her tent, the total surrender of that small-boned, supple body, those hands which fiercely demanded even as they caressed . . .

Caro's a strong woman—perfectly capable of taking

care of herself. She'll find somewhere to shelter until the rain stops, he assured himself. Gul Mohammed would see to that.

But as his company trotted on down the river bank with the lightning flashes overhead echoing the spurts of flame from Willie's six-pounders, Rowland kept glancing back toward the hilltop where he had last seen Caro.

The rain ceased as suddenly as it had begun, and the setting sun brought steam from Nuri's coat and Gul Mohammed's wet tunic. The noise of the bombardment came clearly to them now, and Caro looked about her uneasily, realizing how far they had strayed from the hilltop.

It will soon be dark, she thought. Rowland could not have meant me to spend the night on that bleak hilltop. We will be far more use to him if we alert the British garrison to what he means to do. She firmly pushed out of her mind the uncomfortable fact that he had instructed her to remain on the hill.

Rebel sentries were on guard in this part of the native town, but Gul Mohammed still set a steady pace, padding down the darkening, refuse-strewn streets and avoiding the campfires flickering in the dusk. At last he stopped, and drew Nuri into a roofless mud hut.

"Wait here," he whispered. "I look for the way," and was gone like a white-robed ghost.

Caro tried to get her bearings. She could see the bulk of the Moti Masjid about a mile away to the left, and estimated that the fortified ditch surrounding the Judge's residence must be another half mile to her right. Between the two lay the untidy crescent-shape straggle of the native town with the single remaining British outpost—once the courtrooms but now the emplacement for General Elliott's few twelve-pounders—overlooking the bridge of boats directly ahead. She knew from her earlier visit that these guns were manned by the sepoys of Captain Lewis's 94th Bengal Native Artillery—the only company to remain loyal when their comrades deserted—while the front wall of the Judge's residence was guarded by Tom Hamilton and those soldiers of the 42nd Queen's who had manhandled her and Bulbul. She was glad that Gul Mohammed had elected to guide her to the courthouse and General Elliott rather than to attempt crossing the open parade ground again.

Here, at least, there was plenty of cover. Damaged buildings and heaps of rubble extended nearly up to the wall of the courtrooms, leaving only a gap of cleared ground a few hundred yards wide in front of the gate itself, to discourage snipers. They would have to cross that before reaching the central archway with its barred gate.

A rustle of cloth, the whisper of bare feet, and Gul Mohammed was beside her again, wiping a long curved knife before replacing it in his sash.

Taking Nuri's rein, he led her past a campfire, where four sentries sprawled, their throats cut; ahead in the gathering gloom was the courthouse, nearer than she had estimated. But barely had they begun to cross the open space than they heard shouts behind them, and running feet.

The murdered sentries had been discovered. Flame flashed yellow, and a bullet whistled past Nuri's head.

"Ride!" hissed Gul Mohammed, and gripped Caro's stirrup leather. The mare bounded forward at a gallop, as eager as they were to escape the shot that kicked up pockets of mud all round them, and the Mussulman leaped along beside her. In no time they were at the iron grille of the Courthouse, with its guard room above.

"Open the gate!" shouted Caro.

"Open with grape!" echoed a singsong voice within the walls.

"No, no! The *gate*. Let us in. We bring a message from Captain Rowland Steel."

There was a murmur of astonishment from the guard and slowly—too slowly—the gate swung open, but just as it did, a bullet struck Gul Mohammed in the back and he fell with a queer little grunt, blood gushing from his mouth.

"Let us in!" screamed Caro. She flung herself off Nuri and bent over the Mussulman, but he had died almost instantly.

A moment later, strong hands hustled her inside, pulling the mare after her. The heavy gate swung shut again with a sonorous clang; she was safe.

Emily Drinkwater wiped the sweat from Philippa's face, then flinched involuntarily as a charge of canister struck the boarded-up window of the upper room. The firing had been intensive all day, and everyone within the Judge's compound sensed that the end was near. The battered building could not stand much more of this continuous bombardment; it seemed that the enemy was working up to a final all-out assault.

Well, thought Emily wearily, let them come. Nothing can be worse than what we've been through already.

In the last week, the physical condition of the besieged garrison had deteriorated sharply as lack of fresh food, sudden downpours alternating with steaming heat, dirt, sleeplessness, and worst of all, the slow erosion of hope combined to take their toll. Of the eighteen children who had taken refuge in the Judge's house, only five survived: pitiful waifs with the bones showing sharply in their pinched, anxious faces. Their mothers were in little better condition; quite three-

quarters of the small community was suffering from
dysentery and many from outbreaks of boils as well.
Sunstroke had laid low Doctor Williams, and General
Elliott faded daily as if he lacked the will to live. Major
Symington, paper-thin and yellow as a Mandarin, had
taken temporary command.

Only Tom Hamilton and Emily herself seemed to
have the strength to fight off disease—and that for
opposite reasons. Emily's placid, optimistic nature
made her less prone to fears and nervous upsets than
the other women, while Tom Hamilton lived in a
perpetual white-heat of rage at everything—the
mutineers, the monsoon, the garrison's weakness, the
situation in which he was trapped—a rage which
endowed him with apparently inexhaustible energy.
Most of the women and all the servants were terrified
of him, but Emily refused to be frightened or
browbeaten.

When Philippa went into labor unexpectedly, Emily
calmly informed Captain Hamilton that he must find
another lady to manufacture cartridges for his men's
rifles until the baby was delivered.

"Damn it, Miss Drinkwater!" Tom exploded. "Are
my guns to be idle all day because that whey-faced
bitch has decided to whelp at last?"

"I must beg you to moderate your language,
Captain Hamilton," she replied, deliberately starchy.
"Lady Philippa's health and that of her child are of *far*
more concern to me than your guns. I will make a
collection of stockings among the ladies," she offered,
relenting a little, "if you wish to fire canister instead,
but I cannot make any cartridges for you today. Why
not instruct Miss O'Reilly in their manufacture?"

He groaned. "That clumsy old tabby would never
learn. No one else has your touch. Surely Doctor
Williams can attend Lady Philippa without your
assistance?"

"He is too weak to leave his bed. No, I am sorry about the cartridges but the baby must come first." She added with a touch of waspishness, "It would be no use for me to beg *your* help, yet you never scruple to ask for mine."

He surprised her by putting out a hand to detain her. "Wait: of course I will help, you ninny, if there is anything I can do! Don't look so amazed. I've attended the birth of plenty of foals, and I don't suppose a child's is so very different. If all's well, the matter is quickly over, and if anything is amiss the poor creature will be spared this vale of tears, at least. A baby!" he added angrily. "As if we had not enough to do keeping grown men alive without caring for a squalling infant as well."

Emily was too relieved at his offer of assistance, however qualified, to upbraid him for his insensitivity. She smiled and thanked him, offering in her turn to work at making cartridges until Philippa's pains became acute, and they parted on better terms.

Now, as evening drew on and still Philippa writhed and twisted on the charpoy, the great mound of her stomach grotesquely outlined by the lamplight on the bullet-pocked walls, Emily feared that something was amiss. The waters had broken long ago, but still the child's head had not appeared, and until it did, there was nothing she could do to help.

She smoothed back Philippa's hair with a damp rag. "Shall I send for Captain Thynne?" she asked again.

Andrew was on duty at the Courthouse, overlooking the bridge of boats, and Philippa had so far refused to allow him to be informed of her condition.

"No... wait a little longer. Just a little longer." Her voice was decidedly weaker and Emily was tempted to disobey her. What if she should die before Andrew Thynne arrived?

Then Philippa gave a cry and half raised herself

from the bed. Quickly Emily brought the lamp closer and believed she saw the baby's head. A wave of relief swept over her.

"That's wonderful," she encouraged, ignoring the bite of Philippa's nails on her free hand. "It won't be long now." She whispered to the *ayah*, crouched motionless by the door, "Send for Thynne-sahib. Tell him his child will soon be born."

Time passed, and nothing happened. After that single effort, Philippa had relapsed into a semicoma, her breath coming in fast, shallow gasps. Emily grew more and more worried; Tom Hamilton's remark about the poor creature avoiding the vale of tears seemed to echo in her head. If only there was a doctor—a midwife—someone to advise her...Suddenly she thought: Bulbul! Of course Bulbul would know what to do. She sent another servant scurrying over to the annex where Bulbul and Baby Jack were lodged. Bulbul arrived shortly after.

The old woman, swathed in a gold-spangled sari of shocking pink gauze, gave a soft moan when she examined Philippa.

"What's the matter?" snapped Emily.

"*Baba* coming wrong way. Need doctor-sahib quick, quick."

"Isn't there anything we can do?"

Bulbul considered, then shook her head with a helpless shrug. "Doctor turn *baba* 'round"—she gestured graphically. "Memsahib and Bulbul not enough strong."

Strong. Emily's thoughts flashed to Tom Hamilton's powerful hands. "Could Captain Hamilton do it?"

Bulbul nodded doubtfully.

"Stay here," commanded Emily. "I shall fetch Captain Hamilton."

She sped across the landing as fast as her bulk would allow, and encountered Tom Hamilton at the foot of the stairs.

"Hullo, what's up? I was coming to ask if you needed any help. There's a smart outbreak of firing over at the Courthouse, so Andrew Thynne can't come across. How's his wife doing?"

"She's bad—very bad. It's a—a breech birth, and Bulbul wants the baby turned into a better position. She thinks you can do it."

Tom's eyes widened. "Heaven help us."

"Bulbul will show you what to do. Please, Tom. It's the only chance for her—for both of them. We can't just let them die." Unexpectedly, tears glistened in her eyes.

"Hell's teeth! There must be some other way."

"There isn't."

"But I don't know the first thing about babies..." She dragged him, still protesting, into the hot, airless room, stinking of blood and tallow, and stale sweat, and plunged his hands into the prepared basin of chlorate of lime.

"Scrub your nails—that's right. Rinse them. Now do as Bulbul tells you."

She turned away and stood with her forehead pressed against the wall, eyes squeezed shut but still unable to shut out the sound of Philippa's moaning and the steady flow of barrack-room curses that spouted from Tom Hamilton's mouth as he tried, and failed, and tried again to do as Bulbul bade him.

Chapter Fifteen

THE THICK WALLS at the front of the Sultanbagh, ancient fortress and palace of the Princes of Baburpore, had withstood many an assault, but against an attack from within they were useless.

When the trumpets of Nana Sahib's heralds screamed a demand for entry, the Ranee of Baburpore—a slender, slant-browed woman whose large eyes were heavily ringed with kohl—laughed aloud and called her solemn eleven-year-old son, the puppet Rajah, to join her on the battlements.

"Listen to the jackals singing for their meal!" she jeered, and ordered her archers to fire upon the horsemen below. It was the last order she ever gave, for her men-at-arms, who had fed greedily on the bazaar-born stories of Nana Sahib's exploits at Cawnpore, and who hated their mistress as much as they hated the Honourable East India Company which had set her over them, spun around with one accord and loosed their arrows upon the Ranee and her son.

The young boy, his eyes wide with disbelief, clutched at the shaft sticking out a foot behind his head, and toppled slowly over the low battlements, his body turning limply in the air as it fell. The Ranee choked on a gush of blood, and died without another sound.

Outside the great gate, Prince Chandranaya's cavalry gave a wild yell of triumph and surged forward into the main courtyard.

Rowland heard the cheer as his column moved quietly down the river bank, and knew that he was too late. The enemy had overrun the Sultanbagh without a shot being fired. He turned to Brook Vyner, who rode at his side.

"We need reinforcements, Mr. Vyner," he instructed urgently. "A body of the enemy has occupied the Sultanbagh, no doubt through some treachery. Kindly return at your best speed to Captain Arbuthnot and request him to withdraw from the Moti Masjid and join me here."

Brook was only too glad to obey. A cavalry attack on a strong position without the support of artillery was military madness in his view, and the farther he escaped toward the rear the better.

Hurrying back, he delivered the message to Willie, who sat among his begrimed, triumphant Highlanders in the stronghold surrounding the Moti Masjid, from which the last of the mutineers had fled, and was appalled when the captain gave orders to move at once.

"But you cannot march in the dark!" Brook protested. "Your men must be tired as well as hungry."

"True; but they'll sleep softer in the palace than in this damned drafty temple," declared Willie.

"But they've been marching all day!"

Willie fixed him with a cold eye. "Look here, Twyner—Vyner—whatever your damned name may be: when my cousin Rowland requests my support he doesn't mean tomorrow, or in a fortnight's time. He means *now*. Understand?"

Speechless with fury, Brook turned away. The guns were limbered up and the column began to move before he could effect an escape. Leaving only a picket to occupy the Moti Masjid, they followed in Rowland's tracks and caught up with him in the early hours of the morning, bivouacked in a dip of the ground about three-quarters of a mile from the Sultanbagh.

"Good work, Willie," said Rowland warmly. "My scouts say the Nana Sahib's behind those walls as well as Prince Chandranaya of Patelbar. Apparently they crossed the lower ford with an advance guard earlier this evening, *leaving their guns on the far side of the river*. They never dreamed we'd be after 'em so quick. We've got them, Willie, old son! We've got 'em as tight as a pair of rats in a trap."

That the rats could still bite was evident next morning when they took their combined forces in to attack the Sultanbagh.

Sergeant Forbes of the 96th, reconnoitering carefully under cover of darkness, had made an interesting discovery—a breach in the rear wall of the Sultanbagh—and through this Willie's company climbed silently in the hour before dawn.

When Rowland's Sikhs charged with blood-curdling yells at the Patelbar Irregular Cavalry, which had camped in colorful disarray on the flat ground in front of the palace gate, the Highlanders suddenly appeared in the inner courtyard, bayonets fixed and huge feather bonnets fluttering in the dawn breeze.

Screams of terror echoed from the battle-scarred walls as the mutineers realized their peril. Wielding his claymore like a giant ax, Sergeant Forbes cut his way across to the main gate and swung it open; a moment later Rowland's charge burst through the ranks of the Patelbar Irregulars, sweeping them all together into the shrieking melee within the courtyard. Hand to hand, with no room to use their guns, brown men and white struggled and slipped on the blood-spattered mosaic floor, were split asunder by Damascus steel or trampled by rearing, wild-eyed chargers.

Alone in the angle of the walls, deserted by his ally, the Rajah of Bithoor, who had urged him into this trap, Prince Chandranaya whirled his sword with the fury of despair. His green silk turban, half unrolled, hung down his back; his yellow quilted coat was rippled and torn in a dozen places. Was this to be the end of his dream of glory—the end of the new Mahratta Empire promised him by Nana Sahib? Had he schemed and murdered in pursuit of his lost inheritance only to have it snatched from him in his hour of triumph by a handful of red-faced cow-eating Feringhees calling themselves sahibs? Where were his fighting men? Where was the Rajah of Bithoor, who had called him cousin, and promised eternal friendship? Gone: he was alone. But before he, Chandranaya, joined his fathers, he would take a dozen of these English dogs to bear him company.

Recklessly thrusting through the struggling, cursing mob, Chandranaya reached Rowland's flank, and struck at him from the rear.

"'Ware behind you, Rowland!"

Willie Arbuthnot's cracked voice reached Rowland through the din. He turned swiftly, in time to see his cousin deliberately interpose his own body between Rowland and Chandranaya's deadly thrust. The long dagger pierced straight through Willie's chest as Rowland, with a groan of mingled sorrow and anger, whirled his own blade and severed Chandranaya's snarling head from his shoulders.

The blow came too late to save Willie. Rowland half dragged, half carried him to an embrasure in the wall, clear of the fighting, and unbuttoned his tunic. Willie was deathly pale, but his eyes fluttered open and he recognized his cousin.

"It was a good scrum, wasn't it?" he whispered. "I think I'm done for, but it was . . . a good scrum. Can't feel anything . . ."

"Nonsense; we'll get a surgeon to you right away. We'll soon have you stitched up and comfortable."

Slowly Willie shook his head. "No good," he grunted. "Fellow got me fair and square." He was silent a moment, then, "Hark at 'em cheerin'! That means we've won, don't it?"

"Yes, we've won," said Rowland unsteadily. "Now you just take it easy, old lad. The surgeon's coming, and you'll be all right."

But Willie's blood was beginning to well out around the handle of the dagger, pumping his life onto the mosaic of the courtyard floor. He sighed deeply, and his eyelids drooped.

"A good scrum...," he murmured again.

He was dead. Rowland laid him down gently. No time to grieve now, but a yawning gap seemed to open in his vitals as he remembered the good times he and Willie had shared. Catching their first trout in the stream behind Willie's Hampshire home; smoking their first cigar in the school shrubbery, scoring a half-century apiece in that wonderful game against Harrow; climbing trees, flighting duck, quarreling over their first girl... Willie had been part of all Rowland's best memories of England: volatile, happy-go-lucky Willie, given to puns and terrible enthusiasms... All gone now, nothing left but the drawn, paper-white face above the dark-green jacket, the body stretched on the inlaid marble of an Indian palace. No time to grieve now.

Blindly Rowland turned away and blundered down the colonnaded passage that led away from the courtyard. Behind him he heard the sergeants calling the roll, mustering prisoners, marshaling survivors; the fight was over, but Willie was dead, and just for a moment he had to be alone.

The Nana Sahib, Rajah of Bithoor, hurried away from the scene of battle as soon as he realized that the Highlanders were within the palace walls. He watched the beginning of Chandranaya's desperate rear-guard action, and knew that if he were to save himself, and his hopes of a new empire for the Mahrattas, he must escape from the Sultanbagh without delay. At a side gate two horses waited saddled, ready to speed him to safety, but first he hastened in the direction of the treasure house, where the gold and jewels amassed by generations of Chandranaya's forebears lay stored in a great circular chamber, guarded by the hereditary Keeper of the Jewels and his son. Money he must have, to bribe his way through the enemy lines and rejoin his army.

Panting from the unaccustomed exertion, his sallow, plump cheeks quivering and his drooping eyes darting here and there as he hurried through the deserted apartments, Nana Sahib was unaware that someone had watched him leave the scene of battle, and was following where he led. Brook Vyner, too, knew where the treasure chamber lay, and was determined to lay his hands on some of it before the soldiers searched the palace.

At the foot of a winding stairway, Nana Sahib came at last to the iron-bound wooden door and scratched softly.

"Open!" he commanded. "It is I, the Rajah of Bithoor, who seek entry."

Barely were the words out of his mouth than the door swung smoothly inward, and there on the threshold stood the white-bearded Guardian, his son beside him. Behind them a locked iron grille provided the treasure's last bastion, and through it could be seen a winking, glinting heap of rubies, sparkling rivers of diamonds, ropes of pearls, and sapphires as deep and blue as the sea off Cape Comorin.

"Presence!" said the Guardian, trembling.

Nana Sahib pushed quickly past him into the chamber. "The accursed sahib-log is within our gates, and will seize the Nau-lakha and all your treasure.

Only help me to load these chests and carry them to safety..."

The Guardian hesitated, twisting his gnarled hands.

"The key, fool!" urged Nana Sahib. He snatched it just as two shots in quick succession exploded with a deafening double crash in the confined space.

Nana Sahib whipped around, his mouth slack with fear, and saw the Keeper of the Jewels and his son writhing on the stone floor in their last agonies. Over them stood Brook Vyner, a smoking pistol in either hand. The Rajah of Bithoor stared at him, unable to move or speak.

"Good day, Your Highness," said Brook pleasantly. "It is a long time since I had the honor of attending a soiree in your palace at Bithoor. No; don't attempt to escape. As you see, I have another weapon which I shall not hesitate to use. Now if you will accompany me, I know that Captain Steel will be glad to renew his acquaintance with you."

Nana Sahib found his voice with an effort. "Mr.— Vyner, is it not?" he said shakily. "Yes, I remember you, as you will remember me. Look there, Mr. Vyner"—he pointed to the iron grille with its sparkling contents—"there lies the wealth of Baburpore: gold and jewels the like of which no Englishman has ever dreamed of, let alone possessed. I hold the key that will unlock that door."

"Give it to me."

"No, no, Mr. Vyner." Nana Sahib thrust his hand through an arrow slit in the chamber wall. "I have only to open my fingers, and the key will be lost to you forever. But if you will do me one small favor, I will give you the key, and make you master of all you see there."

Brook Vyner licked his lips. Far away a muffled thumping told him that the soldiers had begun to search the palace; time was running out, he must act fast. "What do you want me to do?" he asked.

In the fierce heat of noon, the survivors of the battle for the Sultanbagh marched up to the gates of the Judge's residence, and the sepoys within the walls, who had remained loyal to the British, greeted their comrades with a ragged cheer.

"Jai Company *hai*!"

Behind the Sikhs marched Willie's Highlanders, commanded by young Lieutenant Frederick Alexander, his right arm bound up in a rough sling. The sight of their feather bonnets and swinging kilts sent the English ladies who still had the strength to move scurrying to tear down the bullet-pocked boards over the windows and lean out, waving frenziedly with tears streaming down their unwashed cheeks.

"Our own brave lads!" exclaimed Emily Drinkwater emotionally. "Now I know we really are saved!" She held the tightly wrapped bundle she was cuddling up to the window. "Look, baby: there you see the heroes of Baburpore!"

Caro slipped away from the crying, exclaiming throng at the upper window, and ran down to the parade. General Elliott, shrunk and wasted, had just been carried out on a litter to greet the relieving force, but the dusty, hollow-eyed soldiers who had fought two engagements after a forced march of nearly fifty miles wanted nothing so much as to strip off their sweat-soaked flannel shirts and lie down to sleep. They could hardly stand to listen to the General's congratulations; whereupon he ordered a double ration of grog to be issued and dismissed them to their rest.

Caro edged through the crowd until she could see Rowland. The relief of knowing he was safe and unhurt made her suddenly dizzy, and she leaned against the redstone wall, waiting her chance to speak to him. How tired he looks, she thought. His cheeks are positively hollow... he looks older: can it be only twenty-four hours—a single day—since we said good-bye on the hilltop over there? It must have been a terrible battle, but at least I saved him from our own guns as he crossed the river. Pride in this achievement glowed at the back of her mind; she could hardly wait to find out if he knew who had insured him a safe passage across the river. The moment his men were marched away toward their billets, she ran forward and grasped his stirrup.

"Oh, Rowland!" she exclaimed joyfully, "How glad I am that you are safe!"

Under the dust and grime, his face set hard as he looked down and saw who was speaking. "Safe, yes; no thanks to you, Lady Caroline," he snapped.

It was as if he had thrown a bucket of icy water over her. The glow faded from Caro's face and she stared at him with huge, bewildered eyes.

"No... thanks?"

"Why did you not remain on the hillside as I commanded? Why did you disobey my orders and lead my servant into such peril? Because of your recklessness, Gul Mohammed is dead, and my men half dead with fatigue from searching for you."

Could this be Rowland speaking—to *her?* She had never heard him use that hard, cutting voice before. The injustice of his accusation brought angry tears stinging to her eyes.

"But—you do not understand! It wasn't I who led Gul Mohammed into danger—rather the reverse. He wanted me to make contact with the British outpost. He was afraid—we both were—that the guns would fire on you as you crossed the river, and we took the only course open to us to prevent it."

"Although I had expressly forbidden you to do so. Gul Mohammed is not here to contradict you," said

Rowland stonily, "but I know very well that he would never have left his post against my orders. *Never*. It must have been your doing."

"Your orders!" Now she was angry too. "What kind of orders were those? What sort of a man are you to leave me on a bare hilltop in drenching rain, with only a Pathan cutthroat for protection? Orders! I am not a soldier, Rowland, and neither am I subject to your orders. I did the best I could to prevent your men being blown to bits by our own guns, and now you storm at me for disobeying orders."

"Gul Mohammed was no Pathan cutthroat. He was my loyal servant and good friend. No, Caro," he said in a tired voice. "I am not storming at you. It's true that I have no right to give you orders, but even if it was too much to hope you'd have the self-discipline to do as you were told, I thought you would have more sense than to go precisely where I'd told you not to, and drag poor Gul Mohammed with you."

"I *didn't* drag him with me."

"How you persuaded him to disobey me is beside the point. Whatever the reason, it makes no difference, for the facts speak for themselves. Didn't you realize that Gul Mohammed would feel bound to follow where a memsahib led, even though he could see the danger and you couldn't? If only you had done as I ord—asked, he would now be alive."

"Though *you* might not be."

Caro tried to cast her mind back to the scene on the hillside in the hour after the Sikhs and Highlanders had vanished. *Had* it been as Rowland imagined? Had she been the one to lead Gul Mohammed from his post of duty? She recalled the sneering elongated eyes, heard in memory the repeated demand that she should go to the British outpost. "I guide memsahib. No one see..."

"He *wanted* to go," she broke out indignantly. "He

offered to guide me through the native town. I said we should stay where we were."

"Yet you allowed him to persuade you? I find that strange, I must say. I had known Gul Mohammed many years, and I would have trusted him with my life." His face was shuttered; she could tell that he didn't believe a word she said. She wanted to scream at him that he was wrong, what she said was true; but there were people too close. Lewis Allan hovered nearby, waiting for orders. He looked curiously at Caro as she blinked back her tears. She would not cry in front of him.

Rowland said curtly, "Now, you must excuse me, Lady Caroline, for I have to see that my men are comfortable."

No smile, no word of affection; just a cold nod as he rode away. Rowland had not believed her. Yet she could see, as he could not, that it was because Gul Mohammed was both loyal and faithful to him that he had been unable to wait idly on the hillside while Rowland rode into danger. It had not been her fault that the Mussulman died, yet the bullet that struck him had blasted the love that was growing between her and Rowland as a sudden frost withers a young plant.

Perhaps it hadn't been real after all, she thought bleakly. Perhaps their lovemaking meant nothing more to Rowland than an appetite satisfied, a return to carnal pleasure after the enforced abstinence of patrol.

Anger stirred once more in Caro—anger at herself for so readily succumbing to the embraces of this hard, cold man; fury at him for inviting her love, making use of her, and then tossing her aside.

She drew herself up proudly. She, too, could be hard and cold. He should never know how he had hurt her, nor should he ever again catch the faintest glimpse of Caro the Silent One. I won't be deceived again, she vowed, staring at his retreating back. Caro the Silent One was a vulnerable fool, ready to give her heart to the first man to hold her in his arms and whisper sweet nonsense in her ears. But now I am Lady Caroline March once more, she told herself, resolutely ignoring the treacherous small voice at the back of her brain that mourned the freedom the Silent One had enjoyed. I shall never throw myself at Captain Rowland Steel again.

"No, Caro, I cannot go," said Philippa.

"If you won't, I shall not go either."

"Don't be a goose. Andrew will be only too pleased to escort you, and you would enjoy it."

Caro laughed. "That would provide a fine tidbit of gossip for the ladies of Baburpore! Lady Philippa left to languish at home while her husband diverts himself with his sister-in-law? The tongues would wag all night, I promise you. No, seriously, Phil, it is time—*high* time—you rejoined the social whirl, before someone less scrupulous than I removes your attractive husband. Bulbul can look after little Rowley without your help for a single night—you know how she loves to spoil him!"

"Oh, very well; I'll come if you insist," said Philippa with a little sigh. She had taken a long time to regain her strength after the birth of Andrew Rowland Thomas Thynne—more generally known as Rowley—who now lay gurgling and kicking under a frilled muslin flynet on the veranda while his mother and aunt sipped their jasmine-scented tea and discussed the ball.

Peace had returned to Baburpore and the surrounding countryside in the six weeks since the battle at the Sultanbagh; the scattered remnants of Prince Chandranaya's army had fled into the jungles and their late comrades-in-arms, the mutinous sepoys of the 186th Bengal Native Infantry, tore off their incriminating red jackets and hid their weapons where the avenging sahib-log would not find them.

Day after day Tom Hamilton's patrols brought in natives suspected of involvement in the Great Sepoy Revolt, as the newspapers in England had begun to call the mutiny, and now a civil court had arrived in Baburpore to try these prisoners.

A ball in the redecorated assembly rooms was planned by the ladies, to entertain the visiting lawyers; Caro and Andrew were both determined that Philippa should attend it.

"If she don't go to this ball, she'll find one excuse after another to stay at home all through the 'cold weather,'" said poor Andrew, who dearly loved a party. "But once she finds she's up to it again and the baby's all right without her, she won't be so hard to persuade a second time."

"I'll bully her into going—you wait," said Caro. She was looking forward to the ball, which would bring a breath of life from outside into the tight, cloistered little world of Baburpore. From time to time in the past six weeks they had received news from other stations. They heard of the relief of Lucknow on the twenty-fifth of September, and the chase that followed as the "Gwalior Contingent" with its leader Nana Sahib was driven back to Cawnpore and bombarded across the river by the guns of Sir Colin Campbell's 93rd Sutherland Highlanders; but information was still scarce and sketchy. The mail *dak* frequently fell prey to marauding bands of ex-mutineers, and could not be relied upon.

After the freedom of her life as a native, Caro found it hard to submit to the taboos and restrictions that governed the conduct of an unmarried English lady in a small station. Nevertheless she held firmly to the promise she had made herself, and forced herself to think, feel, behave as Lady Caroline March should.

She saw little of Rowland, whose military duties often took him away from the town, and was careful on the occasions when she did meet him not to be alone with him. Once or twice lately she had sensed that he wanted to get back on their old easy footing, but she was determined not to risk a second rebuff.

He called one morning in October with a silver mug, a present for his godson, little Rowley, and when Philippa went to summon Bulbul, who was rocking the child under a tree in the garden, Rowland turned swiftly to Caro.

"At last I can speak to you alone. For weeks now I have been wanting to apologize for my boorish behavior after the battle at the Sultanbagh. I said things to you that day of which I feel deeply ashamed. Please say you forgive me."

"Ashamed, Captain Steel?" Caro said brightly, giving him no help. "I am certain there is nothing for you to be ashamed of. Why, I have heard you described as the Hero of Baburpore, no less, on account of your exploits that day. As for apologies: don't you agree that it is much too late to withdraw anything you may have said to me on that occasion?"

"Please, Caro," said Rowland in a low, rapid tone, watching Philippa, who had begun languidly to return from her errand, "please don't do this. I know I spoke hastily and you had every right to be angry. I was still stunned by poor Willie's death, and to find that Gul Mohammed had perished, too, was the final straw. Besides, I was sick with anxiety about you. When we failed to find you on the hillside, I imagined the worst, and my anger was caused partly by relief after a bad fright."

And partly by exhaustion, heat, sorrow, guilt for Willie's death, rage at the Nana Sahib's mysterious escape, he might have added, but still Caro would not give in to the old attraction that was making her heart race and her legs feel drained of strength.

Rowland wanted to shake her. He knew she was playing a part; he believed that behind the bright social expression and glib speech the real warm, passionate Caro was still to be found—only he had lost the key. That damned ill-considered speech when he had vented his fatigue and fury on her had driven the woman he loved underground, and replaced her with this correct, guarded puppet of a girl who carefully kept him at arm's length and used her sister's fragile state of health as an excuse to avoid his company.

"Set your mind at rest, then," said Caro with a light, brittle laugh, "for my memory of that entire day is extremely hazy, and I really cannot recall a single word you said to me. There is not the least need for you to apologize."

"Still, I do," said Rowland, who strongly doubted the truth of her last statement. "I shall not be happy until you tell me you forgive me." He smiled at her, willing her to respond in the old way, but there was no answering spark in her velvety violet eyes as she answered abstractedly, "Of course. Ah, here's Philippa with little Rowley. Isn't he enchanting? Please do not speak of it again..."

Rejoining them on the veranda, Philippa found them sitting in silence: Rowland staring at Caro while she gazed blankly at the surrounding trees. Oh dear, she thought, I believe they have quarreled, and she hurried to fill the awkward pause with a lively description of little Rowley's appreciation of his lovely christening present.

The one person delighted to observe the coolness between Rowland and Caro was Brook Vyner, and he lost no opportunity to worsen the situation.

"Strange the way that fellow Steel brings in only half as many prisoners as Tom Hamilton's patrols do," he remarked one morning, meeting Caro exercising

Nuri in the tree-lined sandy avenue known as the Mall. A party of Rowland's Sikhs trotted smartly past as he spoke, and Brook lifted a perfumed handkerchief to his nose.

"Beats me how any white man can stand that rancid butter they rub on their hair," he drawled. "Most of 'em haven't seen soap and water for years."

Privately, Caro found the sharp, almost ammoniacal smell far from disagreeable, but she suppressed her instinctive impulse to defend Rowland's men. He could look after his own without her help.

"An old India hand like Steel ought to be able to spot a mutinous sepoy sooner than a newcomer like Tom Hamilton could," pursued Brook, "but they say Steel gives far too many blacks the benefit of the doubt. He talks to them like a Dutch uncle and lets 'em go. Still, I suppose it's all you can expect from a nigger-lover. He's scared to make an example of a native who might turn out to be his half-brother!"

"Brook, stop this talk at once!" Caro burst out hotly before she could stop herself. Then she shut her lips firmly and turned her face away.

Brook considered her averted profile for a moment or two, then tried another tack.

"Did you see the bullion carts bringing in the treasure from the Sultanbagh? A rare haul there for Her Majesty's Government. They've promised a bounty to every soldier who fought at the palace, but of course the cream of the treasure had been removed before they got there."

Caro was interested despite herself. "What do you mean? Surely the soldiers themselves were the first inside the palace? Or do you think the Ranee removed some treasure before they captured it?"

"No, no. Not a bit of it. The Ranee wouldn't have shot the two Guardians of the Jewels and left their bodies lying in front of the unlocked door of the

Treasure House. That was how young Lewis Allan told me he found it. Two dead bodies, an unlocked door, and jewels scattered all over the floor. He set a guard at once, of course, but he said that amounted to locking the stable door after the horse had bolted, for most of the finer pieces—the religious regalia, for instance—were already gone."

"But who could have—?"

"One doesn't like to mention names, of course, but they say that Rowland Steel was missing just then. It was an hour or more before anyone set eyes on him again, and then he ordered the search of the palace and William Allan was sent to put a guard on the Treasure House."

Caro said slowly, "How could Captain Steel have known where the Treasure House lay? I'm told the palace is like a rabbit warren."

"Bless you, he's been there a dozen times. The Ranee used to invite a few officers from the garrison to dine with her now and then. She wanted her son to learn all about the ways of the sahib-log. After dinner she used to take her guests down and show them the jewels: it was her party piece, poor lady."

"Did you ever dine there, Brook?"

He wondered whether to deny it, but there were too many people who knew that he had, so instead he nodded. "Once or twice," he said offhandedly, "but we weren't shown the treasures. Civilians were treated to a display of *nautch* dancing, and very tedious it was, I recall."

They trotted on for a few moments in silence, then Caro asked directly: "Are you telling me that Captain Steel has stolen the Baburpore regalia?"

"No, no; I didn't say that—not a bit of it. You mustn't put words into my mouth, you know," said Brook, delighted with the effect of his scandalmongering. "Looting's a very ancient practice among soldiers.

Frowned on officially, of course, but quite different from stealing."

"I see no difference. Taking valuables that do not belong to you is stealing, call it what you will."

"Ah, well, that's a woman's point of view, if you'll excuse me saying so. No soldier would agree with you. Anyway, there's no evidence that Steel's done anything of the kind, though I've heard it said that the *beebee* he keeps down at his nice, secluded bungalow has cost him a pretty penny. Lord, though—I shouldn't let my tongue run away with me. My apologies, Caro!"

"You seem to have heard a great many things about Captain Steel lately," said Caro, trying hard to hide her shock. What business was it of hers if he kept a native girl? He could keep a whole harem for all she cared.

"Ah well, word gets around, y'know," said Brook, watching her keenly. "I thought you'd be interested, seeing that he's such a particular friend of yours."

"How could you imagine I should enjoy hearing such stories about a—a *particular* friend? At all events, you are quite mistaken. He's hardly a friend at all."

"I am so very glad to hear it." Brook urged his horse closer. "Does this mean—Caro...? I must know—have you thought any more of what we said, that night by the campfire? When you allowed me to hope?" Her closed face made him fear he had been too precipitate and he added, "I have no wish to press my suit too hastily, but I shall have to leave for Vanyasi next week, after the trials are over, and I dream of taking you with me."

"Next week!"

"Oh, never fear, I am not asking you to marry me next week. I meant I would take you with me in my heart. If I only knew that on my return you would consent to allow me to address you, I should go away happy."

Was that really all he wanted? Caro wondered how

much Brook knew or guessed of her relations with Bulbul's customers—and with Rowland Steel. An instinctive awareness of Brook's capacity for self-deception, about her as well as himself, warred with Caro's desire to laugh at the stuffy, old-fashioned language he seemed to feel was necessary when discussing affairs of the heart. "Address," "nuptials," "proposal"—she would not be surprised if he referred to "hymeneal felicity" before long. Other men who had wanted her body had grabbed for it. Brook, on the contrary, asked nothing more than to be allowed to hope that in the dim, distant future he might address his respects to her. Surely it was safe to agree to this?

She gave him a dazzling smile. "I should be sorry to think you had gone away unhappy," she assured him.

He leaned over and squeezed her hand. "Dearest Caro, I will return as speedily as I can."

Try as she might, Caro could not get Brook's casually dropped words out of her mind. The poison he had injected into her thoughts of Rowland Steel spread and festered until she could think of nothing else. The accusation that he was neglecting his duty in the pursuit of former mutineers meant nothing to her. Already she was sickened by the savage parody of justice, the four-at-a-time hangings, floggings, and systematic debasement of the dejected native prisoners that Tom Hamilton dragged triumphantly through the streets on their way to execution. Caro could remember those same natives proud in Company uniform, trusting in and trusted by their British officers. She realized that Captain Steel, who had known and served these men all his life, would find their degradation a thousand times more painful than she did. "'*Les represailles sont toujours inutiles,*'" she had heard him quote, and could not help agreeing with him that reprisal did seem a useless enterprise.

The ridiculous tale of Rowland stealing the

Baburpore regalia she could laugh at too. Such jewels were easily identified, and if Rowland suddenly indulged in an orgy of spending his ill-gotten gains, the news of it would be around the station in a flash. She simply could not imagine him doing such a thing. No, it was the story of the native girl in his bungalow that came between Caro and her sleep, for that had the ring of truth about it.

What was she like? Young and dazzlingly beautiful, I'm sure, thought Caro wretchedly. The full weight of her own nineteen years lay heavily on her shoulders. Had Rowland loved her only because she reminded him of his Indian *beebee?* How could she, Lady Caroline March, ever draw back to her, on her own terms, a man whose bed was warmed by a dusky, doe-eyed beauty who asked no more of him than the honor of sharing his couch?

But perhaps she *did* ask more of him. Caro's spirits revived a little, for Brook Vyner had hinted that the girl was expensive—was, indeed, running Rowland into debt. Now Caro began to imagine a predatory, feline enchantress, swathed in cloth of gold, her long nails clutching, demanding, begging for jewels with which to deck her beauty—jewels which could not be bought on a Company officer's pay...

"Is it customary nowadays for—for unmarried gentlemen to keep native girls in their quarters?" she asked Philippa after much thought.

Her sister blushed fiery pink. "Really, Caro, what an indelicate question!"

"I wouldn't ask anyone but you," Caro reassured her. "Do they?"

"No, thank goodness! That old custom has quite gone out of fashion. Fifty years ago it was a different matter, but I'm glad to say that nowadays gentlemen have more respect for their wives than to admit those fallen creatures to their households."

"Of course," said Caro soothingly, for Philippa's feathers seemed ruffled by the very mention of kept women. "But in the case of a man without a wife...?"

"Are you thinking of Mr. Vyner? Put your mind at rest. I am sure his taste is far too refined for him to allow any *beebee* into his quarters—let alone his bed," Philippa answered furiously. "Besides, his superiors would not approve."

But Captain Steel's superiors would neither know nor care, thought Caro, and Philippa does not consider *his* taste in the least refined. His father was known to keep a number of handsome native girls in his compound; no one would be astonished if Rowland did the same. Like father like son. But Caro did wonder what kind of a woman she was.

The matter continued to nag at her all through the preparations for the ball.

Chapter Sixteen

ROWLAND STEEL'S BUNGALOW lay apart from the main row of neat, verandaed dwellings that made the station as like a corner of England as the unremitting efforts of a dozen homesick memsahibs and their diligent native gardeners could do.

When compared with the trimmed and manicured front lawns, the marigold borders and rigorously trained climbing roses of his neighbors' compounds, Rowland's quarters looked at once untidy and exotic. Chickens scratched in the reddish dust that lay thickly up to and on the steps of the veranda, and he had made no attempt to create an English-style garden to soften the bungalow's harsh exterior. Instead he had built an inner courtyard in the Mussulman style, paved with mosaic tiles of green, blue, and gold. A fountain played into a marble basin, and a pair of white peacocks strolled, shedding feathers, around the single smooth-trunk tree that cast a deep shadow over one side of the courtyard.

Beneath the tree, cushions were scattered, with long cane chairs and an assortment of round copper-top tables, for it was here that Rowland preferred to eat his meals in company with the peacocks, some yellow-beak mynahs, and a sly, scavenging squirrel.

It was no accident that Caro went cantering past this bungalow at eleven o'clock on a hot October morning when Rowland was not at home. She had taken care to choose a time when he was away, for on her two previous visits to his quarters—invited, announced, and accompanied by her sister in the sedate pony-trap—she had been offered no opportunity to explore beyond the courtyard where Rowland had entertained them.

She had felt, or imagined she felt, sultry kohl-rimmed eyes watching from behind some trellis or screen as she and Philippa sipped tea and nibbled wafer-thin sandwiches. She heard, or imagined, the tinkling laughter of Rowland's hidden concubine, but on each occasion she came away with no solid proof that the native girl Brook had spoken of was more than malicious gossip on his part. Sitting in the cool, tranquil courtyard, Rowland exerted himself to please his visitors, and Philippa was quite won over.

"He has changed a great deal for the better in the last months," she had commented as they drove home. "He was always agreeable, but before the rebellion there was something wild about him that made me uneasy. Now he seems more settled, and I cannot help liking him the better for it." She added with a touch of archness, "I daresay he is contemplating marriage, and thinks it is time to mend his ways."

"Marriage?" Caro was disagreeably surprised by the idea of Rowland marrying. "To whom?"

"Oh, Caro, are you blind? Haven't you noticed the way he seeks your company, and the look in his eyes when he speaks to you? It is the talk of the station."

Caro blushed and said nothing more, but she had hoped that Philippa was right. All the more reason to settle the matter of the native concubine, once and for all. And so it was that on a bright October morning, she found herself at Rowland's lodgings.

As she drew level with the gate of the compound, Caro halted Nuri and slowly passed a hand across her face as if overcome by the heat. He *syce* regarded her with surprised alarm.

"Oh dear," said Caro. "I don't feel very well, suddenly. The sun... *Syce*, ask Captain Steel if I may come in and rest for a few moments."

The boy ran off and soon returned with Bakti Bahadur, the butler who had taken Gul Mohammed's place. He bowed with joined palms.

"Steel-sahib not at home. Him going in Sultan-ganj," he apologized.

Caro closed her eyes and swayed artfully in the saddle. "I—I feel so faint," she murmured. "I'm sure Captain Steel would allow me to rest here until I recover."

"Yes, yes, miss-sahiba. Come into house," urged Bakti Bahadur. He helped her to dismount and told the *syce* to run home and bring back the miss-sahiba's *ayah* in the pony cart. Leaning on his arm, Caro entered the cool, darkened living room.

Bakti Bahadur installed her comfortably on a chaise longue and shuffled away to summon more help. She heard his voice echoing down the long passage, then silence.

This was her chance. Caro sprang up softly, flinging aside the cashmere shawl the butler had placed over her knees. On tiptoe she crossed the hall and opened the first door she came to. A library: bookshelves to the ceiling, a desk, filing cabinets, a glass-front case full of ivory figurines. Softly she closed the door and opened the next one.

Ah, this was the bedroom. The *punkah*, suspended over the wide bed with its richly embroidered silk cover that stood in the center of the room, swayed gently in the breeze from the door. A cord attached to its corners disappeared through a hole in the louvered doors that opened on to the veranda, where, no doubt, the *punkah-wallah* spent the night. Across the single curved-back armchair lay a long, loose robe of dark-green silk such as a rajah might wear, with a pair of soft, curly-toed slippers ready on the floor beneath, awaiting the master's return. A large tin trunk with double handles occupied one corner of the room, an austere, country-built dressing table another, while in the third stood a round washbasin supported on a tripod.

A typical soldier's bedroom, thought Caro, hovering in the doorway, with only the extra-large bed with its silk covering and the green robe to hint at a taste for Oriental luxury. Yet there *was* something un-English about the room: a faint aroma—not of soap or tobacco, not the compound of garlic, musk, sandalwood and turmeric, the very perfume of India that had first struck her senses on the Bombay waterfront—but another, subtler scent, indefinably yet unmistakably feminine. Caro's nostrils flared like a horse scenting danger. A woman had been in this room, and not long ago.

A soft touch on her ankle made Caro spring back, her heart thundering, but it was only an orange cat, rubbing and winding round the looped-up hem of her riding habit. Far down the passage, she heard the patter of bare feet, and hastily slipped back to the darkened living room. She had just settled herself on the chaise longue and closed her eyes when a woman's singsong voice spoke from the other side of the room.

"Has Ladee Caroline finished look-see in Steel-sahib's rooms? Has she found what she was seeking?"

Caro's eyes flew open and guilt at having been observed in her prying made the blood rush to her face. "I called and no one answered; I went to see if Steel-sahib's servants were dead or had run away, for none came to attend me," she said crossly.

The woman laughed. "Servants do not hide in Steel-sahib's bedroom," she mocked. "And all the while I waited here to attend your pleasure."

How long had the sly creature been watching? "Who are you?" Caro asked.

The woman stepped forward, an ice compress in her hand, and for a long moment she and Caro stared at one another. Caro saw a Eurasian girl only slightly older than herself, slender and golden-skinned, with wide eyes of an almost ebony hue that tilted up a little at the corners, a delicate straight nose, and full-lipped mouth. Bracelets tinkled on her smooth bare arms, and as she bent toward Caro to lay the ice pack on her forehead, Caro caught a whiff of that strange, subtle scent she had detected in Rowland's bedroom: flowery, expensive, and undoubtedly French in origin. There could be no doubt about it: this was the *beebee* who was costing Captain Steel a pretty penny. But what startled and annoyed Caro far more than discovering that Brook had told the truth was the way this girl resembled herself. They might have been sisters, almost twins. Far from finding a bond in this physical likeness, Caro strongly resented it.

A wall of antipathy seemed to spring up between the two women.

The Eurasian wore her hair piled high and gathered in a comb on the crown, with the back hair hanging in heavy ringlets. It was exactly the style Caro had worn on her last visit to Rowland's house. Her gown, too, was familiar. Caro looked closer and recognized an old flowered muslin which she had given to her own *ayah* when she had tired of it.

"Who are you? Where did you get that dress?" she demanded.

"I am Serindar, and the dress was given to me by Steel-sahib." The girl stared at Caro, taking in every detail of her appearance.

"Why are you here?" Caro knew she had not the shadow of a right to ask such a question, but some

389

angry demon urged her on.

Serindar knew it too. "I serve Steel-sahib," she said with scarcely veiled insolence.

"How do you serve him?"

Serindar tittered, one hand over her mouth. "So many questions, Ladee Caroline! I sing, I play, I make Steel-sahib happy. I tell the servants to make clean, to buy good food, look after bunglo..." She stretched out one slender hand, admiring the rings on it.

In short, you behave as a wife to him, thought Caro. A dull rage consumed her. "You're a servant yourself," she said curtly.

"Yes; I am a good servant. Steel-sahib does not have need of a white memsahib while Serindar is here to look after him."

She threw it down like a challenge.

We'll see about that, thought Caro, rising and pulling on her gloves with quick, angry tugs.

"You are going alreadee, Ladee Caroline?"

"Be so good as to tell my *ayah* that I have ridden on home. I can stay here no longer, but mean to tell Steel-sahib what you have said to me."

Serindar's almond-shape eyes glinted with mischief. She clapped her hands and ordered Bakti Bahadur to fetch Caro's pony. Then she extended two fingers in graceful parody of leave-taking.

"Good-bye, Ladee Caroline; so veree kind of you to call," she mimicked, and broke into tinkling laughter.

The sets were already forming for the first cotillion of the Lawyers' Ball supper, and Rowland Steel had still not arrived. Caro glanced anxiously past Henry Vane's blue-jacketed shoulder, across the shining floor under glittering, newly polished chandeliers and the undulating snowy-white *punkah* with its gallant scarlet flounce, to where Philippa sat on a small gilt chair beneath a star formed of bayonets and the regimental colors of the Bengal Native Infantry, stifling yawns and yearning to be back with little Rowley. Her face was white as the lace fichu round her shoulders, and her dark-circled eyes looked very tired. Caro knew that she ought to release her sister from her self-imposed chaperonage and insist on Andrew summoning the carriage to take them home.

Where was Rowland? Some few days before, he had asked to be her partner for the dance which would be next, and though there were plenty of dashing young subalterns clamoring to lead her out in the few remaining sets, Caro could not prevent her eyes from searching the crowded assembly rooms in the hope that Rowland would suddenly appear. Oh, yes; she had something to say to him! She listened with only half an ear to Henry Vane's lively account of a tiger-shoot in Bengal.

It had been a long, hot, exhausting evening. Having made up her mind to attend the ball, Philippa had decided to give a dinner party as well. It was Caro's first experience of an upcountry *burra-khana* and before the heavy meal was half over she hoped profoundly that it would be her last.

Her *ayah* had laced her tightly into a low-cut ball dress of rose taffeta with wide flounces that flattered her small waist but gave her little room to breathe, let alone eat.

The company consisted of the Judge and his lady, Major and Mrs. Symington—the latter round and jolly, with shining inquisitive boot-button eyes, a sharp contrast to her gaunt, parchment-skinned husband, Caro, Brook Vyner, Henry Vane, a fresh-faced subaltern in Rowland's regiment with a passion for practical jokes, and his shy, dark-haired wife Alice, and Meredith Foster, a bespectacled visiting lawyer with a didactic manner and a fondness for hearing his own voice. His mouselike wife, in a high-neck gown of dove-gray silk, seemed to have no function in life beyond agreeing with her husband's opinions.

It took an age before they were all assembled, with the gentlemen discussing the trials at one end of the drawing room, and the ladies grouped in a tight semicircle round the sofa at the other, offering sprightly compliments on one another's looks and casting arch glances across at the men as they speculated on the delights of the ball to come. There was a curious sense of constraint among these women, who knew each other's lives inside out and yet felt obliged, because of the splendor of the occasion, to converse in the most formal and stilted manner.

"When does your son return to us from England, Mrs. Symington?" asked Philippa, who did not in the least wish to hear the answer to this question, which she already knew, via her *ayah*, but was instead passionately interested to discover if it was true that there were two cases of suspected typhoid among the Symington servants, as her *ayah* had also reported. If it were true, Mrs. Symington would certainly delay the homecoming of her delicate, adored only son.

Mrs. Symington's button eyes twinkled, and she launched into an animated recital of her son's successes at school in England, while Philippa cast agonized glances at the clock.

From the dining room came the jabber of native voices and an occasional crash. Philippa made desperate signals to Andrew, who eventually left the room. A moment later they heard his loud voice rating the table attendants as a set of lazy good-for-nothing black heathens who deserved to roast in hell for their efforts tonight. The ladies pretended not to hear, and resumed their conversation quickly.

Beside Caro, Alice Vane, and Mrs. Peabody, the Judge's wife, who had stood shoulder to shoulder firing muskets during the siege of Baburpore on terms of perfect equality, now sat in tongue-tied silence, as if the great chasm of rank between their husbands was too great to be bridged by idle chatter.

Henry Vane was the first to cross the invisible barrier between the sexes, and came over to stand by Caro—she suspected for the express purpose of annoying Brook Vyner, whom he heartily disliked. Leaning over Caro's chair, he engaged her in easy conversation until dinner was announced, whereupon he seized her arm and wheeled her into place at the back of the procession, leaving Brook, the scowl all too ·clear on his face, to bring up the rear with poor Alice Vane.

"Can't allow that pompous Civil to monopolize the prettiest girl at the party," he whispered gleefully as he whisked Caro to the far end of the long table set with vast platters bearing whole turkeys, hams, and other savory meats. Caro felt her stomach contract at the mere sight of so much rich, greasy food. Oil lamps flared on the walls and table, contributing to the general stuffiness, and the background was a constantly shifting crowd of turbaned, white-robed, and splendidly sashed servants.

"I'd be obliged if you'd give me a few hints on carving, Lady Caro," Henry went on. "Last time I had to deal with a turkey I sent a couple of pounds of stuffing flying into my neighbor's lap."

Andrew and Philippa took their places opposite one another at the center of the table, and Brook—as the youngest of the remaining men—was obliged to steer Alice to the far end and prepare to do battle with a giant roast which had been placed—together with a blunt-looking carving knife—directly in front of him.

Corks popped. Brown hands with spotless white sleeves placed heaped plates in front of the diners. The pitch of conversation rose higher as the champagne did its work, and the atmosphere grew steadily thicker.

Caro pecked at her food and in the intervals of saying "Yes" and "No" and "Not really!" in response to the talkative Mr. Foster, she brooded on her encounter with Serindar. A thousand times she rehearsed the cutting phrases with which she would lash Rowland Steel for his infamy. To keep a harlot in his quarters and dress her to resemble Lady Caroline March! It was abominable—a scandal—how dared he treat her so? Her stays pinched as she drew deep, indignant breaths, and she saw with disgust that a blob of gravy from Mr. Foster's gesticulating fork had landed on the bosom of her rose-silk dress.

Mr. Foster saw it too. "A thousand apologies, Lady Caroline! Here, let me remove it for you."

Gallantly he flourished a snowy handkerchief, but just as he bent to remove the offending spot a roar of rage from Andrew Thynne halted the conversation. Caro looked up quickly. The flounce of the swaying *punkah* had come loose, and drooping too low over the table, had whisked the gauze protector off one of the oil lamps and deposited it neatly on Andrew's head.

Chaos ensued. Andrew leaped up with smoke rising from his hair, and the sharp smell of singeing filled the room. Servants rushed to and fro, moaning and getting in one another's way.

"Put out the lamp, damn it!" bellowed Andrew. "D'you want to set the place on fire? God's teeth, I'm burned to a cinder!"

A servant hastily extinguished the flame and black oily smoke from the wick assailed every nose.

"Stop the *punkah*," cried Philippa shrilly, as the waving flounce, billowing like an unreefed sail, threatened the second tall oil lamp. A solid wall of heat seemed to descend on the room as the *punkah* was arrested in mid-flight and hung motionless over the table. The men mopped their faces and the ladies wriggled surreptitiously as they felt sweat trickle between their tightly encased breasts and buttocks.

Two more courses yet to sit through, thought Caro. However shall I manage it? Henry Vane gave her a mocking grin and she wondered immediately if he were responsible for the disintegration of the *punkah*. It would be his idea of a good joke.

As if guessing her thought, Henry held his hands palms upward in a gesture of innocence. "Not me, I swear, Lady Caro. But don't you just wish you were shivering at a London dinner now?"

Three hours later Henry was still glued to her side, chatting with Philippa while Caro danced, but always there to engage her attention as soon as she was escorted back to her chair.

"... And at that moment the *howdah* gave a great lurch. I looked around and there was the tiger—an enormous man-eater—in the very act of climbing up my elephant's rump!"

The ladies gasped suitably. "How dreadfully alarming. What did you do then?" Caro questioned.

"I was in a blue funk, I can tell you, Lady Caro," said Henry in a tone that indicated that he had been in nothing of the sort. "I put the muzzle of my Winchester between the brute's eyes—Hallo!" he broke off, looking across the room beneath the swaying *punkah*. "Here's Rowland Steel after all. Curse the fellow—I was beginning to hope you'd give me his dance, and now here he is to claim it. I wonder where he's been all this time—he looks like a cat that's swallowed the cream."

"My dance, I believe." Rowland suddenly appeared before Caro, bowing. His eyes glowed, complimenting her appearance, and a smile hovered on his lips. He looked, as Henry had remarked, uncommonly pleased with himself.

The next thing she noticed was that, far from wearing ball dress, Rowland was still clad in boots and breeches. White dust clung to the shining leather.

"Hang it, Rowland," said Henry, looking him up and down. "You can't dance with Lady Caro in that rig. You're improperly dressed, man. Go away and change and leave me to look after your fair partner."

"Oh no, you don't, my little peacock," countered Rowland, laughing down from his full six-foot-two on Henry's small and immaculate figure. "Yes, we're very fine tonight, to be sure." He flicked a careless fingers against Henry's pale-blue watered-silk lapels. "Don't tell me this was made for you by Chouse Lall, for I won't believe it. Jermyn Street, at least—and are those white gloves? God save the mark! Well, make the most of your finery, for you won't get much chance to wear it where we're going, my lad."

"We're—we're ordered out?" Henry stuttered in his excitement. "W-wait, Steel, you rotter; come back and tell me what you mean?"

"Later, old boy. Time and the Baburpore band wait for no man," said Rowland over his shoulder, steering Caro through the dancers' whirling flounces and twinkling patent-leather boots. He swung her into the waltz that had just begun, and for a moment forgetting how angry she was with him, she abandoned herself to the pleasure of moving in rhythm with him, of being in his arms once again.

The hard grip of Rowland's ungloved hand on Caro's waist shifted slightly. He smiled down at her.

"Ah, that's good. So very good. I was afraid you'd given away my dance."

"Another minute and I'd have given in to Henry's entreaties," she said lightly. "Where were you?"

"I was summoned to attend my General at Fatengarh. I pleaded with him, Caro. I said that tonight of all nights pleasure must come before military duty, but he swore I'd thank him for spoiling my dancing when I heard what he had to say."

"What had he to say?"

The music had stopped, and other couples began to leave the floor. Rowland still stood clasping Caro, looking down at her with that mixture of excitement and elation. He looks...almost possessive, she thought uncomfortably, and moved, trying to break the spell. People were staring at them; this meeting wasn't going at all as she had planned.

Over Rowland's shoulder she saw Brook Vyner approaching. The band struck up a lively schottische.

"My dance, Steel," said Brook.

Rowland did not appear to hear him.

"Excuse me, Steel, but this schottische is mine. Caro...?" He took her hand to lead her across the floor, but Rowland's fingers suddenly tightened on her other arm. She stood, absurdly pinioned, torn between the two men.

"Brook. Rowland. *Please*. I must go to my sister."

"Not just yet," said Rowland decidedly. "Sorry, Vyner, but you will have to allow me this dance. I have something very important to tell Caro. In private."

Brook's hand dropped and his mouth opened in outraged astonishment as he watched Rowland threading rapidly through the throng, almost dragging Caro with him.

"One in the eye for you, eh, Brook?" Henry Vane joined him. "You're not alone, you know. He did just the same to me. Beats me how he gets away with it."

"But it was *my* dance!" said Brook angrily. "He had no right—his manners are impossible."

"He has no manners. Don't let it bother you. From a hint or two he let drop just now I gather that Baburpore won't be seeing much more of Captain

Steel. He's—we're—ordered out."

"Good riddance; I hope he never returns," said Brook viciously.

It was cool on the veranda after the stifling heat of the ballroom, but Caro's cheeks were on fire. What would her sister think? What would the tattling gossipmongers of Baburpore have to say after hearing Brook insulted and seeing Caro dragged from the dance floor like a Sabine maiden?

Rowland didn't seem to notice her angry face and snapping eyes. He said, still clasping her hand too tightly for either propriety or comfort, "Well, don't you want to hear my news? Sorry I had to give poor old Vyner the rightabout, but I'm pressed for time. We're ordered out at dawn and I have to see my men are prepared. But I couldn't leave without telling you. Caro; I've been posted to Nepal—my father's old command. We're going to hold the frontier against any attempt by the Nana Sahib to gather support in the hills there."

"You're going to Nepal—at dawn?" Caro said slowly.

"No, no. The posting comes later. At dawn we ride to Bithoor, where they say the Gwalior Contingent has raised a new force. But even if we catch the Nana on home ground, as I hope we shall, my posting is secure."

He glanced around, taking her other hand in his and lowering his voice a little. "Caro, ever since that wonderful night in camp, I've been dreaming that this would happen. That I'd be able to ask you to marry me, and could afford to give you the kind of life you deserve. Color, excitement, adventure. And now it's all happened at once. I've been gazetted a major, and I'll be commanding the station on the Nepalese frontier. It's a wonderful country, like the roof of the world. Caro, will you marry me and come there, too?"

It couldn't be true. Surely no one, not even Captain Steel, would have the impudence to propose marriage to an English lady while at his quarters lived a painted native hussy dressed to resemble her. All the hot, angry words that had festered since her meeting with Serindar bubbled to Caro's lips.

"Marry you? I wouldn't marry you if you were the last man on the subcontinent. Do you think I'm a doll, to be picked up or dropped at your whim? Dragged here and there without a chance to speak for myself? I tell you, Rowland Steel, if you'd asked me to marry you two days ago, I would have considered your proposal, fool that I was. I thought you loved me once and might again. But not now. Oh no."

In the light of the paper lanterns that glowed around the veranda she saw Rowland's eager expression change as her words hit him.

"But Caro...what's happened? I thought—I hoped..."

"That you could pick up where we left off? I'm afraid that's impossible, Rowland. That night in the camp"—she swallowed. She could not bring herself to pretend it had never happened, or that she hadn't been his willing partner—"that night changed matters between us. Don't you realize that? I regret—I shall always regret my behavior then, and if you were a gentleman you would forget all about it."

"Forget? How could I forget the night when my dreams came true? Caro, something's happened. Tell me what it is. You're not still worrying about the way I blamed you after Gul Mohammed was killed? I thought that was settled between us."

She was silent, fighting tears, struggling to keep her voice under control. She longed to respond to the pressure of his hands on her bare shoulders, to feel his mouth on hers setting her skin tingling and her blood on fire. But the image of Serindar with her jingling bracelets and sly, insolent smile stood between them.

She said in a choked voice, "I don't wish to speak of it."

"Come, Caro." Rowland shook her gently. "I can't ride away leaving matters like this. When I saw you last I was encouraged to hope that you were beginning to forgive me for—for taking advantage of you on that occasion. Now I am trying—however late—to make amends, and you turn me down. Why? Caro"—he gripped her arms with sudden urgency—"is there something you want to tell me about that night? Something that has changed your attitude toward me?"

"I am not carrying your child, if that is what you mean," said Caro coldly. "You may rest easy on that score. Now let me go." Caro tugged against his hands but their grip tightened cruelly.

"Not until you tell me why you refused me in such terms."

"Very well then." Caro raised stormy eyes to his. "I want to know how you, an English officer—supposedly an English gentleman—can have the effrontery to ask me to be your wife when in your bungalow, in your very bedroom, you keep a—a creature!"

To her chagrin, instead of looking guilty or abashed, Rowland laughed robustly. "So that's it! I am glad to have it in the open at last. But tell me, Caro, how can you, a delicate English female—supposedly a lady—know who or what lives in a poor captain's bedroom? I confess that puzzles me. It is not so strange that you should have seen Serindar, for the monkey likes to imagine herself mistress of my household when I am not there to rid her of the notion. But in my bedroom!"

Caro found his teasing laughter intolerable. How dared he put her in the wrong! She was not going to confess that she had stood like a bloodhound sniffing the air in his bedroom. She said angrily, "You may find it amusing. I do not. To me, your behavior is entirely reprehensible."

"Come, Caro; confess that you are making a mountain out of a molehill! Serindar is of no consequence. We can't quarrel over *her*. After our marriage she would, of course, cease to be a member of our household—in fact I'll send her away tomorrow, if that will satisfy you."

"So you'd turn out the wretched girl without a shadow of compunction—just as your father turned out poor Bulbul?" cried Caro indignantly, quite forgetting how much she had disliked Serindar. "Rowland, you are a *monster!* How could you contemplate such a cruel action?"

"Well, *I* don't mind if she stays," said Rowland with irritating reasonableness. "I only suggested turning her out on your account. As I say, it matters very little to me one way or the other. I took her in because a man has certain needs and . . . because she resembles you a little."

"A little! You have contrived to make that girl look like my double."

"Ah, Caro, you exaggerate," he murmured, but she cut him off, her anger back in full spate.

"As to the *needs* to which you refer, you do not have to explain those to me. Serindar assures me that while she lives with you, you have no need of a memsahib. Those were her very words."

"But if she goes, I shall have," he pointed out.

"Then you must look elsewhere for someone to satisfy those needs, for my hand is already promised," she said coldly.

Rowland caught her by the shoulder. In the lantern light his face was suddenly grim, his dark eyebrows drawn together in a straight line.

"What did you say?"

Caro lifted her chin defiantly, determined not to be intimidated by his obvious anger.

"I am already engaged to be married."

"I don't believe you," he said flatly. "You are mine, Caro, and you know it. No one else can have you."

She flared up at that. "I am not yours and never shall be. Do you think you can order my life as you order Serindar's? You are very much mistaken."

"Just whom have you engaged yourself to marry?" he said mockingly. "Not one of my more impressionable subalterns, I trust?"

Caro took a deep breath, waiting for the explosion. "Brook Vyner."

She was not disappointed. "That pompous little Civil with no more guts than a rabbit?" he gasped incredulously. "I don't believe it. You could not—*could not*—marry such a fellow."

"It is no business of yours who I marry."

"You cannot love him. And, my God, you cannot *want* him!"

The truth of the words stung her almost to the point of tears, but pride kept her composure. "Well, Captain Steel"—Caro looked him straight in the eye—"you are wrong. I both love—and want—him!"

"Never! I will never believe that!" Rowland spat out the words.

"That, Captain Steel, is your problem," Caro announced as she turned back toward the ballroom, but was stopped by the presence of his hands on her arms.

With a roughness born of desperation, Rowland spun her around, caught her up, and forced his mouth upon hers. She was stunned by the brutal pressure of hands, kneading her shoulders and furrowing her back. The gentle kisses she had enjoyed but too briefly; now he was ravaging her mouth, driven to distraction by the shock of her words. For the first time, Rowland Steel had caused her pain, and it was on that, not on the mindless ecstasy of being in his arms, that Caro concentrated all her will. Managing to struggle away, she dealt him a ringing slap on the cheek. The marks of her fingers stood out clearly against his pale skin.

"You—you little hellcat!" said Rowland distinctly. "Yes, I suppose I should have expected that." He released her, rubbed his cheek, and then gave her a mockingly formal bow.

"Permit me to felicitate you, Lady Caroline, on your approaching nuptials, and to wish you every hymeneal bliss! But please don't ask me to dance at your wedding, for I would sooner be hanged!"

He turned on his heel and strode away, leaving Caro to make her own way back to her sister's side.

"Where *have* you been?" asked Philippa anxiously, but Caro was spared the need to reply by Brook Vyner, who appeared out of the noisy, jostling throng, asking her to stand up with him for the next dance.

Philippa nodded and smiled; she approved of Brook and his prospects and wished that Caro would become a little more aware of how powerful a friend young Mr. Vyner could become.

Caro's heart ached, her feet ached, her head felt ready to burst with the heat, the noise, and the champagne she had drunk at dinner. But above all these discomforts she knew an overriding anxiety: Rowland must never guess that she had lied to him. Somehow she must wring a proposal of marriage out of Brook before the story of her fictitious engagement went the rounds of the coffee shops in the morning and made her the laughingstock of the entire station.

She stole a look at her programme. The last three numbers had no names written against them, for she had hoped to dance them with Rowland; there was nothing to stop her transferring them to Brook. A polka, followed by the "Lancers," and then the "Last Waltz." The polka's lively rhythm was hardly conducive to serious romantic discussion, and it was hard to talk at all during the intricate figures of the "Lancers."

"I am a little tired. Shall we sit this one out?" she suggested.

"Of course. That would be delightful. Come, let me procure you a reviving glass of champagne."

He led her to an alcove decorated with regimental colors, fussing over her, making her comfortable. Caro smilingly thanked him, though her thoughts were whirling in near panic. How? How can I begin? How shall I maneuver him into proposing to me— *now?* This polka won't go on much longer, and Rowland is watching me. Before they strike up the "Last Waltz," I must be truly engaged to be married.

She gazed at him as soulfully as she could. "I wish you were not leaving us so soon, Brook. Baburpore will be a sad place without you."

He looked delighted, if a trifle surprised. "You will miss me?"

"More than I can say."

Across the room, Rowland's dark eyes seemed to be boring holes in her back. She hunched her shoulder, trying to escape them. Anger at the way he had treated her, at his absurdly arrogant declaration that she belonged to him alone, stiffened her resolve to show him she was not the puppet he seemed to think her.

Stretching out her gloved hand to clasp his, she gave Brook her most beguiling smile.

"Tell me, dear Brook, how soon can I start counting the days for your return?"

"Caro, you don't mean you've changed your mind? You'll accept my offer? Oh, this is a wonderful surprise. I have been waiting and hoping for so long, and nothing you said or did gave me the least hint that my suit was not in vain. Tell me it's true, and I shall be the happiest man on earth."

The ease with which she had gained her objective made Caro a little dizzy—or was it the champagne? She stole a glance past Brook—whose incredulous smile and slightly popping eyes reminded her lamentably of an overjoyed frog—to see if Rowland were observing the scene. But he had gone, and suddenly her victory was dust in her mouth. She had a wild desire to jerk her hands free of Brook's insistent, proprietary fingers, to beg him to forget everything she had said in the last few minutes, to awaken and find that the whole of this horrible, disastrous evening had been nothing but a dream.

Instead she heard her own voice quietly accepting Brook's proposal of marriage just as the band began the sonorous roll of drums that heralded the "Last Waltz."

Chapter Seventeen

BARBURPORE HAD NEVER seen such a wedding. For days the *durzees* had been sewing frenziedly, hands and feet working nineteen to the dozen, on every veranda in the quarters under the eagle eyes of memsahibs each of whom wished to be the best-dressed guest at the wedding of Lady Caroline March.

Philippa had cast off every trace of post-natal lethargy and depression as she bustled and planned and ordered and contrived to make the occasion a memorable one; she reminded Caro rather forcibly of their mother on the eve of a soiree. Her sister regarded this as a compliment.

"If only Papa and Mama could come! They are so pleased to hear of you making such an excellent match," she exclaimed, and dropped her voice confidentially although the servants were nowhere in sight. "Really, Caro, although I was worried now and then that you were paying too much attention to members of the military, I must now admit that you have played your cards very cleverly. Brook Vyner is a most exceptional young man, and I am convinced that he will go far in the Service. He is his uncle's heir, he tells me, and his uncle has the ear of Lord Palmerston himself. One could hardly look higher."

Caro assented, but listlessly. She was glad that Philippa was pleased, and it was kind of her to throw her heart and soul into the wedding preparations, but Caro herself could not arouse much enthusiasm for them. A curious apathy possessed her; a strange feeling of being outside herself, of watching Caro March as she visited and wrote notes and tried on dresses and did all that was expected of a bride-to-be, but without any sensation of taking part in these activities.

Rowland had ridden away immediately after the ball, and now Brook too, still slightly stunned by the way a courtship he had expected to take years had been abbreviated to mere weeks, had been obliged to attend to urgent matters in Vanyasi in order to leave himself free thereafter to take a honeymoon in Delhi before returning to his post.

"Well, I wish you had settled for Steel, myself," said Andrew, glancing at his wife with a touch of defiance. He had just returned from his early ride and they were breakfasting together on the shady veranda. "You've cost me close on a thousand rupees with your sudden change of heart. Fellows at the Club wouldn't give me better than seven to four against your marryin' Steel, because they said I'd be bound to have inside information. Damn it, I wish I *had* had, that's all. Here, what's up, Caro? Come back, you ninny. I was only joking, you know!"

But Caro had suddenly burst into tears and rushed from the veranda into the sunlit garden.

"Oh dear," said Philippa, "she's forgot her bonnet again."

Andrew was mildly aggrieved. "Dashed if I'll ever understand you females," he grunted, helping himself lavishly to marmalade. "Don't she want to marry the fellow after all?"

The ceremony took place at dusk after the heat of the day had abated, at the little white-washed church which had, by some miracle, entirely escaped the mutineers' bombardment. An arch of marigolds ingeniously contrived by Pir Ali, the gardener, was fastened to the wooden portico, and promptly at five o'clock a smart yellow phaeton bearing the bride-groom and his best man, the fork-waving Meredith Foster, rattled under the arch and deposited its occupants on the church steps.

Soon after the pews began to fill with the cream of Baburpore society, the men sweating and wincing in high, stiff collars, and their ladies a dazzle of new silks, velvets, and nodding, beplumed bonnets. A subdued murmur, like the buzzing of many bees, rose to the rafters.

It gradually increased in pitch and volume as twenty hot minutes crawled by with no sign of the bride. Ladies waved their fans and twisted around to look behind them, but to no avail.

"Think she'll leave you standing at the altar?" asked Meredith Foster in a loud, jocular whisper.

Brook shot him a venomous glance.

"All right, old chap, no offense," said the best man hastily, feeling in his vest pocket for the hard circle of the ring. "I daresay the lady will be here in just a moment or two."

Little did he know how accurate his first guess had been. At the Thynnes' bungalow Andrew, splendid in full regimentals, stood waiting beside the favor-decked open carriage, staring gloomily at his watch. In Caro's bedroom, Philippa and Bulbul were trying to calm the bride, a vision in white satin embroidered with tiny pearls to match the pearl tiara which Mrs. Elliott had insisted on lending her. Caro sat at her dressing table with a small box open on her lap and tears streaming down her cheeks.

"*Baba, baba*, don't cry," begged Bulbul. "Too late now to cry."

"Pull yourself together, Caro dear. You are ruining

your face and keeping everyone waiting," said Philippa. She whispered to Bulbul, "Go and fetch my laudanum drops, quickly!"

"I was wrong," Caro wailed. "I should never have sent him away and now I shall never see him again. Oh Philippa, I've made a terrible mistake!"

"No you have not," said Philippa firmly. "You are feeling the strain of the occasion, as brides often do. But now you must think of your guests, who are waiting to see you married, and of Brook, who is probably just as nervous as you, did you but know it. Here, drink this," she added, taking the small flask from Bulbul and measuring out a large dose, "and then try a little rouge on your cheeks. There, that looks a great deal better. Give me that box."

She tried to take possession of the small box that had caused Caro's sudden collapse, but her sister's fingers closed over it obstinately.

"No, I want to wear it. Please, Phil." She looked up with swimming eyes.

"Oh, all right; anything so you do not begin weeping again," said Philippa briskly. "Now come; I will carry your train myself as far as the carriage. Bulbul, take the bouquet and mind no one steps on the miss-sahiba's veil."

Caro carefully pinned the small pearl brooch in the shape of a horseshoe to her bosom and picked up the card that had accompanied it. *To bring you luck on your wedding day. Rowland Steel.* Not a word of warmth, not a hint that they would ever meet again. He had gone, vanished into his frontier post on the roof of the world, and she of her own free will had chosen to marry Brook Vyner. Tears or laudanum made the firm black pen strokes on the shiny card blur before her eyes and she tucked it quickly in her white reticule.

"I am ready," she said.

The laudanum supported her all through the

ceremony and the feast that followed. Voices seemed faint and distant, nothing to do with her at all, but like an obedient child she smiled and made the right responses, and no one seemed to notice that in spirit she was miles away. As if in a trance, she saw Brook's expression of wild anxiety dissolve into complacency as she floated up the aisle on Andrew's arm. Remotely she heard the Reverend Caleb McCulloch's rich tones instructing her on the purpose for which holy matrimony was ordained, and referring to the miracle at Cana of Galilee. She wondered vaguely why he chose to speak of that now.

Later Brook's clammy hand touched hers as he fumbled to push something hard on to her finger. She looked down: a ring. Why was he giving her a ring? With a great effort her mind struggled back from the limbo in which it had been wandering and she knew that Bulbul had been right. It was too late to weep for Rowland Steel and what might have been. She and Brook Vyner were now man and wife.

Mr. Peabody, the Judge, was the first to call her by her new name, back at the Thynnes' bungalow, where a magnificent spread awaited the wedding guests.

Caro stood with Brook at her side in the receiving line, the train of her dress spread around her feet, while the gentlemen kissed her heartily and the ladies bumped cheekbones and exclaimed in admiration of her looks, her toilette, and told her over and over again how beautifully the church had been decorated and how superb was the wedding feast. She smiled back at the happy, well-fed, well-meaning faces, shiny with alcohol and heat in the sultry evening, and wished herself anywhere but at her own wedding.

"A glass of champagne, my dear. The Judge is about to address us." Brook, very dignified and correct, loving the ritual as much as she detested it, pressed a tall glass into her hand. Since leaving the church, they had hardly had the opportunity to exchange a word, but now she thought with alarm of the long hours together that stretched before them once they left the wedding and journeyed downriver to Delhi. Hours? No; a lifetime together, and I don't understand him or he me. What a blind fool I've been not to recognize that Rowland spoke the truth when he said I belonged to him. Her hand stole to her breast and touched the little horseshoe of pearls, and even in her dazed unhappiness it seemed to bring her comfort.

With an effort she raised the glass and smiled at Brook, toasting him. "My husband!"

A faint look of annoyance crossed his face at her words and she wondered why. Oh, that old bore the Judge was still droning on. She shouldn't have drunk until he proposed the toast. Defiantly she drained the glass and felt sweat break out beneath her tight corsage. Surely it must be nearly time for her to slip away and change into traveling costume?

Brook replied to the Judge's toast in graceful, flowery phrases that must, Caro thought as she fidgeted at his side, have cost him many an hour to rehearse, probably with the aid of a mirror. The loquacious Meredith Foster attempted to launch into a speech too, but the young officers soon tired of him and drowned his opening sentences with loud "Huzzas!" and stamping of feet. The party was getting noisy and Philippa signaled to the band. Then she took Caro's arm.

"Come, my dear. The *palanquins* are ready to carry you to the boat."

The ordeal was over, but Caro hesitated, reluctant to leave these familiar faces and launch out on her new life. She dreaded the moment of farewell to Bulbul.

In her bedroom, Bulbul's face reflected in the mirror was gray and lined as she unhooked Caro's basque and let the shimmering folds of the wedding dress slip to the floor. Silently she eased the apricot velvet jacket of the traveling dress over Caro's shoulders. Mists rolled away from Caro's brain as she recognized the old woman's distress.

"Bulbul, will you come and live with me at Vanyasi when I return from our honeymoon?"

Bulbul's head was bent now, her face hidden. "No, *baba*. I must go back to Patelbar. I have stayed away too long."

"But your house—your lovely house, is burned! Your girls are scattered. You cannot go back there; the British have annexed the whole of Chandranaya's territory, you know."

"Even so, little one, I must go back. What I built once I can build again. Oh, *baba*!" Suddenly her face crumpled and tears coursed down her fat cheeks. "What I hoped for you was not to be. Once, I would have lived with you, but that time is past. It is willed otherwise. Now, you must go." Gently she embraced Caro. "Be happy," she murmured softly, and slipped away, the pale ghost of a dancing girl called the Silent One trailing in her wake.

Caro lay back against her pillows, bare shoulders rising from a foam of creamy lace, watching the cabin door with a mixture of apprehension and perplexity.

It was over a week since her wedding, and in all but one respect marriage to Brook was proving more agreeable than she would have believed possible. They journeyed in the greatest luxury by river from Baburpore, stopping two days at Agra en route. Brook returned with her there to see the world's greatest monument to love, the Taj Mahal, built by the Mogul emperor Shah Jahan in memory of his wife Mumtaz Mahal. Like thousands of lovers, they had stood in the moonlight to marvel at the glimmering marble dome that seemed to float above a shining ribbon of ornamental water, perfect and insubstantial as a dream. Only they were not lovers.

Brook was at his best as a guide; his keen eye for beauty and desire to share with Caro his knowledge of Indian architecture and history made him the perfect companion on a sightseeing tour. It was only when beggars pressed him too closely, or he suspected a native of overcharging, that a look of sullen moodiness overshadowed his face and his manners became rude and overbearing.

While he was happy and interested, whisking Caro from one monument to another with infectious enthusiasm, she found it easy enough to play the part required of her: the docile, well-bred, eager-to-please wife that he wished her to be. The trouble was that all the time she was perfectly conscious that she was playing a part, and knew that sooner or later her true self would grow impatient of this milk-and-water marriage.

Her own ideas of conjugal life had suffered a shock on the wedding night, after they had boarded the riverboat. In their luxurious stateroom, with its great window overlooking the water, neither of them had been able to eat more than a few mouthfuls of the roast quail and creamy syllabubs that the cabin staff set before them. Brook drank most of a bottle of champagne, and then called for brandy. Why, Philippa's right: he *is* nervous, thought Caro, and she did her best to put him at his ease.

Conversation became more and more difficult to sustain, however, and when Brook rose unsteadily and announced that he was going to bed, Caro could not help feeling relieved.

"I've a devil of a head, Caro," he said blandly. "I think I may have taken just a touch of fever. If you'll excuse me, I think it's best that we occupy separate cabins tonight. There is no sense in taking unnecessary risks."

She smiled up at him, trying not to let her surprise show too clearly. "It has been a long day," she agreed. "I hope you'll feel better tomorrow, after a good night's rest. Is there anything I can do to make you comfortable?" she added, feeling more like a nurse than a new bride.

"Oh no, thank you. My man will do all that's needed," Brook assured her hastily. "He's used to these fevers of mine. You have a good night and don't worry about me. Tomorrow we pass Chattigarh, where there's a temple I've always wanted to see. We'll explore it together—if I'm recovered, of course."

Puzzled but obedient, Caro spent her wedding night alone.

Next morning, Brook appeared in excellent spirits and greeted her with a chaste kiss on the cheek before settling down to a hearty breakfast of deviled kidneys and boiled eggs. They spent an agreeable morning scrambling about the ruins of the Hindu temple, examining the bas reliefs. Brook made a few small sketches and Caro was surprised to discover that he had a talent for drawing.

"I did not know I had married an artist. These are truly excellent," she exclaimed, idly leafing through the portfolio that lay where the coolie had deposited it. "Oh, here's a sketch of me in my sowar's uniform. They're wonderfully clever!" And, moving on, "Oh, what is this beautiful necklace? It must be a maharajah's jewel, at least!"

Brook was at her side in a flash, almost snatching the paper away from her. He shuffled it into the folder with fingers that trembled slightly. "Oh, that's nothing. Just a bauble I once saw a native girl wear. Colored glass, of course, but I thought the design attractive."

Caro stared at him through narrowed eyes. She was sure he was lying, but what good would it do to say so? No one would draw in such loving detail a necklace made of colored glass. She determined to have a better look at the sketch if she got the chance.

Toward sunset, as they glided quietly on the dark, smooth water, with the blue woodsmoke from dozens of cooking fires along the back sharp and aromatic in their noses, Brook again began to complain that he felt less than well. As before, he refused all offers of help, and after supper retired alone to his cabin. Caro spent a second solitary night.

Why did he marry me? she asked herself when this routine had been repeated throughout the week. Won't he ever want to make love to me? She felt humiliated now as well as puzzled; she had failed to attract her husband to her bed. But that was absurd, she thought. No wife should have to play the harlot and lure her husband into sleeping with her when they had been married only a week. Brook must be unwell. Perhaps an undulant fever that struck as the sun went down and vapors rose from the river. But if so, how strange that he seemed perfectly healthy during the daytime. I'll persuade him to see a doctor when we reach Delhi, she thought. Meanwhile...

Meanwhile, the *ayah* that Philippa had sent to attend her was beginning to make sly comments on Brook's continued absence from her bed. Caro resolved to risk a rebuff and bring her disquiet into the open.

"I hope your 'sunset fever' will spare you tonight," she said boldly one morning as Brook joined her at breakfast. "I am growing lonely at night in that great bed. My *ayah* thinks it strange that we continue to sleep apart, and I hardly know how to answer the questions she asks."

"Questions? The impertinent wretch! I hope you are

not in the habit of talking to native servants, Caro."

"Of course I speak to her. I don't wish to live in complete isolation, and I find her a most useful source of information."

Brook looked thoughtful, though she could tell he was not pleased with the turn the conversation had taken.

"Do you think the fever has left you?" she pressed him.

"Yes, I believe I am somewhat restored today," he said grudgingly, and sure enough, sunset passed and darkness fell with no complaint of ill health from him.

Caro ordered his favorite *tandoori* chicken and a *pilau*, followed by tiny, sweet bananas and silver-coated sweetmeats. She felt unaccountably nervous, and matched Brook's drinking, glass for glass. He observed this with disapproval.

"One glass of champagne is generally considered sufficient for a lady," he commented. "I noticed at our wedding that you seem to have acquired a marked taste for alcohol."

"It is so reviving in this climate," she agreed, smiling. "Yes, just a little more, if you please. Andrew assured me it is safer to drink than water anywhere in India."

"Be that as it may, I do not like to see my wife quaffing strong drink like a trooper's woman."

Caro opened her eyes wide. "Surely you would not have me go thirsty, Brook? Especially since as yet I am your wife in name only."

The gibe cut him. He stared at her, white-faced.

"So that's what you want, is it? That's what your sly hints are aimed at. Very well, Caro; I'll see you get satisfaction tonight in a way that will silence that damned *ayah* of yours for good."

He stamped out of the room and slowly, pensively, she prepared for bed in the large cabin with its silk-hung fourposter. Did she regret rousing him to action by such crude means? No, she thought firmly. I'm tired of pretending in this way. Life in Bulbul's house has shown me that lying with a man is a habit I can't willingly forgo—and why should I? There must be some compensation for the loss of my freedom. Now I am married it should be a perfectly legitimate pleasure for me, unlike strong drink, which Brook disapproves of so heartily. I may not love him yet, but who knows what will happen tonight? Sometimes the least attractive of Bulbul's clients had proved to be the best lovers.

She waited nearly an hour, carefully arranged on her pillows so that the light fell on her gleaming shoulders and long dark hair, before the cabin door crashed open suddenly and Brook stumbled in. Dear Heaven, he's drunk, she thought. No, worse than that—he's been taking opium again. His eyes were glazed and staring, their pupils contracted to tiny pinpricks. They focused on her bare shoulders and an expression of revulsion twisted his features.

"Turn out the lamp!" he said hoarsely. "By God, Caro, have you no shame? Turn it out, I say."

Her eyes widened in amazement. Didn't he want to look at her—his bride and wedded wife? How different from Bulbul's customers' "Show me your jewels!"

"Brook, we are man and wife. There is nothing to be ashamed of," she began, then gasped in pain as his fingers bit into her upper arms. The attack was so sudden that she was pinioned before she realized he had moved the bed.

"You asked for this, you bitch," he sobbed, and hardly had her mind registered the insult than she was struggling, it seemed, for her life. He was mumbling disjointed sentences as his free hand ripped at her nightdress: "I didn't want to do it, but you made me. You women are all the same. You look so pure and innocent, but underneath you're nothing but a pack of bitches in heat and that's how you'll be treated."

He twisted her arm behind her back and pinned her face down on the bed. Caro fought to free her mouth from the suffocating pillows.

"Brook!" she gasped. "What's wrong with you? I don't... I didn't mean... Please stop it. Let me go! You're hurting me. Help!"

She realized with terror that nothing was getting through to him. He was temporarily insane and capable of murdering her in this fury. She was wiry and fit, but he held her easily, his hands tearing at the filmy nightdress, forcing her legs apart. His breath rasped in her ears, and her terror mounted as she became aware of his intention. "Don't, Brook," she cried out, "that's not the way..."

But she could not stop the unnatural violation. "It's my way," he groaned, forcing himself deeper and deeper into her tenderness, pushing her past pain to the edge of agony, his words coming with his thrusts. "It's the way... I treat bitches... who come whining and begging and bothering... Who won't let a man alone... I tried—to warn you... to show you... But you want it... *You asked for it!*"

Suddenly Brook moaned and his grip slacked. He rolled away from her as she lay face-down on the bed, trembling. When, after a moment, she managed to maneuver herself over so that she could see his face, he burst into tears. "Oh, what am I doing?" He wept. "What have I done?"

Caro sat up quickly, her arms hugging her knees. She was beginning to understand, though her mind found it hard to accept, that her husband had no experience with women at all. Rather than admit it, he had screwed up his nerve with drugs and then taken her like a wild animal.

She said, almost pitying him, "Brook, you're wrong. It can be... beautiful."

"Never!" He shuddered. "You cannot know that,

Caro. What you have read or been told about it is all part of a vast conspiracy, hiding the filthy truth."

"No, it's not. If you love someone—"

"Love!" he interrupted. "Love has nothing to do with this. Love is noble, an inspiration that lifts the soul, not one that drags it down to the level of lower beasts."

Caro felt bewildered. "Can it not do both?"

"Not for me. I love you, Caro, never doubt that; but not in *that* way." He had turned away from her and his voice was muffled. "You see, I—I am not like other men. When I was fifteen, a mere boy, I was tricked into a woman's arms . . ." How clearly he remembered it: the gasping, sweating whore with frizzy blonde hair who had squeezed him so painfully he thought he would vomit; his friends giggling outside the door and running away; the terrible feeling of being trapped in the frowzy room that smelled of cheap scent and garlic and stale urine; and when he had failed and could not pay, the pock-marked bully who had flung him out on the street's filthy cobbles in the gray light of dawn.

"I found the experience . . . distasteful. Since then, I have avoided intimate contact with women; but you were different. You look so pure and remote, I could not believe you would have the gross carnal desires of other women."

How looks could deceive, thought Caro sadly. Do I really look pure and remote after all I have been through?

Brook went on, more confident now: "When I came to India, I was warned to stay away from native women, so I turned to other company."

"What other company?" she asked, although she could guess.

Brook said hurriedly, avoiding the question, "My uncle heard of it. He sent for me and made it clear that such practices must stop if I wished to rise in the

Service, since it made me vulnerable to blackmail. There can be no breath of scandal attached to the higher echelons of the Indian Civil Service. Lord Canning is adamant about it."

"So you resolved to marry and become respectable! I wish you had warned me of your ... particular problems before we married."

"I meant to, Caro. I thought we would have a long engagement and gradually I could accustom you to my way of thinking. But you were so eager for the wedding to take place soon that I gave in to you. At times I even thought that you might have a particular reason for desiring a speedy wedding."

The blood rushed to Caro's face. "Why did you think so?"

"I am not blind. I saw Steel leave your tent that night we camped on the Patelbar border. I thought that the scoundrel had forced his attentions on you and then, when you turned to me at the station ball, that he had refused to marry you."

Oh, what a mess I've made of things, thought Caro bleakly. Both men had believed her pregnant from that night and still wanted to marry her, but she, fool that she was, had chosen the one with no use for women. It was as much her fault as Brook's, and she could not deny his chivalry.

She asked, "Would you have minded, if I had come to you bearing Rowland Steel's child?"

In the dark she felt the movement as Brook shrugged. "I would rather it had been anyone else's," he admitted, and now his voice was sleepy. "But no, I would not have minded. You see, I love you, Caro. I can't stop looking at you. I don't want to sleep with you any more than I would want to sleep with the Mona Lisa, or the Venus de Milo, but all the same I love you. I want to set you on a pedestal and deck you in jewels. I don't want anyone else to touch you."

You wanted a statue, not a wife, she thought. "Don't put me on a pedestal, Brook," she begged. "I would not be comfortable there."

Brook said dreamily, "I imagine you all in white—pure, radiant—with just one jewel: a single, blazing ruby at your throat..."

He was drifting away from her into some private world. She said urgently, "What made you treat me so tonight? You were not yourself; you were like a man possessed. What had you taken to drive you into such a state?"

It was no use. He had fallen asleep, but she knew with cold certainty what the answer to her question would have been. When Brook was afraid, or life made too many demands upon him, he resorted to opium, and under its influence he could lose all control over himself. She vowed to herself that never again would she raise the ghost of that "distasteful experience" that had set her husband against the whole female sex. He had been a boy then, but the festering violence had grown in him over the years and might, when opium unleashed the fury within him, drive him to kill without compunction.

The next morning it was as if the night had never been. Brook entered the breakfast cabin calm and clear-eyed, the model of a devoted husband. He kissed her cheek, inquired how she had slept, and helped himself largely to eggs and bacon before groping in his waistcoat pocket. He handed Caro a small, hard lump wrapped in tissue paper.

"For you, my love."

She unwrapped layer upon layer of tissue and discovered a soft leather pouch. This she tipped open on the table, and caught her breath at the contents.

"Oh... Brook! Thank you. It's beautiful."

It was a single huge ruby set in a gold pentagram, like a star, attached to a thin gold chain. This was what he had been describing just before he fell asleep last night—the single ruby to blaze at her throat.

"It's a beauty. It's so *big*," she whispered. "Can it be real?"

"Certainly," said Brook briskly, picking it up and holding it to the light. The ruby glowed like fire. "I would not insult you by offering you a counterfeit jewel; allow me that much pride! I bought it some time ago, as an investment, and have been meaning to give it to you. As you see, it must originally have been a turban jewel, but I thought you would prefer a necklace, so I had the chain made in Agra. Wear it tonight, my dear: I believe it would look well against a dress of plain white satin."

Was it a peace offering, a conscience gift, a tacit reminder that she must lock the door of memory on last night's revelations—but never forget them, Caro wondered. She was learning that dealing with Brook was seldom straightforward. He would hint at what he wanted her to do or say, but never command outright. If she failed to pick up the hint, or disobeyed his wishes deliberately, his chilly displeasure lasted for hours. But if she did as he wished, he could be as open-handed as a favorite uncle distributing bonbons.

The house he had hired for the duration of their honeymoon was in Delhi's most desirable quarter, near the Queen's Gardens, and barely were they installed there, with the servants scurrying to and fro unpacking trunks and hanging curtains under Caro's supervision, than she received a caller.

Brook was out riding when the card was brought in, and Caro knew a moment of panic. She looked wildly round the half-furnished drawing room. There was nothing she could do to improve its appearance before her visitor entered, so she quickly dismissed the servants and tidied her hair with rapid, nervous gestures.

"Show Mrs. Vyner in, please."

She had just removed the dusty pinafore that had been protecting her sprigged muslin gown, when the double doors were flung open and the butler announced, "Mrs. Vyner!"

There was a swish of silk skirts and a statuesque, full-bosomed lady in a high-crowned bonnet with nodding green plumes swept through the door like a ship in full sail. Her squarish, strong-jawed face was high-complexioned, but she was still a handsome woman in her late fifties, with beautifully arched dark eyebrows beneath which sparkled a pair of the friendliest brown eyes Caro had ever seen.

Her outstretched hand was ignored, and the next moment Caro was enveloped in a cloud of silk and green plumes and lavender water as her visitor enfolded her in a warm embrace.

"My dear child!" she exclaimed, "I am so very happy to meet you, and only sorry that I could not be present at your wedding in Baburpore. I am Brook's stepmother, as you will have guessed, and as soon as I heard you had arrived in Delhi I could not wait a moment longer, but ordered my carriage to bring me here at once. I hope you will forgive my lack of formality, my dear, but I was so very eager to meet Brook's bride."

Could this really be her mother-in-law? The wide smile on her full, generous mouth and the warmth of those eyes indicated a very different nature from the chilly correctness of her son. Caro was drawn to her at once.

"I am delighted to meet you, too," she said, and did not mention that Brook had never once referred to his stepmother's presence in Delhi. "I am afraid the house, as you see, is still at sixes and sevens, but there is so much to arrange that I barely know where to begin."

"I'd advise you to leave all that to the servants," Mrs. Vyner suggested, laughing. "Ten to one Brook will rearrange everything to suit his own taste as soon as he sees it. Why do it twice? That's one thing to be said for Brook: he has excellent taste, though dear knows where he got it from, since neither his father nor I was ever much interested in the visual arts. More taste than money, poor boy; but at least it has brought him a beautiful wife." She gazed at Caro with evident approval. "I would dearly have loved to have traveled to Baburpore for your wedding, but the powers-that-be (that is to say, my brother) declared that the country was still too unsettled for travel—such nonsense!—so I had no alternative but to await you here. I am spending the "cold weather" with my brother—the Governor—you will have heard Brook speak of him, no doubt. Tell me, where is the dear boy?"

Was there a touch of irony in her tone? Caro could not decide, but she was left with the impression that the ebullient Mrs. Vyner was faintly contemptuous of her stepson.

"He went riding an hour ago, ma'am. I daresay he will soon be back."

"How delightful! Then we can have a pleasant chat and get properly acquainted with no one to bother us," said Mrs. Vyner, plumping herself comfortably on the still-uncovered sofa. "I want to know all about you, and hear of your adventures during the sepoy rebellion. No—no modesty, I beg of you! I had it on very good authority that you were the real heroine of Baburpore, and disguised yourself as a native to bring the relief force. Is it really true?"

She was remarkably well informed, Caro found, and when Brook returned she already felt that she and her mother-in-law were old friends. Before Mrs. Vyner left she arranged to take Caro on a shopping excursion the following morning and show her some of the sights, and also invited them to a little soiree to be held at her brother's house the next Thursday.

"La Melusine has promised to sing, and I am told she is superb, if she does not throw a fit of hysterics! I do hope you will come," she said, pulling on her gloves. "*A demain,* Caro dear. I will send the carriage at eight o'clock. There is so much I wish to show you."

"I hoped to show Caro the sights of Delhi myself, Mama," objected Brook. There was an edge in his voice which made Caro glance at him sharply. Surely he couldn't be jealous?

Mrs. Vyner heard it, too. "Why, you silly boy," she cried gaily, "I don't mean *your* kind of sights. I am not going to make Caro trudge round a collection of odoriferous temples and overdecorated mosques! I'll gladly leave all that to you. No; I mean to show her the race course, the *gymkhana,* the shops, the *modistes*... She will need an entire new wardrobe before she travels to the wilds of Vanyasi, you know!"

Before this catalogue of pleasure, even Brook was obliged to smile. "Very well, Mama. I hope you will both enjoy it."

Between her husband's and her mother-in-law's efforts to entertain and instruct her, Caro's honeymoon passed in a whirl, and it seemed no time at all before she was directing the servants to pack all their new possessions for the long journey upcountry to Vanyasi.

One of the delights of her month in Delhi had been the discovery that Brook was extremely rich. He constantly gave her presents and expected—positively encouraged—her to spend money as fast as he gave it to her.

"Nothing but the best for you, my dear," he would

say, and she marveled at his generosity.

So did his stepmother.

"At least he's not as close-fisted as his poor papa," she remarked cheerfully after helping Caro to choose half a dozen neat-legged polo ponies from a bankrupt subaltern's stable. "Brook was always clever with money—but careful, too. Ah well, that's love for you. Make the most of it, my dear. I expect he's been lending *lakhs* of rupees to some poor rajah, to pay his troops. Two percent per month, I believe some Civilians charge. No wonder they call them the Heaven-Born—they're simply made of money!"

Caro took her advice. She bought furniture for the bungalow in Vanyasi she had not yet seen; soft furnishings for the bedrooms, china, glass, and silver, besides a number of gleaming sauce pans, egg whisks, soup ladles, and other kitchen equipment.

Brook smiled indulgently when he saw these. "You won't get my fellows to use those new-fangled gadgets," he predicted. "There's never a more dyed-in-the-wool traditionalist than your native cook."

"They'll use them if I tell them to," said Caro with spirit. She was feeling her oats.

Brook shook his head. "A word of warning: don't go interfering with my native servants up at Vanyasi, Caro," he said seriously. "They know my ways, and I know theirs, and I don't want them upset. They're bound to resent a new memsahib—it's only natural—and the most tactful thing you can do will be to stay right away from the kitchen and the servants' quarters until they all settle down."

"Then I'll have nothing to do!"

"Don't worry; there'll be plenty for you to do, my dear. Entertaining, social calls, all that sort of thing. I don't want my wife lumbered with a lot of domestic chores she can perfectly well leave to the servants."

Caro wasn't convinced, but she said no more,

turning the conversation to her new dresses, and the presents she had sent for Andrew and Philippa, Little Rowley, and Baby Jack back in Baburpore.

It was a Thursday, the last evening of their honeymoon. As they mounted the long staircase to the great room hung with chandeliers, where Mrs. Vyner was holding her weekly soiree, she swooped like a bird of prey through the chattering throng and seized Caro's hands with cries of admiration.

"My dear, you look too, too lovely tonight! That white satin—superb! And the pendant..." Her voice died away and slowly the color drained from her face. "Where did you get that ruby?" she asked in shaken tones.

"Why, from Brook. He gave it to me only a few days ago." Caro was both bewildered and frightened by her hostess's fixed stare at the great ruby star. "Dear Mrs. Vyner, are you unwell? Let me get you a glass of water."

"That jewel you are wearing," said Mrs. Vyner in a strained, unnatural voice, "once belonged to a murderer. I know, for with my own eyes I saw it in his turban during a reception at the palace of Bithoor. Take it off, Caro: take it off and hide it. Never, ever mention it again, even to Brook. That ruby is accursed, stained with innocent blood; it has been worn by the Butcher of Cawnpore—that fiend in human form, the Nana Sahib!"

Chapter Eighteen

THERE IS NO drug on earth more addictive than danger, and after her free-and-easy life with Bulbul and the exciting, perilous days at the end of the mutiny, Caro found it hard to settle to the monotonous existence of the wife of a conventional young Assistant Collector in a small, dull upcountry station.

Not that she didn't try . . . Perhaps if Brook had been an ardent, passionate lover as Rowland had been, perhaps if she had not been shaken into distrust of her husband by the episode of the ruby, perhaps if she had been busy from morning till night—as he was, as the missionaries and the schoolteacher and the Forestry Department manager, and the Collector and the Judge and the young officers on leave, and the wives of all these officials were—she might have developed a proper pride in her home and an interest in her surroundings. She might even have been happy, and learned to enjoy, as Brook did, the sensation of being a big fish among smaller ones.

For if Baburpore had been a small pond, Vanyasi barely qualified for the title of a puddle. Perched on a slope above a mountain stream whose clear green water sometimes turned pewter gray with alluvial silt, Vanyasi boasted only a dozen neat European bungalows grouped around the slightly larger building of the Shikar Club, where members of the European community met to gossip and drink in the cool of evening. Sporting young officers who spent the daylight hours of their leave hunting wild game in the hills above Vanyasi formed the hard core of attendance at the Shikar Club, and their jokes and cheerful chatter could have done something to bridge the chasm of isolation in which Caro felt herself trapped. But Brook did not approve of ladies sipping *chota* pegs at the Shikar, and reacted so violently when Caro suggested a visit that even this small safety valve of pleasure was denied her.

"You may invite officers to dine with us here," he said, as if bestowing a vast favor on her, "but I cannot allow my wife to be seen drinking at the Shikar. It would not make a good impression. Here in the wilds it is even more important to keep up civilized standards of behavior, and resist the temptation to 'go native' than it would be in a more populous station. Yes, I think it an excellent notion that you should begin to do a little modest entertaining at home."

"Who is there to entertain?' she asked despairingly. "The Collector and Mrs. Williams dined with us last week; we have dined at the Fowlers' and the Byles'; I went to Margaret Ramsay's tea party . . . There *is* no one else."

"Then by all means invite one of the young officers, if you wish to see a new face," said Brook impatiently. "Mr. Moncrieff of the Queen's 62nd is perfectly presentable. Upon my word, Caro, you are hard to please these days. You live in the lap of luxury and have nothing to do but enjoy yourself, yet you persist in bothering me with these petty problems. Why don't you join in the diversions of the other wives? They find plenty to occupy their time."

"They have their children," Caro pointed out.

"Miss Ramsay has no children."

"She has her little school to run. Oh, Brook!" she exclaimed, remembering. "She told me yesterday that she wants to expand her class and divide it so that the younger children get a chance to learn. She asked if I would like to help her."

"My wife to teach native children!" said Brook with a short, angry laugh. "Miss Ramsay aims high indeed."

"I *would* like to." Caro saw the words of refusal begin to form on Brook's lips, the usual petulant crease appear between his eyebrows, and added quickly, "I must have something to occupy my mind, Brook, or I think I shall go mad. Since you forbid me to direct the servants, I feel perfectly useless in my own house. I cannot sit idle all day, or knit socks for lepers or whatever it is that Mrs. Fowler and Mrs. Byle do at their Ladies' Sociable Evenings. If you love me, Brook, please allow me this."

"Of course I love you," said Brook irritably, "but I cannot be forever telling you so. Oh, all right. I do not see that it will do any good to those poor benighted children to have their heads stuffed full of nonsense, but if the Collector has no objection, I daresay you may please yourself in the matter. I shall be away most of next month, in any case, making my tour of the District, as Mr. Williams' health is so uncertain."

He spoke with a certain satisfaction. The more uncertain the Collector's health, the better his own prospects of promotion.

"Touring the District! Oh . . . can I come with you? I would like nothing better than to see the country beyond this valley."

"What—and rough it in camp for a month? Certainly not," said Brook emphatically. "I do not wish to have my wife tanned as brown as a native, eating around a campfire with a lot of gawping servants."

She could not help but recall the happiness of those days in the wild with Rowland, how he had loved her brown and strong, treating her with gentleness but allowing her no privileges of food or comfort not enjoyed by his men.

No, thought Caro bitterly, Brook would like to keep me in a pretty little casket, wrapped in cottonwood, so that he could occasionally take me out to show to admiring guests. Will he ever realize that I am a human being, not just an expensive toy?

Fortunately for her, even the contrary Collector could find no objection to Caro assisting at Margaret Ramsay's school, and although Mrs. Williams sneered at these efforts to teach native children to count and read, Caro soon found the work absorbing.

The schoolteacher, Margaret Ramsay, was a tall, spare, strong-featured woman of forty-five, who had lived in India all her life and spoke every dialect for hundreds of miles around. Brook thought her unfeminine, and disapproved of her sturdy independence of spirit and forthright way of speaking. She had level blue eyes and crisply curling gray hair cut short and swept back from her forehead in a severe, almost mannish style, but Caro liked her direct, no-nonsense manners and sense of fun, and greatly admired the endless patience she displayed toward her small pupils.

Caro's knowledge of Hindi now proved useful, and with Margaret's help she soon mastered the local dialect. Nearly every day an extra child or two would straggle up to the wooden schoolhouse and squat patiently in the courtyard until Miss Ramsay rang the bell and opened the doors. Soon the small schoolroom became so crammed that Caro was obliged to take her class under the great peepul tree in the courtyard. While Brook was away, she often spent the night at Margaret's bungalow next to the school, and before the day's work began the two of them would climb the hill behind the house, for Margaret's passion was hunting butterflies, and the steep slopes above Vanyasi furnished a rich field for specimens.

"Certainly it is not cruel!" exclaimed Margaret, flushed with exertion after a successful chase. She gently crushed the thorax of a magnificent ornithoptera whose wingspan must have measured a full seven inches. "Nothing makes a human more compassionate toward his little fellow creatures than a close acquaintance with them. I gain this acquaintance, and gain it cheaply, by sacrificing the lives of a few to add to my knowledge of the many."

She placed the brilliant insect between the folds of a sheet of thin letter paper, and placed it carefully in her satchel. "Oh, there is a black swallowtail. After him!" She was gone in a flurry of skirts, her long springy cane with the green-dyed gauze bag whirling round her head as she swept after the elusive prey.

Caro laughed and followed. She was not convinced by Margaret's argument, and preferred the butterflies alive, but how much pleasanter it was up here in the early-morning freshness, where birds sang and frozen green beetles clung to the scented grass, than it was facing Brook across the breakfast table on the veranda, listening to the hoarse croaking of crows and her husband's interminable advice on how the wife of a promising young Civilian should comport herself.

It was not long before Brook became jealous of the time she spent up at the school.

He returned from his month on tour with a batch of new servants, and a drawn, anxious face. Caro thought he had lost weight.

To her questions about his journey he gave abstracted answers, and sometimes seemed so ignorant of the places he had visited and the land settlement problems he supposedly had investigated that Caro began to doubt that he had ever been out of the valley.

"Did you see the Buddhist monastery, when you camped at Panchitana? Margaret says it is very fine," she said, trying to take an interest in his affairs, as a good wife should. "Do you know, I have been following your progress on the map she gave me. Her father was once Collector here, and she used to accompany him on all his tours."

Brook regarded her thoughtfully, almost as if seeing her for the first time. Not only seeing her, she thought with a sudden chill, but seeing her as a problem—a danger. "You know, Caro," he said slowly, "you must not pay too much attention to what that old—to what Miss Ramsay tells you. She is well known to be eccentric, but since her father was greatly respected in these parts, people here make allowance for her... strangeness. But I own I was a trifle disturbed to hear how much time you have been spending in her company. I do not want you tarred with the same brush."

That meddling butler, Gopal, thought Caro angrily. Always spreading tales. Aloud she said, "What nonsense! Margaret is quite as sane as you or I."

"Oh, I don't doubt her sanity. It is simply that, living on her own so long, she has developed certain undesirable characteristics..."

"If you mean she is capable of taking care of herself, I admire her for it," cried Caro, angry in behalf of her friend. "I wish you would allow me the same freedom to manage my household."

This was a recurring argument. Try as she might, she could not persuade Brook to allow her any responsibility in the running of the bungalow or its garden. It was true that the servants kept the house clean enough, the *mali* produced a few stringy vegetables from time to time, and the boy who tended the poultry brought eggs that competed in size with a hazelnut in addition to the tough carcass of fowl that they ate almost daily. But Caro would have liked to have added sheep, goats, and cows to their establishment, to improve the garden's primitive irrigation system, and to handle the household accounts as she knew Philippa and every other memsahib in British India made it her business to.

"I am sure that Gopal cheats you in every way," she told Brook at the conclusion of dinner one evening. Flying insects whirled around the oil, and the heavy heat made Caro reckless. "Just let me order the household supplies for one month, and see what a difference it will make."

"Certainly not. There is not the least need for you to meddle in matters that do not concern you."

"But they *should* concern me. Margaret says that every lady should know the price of food, and pay the *dhobi* and the *durzi*. How else can she see that they do their work properly and charge the proper price?"

"Margaret again. Always Margaret," he exclaimed scathingly. "Do you discuss every intimate detail of your married life with Margaret Ramsay? I thought you would have had more pride."

She was cut by his tone. "You know very well I do not!" she said hotly. "Thanks to you there is no *intimate* side of my marriage to discuss. We are living a sham, Brook; pretending to be man and wife when we do no more than share the same roof! It is intolerable to be lectured on every petty detail of my conduct, to be obliged to tread a positive tightrope of convention and respectability when it is all a charade. I am less your wife than I was wife to the men who came nightly to Bulbul's house in Patelbar, for *they* were at least men. *You* are nothing but the shell of a man, a shadow-husband, and I will not obey you any longer."

The words were out, and she could not regret them. The resentment that had built up in her like a black boil over the past months had at last burst, and she was conscious only of relief. But she had forgotten the strength of Brook's temper when aroused. He seized her and shook her, slapping back and forth across her face until her head spun.

"Take that back, you slut," he hissed, "you filthy-minded, foul-tongued slut. I made the worst bargain of my life when I married you."

"Bargain?" she said dazedly. "I made no bargain."

"Trust a woman to forget anything that inconveniences her," he sneered. "Think back, my dear. Back to the night beside the campfire when I first offered you my protection. My silence in exchange for yours."

"Silence?" Dimly she remembered Brook saying that if she were his wife he would never permit anyone to refer to her past. She had thought him pompous and presumptuous to suppose that she could not fight her own battles, and had dismissed the matter from her mind. Was this what he had meant? That he would conceal her past as long as she kept silent about the sexual peculiarity of their marriage?

His next words confirmed this. "Have I ever spoken of the scandal that drove you from England, or your degradation in the Joyhouse of Kali?" he demanded. "You know I have not. I have kept my side of the bargain: it was too much to hope that you would do the same. I should have known better than to trust to your discretion or honor, since plainly you lack both. I must have been bewitched when I offered you my name, but now that you bear it I will not allow your evil tongue to blacken it, or hinder my career. With or without you, I intend to rise to the very top of the Service, and I'll teach you never to speak like that to me again."

Wounded vanity, fear of exposure, and threatened ambition turned his hands into steel hoops around her throat, squeezing pitilessly, and suddenly the scene in their cabin on the riverboat, when he had abused her for making sexual demands on him, was back in her mind with horrid clarity. In his rage, Brook was quite capable of killing her.

"No!" she gasped, tearing at his fingers. "I won't speak of it again. I swear!" A red mist swam before her eyes. Dimly she was aware of a rustle of cloth and padding feet. Someone stood in the doorway watching them, gesturing urgently.

"Stop!" The single soft Hindi command was enough to slacken Brook's grip. The madness died from his eyes, and he let her slip to the floor, from where she tried to get a glimpse of her rescuer. It was too late; the figure, as if divining her intent, had swiftly turned its back. All she saw was the flick of white robes disappearing through the door of Brook's study before blackness overwhelmed her.

Later that night she woke in bed, her throat bruised and aching. Beads of sweat stood on her forehead, and the heavy, damp braid of hair clung to her neck. For a moment she lay, shaking off evil dreams, wondering what had awakened her. Far away to the south thunder rumbled, but she knew it would be weeks yet before the monsoon winds brought the relief of rain to Vanyasi's parched soil.

When the rains did come, they would probably wash away the bridge that the Forestry Department coolies had just completed, and sweep into the river thousands of tons of precious earth from the tiny terraced fields above the bridge, but no one would complain. Such annual disasters were a part of life, accepted and expected by the patient, fatalistic people of the valley.

Two monsoons, thought Caro. She knew how often the second monsoon was a white man's last. Few European constitutions could withstand for more than two years the dirt, disease, and fatal climate of India. Numerous headstones in every Christian cemetery bore the names of English men, women, and children whose lives had been claimed by their second monsoon. She had been lucky, so far. The fever through which Lady Marvell had nursed her in Cairo had been her sole experience of the burning devil of the East, but now, sweating and shivering by turns in the hot, still air of her bedroom, Caro felt that her luck was running out. Her health was being undermined by isolation and unhappiness—she felt far from well.

Then she realized why—or partly why. The *punkah* that usually stirred the air hung motionless over her bed; the coolie on the veranda must have fallen asleep. It was old Abdullah, deaf as a post and nearly as blind as a bat, but usually a most reliable *punkah-wallah*. The curious thing was that she seemed to hear the monotonous creak of the pulley still operating, although the flounce above her did not move.

Fully awake now, Caro tested her throat and found it far too sore to risk a shout. Shouting at Abdullah was an unprofitable exercise at any time, so instead she groped beneath the bed for a slipper to hurl at his head to remind him of his duty. Just as she took aim at the spot where he should be crouching, slightly to the right of the window onto the veranda, she heard the *punkah* again. *Ker-krunk! Ker-krunk!* The coolie was certainly still at work, but in another room.

Automatically she shook out each slipper to rid it of slumbering centipedes, scorpions, or other unwelcome visitors, then slid her feet into them and padded out to the veranda. Its long side, onto which her bedroom faced, was deserted, but walking softly around the corner of the bungalow, outside Brook's study, she almost stumbled over Abdullah's hunched form. His back was toward her and he pulled his rope as if in a trance, oblivious of her presence. The study window he faced was open, and behind the curtains voices rose and fell.

Caro strained her ears, but from where she stood she could distinguish no words. Nor, because of Abdullah, could she approach more closely. One voice was certainly her husband's; the other was high-pitched, rather querulous in tone, faintly familiar. Through the window drifted cigar smoke, combined with another sweetish, sickly aroma. Caro wrinkled her nose, and memory nudged at her. Brook's visitor was smoking *charrah*—hemp: where had she smelled that within *Shikar* doors before? Oddly enough, she remembered the odor from before the Joyhouse. She associated it with Andrew, who never smoked tobacco, and groping slowly after the recollection, she pinned it down. It had been in Patelbar, in the guest rooms of Prince Chandranaya's palace. Andrew had come back from a hunting foray with the princes, and Philippa had scolded him, refusing to kiss him while the smell of *charrah* hung about his clothes. How long ago that seemed! How carefree they had all been before the mutiny. It was odd that she should remember it now.

The *punkah-wallah* shifted his position, and Caro stepped softly back out of sight. She returned to her room, greatly puzzled as to whom Brook's midnight visitor could be. Certainly not a woman, nor a European, for the wearer of robes who had prevented Brook throttling her earlier that evening had spoke in Hindi, and it seemed likely that it was with him that Brook was now so deep in talk.

Next morning she challenged him directly.

"Why did you allow the *punkah-wallah* to leave his post outside my room? I woke and the place was like an oven. If you wish to sit up late in your study you should instruct another coolie to work your *punkah* and leave Abdullah at his usual post."

To her surprise, Brook looked abashed. "Oh . . . you awakened? I am sorry, my dear. It was some religious festival last night and only Abdullah, who is too blind and deaf to care about such junketings, was available when I needed him. It will not happen again."

"Who were you talking to, so late at night?"

Brook busied himself with his toast for a moment before he answered. "It was one of my clerks. He had some problems of a...ah, confidential nature he wished to consult me about. Late though it was, I could hardly refuse the poor fellow a hearing."

"Do you customarily allow your clerks to smoke *charrah* while they speak to you?"

Brook took refuge in anger, as she had known he would.

"Really, Caro, it is none of your business what I do or do not permit among my staff. As it happens, I had the greatest difficulty in persuading the unfortunate fellow to confide in me, and I suggested he smoke to calm his agitated mind."

"How thoughtful of you."

Brook looked quickly up from his toast, suspecting her of irony, but she continued in her most guileless tone, "Since you were so obliging as to forgo your sleep on your clerk's behalf, it is perhaps churlish of me to begrudge him Abdullah's services. Will you warn me if you have occasion to need them again?"

"Naturally, my dear." Brook's eyes moved thoughtfully over her face and the high-necked muslin blouse that hid her bruised throat. He said, with a blandness matching her own, "I am sorry to have deprived you of them so unexpectedly, but after last night's unfortunate—er—argument, I believed you would sleep through more than a quiet conversation in my study. How much did you hear of it? I trust we did not keep you awake long."

Caro was glad then that she had not eavesdropped more successfully; a muscle ticking at the corner of Brook's eye warned her how dangerous it would be to admit hearing anything. She said, as if the subject bored her, "Oh, no. I heard nothing but distant voices. As soon as I realized where the *punkah-wallah* had gone, I lost interest and went back to bed."

Nothing altered in Brook's face, but Caro saw the fingers that had been gripping his knife until the knuckles were white slowly relax. "Very sensible, my dear. Now, let's speak of more pleasant matters. I'm told that the Nawab is giving a dinner in honor of the Lieutenant-Governor when he visits us next month, and we are to be invited. What do you say to that?"

"Durlah Sultan?" asked Caro. She had met the rotund, polo-playing Nawab twice at official receptions, but had never been to his palace. "Oh, that will indeed be something to look forward to."

Brook nodded approvingly, little knowing that his mention of a visit by the Lieutenant-Governor had set bells ringing and birds fluttering in Caro's heart, which beat so fast she had difficulty in controlling her breath. For Margaret Ramsay had heard in a letter from a friend whose husband was in charge of staff appointments at Government House that the newly promoted Major Rowland Steel had been taken back into the Lieutenant-Governor's staff at the latter's express wish after only six months at his Nepalese frontier outpost. If the Lieutenant-Governor were to visit Vanyasi, it was entirely possible that his escort would be accompanied by Major Steel, and that he, too, would be present at Durlah Sultan's banquet.

But a few days later two things happened that pushed thoughts of the Nawab's feast to the back of Caro's mind.

A man-eating tiger was reported at Kalipatam, a small village only five miles to the east of Vanyasi. In a single night the great cat killed an old woman who was collecting firewood and two small herdboys. The terrified villagers formed a deputation and begged the Collector to send word at once to the sahibs at Baburpore, so that a great hunter might come with all speed and shoot the marauder. Two days after that Captain Tom Hamilton arrived in Vanyasi.

Brook had ridden over to Kalipatam to inspect the remains of the tiger's victims and consult with the headman there. The first Caro knew of Tom's presence in Vanyasi was when his card was brought in to her as she sat languidly writing letters one muggy, hot May morning.

Her lethargy vanished in a flash. "Show him in," she told Gopal, the butler.

Tom looked even bigger than she remembered, bronzed and fit, towering over the diminutive white-turbaned figure of Gopal. Caro could not stop herself: he was a brute, but the sight of his familiar face in this house of strangers filled her with joy. She flung down her pen with a cry of pleasure and sped across the room to greet him.

"Tom! By all that's wonderful! Where have you sprung from?"

Laughing, he caught her under the arms and lifted her up to kiss the tip of her nose, regardless of Gopal's disapproving stare.

Over his shoulder, however, Caro saw it, and drew back a little, blushing as she realized how Brook would disapprove of this manner of greeting an old admirer. More formally, she offered him her hand, but he ignored it and pulled her toward him again for another, more emphatic kiss, saying, "No—no; this is more my style, you know! Don't pretend you've turned into a lady, Caro, for I won't believe it. No need to put on airs and graces with me, after all we've been through together." He hugged her with burly, bearlike enthusiasm. "By Jove, but it's good to see you. How's married life suiting you?"

His manner was so blunt and friendly, his delight at seeing her was so very clear, Caro could not help welcoming him. Looking at the warm, admiring glow in his dark eyes, listening to his easy flow of gossip, she could ignore the misery of moments when she had seen the darker side of his nature—his murderous rages, his pleasure in tormenting the weak.

Here in her own house, surrounded by her own servants, she had no need to remember—or to fear him. During the past weeks since Brook had forbidden her to teach at Margaret Ramsay's school, Caro's isolation had been so complete that she would have been glad to see any old acquaintance who could reassure her that the world outside had not forgotten her. Now she gulped down the news and gossip about her friends as a starving person gulps down food.

"Tell me more. About Philippa. And little Rowley—how big is he now? And Baby Jack? And dear Andrew? I am pining for news of them all, for they are the wretchedest letter writers you can imagine. It's been two months since I've heard from my sister, and then it was the merest scrawl. Is your regiment still at Baburpore, or have you a new posting? You must tell me everything, for I know nothing that is not six months out of date. We are so cut off here that I warn you I shall keep you talking until I have extracted every particle of information you possess. But first you must have some refreshment."

She clapped her hands and gave the order. Tom looked at her curiously, recognizing the symptoms of strain in her rapid, overbright speech. He began to answer her questions as best he could, studying her carefully meanwhile. He thought she was prettier than ever. Pretty? No, damn it, she was a beauty; though thinner than she should be and with a disturbing air of fragility. He wondered fleetingly if she was breeding— that might account for her pallor—but then he recalled that if half of what he'd heard in the mess about Brook Vyner was true, the fellow was incapable of getting anything with child.

Tom, who usually acted first and thought afterward, could read the language of the body more fluently than he could interpret words. He saw behind Caro's bright, social manner and the nervous, restless movements of her hands, the cravings of a frustrated woman, and he guessed, with an instinctive, primitive awareness, that married life had not brought Caro all she sought from it.

But I'll see she gets all she needs while I'm here, he promised himself. It may be a week before the man-eater strikes again, he thought comfortably, and there's no sense in sitting up in a damned chilly *machan* night after night until it does. He began to tell her about his quarry.

"I haven't seen the pug marks for myself, but they say it's a lame tiger—probably turned to man-eating because it's too slow to catch *sambar*. We'll try to beat it out of covert."

Brook returned to find them sitting too close together on the settee for his liking. His jaw tightened and a muscle beneath his eye twitched spasmodically, but he forced a smile.

"It's good of you to break your leave in this way, Hamilton," he said formally, "but we need your help, and no mistake. This cat's a real killer."

"My pleasure, Vyner; my pleasure," Tom assured him. "Caro here's been tellin' me all about your excitin' life up here in the hills; I can't wait to see the lie of the land at Kalipatam."

Brook glanced suspiciously at Caro. *What* had she been telling Tom Hamilton? And how much did she know to tell? He wished that anyone else had been sent from Baburpore to deal with the man-eater, but beggars couldn't be choosers; bagging the man-eater wasn't a task he cared to take on himself, and Hamilton was reputed to be a deadly shot.

"We'll go up there when you're ready, and I'll introduce you to the headman," he told Tom. "He'll provide beaters, a *machan*, anything else you need."

"May I come too?" asked Caro, with an eagerness she had not displayed for months.

"Of course."

"Certainly not."

Tom and Brook spoke simultaneously, then glared at one another.

"Why shouldn't she?" demanded Tom. "There's no danger at all today; the wretched brute is full-fed and is bound to be lying-up in thick jungle to sleep off his meal. It's tomorrow, and the next day, that we'll have to take care. If Caro wants to see how a tiger-hunt is organized, now's her chance."

Brook raised more objections, but Tom, from his unassailable position as the expert on tiger shooting, easily overrode them. Brook's sullen expression clearly indicated to Caro that he was about to indulge in a fit of the sulks, but today she did not care. She felt alive for the first time in weeks, and the thought of how her husband would lecture her when they were alone made her determined to put off that moment as long as she possibly could.

The three of them rode out an hour later, and reached Kalipatam before noon. The headman showed Tom the *nullah*, the deep ravine where the tiger had dragged the bodies of his victims, and together they selected a suitable tree overlooking a small pool at the narrow end of the *nullah*, in which to position the *machan*—a platform of stout poles lashed into the fork of the tree—from which Tom hoped to shoot the man-eater. He engaged a score of beaters, who would drive the tiger toward him through the undergrowth, and bought a young buffalo to use as bait, securely tethered to a tree by the pool, within easy shot of the *machan*.

Tom was in his element as he made arrangements for the drive. Hunting was the sole occupation that satisfied all the primitive savagery in his nature; the thrill of pitting his wits and skill against the cleverest, most powerful killer in the jungle keyed him up and made him happier and more sensual than Caro had ever seen him. She could not help contrasting this keen, alert, resourceful man with the brooding, withdrawn Tom Hamilton who used to cast a shadow over his wife's gayest soirees.

Tom should never have married Amelia, she reflected, nor tried to live the life of a gentleman of fashion. It was not his style. This was where he belonged, among men and animals as simple and ruthless as himself.

Had he really killed his wife, she wondered yet again. Rowland believed he had, despite the jury's verdict.

"One can't forgive the man who murdered one's sister," he'd said to Caro, "and I don't deny it was all I could do to keep my hands off him when he showed his face at Baburpore. But after all there's nothing I can do about it and now, after all this time, I can understand *why* it happened. Amelia was the most feminine creature you can imagine, and she could no more stop herself teasing Tom Hamilton than she could stop breathing. She had begun to think him loutish, compared with all her smart new friends. I remember she referred to him as a 'rhinoceros' in one of the last letters she wrote to me. She was joking, of course, but such mockery must have touched his pride. I should have warned her that teasing a wounded rhinoceros is apt to have ugly consequences." Rowland's evaluation had undoubtedly been correct, but not until now had Caro been able to appreciate his wisdom.

On the ride home, Brook reviewed Tom's preparations with an icy rage gnawing at his heart. How dare that hulking jailbird come here and start lording it over his, Brook's, domain? How dare he address Caro in that arrogant, familiar fashion, and encourage the empty-headed little ninny to defy her husband after all the care he had taken to bring her to heel? Well,

Hamilton should regret it; and Caro, too, should rue the day he set foot in Baburpore. He will rid Kalipatam of its four-footed scourge—that will suit me well, thought Brook; but somehow I'll prevent him from returning to brag about it in the mess at Baburpore.

That night the man-eater killed the tethered buffalo.

Brook received the news at dawn, and immediately summoned Tom.

"I understood you to say the tiger would lie quiet for a day or two," he sneered. "How do you explain this?"

"There must be a second tiger," said Tom after a moment's thought. "It's all right, Vyner; there's no need to get steamed up about it. It's unfortunate, but it alters nothing. We will go ahead with the beat tomorrow as planned."

To Caro's surprise and delight, Brook put no difficulties in her way when she asked tentatively if she might accompany the hunting party. Oddly enough, it was Tom who tried to dissuade her.

"I don't want to appear a croaker, Caro," he said with a lop-sided grin which was disarming because it was so rare, "but I wouldn't recommend it. Tiger-hunting's a chancy business, especially if there's more than one of the big brutes on the move. Besides"—he looked a little self-conscious—"Miss Drinkwater and her parents are arriving in Vanyasi tomorrow, to stay with their cousins the St. Legers, and I know she would so enjoy visiting you."

"She will not want to come visiting the very day she arrives," Caro pointed out, and Brook said unpleasantly, "I thought you said that this latest kill alters nothing!"

"Well, it doubles the risk, of course." Tom was surprised that a clever chap like Brook Vyner could not work this out for himself.

"Oh, Tom!" Caro's disappointment showed plainly in her face.

Brook said with false heartiness, "Of course you

shall come if you want to, Caro. Why should you miss all the fun? With a mighty hunter like Tom to protect you, you'll be as safe at Kalipatam as you'd be here in your own drawing room, chatting to Miss Drinkwater."

Tom suspected that he was being mocked, and his heavy head lowered in the old familiar bull-like stance.

"Don't know that I'd call it fun, m'self," he growled. "It's a dangerous business. Bound to be. No place for the ladies, as m'father always said, and he was a great *shikari*, if you like. They still remember him in these parts, though he died twenty years ago."

"Please, Tom." Caro laid a hand on his arm and gazed beseechingly at him. "I never would have thought you were a croaker. Brook takes such—such special care of me that I never get any excitement nowadays. If he says it's all right, I'm sure it must be. I promise I'll stay well out of danger. And I'm used to living in the rough! Please let me come."

They might be alone for all the notice they take of me, thought Brook. Tom looked into Caro's eyes and was vanquished.

"Oh, very well," he said crossly. "If you're so set on it, I won't be the one to stop you. Damn it, Caro, you always could twist me around your little finger. But I insist on one condition. You must sit up in the *machan* with me, for it's the only place I'll know that you're safe. If I have to worry about you, I won't be able to concentrate on shooting straight, and like as not I'll miss my chance at the tiger. How about it, Vyner? Will that suit you?"

"Perfectly," said Brook coolly.

"Oh thank you! That's wonderful. Far better than I dared hope." Caro smiled radiantly at Tom and Brook turned abruptly away, afraid that Hamilton would read murder in his face.

That evening, Caro tried to thank Brook for

allowing her this unexpected treat, but he was in a mood to find fault with everything she said.

"What else could I do, after you had made me out to be some kind of monster who shut you up in the house and denied you any amusements? God knows, I'd be glad enough if you would take part in the social life here—help with the amateur theatricals and so on. But no, you refuse to stir yourself unless some handsome officer begs you to—then you're eager enough to oblige him."

Caro smiled faintly. "I don't consider Tom handsome, exactly."

"No? Gopal told me you seemed to find him attractive enough."

"Gopal has no business to carry tales to you," she said sharply, "and I am surprised that you pay attention to what he says after telling me I must never listen to servants' gossip."

Brook flushed darkly, and she went on: "Tom is simply an old friend and I was pleased to see him. I greeted him as I would any other old friend."

"By allowing him to kiss you like a common trollop! I'd have thought that you, of all people, were well aware of Captain Hamilton's unsavory reputation where women are concerned. "Whoso toucheth pitch. . . ," you know. Well, let it pass. But I warn you, Caro, that if I hear any more gossip concerning your relations with Captain Hamilton, I'll see that he leaves Vanyasi immediately, and looking less attractive than when he arrived. So be very careful."

The picture of Brook threatening Tom Hamilton with physical violence made Caro laugh aloud. "Isn't he just a trifle over your weight?" she inquired mockingly. "I wouldn't advise any rash attacks on his person, Brook dear, for he knows better than most how to defend himself. Anyway, you have nothing to fear, for Tom Hamilton has no interest in me, nor I in him."

Only two days ago, this last statement would have been entirely true, but now the thought of Tom alone in a bedroom so close to hers, of Tom's powerful body close beside her in the tiger-shooting *machan* on the morrow, made Caro's heart race and her cheeks burn in a way they had not done since leaving Baburpore.

The beat was planned to cover a rough triangle of jungle bisected by the deep *nullah* in which the tiger had made his first kills. Tom's *machan*, with the dead buffalo lying by the pool below it, was at the apex of the triangle. At the sides, stops were posted in trees with instructions to tap the trunks to prevent the tiger from breaking away from the path they intended it to take. Brook Vyner, armed with a twelve-bore shotgun, was in charge of the beaters, and had agreed to fire both barrels as a signal to his men to take to the trees if anything went wrong.

In the heat of the day, the drive began.

Caro and Tom, accompanied by Tom's orderly, Narba Singh, had climbed up to their platform an hour before Caro's sharp ears caught the faint throbbing of tom-toms and the far-off shouts of the beaters, the cackle of disturbed jungle fowl, and the rap of *lathi*s on tree trunks about a mile away.

Around the *machan*, the jungle dozed in a heavy afternoon torpor, and in spite of her eagerness to see everything there was to be seen, Caro herself felt sleepy. At the edge of the little pool lay the dead buffalo, a black hulk against the shining water. On a rock nearby a huge black cobra lay in motionless coils: she would never have spotted it had not Tom's trained eye picked it out.

The shouts drew nearer. A curtain of creeper on the far side of the clearing swayed apart, and a herd of elephants, stomachs rumbling, filed swiftly across Tom's field of fire. He drew an imaginary bead on the leader, a magnificent bull standing fully nine foot at the shoulder, and Caro gave a tiny gasp.

"Oh no. You couldn't."

Tom shook his head, smiling, and put a finger to his lips. The elephants vanished like ghosts into the jungle.

Now the beaters were close. The cobra woke and slithered off into the undergrowth, and a moment later a party of spotted deer crossed beneath the *machan* in alarmed, jerky bounds. A pea-fowl arose with an ugly screech and a great flurry of wings.

"Keep very still," Tom whispered in Caro's ear. He sat alert, yet relaxed, the rifle ready, scanning the patches of sunlight and shadow below them.

Suddenly a scream tore the air. Then another, and another. A few seconds afterward came the double explosion of Brook's twelve-bore, followed by a pandemonium of voices.

Tom cursed. "He's broken out," he guessed, "about a hundred yards down the *nullah*. Keep close, Caro. We must go and see what's happened. It sounds as if someone's hurt."

The screams had changed to a continuous moaning when they reached the spot. Beneath a tree overhanging the *nullah* they found Brook and a crowd of jabbering, excited villagers engaged in lifting down the guard who had been posted in the fork of the tree some fourteen feet above the steep bank of the ravine. The man's face was gray with pain and below the knee his leg was a bloody pulp. The tiger had not only clawed its way out of the steep ravine, but had also made a tremendous leap up the smooth-trunked tree and reached high enough to seize the dangling leg of the man seated there before the noise of Brook's shots drove him away from his half-fainting victim.

After the mauled villager had been laid on a litter and carried away to the surgeon in Vanyasi, Tom carefully examined the scene of the accident. Nine feet above ground, the bark of the tree was scored and slashed by the marks of the tiger's claws, and the impetus of its leap must have carried the great cat the few extra feet upward to reach the unfortunate man's leg.

Tom gave orders for another *machan* to be constructed in the fork of this tree. "I shall shoot from here tomorrow," he said.

Sweat dripped under the brim of Brook's helmet and his shirt clung to his back. Ahead he could hear the excited shouts of the beaters, telling him that once again both tigers were on the move.

He paused, cradling the shotgun under one arm, and stared around him. On either side the banks of the ravine rose, rocky and forbidding, with thorny scrub growing right to the top. It seemed incredible that a tiger would choose to climb one of those uninviting banks when he could escape far more easily down the dry bed of the stream, but that was what had happened yesterday, and that self-confident lout Tom Hamilton was banking on the pattern repeating itself today.

A fine fool he'll look if the beast chooses the other route, thought Brook. Tom had offered him his second rifle if he wanted to try for a shot from the original *machan*, but Brook had claimed it was more important to keep the beaters under control. It was, too, he thought angrily. One beater going the wrong way could ruin the whole careful operation. Only Tom and Caro, two people, would have read into his refusal any notion that he was afraid to take the chance of a shot. They had exchanged a laughing glance which Brook had intercepted, and now he burned with rage.

Brook wiped his face. His tongue felt thick, clinging to the roof of his mouth, and he yearned for a cool drink. Why hadn't he remembered his hip flask? Oddly enough, he seemed to hear running water close at hand.

He followed the sound and found himself peering into a deep, narrow fissure, almost a cave, in the left bank of the *nullah*. It was wider at the bottom than at the top, and sure enough a thin trickle of water ran out of the rock face and dripped into a pool on the floor of the cave.

As he stepped out of the sunlight between the sheer walls, a rank, acrid stench caught at his throat. Tiger! This must be where the beasts had their lair. He could see that the cave was empty now; the tigers must have slunk out of it to get away from the noise of the beaters. There was no danger from them, but all the same, Brook moved cautiously, straining his eyes in the dim light. He was bending over the pool with cupped hands, about to drink, when he heard droning above him. Looking up, his eye was caught by an odd shape against the rock: a large, black, symmetrical inverted cone, alive with thousands of deadly black bees, clinging to a jutting outcrop only a few feet above the little pool.

Brook's heart seemed to miss several beats and he froze, still as a statue. If he had taken two steps further before bending down to drink... If he had bumped into that...

Very slowly, shaking as if with ague, Brook lowered himself onto hands and knees and crawled back the way he had come, taking the utmost care to make no noise. Just as he reached the sunlight and stood upright again he heard, closer than he expected, the heavy crash of Tom's rifle.

It was then that he remembered that he had left his own gun lying by the pool inside the cave.

Caro was not surprised when Tom refused point-blank to allow her to sit in the *machan* next day. Since the latest accident, hunting the man-eater had become a grim business and, after spending the night helping the surgeon and Emily Drinkwater in their fight for the life of the native whose mauled leg had had to be amputated, Caro was glad enough to spend the day quietly at home, resting and gossiping with Emily.

Though freckled, thick-bodied, and homely, Emily had a sturdy spirit and a plain way of speaking that appealed to Caro. And under all the good sense there was a romantic side to her nature which few people would have imagined. Shyly but resolutely, she explained to the astonished Caro that she was in love with Tom Hamilton.

"I can't help myself," she said simply. "It is really too absurd, for I've always been considered level-headed, and I've *always* taken Mama's advice—until now. But the more she tells me, and the more I tell myself, what a wretched husband dear Tom would make, the more anxious I become to marry him. Never fear"—she went on, seeing Caro about to speak—"I know *all* about his past: kind friends both here and in England have supplied me with every detail. I know, for instance, that he once tried to abduct you, and ruined your good name when you were barely out of the schoolroom. I know he's stood trial for murder, and I'm aware that he's got the blackest temper any man ever possessed when things go against him. But I am confident that I can—tame him. You see, I understand him so well. Does that sound to you like wishful thinking?"

Caro considered. She, too, had thought she could bend Tom Hamilton to her will, and had discovered her mistake too late. But that was years ago. Tom was a changed person here in India, and besides, she recognized beneath Emily's quiet exterior an even more determined nature than Tom's. He might bluster and threaten, but she would get her own way in the end.

She said, forcing an enthusiastic warmth into her voice, "No—I believe you can do it, and I wish you every happiness. Have you announced your betrothal?"

Emily's face flushed unbecomingly. "There!" she exclaimed. "I'm letting my tongue run away with me again and giving you quite the wrong impression. Promise you won't breathe a word of what I've said to anyone, Caro—not even to your sister—for the sad truth is that Tom hasn't asked me yet! But it makes me truly happy to have your good wishes and approval, because if I felt that I was in any way stealing Tom away from you, I would not be at all easy in my mind."

"From *me*? What can you mean?"

"Oh, I know you're married," said Emily calmly, "but that doesn't alter the fact that Tom cares for you still. He always has. When the chance came for him to travel to Vanyasi, he seized it at once and positively forbade any other officer to come with him. On his pay, you know, he can't afford *shikar* in the normal way. You may be sure I made my plans to follow with no delay, for I knew at once that it was not the chance of shooting a tiger that drew him—it was the opportunity to see you."

"Oh no—you must be mistaken," murmured Caro, but she could not suppress the leap of pleasure her heart had given. Brook's indifference to her as a woman had badly shaken her confidence in her own power to attract men: to hear from Emily that Tom, at least, still cared for her was strangely heartening. If only Rowland . . . she thought, but Emily was rattling on, almost as if she feared that if she didn't unburden her heart now, she would never again pluck up courage to do so.

"It's easier to talk to you than I expected," she was saying, "and I'm thankful for that, because it's a hard enough matter to put into words. But the fact is this: I love Tom, and I think I can make him care for me as long"—she hesitated and then rushed on—"as long as you don't call him back. Oh yes, you could, and I'd be deceiving myself if I didn't admit it. You'd have only to crook your little finger and Tom would fly to your side, married or not. So that's why I'm putting my cards on the table *now*, and asking, do you want him or will you let him go? If I thought you weren't happy in your marriage, or felt the need of Tom's devotion, I'd go home quietly and never let him know I'd lost my heart to him. But you've got Brook, and you're content, aren't you, Caro?"

Caro gazed at the square, freckled face with its broad nose and small, steadfast eyes, wondering what it had cost Emily in pride to make that speech. To beg for her man. Of course Emily was right: it was better to speak frankly now rather than risk heartbreak later. But could she do as Emily asked, and renounce all place in Tom's affections just when she had rediscovered how sweet they were to her? Happy in her marriage! With an effort Caro suppressed the bitter, hysterical laughter that bubbled up inside her.

There had been a time, during the siege of Baburpore, when Emily had set her cap at Brook with a good deal of success. If Caro had not returned, apparently from the dead, it might now be Emily who was the wife of the Assistant Collector of Vanyasi. She was lucky to have escaped such a fate. Life with Tom Hamilton, temper and all, would be a paradise compared to this limbo of frustration and loneliness in which Caro was trapped.

Emily's expression grew anxious. Caro wrestled with her conscience in silence. Ever since Tom had arrived in Vanyasi, she had felt young and light-hearted again, ready to joke and flirt, to fling off the heavy middle-age decorum that Brook wanted to force on her. How simple it would be to take Tom for her lover, and prolong this delightful game of cat-and-mouse, advance-and-retreat. The dangerous pleasure of conducting an illicit liaison under Brook's very nose made the prospect even more attractive. But if she did, what would become of poor Emily?

Caro was about to say she couldn't send Tom away, but at that moment they heard a commotion outside in the street. There was a confused shouting; then came a flurry of knocks on the front door. Caro hurried to open it before Gopal got there. On the doorstep stood Narba Singh, Tom's orderly, swaying with fatigue. Sweat coursed down his face and his mouth worked speechlessly.

"What is the matter, Narba Singh?" asked Caro in a bantering tone. "Has the tiger chased you here from Kalipatam?"

The man ignored her and spoke directly to Emily.

"There is... bad accident, miss-sahiba. Ham'ton-sahib he hurt bad. You come quick with doctor."

"Tom's hurt!" Emily turned dead white, but she wasted no time asking for details. "Take me to him at once," she directed. "Mrs. Vyner will follow with the doctor. Are you all right, man? Caro, be so good as to order him a drink, or I fear he may faint with exhaustion. He must have run all the way from Kalipatam."

Caro shouted for the servants, who hurried up wide-eyed. She sent Gopal to fetch the doctor to the bungalow at once.

Narba Singh was nodding, his chest still heaving from his long run. "Bearers bringing Ham'ton-sahib. I run first to get doctor."

"Was it the tiger?" Caro asked, fearfully recalling the villager's mauled leg. "Was Captain Hamilton wounded by the tiger?"

"No, memsahib. He shoot tiger, one-two. All dead. Vyner-sahib come, say look in cave where tiger live. Fetch gun I leave there. Ham'ton-sahib he go in cave, black devils come after, hurt him bad."

"*Devils...?*" began Caro, but just then a litter carried at a swinging jog by half a dozen bearers appeared around the bend in the road. They hurried to meet it and escorted it indoors.

"Lay him down on the bed. Gently now," directed Caro, staring appalled at the motionless, unrecognizable figure of Tom Hamilton. His face, neck, and hands were grotesquely swollen and hundreds of tiny black darts, like coarse black hairs, sprouted from every inch of uncovered skin. His eyes and mouth were mere slits in the red, puffy flesh that had been his face; his jaw and neck were merged into one, and he seemed to swell up even more as they watched. He no longer looked like a man; he had become some hideous monster from a nightmare.

"What has done this?" she whispered.

Emily picked up the hot, tight, shiny balloon that had been Tom's wrist and sought for the pulse.

"Black bees," she said somberly, "the smallest and deadliest creatures in the jungle. We shall need more than a doctor to save his life. We must find a bee-wizard at once, or the shock will stop his heart."

Chapter Nineteen

AFTER A CONVALESCENCE of several weeks' duration, Tom Hamilton went back to Baburpore on a litter, his face and hands still a suppurating mask of lymph, despite the bee-wizard's skill. The old man's gnarled fingers had gently pulled out the stings, one by one, and as he worked he made a soothing low-pitched hum like a murmur of faraway bees. Emily's devoted nursing and Tom's own strong constitution had combined to pull him back from the threshold of death, but it had been a near thing.

Again and again Caro tried to convince herself that Brook's threat that when Tom left Vanyasi he would look less attractive than when he came had been nothing more than a strange coincidence. How could Brook have known that the cave was full of bees, she reasoned. According to his own story, he had drunk from the same pool without mishap, and it was only when Tom blundered against the nest itself that the bees exploded from it. Yet there were a few points that disquieted her. Brook had left his gun in the bees' cave, and asked Tom to bring it out for him. Why had he not gone back himself? Did any man abandon a valuable weapon so carelessly when tigers were about?

Resolutely, Caro pushed away from her the horrible suspicion that he had engineered the whole accident. Before Emily left, she had found an opportunity to press her hand and whisper a promise that she, Caro, would never, *never* call Tom back to her. Emily's tremulous smile at this undertaking had made her plain face almost beautiful for an instant, and Caro hoped that she and Tom would be very happy together.

For herself, it no longer mattered that Brook was brusque and abstracted, and only roused himself to play the part of a correctly devoted husband when they were in company. Caro preferred it that way. When they were on their own, he ignored her and spent long hours in his study, from which he would emerge with glazed eyes and the smell of *charrah* heavy about him.

Like a child anticipating Christmas, Caro clung to the hope of seeing Rowland at Durlah Sultan's banquet. She thought of him all day long, and lying at night in her hot, lonely bed, listening to the zinging mosquitoes and croaking frogs, she imagined herself once more in his arms. Their angry parting, the quarrel over Serindar were forgotten, and instead she wore his little horseshoe brooch close to her heart and remembered their one night of love in the silk-hung tent on the Patelbar border.

Meanwhile, left increasingly to her own devices, and forbidden to teach at Margaret's school, Caro could not resist trying out a plan that had tempted her for some months. At the bottom of her trunk, wrapped in tissue paper, lay the spangled gauze trousers and bodice of her dancing-girl's costume, together with several saris of more sober hue. Dressing in them one warm night when the door of Brook's study was firmly closed, she pulled back her hair in a single plait and adorned her brow with a modest scarlet dot. She threw the end of her sari over her head and surveyed the result in the mirror.

A light-skinned Indian woman with large, kohl-rimmed eyes smiled back at her, lowering her lashes demurely and then laughing secretly, hand over mouth. She would pass unnoticed—in the dark, at any rate. Caro remembered that Rowland had said, "You don't have to act; you *become* a native," and her spirits rose. She had played the memsahib long enough. Tonight she would shake off the white woman's corsets and chains of convention and enjoy a few short hours of freedom.

Since Brook had dismissed the *ayah* she brought from Baburpore and substituted a sly-eyed local woman, there was no servant she trusted not to carry tales to Brook, so she slipped out of the bungalow alone. Subdued laughter and the rattle of pots came from the servants' quarters as she skirted the corner of the house where the *chokidar*—the nightwatchman— crouched, and vaulted the low mud wall that encircled the garden. The thick, sultry air smelled excitingly of cooking oil and turmeric, dung, and the sweet scent of the struggling roses that their *malee* had managed to nurse this far toward the life-giving rains. Free from her hot, pinching stays and stiff shoes, Caro glided quickly down the steep cobbled alley that led toward the bazaar, adopting almost unconsciously the easy, hip-swinging gait of the native women thronging the narrow streets between frowning, mud-walled dwellings. Nobody stared at her, stopped, or questioned her; she was accepted into the busy, jostling throng as if she had belonged there all her life and for the first time for months she felt confident and happy.

"Oh, lotus blossom, show me your jewels," murmured a Rajput giving her an admiring, sidelong glance as she loitered before a stall selling sweetmeats whose oily, treacly smell seemed to penetrate to the very roots of her hair.

Caro smothered a laugh and twitched the end of her sari closer about her face. "Show me your silver first, brother!"

A party of sepoys swaggered past, shoulder to shoulder, filling the narrow alleyway. Caro shrank into an alcove, hiding her face until they turned a corner.

She wandered into the Street of the Coppersmiths, enjoying the feeling of being part of this press of humanity, listening to snatches of conversation, the raucous shouts of street traders, the shrill bargaining of native women, and, above the general hubbub, the clear, bell-like notes of hammer on copper inside the tiny stalls where the coppersmiths worked, their oiled bodies gleaming in the torchlight. How different was this whole cheerful jumble from the parade-ground stiffness of the British quarters and the neat lines of Civil bungalows at the top of the hill! Caro felt in a strange way that she had come home as she wandered deeper and deeper into the maze of narrow streets.

She haggled for a bunch of plantains from a solemn boy with a round red skullcap on his cropped head. The moment he took the money he darted away to help his father, who was flapping ineffectual hands at a huge white humped Brahmin bull, which had lumbered into the middle of his stall, upsetting baskets left and right. Its mild, contemplative gaze ignored the agitated merchant and fastened instead on the little heaps of grain, peas, and lentils on their round wicker trays at the rear of the stall. Seeing its intention, the merchant moaned, but did nothing to hinder the great beast as it stood swishing its tail across bundles of ruined vegetables and munching grain from each tray in turn.

Caro was sorely tempted to speed it on its way with a prod from the small jeweled dagger she wore tucked into her waistband, but such violence to a sacred beast might, if observed, have aroused more hostility than gratitude from the merchant and attracted undesirable attention. She wandered on, avoiding the mangy dogs that snarled and fought over decomposing bones.

As she moved from stall to stall, she amused herself by making a mental assessment of where she would buy the household goods if Brook ever could be persuaded to change his ridiculous custom of leaving all the shopping in the hands of his steward, that smooth-tongued, tale-bearing hypocrite Gopal. She could see glossy green watermelons and ripe plantains on every stall—yet Gopal had sworn they were scarce when serving her with tasteless, underripe fruit yesterday. She wondered how much he had charged for them in the black account book she was never allowed to see. Oranges, too...

A crowd had gathered round the rug-strewn stall of a Nepalese carpet seller. Caro wriggled through to the front to inspect his wares. As she did so, her eyes fell on a short, stout figure standing immediately behind the merchant, and her heart gave a sudden jolt.

The man was in profile to her, plainly dressed in an ordinary, rather dirty muslin tunic and long wrinkled trousers, and wearing a flattish turban of the Mahratta pattern. His bull-like stance, with heavy head lowered, shoulders slightly hunched, and curving stomach tapering down to absurdly small feet in pointed slippers seemed familiar—too familiar. Caro stood on tiptoe to get a better look, and just then the man she was watching turned his head and looked straight at her.

As she met the flat black eyes under high-arched brows, Caro's mouth went suddenly dry and clammy sweat sprang out on the palms of her hands. She pulled the folds of material closer about her face and bent her head quickly, for she recognized the heavy, pallid features, the cupid's-bow mouth under the thin, drooping mustache of the man whose gaze had first devoured her across the banquet hall in Patelbar. Here, inexplicably, in this small, upcountry station near the Nepalese frontier, apparently alone, was the Butcher of Cawnpore—the man whom every British soldier in India longed to call to account for his crimes. It was the Nana Sahib.

He could not have recognized her, muffled to the

eyes in the enveloping sari, but like a wild beast scenting danger, he looked warily from side to side. Then he left his position behind the merchant and began pushing a way through the crowd before Caro could get a second glimpse of him.

She knew a moment's panic, but one thing was clear: she must not lose sight of him.

Little as she relished the thought of following that monster to his lair, she knew it was her duty to track him down, and then alert the authorities to the presence in Vanyasi of the most wanted man in India. Every instinct urged her to seek help, to run to the Shikar Club and blurt out her story, but dressed as she was, how could she? Native women were not admitted to the club, and even if she managed to bluff her way past the servants, precious time would be lost while she explained her presence in such clothes. Besides, Brook would be furious: she quailed at the thought of his anger.

To return to the bungalow and change her dress would take even longer. If she once lost sight of her quarry in the maze of tiny alleys that bisected and dissected the native town, she would never find him again. He would disappear as completely as a musk-rat into its tunnels and then, even if the military could be persuaded to search the town she knew the chances of finding one man in such a warren would be extremely slender. He would be warned and never risk showing himself in the bazaar again.

No: there was no help for it. She must follow him alone and mark where he stopped. Only if she could point with certainty to his hiding place would her story be believed, though even now she foresaw plenty of difficulty. Her heart sank as she visualized the Collector's prim, skeptical smile when she told him whom she had seen.

"My dear young lady!" she could imagine him

saying, "are you certain this story is not just the product of an overheated imagination. We all see strange things at times, I know, but to claim to have recognized the Rajah of Bithoor in the bazaar at Vanyasi—that must overtax even my credulity. What were you doing in the bazaar at night, in any case? Does your husband encourage such nocturnal expeditions, Lady Caroline? I confess I find it strange if he does. Or was he perhaps unaware of your precise whereabouts? I thought so. Maybe I would be wise to drop a word of warning in his ear."

Well, she would face that hurdle when she came to it. Surely *someone* would believe her, even if the Collector did not! The most important thing now was to keep her quarry in view. Already the portly figure was moving with surprising speed up the steep path between the silversmiths' stalls, while she was hampered by a pattering train of heavily laden donkeys, which had emerged from a side street to block the whole alley.

"Mother of iniquity, do not turn around here!" shrilled the donkey driver, whacking the lead-ass on the rump with energy as she tried to take a shortcut home between the harness-makers' booths. Caro ducked under her nose and tucked the end of her sari into her waistband to leave both hands free as she almost ran up the steep, rough path. It was darker here, away from the main bazaar, though lights shone from upstairs windows where courtesans sat cross-legged on their balconies, each with a candle before her to illuminate her features. Below, at street level, aged crones stirred aromatic cauldrons, and torchlight flickered through fretted shutters in opium dens where smokers sat entranced.

Turn left; turn right; left again. The stout figure of the Nana Sahib kept steadily uphill, and Caro panted with exertion as she tried to keep him within sight without letting him know he was being followed. Where could he be going? The huts of the native town were thinning out now, as they approached the Civil Lines where the Europeans lived, and the Nana Sahib slowed his pace, stepping aside as a solitary horseman rode toward him, raising his joined palms in unctuous salute to the oblivious young officer who passed, his *syce* trotting behind him. Caro recognized him: Mr. Moncrieff, the subaltern whom Brook had classed as "perfectly presentable," and had urged her to invite to dine with them. She wondered why he was riding so late in the direction of the native town. Perhaps he had lost at cards and now sought a native girl to comfort his bed. Perhaps he would spend the night glassy-eyed before a pipe of opium. Whatever his mission, it was no good hoping for help from him. Caro squeezed past his horse on the narrow track and hurried uphill again.

Here was the church, and beyond it the Shikar Club, where every British officer in Vanyasi would now be slaking his thirst and recalling the day's sporting exploits. If only they knew their enemy was passing by the very door of the club.

Caro felt the weight of responsibility heavy on her. The man she followed had betrayed General Wheeler's garrison at Cawnpore, luring them from the battered shell of the hospital they had defended so gallantly, promising them safe conduct by river to Allahabad, and then ordered his men to fire on the helpless refugees as they tried to board the boats. He had imprisoned the survivors, two hundred British women and children, until Havelock was within a few miles of the building that was their prison, then had them savagely butchered and their mutilated bodies crammed into a dry well. He was lost to human decency, more vicious and treacherous than any animal. He must be caught and destroyed, but she wished that anyone rather than herself had been chosen by fate to capture him.

She shivered, even as she told herself she was in no danger. All she need do was follow him to his hiding place and then inform the soldiers. They would arrest him; she need take no further part in the operation. But all the same, as she slipped from one patch of shadow to the next, she was afraid.

Outside the Shikar Club he rested a few moments, and Caro crouched behind him, still as a stone. Had he heard her? Something in his attitude seemed to indicate that he, too, was straining his ears for a footfall, an unfamiliar sound. Then he relaxed and moved on, toward the neat lines of Civil bungalows.

Caro followed, her heart leaping. From her point of view the fugitive could not have chosen a more convenient route, since now he must pass directly by her own bungalow. She would slip in through the unlatched window on the veranda, change her clothes, and then confront Brook with her story.

Determinedly she pushed away the nagging worry that Brook would react as skeptically as she had imagined the Collector doing and ask the same awkward questions. "What were you doing in the native town late at night? If you recognized him, why didn't he recognize you?" Well, she would get around them somehow. Brook was ambitious, and would realize that to catch such a prize as the Nana Sahib would assure his promotion in the Civil Service. And to catch him here, in open country, would not be difficult. They had now reached the limit of possible hiding places, and still Nana Sahib walked on and she followed. Beyond Brook's and Caro's bungalow lay the school, and then the mountain road. It would be hard for a stout man on foot, however wily, to vanish before morning on that desolate track.

Fifty yards ahead of her, plain in the moonlight, Caro saw her quarry draw level with her own bungalow—and all her plans and hopes collapsed into dust. With the ease and confidence of long practice, Nana Sahib opened the garden gate, and she heard the quiet murmur of his greeting to the *chokidar*, followed by the click of the gate. A moment later, an oblong of light showed from the veranda door that opened into Brook's study.

The truth struck her then, and nausea threatened to overwhelm her. It was no use telling her husband that the fugitive Nana Sahib was in Vanyasi. *He knew.* The Butcher of Cawnpore had been harbored in her house, probably for weeks—ever since Brook's tour of the district.

Little things that had puzzled her clicked neatly into place. The new servants, her *ayah*'s dismissal, the refusal to allow her any part in the running of the household.

Caro rose slowly and glided through patches of deep shadow to the veranda door. It was half open, to catch the night breeze, and from within voices rose and fell as they had so many times in these past weeks. Now she knew who talked with Brook in his study so late at night, and the unsuspected depths of her husband's deceit made her tremble with helpless rage. She pressed her ear to the wall and found she could hear the low, rapid conversation.

"Did you speak with the seller of carpets, Highness?" That was Brook's voice.

"He carried evil tidings. Jang Bahadur will not grant me asylum within his domain."

Caro knew that Sir Jang Bahadur was the Prime Minister of Nepal.

"I feared as much," said Brook. "But what of the tribal chiefs? There are many that owe no loyalty to Jang Bahadur, and they would make you welcome. It is dangerous for you to hide here now that the Lieutenant-Governor is making his tour. There are men among his escort who would know you, even in disguise."

As I did, thought Caro. Though Nana Sahib wore servant's clothes, he had not the look of a servant. He would be more at home in the guise of a fat Hindu moneylender.

The rajah laughed unpleasantly. "So you grow weary of my presence, Vyner-sahib. Have you spent the worth of the jewels I gave you from the Sultanbagh at Baburpore? Does your palm itch for more?"

"It would help," Brook agreed smoothly. "It is an expensive matter to keep the mouths of all my servants tightly closed for weeks on end. Thank you. I am sure this will help. It will look well on my wife. So . . . what of the tribal chieftains?"

The other's voice was so low Caro had to strain to hear.

"I saw your wife in the bazaar tonight, Vyner-sahib. I think she knew me. She followed me all the way back here."

Outside the door, Caro froze.

Brook laughed in loud disbelief. "My wife in the bazaar? Impossible—you are imagining dangers where none exist. My wife is here and asleep, and has been these past three hours."

"Go and see," insisted the soft, petulant voice.

Caro fled. She darted noiselessly along the veranda, turned the corner where old Abdullah pulled rhythmically at the *punkah* rope, and flung herself through the window into her bedroom. Heart hammering hard enough to choke her, she tore off the Indian clothes and stuffed them into a trunk. Then she pulled on her nightgown and scrubbed frantically at the *bindi* spot on her forehead. She was not a moment too soon. The mosquito net around her bed was still swaying when she heard Brook's step outside her door, and the creak of the door opening. From the light on her studiously closed eyelids, she knew he was staring down at her, lamp in hand. Whether another figure stood in the doorway, she could not tell.

"Caro—are you awake?"

"Whaa—what is it?" she said sleepily, trying hard to still her panting breath.

"I heard a noise outside. I wanted to see that you were all right. Good night, my dear. I am sorry I disturbed you."

The footsteps retreated; died away. She was safe, for the moment.

"I have a present for you, my dear," said Brook at breakfast a week later.

It was Caro's twentieth birthday, and also the date fixed for Durlah Sultan's *burra-khana* to entertain the Lieutenant-Governor of the Province. Although only just past eight o'clock, the early-morning freshness was already fading, and the air felt heavy and humid. Soon the monsoon wind would blow and the rains release the electric tension that made Caro's head ache and her appetite vanish. She had lost weight and in her thin face her brown eyes looked twice their usual size.

"Thank you, Brook." She took the large flat jeweler's box from him and flipped open the lid without great interest.

Inside lay a long necklace of diamonds, emeralds, and pearls. She guessed at once who had given it to Brook, and her flesh crawled as if at the touch of a snake. She shut the box again quickly.

"Don't you like it? The stones are real, you know. Nothing but the best for you, Caro."

"Oh... of course I like it," she said helplessly. "It's beautiful. But it's too valuable. I'd be afraid to wear it for fear of losing it. You shouldn't give me such presents, Brook. I'm sure you can't afford it."

It was the wrong thing to say. Brook immediately looked offended. "What nonsense! I'm not a pauper, and if I like to give my wife jewels, I expect her to accept them gracefully, not begin raising ridiculous objections. Of course they're not too valuable to wear. You may find it strange, but I like to see you well-dressed. We have a position to maintain here, though you seldom seem aware of it. The Durlah Sultan will bring out all his jewels tonight, you may be sure, but he'll have nothing to match *this*." He patted the box with a satisfied smile. "You'll outshine them all."

"Oh, but I can't wear it tonight!" she exclaimed.

"Whyever not? Do you imagine I gave you that necklace so that it could lie unseen at the bottom of your jewel case? Certainly not. I want you to sparkle tonight. I shall be very displeased, Caroline, if you refuse to wear my gift."

Caro looked at the tight line of his mouth above the weak chin, his bland, rather prominent eyes, and wondered how she could ever have thought him handsome. There was nothing to be gained by quarreling with him, though. She would have to wear the necklace, even if she thought it accursed.

Durlah Sultan's little twinkling eyes surveyed with satisfaction the long table loaded with countless dishes, candles, vessels of silver and glass, heaps of rice, mounds of jelly, pyramids of silver-coated sweetmeats. He signaled once again to his wine-bearer.

By the Prophet, how these British could drink! Three dozen bottles of claret and five dozen of champagne had already been accounted for, and still the goblets were drained as soon as they were refilled.

The Lieutenant-Governor of the Province, Sir Francis Micklethwait, seated as guest of honor on Durlah Sultan's right hand, must alone had drunk more than two bottles of wine. Durlah Sultan hoped that this lavish hospitality would put Sir Francis in an amenable mood toward the various small concessions the Nawab hoped to wring out of him at their formal audience tomorrow. Himself an abstainer, Durlah Sultan did not realize that plying the Governor with liquor might well have the opposite effect, giving him a nasty hangover and consequent bad temper at the audience.

Lady Micklethwait, fat and jolly, always traveled with her husband, to whom she was devoted and, many said, prevented him from making an ass of himself in nine stations out of ten. She was doing ample justice to the syllabubs, custards, and pies that Durlah Sultan's cooks had so painstakingly copied from European recipes, but the Collector's wife, Kathleen Williams, sallow and vinegar-faced in high-necked black bombazine more suitable for a funeral than a banquet, nibbled suspiciously at her food as if afraid it might be poisoned.

On Durlah Sultan's left, Albert Williams, Collector of Vanyasi, coughed dryly and reached for his handkerchief. His dark eyes were sunk deep in his head, giving him the look of a skull. *He* will join his fathers before the end of the monsoon, thought Durlah Sultan confidently, offering him some betel nut; and then, if all is well, they will put Vyner-sahib in his place. Vyner-sahib would, he was sure, be easier to deal with than this dour, correct, sardonic Williams-sahib.

There would be no nonsense about refusing bribes or pestering a nawab to limit the size of his household when Vyner-sahib sat in the Collector's chair. An Englishman who could be bribed like Vyner-sahib was a rare jewel, a gift to an Indian ruler. Durlah Sultan's gaze\fastened on the sparkling necklace which Vyner-sahib's young wife wore. If my eyes do not deceive me, he thought, that is the Nau-lakha, the principal heirloom of the Peshwas of the Mahrattas, worth a crore of rupees at the very least. I wonder how it comes to be around the neck of Vyner's memsahib; and I wonder, too, if anyone else will recognize it.

Caro, seated halfway down the long table, had a wine glass of Waterford crystal, but the plate on which her food congealed was of the cheapest, thickest white china you could buy in the bazaar, chipped and discolored. Mechanically she ate the soup and sweet biscuits that were offered simultaneously by the overexcited servants without noticing anything odd about the combination of tastes. She would have swallowed the fish that followed with equal oblivion had not Angus Moncrieff, seated beside her, laid a hand hastily on her arm.

"On no account touch the fish, Lady Caro," he warned.

"Is it not fresh?"

"Fresh be damned," said Angus, who was not one to mince his words. "It is certain death."

Caro thanked him absently and went on eating the truffled sausages and sugared almonds that next arrived on her plate. She was gazing absently across the clutter of dishes until her eyes fixed on a late-arriving guest too far away for conversation. Angus's eyes followed hers.

"By Jove, isn't that Rowland Steel opposite?" he exclaimed. "I heard he'd been promoted to major after the relief of Baburpore. There's a hero for you! D'you know the story? He stormed the Sultanbagh with just two hundred men, and took it, too! Now what can he be doing here, escorting that fat fool of a Governor about his province? I thought he'd been given his own command on the frontier."

He had Caro's attention now. "Please tell me *all* you know of Major Steel," she begged, her glance never wandering from Steel, and there was an urgency in her voice that made Angus look at her curiously. "Why are you surprised to see him here?"

"Well, he's hardly cut out to be a staff officer; I'd

have thought he'd be bored stiff. Not nearly enough action for a chap like him. Still, he seems to be enjoying himself tonight—and so does Mrs. Keogh, by Jove."

Rowland's curly dark head was bent close at his right, to the mousy brown ringlets of the Irish surgeon's downtrodden little wife, whispering jokes or compliments—it was impossible to know which. She, to Caro's amazement, was simpering and pouting and fluttering her eyelashes with all the vivacity of a born flirt.

Jealousy knifed through Caro. He doesn't know I'm here, she thought. Or he's pretending not to. Oh, if only I could catch his eye and make him realize how vital it is for me to speak to him! But Rowland, splendid in scarlet and gold regimentals that hugged his broad shoulders and narrow waist without wrinkle or crease, continued his whispered conversation with Mrs. Keogh with never a glance across the table.

When her other neighbor claimed her attention, Rowland turned to his other side, his left, and concentrated his charm on Margaret Ramsay, handsome in copper-colored silk. It was too far to hear a word they said, but from Margaret's unusual animation and sudden wild gestures, Caro guessed they were discussing The Chase.

Butterflies! When I have a message of such urgency that I feel I ought to scream it across the table, Caro fumed. When, oh when will this interminable meal be over? When will I get a word alone with him? She felt a little chill and looked up to find Brook staring at her, a look of such cold calculation in his eyes that she shivered. Hypersensitive and critical, he watched every move she made. More and more she dreaded going back alone to the bungalow with him—and their unwelcome guest—dreaded facing the inevitable inquisition to come on the way home.

To whom had she spoken?

What had they discussed?

Why had she spent an entire course mooning at Captain Steel, who refused even to acknowledge her existence?

Why had she not exerted herself to be pleasant to the Governor's lady, the Collector's wife, the people who mattered?

At long last the ladies rose and followed Lady Micklethwait to the tapestry-hung chamber that served tonight as a withdrawing room.

Fluttering and cackling like hens that have seen a fox, they plumped themselves down on silken couches and began to discuss their host, the banquet, the food and the palace as freely as if they were in their own homes, with no regard for the servants who hovered anxiously, offering sherbet fruit juice and fanning the memsahibs' plump shoulders.

"Imagine! The bonbons were filled with chilies!"

"The soup tasted of cinnamon."

"Did you remark the Nawab's turban jewel? A ruby as big as a pigeon's egg. How he can pretend that his pension won't run to feeding all his dependents when he flaunts jewels like that, I'll never know."

"And his zon, Zoltan Shah—I'll swear his face was painted."

"They say there are whole rooms filled with pianos and billiard tables," remarked Mrs. Keogh, giggling and still enjoying her success with the dashing Major Steel. "He keeps them to show his enthusiasm for Western culture, but they are never used and the ants have gnawed all the legs to powder. My husband saw them when he was summoned to attend the Begum's pet deer. Shall we ask for a tour of the palace and see for ourselves?"

"What, trailing our best gowns on those dirty marble floors? No thank you," said the Honorable Mrs. McTavish, looking down her high-bridged nose.

She was the niece of a former governor and considered herself a cut above the other ladies of Vanyasi. She turned confidentially to Lady Micklethwait. "It must be a great trial to you, to be obliged to sit through any number of these upcountry banquets when your husband is about his official duties. You must find them odiously tedious."

"On the contrary, I always enjoy them, and never more than tonight," said the Governor's lady warmly. "I thought our host very charming. Everywhere we go we find different entertainment planned for us, and the kind generosity of our native hosts never fails to astonish me. It is true that their taste—their etiquette—is somewhat different from ours, but who is to say it is any the worse for that?"

Caro saw the worried face of the Vizier, who had been responsible for the evening's arrangements, relax into a smile as he took in the Burra Beebee's words, and her heart warmed to Lady Micklethwait. If only more European ladies were like her—generous, open-minded, ready to be pleased instead of outraged by differences in manners—how much better an understanding there could be between the sahib-log and the natives.

Mrs. McTavish's long, scrawny neck, like that of a plucked fowl, moved convulsively as she digested this gentle rebuff. Shifting her ground quickly, she began to converse on topics designed to show her own familiarity with the great ones of the land. Was it true, she asked (knowing it was), that Hope Fitzmaurice had gone home, and William Lumsden—quite a boy, only fifteen years in the Service—been promoted over the heads of nine of his seniors? What a scandal that was, to be sure! Robert Adams had got the Judgeship of Battapore, she knew, but who was to follow old Doughty, who had died of drink at Shahabbaganj?

Caro fidgeted and fretted, glancing toward the

door, as the ladies gossiped and sipped. She must speak to Rowland—alone. Soon the gentlemen would be rejoining them, and then Rowland would be trapped into acknowledging her!

But when at last the men arrived, smelling of brandy and His Highness's excellent cigars, neither Rowland nor Durlah Sultan were with them.

The Governor was now in rollicking mood, ogling every pretty woman. Caro, to escape his heavy-handed attempts at flirtation, allowed herself to be persuaded to the piano stool by Isabelle Baum, the German missionary's wife, who, it was said, had a voice. Angus Moncrieff came, too, to turn the pages, and while Isabelle was inflating her lungs and clearing her larynx, in preparation for the first thrilling note that would electrify and deafen those of her audience who were possessed of normal hearing, Caro whispered urgently, "Where is Captain—I mean, Major—Steel?"

"Always enjoy hearing Mrs. Baum sing. Capital voice. Capital girl," remarked old Colonel White from his armchair, in the loud, uninflected tones of the stone-deaf. "Wonderful how she gets up to those high notes. Bravo, Isabelle! Give us the *Evening Hymn* from 'The Last Rose of Summer,' to make us think of home."

Angus chuckled softly. "Durlah Sultan said he had something interesting to show him and bore him away in triumph. I had the impression that old Micklethwait would have liked to see it too, but he's a deal too scared of his mem to try any of those tricks."

Isabelle gave them a quelling glance and soared away in fortissimo like a creaking cartwheel under a heavy load, with Caro hard put to it to keep her in time.

Under cover of the polite applause she murmured to her page-turner, "What do you mean?"

"That he's running his eye over the Nawab's bevy of beauties by now," said Angus mockingly, and Caro's hands dropped from the keyboard.

"But he must come back. He must!"

"Next ve sing a little lieder, *hein*?" said Isabelle, flushed with triumph and determined that this captive audience should enjoy her talent to the full. "Lady Caroline, Lady Caroline, you are not attending. The music is here."

"Yes, I am," said Caro faintly. The thought of Rowland in the arms of some dusky enchantress when she needed him so badly was almost more than she could bear.

"So. This is sad; it tells of youth past and death coming. You must play slow, with much feeling."

Caro felt for the chords, but her eyes were blurred and she could hardly read the music. Angus, busily turning pages, was surprised to see a sparkling tear roll slowly down her cheek and drop on to the green silk of her dress.

"I have found nothing," said Durlah Sultan. "Nothing, nothing, nothing."

Nautch girls swayed like ripples on water in front of the cushions where he and Rowland sat, but neither of the men paid them the least attention.

"Yet we have had reports that indicate he is still in this area. I myself have spoken with an emissary of Sir Jang Bahadur, and it seems certain he has not crossed into Nepal." Rowland brought his closed fist down on his knee in a gesture of frustration. "So near! We have come so near to capturing him, time and again, and on each occasion he has vanished as if the earth had swallowed him up. Someone must be shielding him—but who?"

Durlah Sultan gently stroked his chin. His bright, clever eyes were thoughtful. "A sahib?" he suggested.

"Surely not. After the atrocities at Cawnpore?"

"Memories are short and some—even sahibs—have

a hunger for gold that amounts to a sickness." He paused, and then added deliberately, "Gold—and jewels with which to deck their memsahibs and show how great they are."

"Caroline Vyner's necklace?" asked Rowland sharply. "You don't suppose that was real?"

"It was the Nau-lakha," said Durlah Sultan simply. "The heirloom of the Peshwas. I thought that you, also, would recognize it."

Rowland sprang to his feet and clapped him on the shoulder. "Old friend, you have shown me the key to the door," he exclaimed. "Now let us see if I can unlock it."

"Fifty troopers will be ready when you need them," said Durlah Sultan, smiling. "Good hunting, brother, but remember that you hunt a jackal—a bitter, dispossessed jackal—and he will do his best to bite!"

Chapter Twenty

THE CLICK OF Brook's bedroom door latching shut sounded loud in the heavy, humid night. It seemed to Caro that the whole world was tensely holding its breath, waiting for something to happen. Quickly she swung her legs out of bed and moved to the window. She was fully dressed in her native disguise, and had not a minute to spare.

The Collector's compound, where Sir Francis Micklethwait and his escort were quartered, was over a mile away, on the other side of the Civil Lines. She must find Rowland, deliver her message, and return home before the early-rising servants discovered her absence and gave the alarm.

She knew that Brook was already suspicious of her. Once or twice as they drove home tonight he had seemed on the point of asking her something important, but each time he had checked himself, shied away, and gone on speaking of other things.

He had surprised her by showing interest in her daily doings, asking how she occupied her time. "The other ladies complain they hardly see you. I do not wish you to work at Miss Ramsay's school, but all the same you must not be dull. There is no need to stay at home continually."

So you want me out of the house for part of the day, do you, she thought with an inward laugh. What villainy are you planning now? Has the Rajah of Bithoor tired of occupying the servants' quarters and begun to cast covetous eyes at my boudoir? Well, he shall not have it!

Aloud she said in a studiedly weary tone, "In this heat, home is the only tolerable place to spend the day. So much thunder: it makes my head ache, and I am well content in my nice cool boudoir. I find plenty to amuse me, I assure you. I enjoy listening to the servants' chatter; I understand it quite well, you know."

It was tempting to tease him, to make him wonder what she knew or guessed; what she had heard from the servants; but Caro knew it was dangerous, too. When they reached home she went straight to her room, and waited with mounting impatience for her husband to go to his.

Now at last she was free to go. Since that first night, a month ago, Caro had slipped out of the house so often that she had grown careless. She did not notice that deaf old Abdullah had been replaced on the veranda by a young, keen-eyed coolie unknown to her.

Half an hour after her departure, Brook awoke from a deep sleep to find the young coolie standing nervously at the foot of his bed.

"Sahib, sahib!"

"Yes, what is it?"

"Sahib, she is gone. I followed her at a distance, as you bade me, and saw her speak with the *chokidar* at the Collector-sahib's gate."

Brook swore softly and reached for his boots. "You did well," he told the servant, "but there is danger all around now. Rouse the Great One and tell him we must ride at once."

For the first time in months, it seemed, luck was on Caro's side. The *chokidar* at the Collector's compound was a man she knew, uncle to the *ayah* whom Brook had dismissed without consulting her. She cut short his exclamations at seeing her in native dress.

"Tell me, Gulab Singh, where does the Major-sahib sleep? I have an urgent message for him that cannot wait until dawn. It is a matter of many lives."

The rupee she offered vanished silently into Gulab Singh's robes. He looked at her for a long moment, considering; then said briskly, "Come, memsahib. I will show you his room. It is not long since Steel-sahib retired to rest. He may still be awake."

No light burned through the open window of the room he pointed out. Caro's heart sank, but having gone so far there could be no retreat.

"I will wake him," she whispered. "Thank you, Gulab Singh."

The old man tugged at her sleeve. "By your favor, do not disturb the Collector-sahib. He sleeps lightly, and his anger is terrible."

Caro smiled in the dark. "Have no fear," she said and hurried away across the courtyard. Her eyes were well accustomed now to the patchy moonlight, and she negotiated the veranda wall without a sound. The lightly sleeping Collector undoubtedly was going to have a disturbed night, but she could at least ensure that blame for this did not attach to Gulab Singh.

She stepped quietly through the open window and flattened herself against a wall, taking her bearings. She had no wish to stumble over a stool or a pair of carelessly discarded boots and alarm the compound prematurely.

That white blur in the middle of the room must be the bed, draped with mosquito netting. Holding her breath, she listened intently, but heard no other sound of breathing in the dark, silent room. She tried to whisper his name, but her throat was suddenly dry and no sound emerged.

Gliding forward as silently as a ghost, she pushed aside the folds of netting and bent to shake the sleeper's shoulder. Her hand met nothing but a rolled-up blanket: there was no one there. Gulab Singh had tricked her. In sudden panic she started back toward the window then gasped with fright as a huge dark shadow detached itself from the cupboard by the wall and seized her shoulder in a brutal grip. The muzzle of a pistol was jammed in her back, and a hard hand clapped across her mouth, stifling her scream.

"Now, my fine fellow," growled Rowland, striking a light, and fractionally relaxing the pressure on her mouth. "You've got some explaining to do. Why are you prowling about my room at dead of night . . ." The strengthening lamplight illuminated his prisoner's features, and Rowland stepped back, releasing her as abruptly as if she were red-hot metal. "Caro!" he exclaimed furiously. "What the *devil* are you doing here? You must be crazy to come sneaking into a room in the dark. I might have blown your brains out and asked for explanations later. *Why?*"

The moment had come, but she found it difficult to frame the words. "Rowland, I—I—you frightened me!"

"And you frightened me," said Rowland, still very angry. "If I hadn't thought you might be a messenger from Durlah Sultan, I'd have shot you down as fast as a rabid dog. Well? Out with it. What do you want?"

It wasn't how she had imagined their meeting, during those long, hot, loveless months. Rowland's hostile face told her he had not forgiven her for the way she had rebuffed him at the dance at Baburpore, that his behavior at the banquet had been no oversight. There was to be no reconciliation. No wordless falling into one another's arms, past differences forgotten. How could she have been so naive as to think there would be?

She pulled herself together and said quietly, "I had to see you. I have urgent news for you and had no chance to speak to you tonight at the Nawab's party."

"Durlah Sultan is not a Nawab," said Rowland in an irritated tone, "but no matter. What was this desperate message that could not wait till morning?"

He was mocking her, making her mission appear trivial, but even so she had to deliver the news. "The Nana Sahib is here—in Vanyasi. I have seen him with my own eyes. If you move quickly you can capture him."

She had expected—what? Astonishment, possibly disbelief—certainly not laughter. But Rowland threw back his head and uttered a laugh that had no amusement in it.

"By heaven, that's rich! Poacher turning gamekeeper, eh? I find this very interesting—very interesting indeed. Tell me, what's your game, my fine lady, breaking into my room to inform me of something I knew already and—if my guess is right—*you knew* I knew?"

"You knew?" She was bewildered. "Then why have you not arrested him?"

"Because I want to kill more than one bird with my stone. Because I want him to lead me to his hiding place. We believe that someone with a certain degree of power—possibly a native ruler or even a Company official—has been shielding Nana Sahib for a long time, and we want to catch him—red-handed. Since you know so much, perhaps you can give me a hint as to whom it is."

She stared at him in silence. So he did not yet know of Brook's involvement. He might suspect, but he would not know for certain unless she deliberately, cold-bloodedly framed the words that would convict her own husband. Those words stuck in her throat: she could not do it. Brook had neglected her, abused her, systematically destroyed her self-respect in his efforts to make her the meek, correct, feather-brained creature he thought a wife should be: she did not love him. But she could not forget his strange, erratic generosity and his love of perfection; his genuine delight in her beauty and desire to enhance it with magnificent jewels. The necklace she still wore, for she had not called her *ayah* to undo its complicated fastening, was warm against her skin. No, she could not betray Brook, since it had been for her, at least in part, that he had plunged ever deeper into this morass of treachery and deceit.

Rowland said impatiently, "Well?"

Caro rose with all the dignity she could muster. "Since you do nothing but insult me and clearly have no need of my assistance in capturing your quarry, I will bid you good night," she said icily. "I regret disturbing you."

She had taken only two steps toward the window when Rowland's hand flashed out, stopping her.

"Not so fast, now. I asked you a question. Since you don't see fit to answer it, I'll try another. Where did you see the Rajah of Bithoor?"

"In the bazaar. Let me go!"

"Answer my questions first. Where is he now?"

She hesitated, trying to find a way out, but his fingers bit cruelly into her arm. "In one of the bungalows in the Civil Lines. Ours. Hiding in the servants' quarters."

Rowland gave a soft whistle and released her. "So *that's* where he vanished every time my agents followed him. They would not think of searching the Assistant Collector's bungalow." In the near-dark, his eyes were like chips of ice as they stared down at her, glittering and diamond bright. "Just why have you and your precious husband decided to give him up now, after shielding him for so long? Does it mean that the pair of you have squeezed him dry—extracted the last rupee and the last string of baubles from the wretched creature and resolved to hand him over to the authorities? You'd have saved me a vast amount of chasing about the country on false trails if you'd reached this decision sooner."

"Rowland, you quite misunderstand. He just happens to have chosen our house to hide in. We have nothing to do with it. Truly! I swear I have never even spoken to him."

"You expect me to swallow that?" said Rowland contemptuously. "Really, Caro, that is doing it a trifle too brown. You ask me to believe that servants in your house can come and go without your knowledge; that a man—a notorious criminal—can hide over a month in your bungalow before you realize it? And when you *do* realize whom you are—so innocently—harboring, do you report the matter to the proper authority, the Collector? Oh no!"

"He would never have believed me. You don't know what he is like."

"A man of sense, from your description. I don't believe you either. My dear Caro, I know your talent for play-acting and I have been taken in by you once already. This is the single, solitary occasion when you are going to tell the truth, the whole truth, and nothing but the truth, if I have to shake it out of you."

"I am telling the truth," said Caro stoutly. "I can't help it if you don't believe me, but you are losing a great chance to catch the man all India is seeking."

"Did your husband send you here?" He was holding her close to him, as he had in the days of their love, but this time his eyes shone only with suspicion. "Did he tell you to trade on the affection I once had for you? Did he suggest that you should creep into my bed for a few hours, to give my quarry time to get clear away? Well, my dear, this time the two of you have miscalculated. I never mix business with pleasure. My business is to catch the Rajah of Bithoor and his protector—and you're coming with me while I do so."

"I shall do nothing of the kind," snapped Caro, losing her carefully controlled temper at last at this willful misinterpretation of her motives. Her eyes sparkled with outrage. "You are a vile, distrustful, evil-minded brute, and I am very sorry I ever tried to help you."

"That sounds more like the Caro I used to know," commented Rowland imperturbably. "Yes, I know you would like to scratch my eyes out or deal me one of your famous slaps across the face. But you're in deep water here, my dear. No display of temper will get you out of it. You've been harboring a wanted criminal and I'd be failing in my duty if I let you go."

"Duty!" She almost spat the word at him. "You don't know what duty is."

"Oh yes, I assure you I do. I also know the meaning of pleasure, and I must confess the sight of you in a rage has brought it most forcibly to my recollection. Perhaps before grim duty calls me, I can show you . . ."

Quick as she was to divine his intention, Rowland moved faster. His strong hands were drawing her close into the circle of his arms, his hard lips on hers before she could whisk out of reach. For a moment she swayed in his embrace, blood thundering in her ears, hating him and hating her own body for the treacherous way it responded eagerly to his touch. Rowland laughed softly, triumphantly.

What had begun in anger turned all too quickly to desire. Her need for him had always been great, but this surpassed her most desperate longings. She could not fight back, would not resist him. Instead, she matched her passion to his: her strokes to his caresses, her kisses to his mouthings. By the time he drew her toward the bed, she had never been so perfectly primed for love.

Abruptly, Rowland cast her down and stepped back.

"So that was what you came for, after all, my lotus. What a pity we have no time to indulge our appetites any further. Grim duty is calling me... *No, Caro!*" Suddenly his voice cracked like a whiplash. "Stay where you are or I'll call in a trooper to guard you."

Too tired, too sick at heart to disobey, Caro sank down on the charpoy, and watched the first green and purple streaks of dawn in the sky. Outside in the courtyard horses whinnied and men muttered, cursing as they struggled with straps and buckles in the dim light. Caro heard the Collector's querulous voice complaining of the commotion, and Rowland's deeper tones explaining.

He returned to his room, fully dressed and accoutered, and she followed him out to the courtyard without a word. He hoisted her quickly to the saddlebow of his big bay charger, and quietly the cavalcade filed out from the compound, heading for the Civil Lines.

"I congratulate you, Caro," said Rowland sardonically an hour later. "You have played your part to perfection and no doubt the Nana Sahib will remember you in his prayers. The birds, as no doubt you have guessed, have flown."

A stone seemed to hit Caro a heavy blow over the heart. "Gone? Impossible!"

"See for yourself."

Caro rose stiffly from the boulder on which she had been sitting, watched by one of Durlah Sultan's Muslim troopers, while Rowland and his men surrounded the bungalow. When all were in position, Rowland approached the door with drawn sword and called on Brook Vyner and the Rajah of Bithoor to come out. Silence answered him. Then the troopers entered and searched every room. The house itself, the servants' quarters, the stables—all were silent, deserted.

Caro made her own inspection. "He's taken my mare!" she cried indignantly.

"Good God, is that all you're worried about?" said Rowland in disgust. "He's taken your jewels too, by the looks of it. Every drawer in your room turned out. No doubt he's hoping you'll rejoin him and claim them, but that hope is destined to be dashed."

"Can't you understand? I had nothing to do with this!" said Caro quietly and desperately. "I tried only to help you."

"Yes, by delaying our discovery of Nana Sahib's whereabouts until he could make good his escape. Vastly obliging of you."

"How can I convince you. . . ?"

"It's not the least use trying to convince me of your innocence while you wear the Nau-lakha round your pretty neck, so spare yourself the effort, I beg."

"The *what?*"

"That gaudy necklace that becomes you so well. Do you mean to say you don't know of its fame? Durlah Sultan recognized it, even if you do not. He told me tonight that it is the great heirloom of the Peshwas; it belonged to Nana Sahib's adoptive father, Bajee Rao, the last Peshwa of the Mahrattas. You must be proud to wear such a treasure."

The heavy rope of emeralds and pearls seemed suddenly to burn her flesh. She raised her hands in an involuntary gesture to tear it off.

"No, leave it there," said Rowland harshly. "It is probably safer round your neck than anywhere else just now, for no one can say you don't value your neck." He looked at her curiously. "Are you feeling quite well? You almost do convince me of your innocence—or else you are an even more accomplished actress than I imagined. Now hurry and dress more suitably for riding. We have no time to lose."

"Rowland, I am so tired. Can't I stay here? I won't try to escape, I promise."

Rowland looked at her white, exhausted face and swiftly quenched the flicker of pity he felt for her. "No. You must come with us. The sight of you in our hands may prompt your erring husband to give himself up."

The absurdity of this idea was such that, despite herself, Caro nearly laughed aloud.

"How can you think so? He cares nothing for me, and never has."

"My dear Caro, you greatly undervalue your charms. No man risks his life and ruins his career for a woman he cares nothing about," said Rowland with absolute conviction. "Go and dress at once. We have wasted enough time already."

Mile after mile, hour after grilling hour, the hill country unrolled itself under the pounding hoofs of Caro's horse. Compared with Nuri's light floating action, the trooper's country-bred horse which Rowland had commandeered for her use was a rough-gaited, short-striding plodder with a mouth of iron, but his stamina seemed boundless. They climbed hills and forded rushing, greenish white mountain streams; they thundered through villages where slant-eyed children ran alongside the troopers, palms extended, and peasants in the tiny terraced fields who turned to watch them ride by replied in almost the same words to their oft-repeated question.

"Yes, sahib. That way. Yes, a great lord, riding fast with his servants. He passed four hours—three hours, two hours ago." And always they pointed towards the snow-capped hills.

Gradually the time interval decreased. They were gaining on their quarry. By ten o'clock, when they stopped to rest and water their horses, Caro was light-headed from lack of sleep. Dimly she was aware of Rowland lifting her from the saddle, laying her in the shade with a rolled blanket beneath her head. She was also aware of the Muslim trooper who watched her, unwinking, his rifle across his knees. She no longer cared. She slept the sleep of utter exhaustion.

Dusk was falling when she awoke, and the sharp tang of woodsmoke filled the air. The troopers squatted around cooking fires, busy with their meal.

"Wake up and eat," said Rowland. Sita Ram was offering her a small bowl of rice and vegetable curry. "Our scouts report that your husband and his party have crossed the Murranbagh pass and are camped beside the river. If we ride fast we may catch them by nightfall."

As they trotted on through the crisp, scented dusk, the thrill of the chase began to infect Caro. She ceased to think of herself as a prisoner, under threat of trial and disgrace; she forgot that the man she was hunting was the one she had promised to love, honor, and obey only seven months before. All that seemed remote, irrelevant. The only thing that mattered was that she was here, once again riding side by side with Rowland into unknown country, with danger ahead and the prospect of action. She felt intensely, absurdly happy.

"What will you do when you come up with them?" she asked.

"Take them alive, I hope. I would be easier in my mind were we not so close to the frontier with Nepal, for strictly speaking we have no business beyond that point, and the Governor was emphatic that I must not risk provoking a diplomatic incident by violating the sovereignty of a friendly power."

"Surely the friendly power would assist you to capture an enemy?"

"Perhaps; if we happened to fall in with men loyal to the central government. But there are many tribesmen in the frontier region who regard themselves as independent, and take a positive delight in undermining the authority of the Prime Minister. The very fact that the Rajah of Bithoor has chosen to flee in this direction suggests that he may have supporters hereabouts."

Caro gazed round at the wild, forbidding hills, which seemed to grow taller as darkness fell. "Where is the frontier?"

Rowland laughed. "I wish I knew precisely. Daffadar-Major, where is the frontier?"

The grizzled native officer launched into a detailed recital of the signs by which they would know they had crossed the border, but it seemed clear to Caro that he knew no more than they did. As the miles passed, she began to notice a certain unease in the faces of the troopers. They muttered among themselves and constantly glanced back over their shoulders. They were farther from home than they cared to be. Night was coming on, and they feared an ambush.

Rowland and the Daffadar-Major rode up and down the line, encouraging them, reminding them of the importance of their mission, and gradually the men took heart again and pressed forward.

"You can't blame them for hanging back a trifle," said Rowland, rejoining Caro at the head of the small column. "The tribesmen in these parts are a wild lot and have unpleasant ways of treating their enemies. It's one thing to go hunting half a dozen defeated Mahrattas, but quite another to encounter a hostile tribal chieftain in his own territory."

"You think we have crossed the frontier, then?"

"I'm afraid so. We've traveled too far to be still on Indian soil."

"Should you go on, then? Your orders forbade it."

Rowland's teeth flashed in a sudden, infectious grin. "Delhi *dur ast*—that's to say we're a long way from the people who gave those orders. What would you do?"

"Go on," said Caro promptly. "They may be no more than a few miles ahead. We *cannot* give up so tamely."

"Good girl!" He gave her a puzzled look and his voice, for the first time, was uncertain. "I wish I knew whose side you were on."

Caro laughed. In her mood of euphoria she no longer felt offended that he did not trust her. "You know as well as I do. It is only your nasty, suspicious *soldier's* mind that won't let you believe it."

"Caro," he began, "if only"—but a shout from a keen-eyed sowar just behind interrupted him.

"Sahib! Major-sahib! They are there."

Clear in the bright moonlight, a small party of horsemen could be seen about half a mile ahead, toiling on weary horses up a steep path that led through a narrow gorge between boulder-strewn slopes. At the bottom of the gorge roared a great river, pewter-colored with silt from the high Himal.

Rowland turned to the Daffadar-Major. "Sound the charge!" he ordered quietly. The bugler set his trumpet to his lips.

As the spine-tingling notes floated up the gorge, the fugitives beat their failing horses, urging them to greater speed. Rapidly the gap between hunters and hunted diminished.

"Stay here, Caro," called Rowland, as he set spurs to his charger. "Sita Ram will guard you."

"Never!" shouted Caro. She didn't know whether he heard or not, but she saw approval in Sita Ram's flashing grin. She was swept along in the glory of the charge, knee-to-knee between two troopers, her hand feeling as if by instinct for the sword that swung at her horse's flank. She was determined to stay near Rowland at all costs, whether he liked it or not. She wanted to be in at the death.

Like a wave breaking over a rock, the troop of Irregular Cavalry swept uphill and engulfed Brook's small party. The servants formed a circle with the Nana Sahib in the center, but they made no attempt to fight although they were armed with swords and *lathi*s.

"Surrender!" called Rowland.

Seated on Caro's gray mare in the middle of his retainers, the Rajah of Bithoor raised his heavy-lidded eyes and looked straight at his captor. His mouth curved in a smile.

"A deen!" he shouted in a high-pitched voice that carried piercingly down the gorge. "Kill the sons of dogs, the defilers of their mothers, the infidel swine! *A deen, a deen!* Kill them all!"

At the shout, armed men sprang from behind the boulders on either side of the path, waving curved swords and leveling their long muskets. A ball whizzed past Caro's ear and chipped splinters from the rock face. The narrow gorge echoed with shouts, shots, and the screaming of terrified horses.

"We are betrayed, memsahib. Follow me!" It was Sita Ram, shouting at her side. He tugged at her bridle, trying to draw her clear of the melee, when a sword hacked at his head and his voice died in a bubbling gasp.

Caro sprang from the saddle and caught him as he toppled. She pulled him into the shelter of a boulder and looked around for Rowland.

He was there in the thick of the fight, still mounted, his sword flashing with the speed of a thresher's flail, but she saw at a glance that his men were outnumbered. As she crouched beside the wounded man, wondering how best she could help him, Caro sensed a movement behind her. The next instant, fingers were tearing at her throat.

She could not scream. Desperately she twisted and clawed up the pistol she had just laid down, swinging the heavy butt with all her strength at the side of her assailant's head. He grunted painfully, losing his grip on her neck, but the next moment the fingers were back again, this time pulling at the necklace she still wore beneath her habit.

"Give me—the jewels—or I'll kill you," he gasped, and through mists of pain she recognized Brook's voice. "I looked everywhere—I knew you must be wearing them. Give...them...back..."

Behind her, there was an explosion so close that the powder scorched her hair, setting off a deafening clamor of bells in her ears that rocked her with the force of a hammer blow. Brook's fingers slackened and fell away from her throat. As Caro turned dazedly to see what had caused it, she found Sita Ram propping himself on one elbow, a smoking pistol sagging in his other hand.

"I kill him," he muttered weakly. "Do not look, memsahib. The *badmash* is no more." He sank back in a coma.

Mercifully, the dark hid the details of what the pistol, fired at point-blank range, had done to Brook's head. Caro felt sick. She staggered to her feet and looked in all directions. Where was Rowland? Where was the Nana Sahib? During her own private struggle in the shadow of the boulder, the skirmish had ended— but how? Dead and wounded troopers and tribesmen lay about the hillside; horses trotted here and there, stirrups flapping; the rest of the fighters had gone, vanished into the hills or back down the valley, she could not tell which.

Aimlessly she wandered toward the glistening pewter river, which slithered like a snake between the steep banks. It seemed to draw her, calling her closer, urging her to plunge in and wash the blood off her hands. Brook was dead. She had not fired the shot, but all the same she had killed him as surely as if she had pulled the trigger herself. A numb chill spread through her body as she stared down at the gurgling water. She sank down on the bank, fifteen feet above the torrent, and shook convulsively. Rowland was gone, dead or captured. She remembered his words, spoken so light-heartedly: "They have unpleasant ways of treating their enemies." What if he were, even now, being dragged off to some mountain stronghold to provide sadistic sport for his captors?

She knew she should go back, to do what she could to help Sita Ram and the other wounded, but still the glistening river held her. How easy it would be to slip down the bank and finish everything in the shimmering, hypnotizing ice-water.

A shadow blacked out the moon; Rowland stood before her.

"Caro, what are you doing there, all alone? Where is Sita Ram? Are you hurt?"

"No," she said blankly. "Brook is dead, and Sita Ram wounded. When I could not find you, I thought— I feared—"

His arms were around her, lifting her up, holding her close. "Why, Caro, what an imagination you have! I'm not killed as easy as that, not by a long shot. Now brace up, like a good girl, for I need your help. We have half a dozen wounded, and three dead, I fear. Worst of all, we've lost our quarry. The tribesmen bore off Nana Sahib in their midst, and though we pursued them they crossed a ravine and flung down the bridge in our faces. I doubt if we'll ever get a chance to catch him now. Still," he added, hoping to bring a smile to her face, "they left your horse behind, you'll be glad to hear. Evidently the Nana will have no need of her where he's going." He put a gentle hand beneath her chin and tilted up her face. "Come, Caro. It's all over now. The villains set a pretty trap for us and we are lucky to escape with our skins. They wanted the Nau-lakha back, and planned to capture you in their ambush."

She shivered. "How did they know I was wearing it still? I might have hidden it before we set off in pursuit."

"If they'd captured you," Rowland said grimly, "you'd soon have told where it was hidden. You couldn't have resisted their methods for long. They knew the necklace was not at the bungalow, therefore it was likely you still wore it. I put your life at risk when I insisted on bringing you with me, but the truth was"— he sounded suddenly unsure of himself—"the truth was I could not bear to leave you behind. I was afraid you would escape me again. I wanted to go back—to bring back those days when we rode together from Patelbar to Baburpore, and the nights... Caro, will you forgive me?"

The numbness was melting away in the warmth of his arms, being replaced by a mounting excitement that made her breath come quickly and the hot blood burn in her cheeks.

"Rowland, you wretch," she said huskily, "I never knew you to ask forgiveness before, and you choose to do it here where there is no one to witness the fact. But—I do, freely, for I would never have forgiven you for leaving me behind. Here"—she fumbled at the neck of her habit—"help me take off this accursed jewel."

It was difficult to free the intricate catch in the moonlight, but she stood patiently, and at last Rowland pulled the long rope of pearls from around her neck. The rubies and emeralds flashed in splendor.

"What will you do with it? I suppose no one has a better claim to it than you."

"I want no part of it." She drew back her arm and flung the sparkling gems with all her strength. The necklace spun in a parabola of winking light and vanished into the steel-gray water below. Caro sighed deeply. "Now I am free," she said.

"Not for long." Rowland set a hand on each of her shoulders, making her look directly at him. He cleared his throat importantly. "Pay attention, Caro. I am about to renew the magnificent offer I made you only seven months ago—though it seems like a lifetime to me. Ahem! Will you marry me? I would like you to make up your mind on this important matter very quickly indeed: in fact, I don't propose to let you out of my arms until I receive a satisfactory reply. Yours is going to be the shortest widowhood that Anglo-India has ever known, and may well involve us in a scandal— though I don't care for that, nor, I believe, do you. Well, what do you say?"

How delighted Bulbul will be, thought Caro irrelevantly. She lowered her lashes in the approved style, wondering how long she dare keep him in suspense. His hands moved impatiently, setting her skin on fire.

"Will you promise to take me with you wherever you go?"

"Undoubtedly."

"Allow me to run my own household and speak to the servants in their own tongue?"

"Willingly!"

"And dress as I like?"

"How can I stop you?"

"And give me"—she hesitated, blushing a little— "half a dozen children who look just like you?"

"With pleasure. Now, Caro, no more conditions. I won't swear my soul away, but I want your answer now: yes or no?"

"Yes," she whispered, and the world seemed to tilt beneath her as he caught her up in his arms.

READ THESE BEST-SELLING
BERKLEY BOOKS

MORE BESTSELLING BOOKS FROM BERKLEY

Send for a *free* list of all our books in print

These books are available at your local bookstore, or send
price indicated plus 30¢ per copy to cover mailing costs to
Berkley Publishing Corporation
390 Murray Hill Parkway
East Rutherford, New Jersey 07073

THRILLING HISTORICAL NOVELS
FROM BERKLEY

Fiona Hill

LOVE IN A MAJOR KEY   (03019-9—95¢)

THE PRACTICAL HEART   (02922-0—95¢)

THE TRELLISED LANE   (03598-0—$1.25)

THE WEDDING PORTRAIT   (03599-9—$1.25)

Jean Plaidy

THE ITALIAN WOMAN   (03262-0—$1.50)

MADAME SERPENT   (03024-5—$1.50)

Send for a *free* list of all our books in print

These books are available at your local bookstore, or send
price indicated plus 30¢ per copy to cover mailing costs to
Berkley Publishing Corporation
390 Murray Hill Parkway
East Rutherford, New Jersey 07073